W9-BAI-804

Single-
minded

ALSO BY LISA DAILY

STOP GETTING DUMPED!

FIFTEEN MINUTES OF SHAME

HOW TO DATE LIKE A GROWN-UP

IS HE CHEATING?

IS SHE CHEATING?

BEAUTY

Lisa
Daily

THOMAS DUNNE BOOKS ST. MARTIN'S PRESS NEW YORK

This is a work of fiction. All of the characters, organizations, and events portrayed in this novel are either products of the author's imagination or are used fictitiously.

THOMAS DUNNE BOOKS.
An imprint of St. Martin's Press.

Printed in the United States of America. For information, address St. Martin's Press, 175 Fifth Avenue, New York, N.Y. 10010.

www.thomasdunnebooks.com
www.stmartins.com

Designed by Anna Gorovoy

The Library of Congress Cataloging-in-Publication Data is available upon request.

ISBN 978-1-250-06044-0 (hardcover)
ISBN 978-1-4668-6565-5 (e-book)

Our books may be purchased in bulk for promotional, educational, or business use. Please contact your local bookseller or the Macmillan Corporate and Premium Sales Department at 1-800-221-7945, extension 5442, or by e-mail at MacmillanSpecialMarkets@macmillan.com.

First Edition: June 2017

10 9 8 7 6 5 4 3 2 1

TO CRAZY AUNT JERRY AND UNCLE MARY,
THE MOST BEAUTIFUL LOVE STORY I'VE EVER SEEN UP CLOSE

Single-
minded

1

You know that feeling when you're suddenly startled out of a deep sleep, and you're in that hazy middle world where you're not sure what's real—like maybe you actually could be chasing after an ice-cream truck wearing only fishing waders and a canary-yellow bridesmaid's dress, or you're just one answer away from winning a year's supply of adult diapers on a Japanese game show?

My cell phone is in my hand, although I have no recollection of answering it.

"Don't panic," says Darcy, as I struggle to rouse myself.

Darcy is my closest friend, aside from my husband, Michael, who's been the love of my life since the first day of kindergarten when I convinced him that the blue Play-Doh tasted *exactly* like cotton candy. He ate the whole can, just to prove me right. Michael was like that.

Darcy is a one-woman hurricane: a fiery, tell-it-like-it-is political consultant who is as hard on the men she dates as she is on candidates. As Darcy likes to put it, "I don't have time for screwups." She never calls me in the middle of the night.

"Oh my God, is someone dead?" I ask.

"Why is that always the first thing out of your mouth?" she says.

"Because someone always is," I say.

It's still dark outside and I check the clock: 5:04. Clumsily, I grope around on my nightstand until I locate the lamp switch and flip it on.

"Darcy, what's going on?" I ask, propping myself up in bed. "Did somebody die? Or not?"

"Ugh. You're about to," she says.

"What do you mean?" I ask, feeling completely freaked without knowing why.

"There's a story on one of the sports blogs. It's about Michael."

"My Michael? What about Michael?" I ask. My intestines do a nose-dive and a nauseating cocktail of dread and adrenaline races through my body. Oh God, is he dead? He's out of town for work, and I haven't talked to him since last night.

And then, the more obvious, "Why are you up in the middle of the night reading the sports blogs?"

Darcy ignores me.

"It's a post about Michael having an extramarital relationship with a twenty-one-year-old college basketball player."

"That can't be true," I say with all the self-assurance a woman can possess while still wearing her pajamas. "What's her name?" Michael would *never* cheat on me. Never. I'd kill him. Kill him dead.

"Alex, it's not a her. It's a him. Bobby something. He plays for Michigan, graduates this year, thanks Jesus after every basket, leads his team in prayer before every game," she says.

"A him? Wait, wait, wait, what? I don't understand. You're saying Michael is sleeping with a man? A *man*?" And then it dawns on me. "Oh gawd. Did you say Bobby? Bobby Cavale?" I ask. "Michael wouldn't shut up about him. How talented he is. What a big career he's going to have. How he was the next LeBron or something. I thought it was just his stupid jump shot."

"Apparently it was his layup," Darcy deadpans. I snort and then giggle involuntarily. Darcy cracks jokes during funerals, scandals, and tragedies. It's her way of helping to break the tension. Because it's hard to contemplate throwing yourself in the path of a speeding termite truck when you're rolling around on the floor laughing.

"Wait, are you saying . . . do you think Michael is gay?" I ask, absolutely incredulous.

"Yes," she says. "Most definitely." I feel my chest cave in.

"No, seriously?" I say.

"Seriously," she responds. The line goes quiet. Which is unusual for Darcy.

"You're crazy! Why do you think that?" I ask.

"Well, even aside from the whole making-out-with-a-guy thing, I always thought he was gay. I've never seen a man more insanely happy, jubilant, even, reporting from the locker room. And then of course there was that crazy Halloween party you guys threw last year. Michael was, hands down, the gayest Count Chocula *ever*. Also, I'm pretty sure he only took up biking so he could shave his legs and gift-wrap his package in Spandex. But that's just speculation."

"Why wouldn't you tell me?" I say, pressing my palms hard against my forehead in hopes of triggering some sort of twenty-minute amnesia, like a reset button for my brain. "Jesus, I feel like such an idiot."

"It never occurred to me that you didn't know. It seemed so obvious," says Darcy. "I mean, you didn't get your psychology degree online or stuffed inside a box of cereal, did you?"

I sigh deeply. This is not making me feel better.

Darcy asks, "Look, do you want me to get my crisis team on this and check it out? My best guess is that it's going to blow up over the weekend, and depending on how it's handled, die out by Monday. Unless there's more. Or video. It's not every day that a top draft pick and an ESPN broadcaster get caught screwing around. Michael is going to need a good publicist if he's going to keep his job. The media loves to devour its own. Tell him to call me if he needs some names."

"Mmmm-hmm," I respond numbly.

"Or you can scratch that and just let him hang on live TV. Your call."

"I don't understand," I say. "Why does some stupid sports blog even care that two grown men are having sex, except for the fact that they both happen to work in sports?"

"Because Michael is married. Because Michael is a basketball commentator and Bobby is a top draft pick. Because Bobby is super-religious and has felt the need to speak to the media extensively against what he calls the sins of blasphemy and homosexuality. And because Michael is higher profile than the average hookup." She snorts. "Between the homosexuality and adultery, all Bobby needs is for Michael to schedule an abortion and he'll have Satan's trifecta."

"Are you sure it's even true?" I ask. "Maybe it's just a rumor." Please, please, let it just be a rumor. A cruel but completely false rumor. A case of mistaken identity. Something we'll all be laughing about a year from now.

"It's true. There are . . . pictures," she says. "I'm so sorry. It was probably bound to come out, one way or another."

"Pictures?" I sit straight up in bed, gripping the phone so hard my fingers began to go numb. What the hell? Was I a serial killer, or a door-to-door magazine salesperson in a past life or something? Outrage and humiliation sear my every thought.

Disconnected sounds dribble from my lips, but my mouth can't form any more words. Like I've been Tasered. Actually, I'd rather be Tasered. At least when you're Tasered things go back to normal after the 18 million volts of electricity hit your heart. You lose your breath, your body seizes up, you twitch around on the floor, you drool, maybe you pee yourself. But you probably recover. There is no way I'm ever going to recover from this.

"Yes, pictures," she says. "Listen to me, you do not want to get involved in this mess. There are plenty of reporters who will be happy to agree you've been wronged and that Michael is a bastard. And then they'll put your puffy face and bloodshot eyes on camera and the story will last a week or a month instead of a couple of days."

"I'm going to kill him," I say.

"No, you're not," she says. "Don't answer any calls on your cell that aren't from people you know. Do you guys still have a landline?"

"What am I, eighty?" I ask.

"Lay low, stay home, order food, or rearrange your medicine cabinet or something. Don't watch TV. Don't surf the Internet. Don't even think about googling 'Craigslist hit men' or 'how to poison my husband with leftover pizza and household chemicals.' Call your web designer right this minute and tell her to put a home page up on your Web site that says it's under scheduled maintenance. Do *not* speak to any reporters. The last thing you want to do in a firestorm is add oxygen. You need to lay low and hope it's not a slow news day."

"On camera? Is this really going to go that far? Michael isn't Steve Phillips, he's just a college basketball announcer. Oh God. I just heard myself."

"Yes," says Darcy in her most soothing voice. "He's a college basketball announcer who's screwing one of the top college players in the country. Not exactly some unknown intern."

I put my head in my hands. Darcy kept talking but I couldn't focus on the words.

"I can't handle this," I say. "What am I going to do?"

"Yes, you can," Darcy says firmly. "Just break out the liquor and pray for a natural disaster."

2

The second I get off the phone with Darcy, I dial Michael's cell. No answer. Asshole!

"Call me," I screech into the phone. "Call me right now!"

Darcy told me not to watch the news, and I should have listened to her. Darcy, after all, has gotten dozens of politicians through prostitution, drug, and undocumented nanny scandals, most of them with their careers still intact. If anybody knows how this is going to play out it's her. I pop in my favorite old movie, *When Harry Met Sally*, to distract myself, a movie I've seen a million times, and I watch ten whole minutes of the DVD before I succumb to the temptation to turn on the news. I can't help it.

That Carrie Fisher line from the movie keeps bouncing around in my brain, when all her friends keep telling her that her married boyfriend is never going to leave his wife: *You're right, you're right, I know you're right.*

I tell myself it's just a blog story, that it can't possibly be true, that it will all disappear in a few days, a page buried under posts about trades and bad coaching and steroid scandals. But just in case, I check FOX Sports. I can't bear to watch ESPN, for fear Michael is calling a game somewhere they play basketball at five-thirty in the morning. I don't want to see him right now, even on TV. I do, however, want to see what Bobby Cavale looks like—no idea why. It can only make me feel worse. If the person your spouse cheats with is a troll, you'd say, *I can't believe he'd cheat on me with them.* If the mistress (or in Michael's case, mister) is gorgeous, perfect, a way better version of you, wouldn't you feel even more depressed? Or would some level of physical perfection make you just shrug your shoulders and say, *Did you get a look at that one? What mortal man could resist that?* What was the reason for wanting to see the person my husband had cheated with? To have a face to tie to the horrible knowledge of betrayal—to give more meat to the memory it? To figure out what he has that I don't? (Aside from a twenty-one-year-old body and a penis.)

HLN doesn't mention anything about it for the first thirty minutes I watch, and I feel a glimmer of hope that they'll skip the story altogether, but then I see the text crawl updating at the bottom of the screen: TOP DRAFT PICK BOBBY CAVALE AND ESPN COMMENTATOR MICHAEL MILLER SEX SCANDAL. Shit.

I switch to MSNBC and they've got basically the same text crawl at the bottom. Oh God, oh God! This cannot be happening! FOX Sports is worse. They do a whole segment on Michael and Bobby Cavale, and one of the commentators mentions that Michael is married and wonders aloud if his husband Alex . . . Wait, WTF, *husband*? FOX Sports thinks I'm a man?

"Alex is short for Alexandra, you hack!" I shout at the screen. "Nice fact checking!"

I'm not sure what's worse—that Michael is having an affair that's making national news, or that the media are under the impression that I'm a dude. Humiliating.

An hour later, I'm still glued to the television set, running back and forth between FOX Sports in the living room, MSNBC on my bedroom set, and hitting *refresh* on my laptop, phone, and iPad every time I make a lap, scanning for breaking stories online. Do I need to set up a Google alert? Both FOX Sports and MSNBC do about a minute on the scandal, showing a blurry photo of Michael and Bobby obviously taken by some pervert with a smart phone. There are no new details, just the stuff Darcy already told me. Top draft pick, ESPN commentator, lots of sex. I do think it's bizarre that the news coverage makes Michael out to be some big ESPN juggernaut. I guess that makes for a more exciting story. Mercifully, there isn't much about me, other than the repeated mentions that Michael is married to a man named Alex. I hope my mother isn't watching. She'll probably think I had a sex change or something. Not that she'll call to find out. She's an attorney with more of a killer instinct than a maternal one. It's 5:30 A.M. in Sarasota, Florida, where Michael and I live, which means it's 2:30 A.M. in San Diego, where my parents live. So one small blessing, at least; they won't hear about it for another couple of hours.

My cell rings at six, six-ten, six-twenty, and six-thirty. A New York number I don't recognize. Letting it go to voice mail, I down two shots of tequila. Who drinks this early? I do, apparently. The phone rings again and again with numbers I don't recognize. Darcy has been right about everything else, there's no way I'm going to let myself get sucked into a conversation with a reporter. So far, I've been pretty much left out of the story other than the mention that Michael is married. And the man thing. Mercifully, there isn't much about me. As far as I know, my last name has not yet been released. At least that is something good. Thank God I kept my maiden name. With every update to the story, I feel like I'm getting seasick on my couch.

I'm humiliated and completely livid with Michael, but there's a part of me that hates to see his career decimated, especially so publicly. Mostly. I helped to engineer it, after all, researching the right internships and plotting the most likely path to get him on air. Michael always says I'm unstoppable, once I get my mind fixed on a goal. Even if that goal is someone else's.

Michael started his broadcasting career while I was in grad school, working his way up from an internship to an on-air gig on the radio, and then two years later, a spot at ESPN. He was the Wiki of sports knowledge, highly ambitious with TV-friendly hair. All our dreams were coming true.

I've always felt lucky to have met Michael so early. Our life together has been practically perfect, thanks to my judicious planning. We fell in love in kindergarten, and attended every single school dance and prom as a couple, dating all the way through college, without a breakup or a blip. I wanted to wait until I'd finished grad school to get married, and so we did. We got married at twenty-six, a week after I finished my doctorate.

I'm an environmental psychologist who consults with charities and businesses to create environments that influence customer and employee emotions and behavior—like helping kids feel less scared at the pediatrician's office, pulling customers to the newest merchandise by employing strategic throw pillows and signature scents, staging inspiring environments for creative types to do their best work, or keeping diners in a restaurant for exactly sixty-eight minutes, the optimum time frame to create a great dining experience, boost liquor sales, and still turn the tables at a quick pace using things you'd never notice, such as table placement and seatback angles. And once, I gave my eighty-year-old swinging-single neighbor Zelda Persimmon a vial of pink grapefruit perfume, which cues men to perceive a woman to be 6.1 years younger than she actually is, because Zelda only likes dating younger men. She's totally like the "It Girl" of her seniors-only salsa dancing class.

I never wish bad things on anyone, even someone I'm really pissed at. But it's hard to resist the impulse to feel a tiny bit of glee as karma comes after Michael's cheating ass. Weirdly, I'm not at all angry at Bobby. He doesn't know me. He never made a promise to love and honor me for the rest of his life. He's young, and obviously naïve, and making some mistakes that all twentysomethings make as they navigate the terrain to adulthood. I feel sorry for him in some ways. This decision is going to follow him around and define who he is, even before he has the chance to define himself. Damn, I'm magnanimous.

I promise myself I'll turn off the TV and all my devices after ten more minutes. And then another five minutes. Finally, I put myself out of my misery and shut them all off. After the blurry image of Michael and Bobby surfaced, the blogs and news coverage started to include more photos of them together and a grainy video of what looked like them kissing in a parking garage. It was tender, really, the way Michael leaned in to kiss Bobby. Michael used to kiss me like that. Then Michael picked up Bobby, and kissed him ferociously. Michael's never kissed me like that.

I can't watch anymore, but I can't tear myself away—those images of my Michael intimate with someone else are already going to be permanently burned into my brain.

The grainy video is looped, unoriginally juxtaposed against Bobby's frequent speeches to religious and conservative political groups, along with snippets of locker room commentary where he rails against the sin of homosexuality and claims that he prays every night for his teammates who have not yet found his personal savior, the LordJesusChristAmen.

I can't stop the tears from coming, so I sit on the floor with a tub of frosting in one hand, clutching our cat with the other. Morley is not exactly cuddling material, so I bribe him to make him stay, letting him lick the strawberry frosting off a spoon while I hug him close.

And that's right where I am when the phone rings yet again.

3

Michael finally calls, two excruciating hours after Darcy, at seven.

"I'm so sorry, Alex," Michael says. "I never meant to hurt you. It just happened. It didn't mean anything. I still love you."

"Why do people always say that when they cheat? Of course it meant something. Maybe it didn't mean anything to you, but it means a hell of a lot to me," I yell. "Did you have sex with that guy?"

"It's complicated," he says.

"Oh, that's bullshit. It's not that complicated. Did. You. Have. Sex. With. Him?"

"Well," he says.

"Don't you Bill Clinton me," I yell. "Yes or no?"

"Yes, but . . ." Michael sighs. One of those long, forlorn, manipulative, *poor me* sighs that makes me want to throw up. On him.

"What?" I ask. If I didn't ask, he'd just keep sighing until he hyperventilated. And once the paramedics resuscitated him, he'd just start the *poor me* sighs all over again. "Stop already. What do you want?"

"I think I'm going to lose my job," he says, his voice all shaky and quiet. "I need your help."

"Are you out of your freaking mind? You have got to be kidding," I say. "You brought this on yourself."

"I know, I know," he says. "And I probably deserve it."

"*Probably*?" Yes, sure, the jury is still out on that one.

"Okay, I deserve it. But if I get fired from ESPN, I'll never get another job in sports or broadcasting again. Please," he says. "You know this is my dream job. It's all I ever wanted to do. You helped me get here."

Locker room access and a clothing allowance, it's freaking homo-nirvana.

God, I'm an idiot.

I get up off the couch and start pacing the great room, desperate to relieve the shock of angry energy buzzing through my body, leaving me feeling like a live wire. I cannot sit back down—I have to keep moving or I'll just fall apart.

"What am I supposed to do?" I ask.

"I need you to fly to the ESPN campus in Bristol with me this morning. We'll meet with the network people this afternoon."

"Are you out of your mind? Why would I go?" I say. "Besides, Darcy told me to lay low."

"I need you to tell them that you knew, and that we were separated when this happened last year."

I sob in disbelief. My mind spins and pitches with the shock of it all, and I drop my head between my knees so I won't hyperventilate, turn blue and die on my living room floor, all alone. I desperately need a paper bag or I'm going to pass out, and the only thing within reach is a decorative glass vase. Grabbing it, I blow in and out of it while keeping my head down, trying anxiously to calm myself. It makes a strange hum every time I exhale. Like the bell choir for the apocalypse.

"Are you saying you're gay? Actually, no, you're not saying it, so I will. *Are. You. Gay?*"

It takes forever for him to answer. "I think so."

"You think so? What the hell are you talking about? How long, Michael? How long have you known you were gay?"

"A couple of months. Or maybe forever," he says. "You're my best friend and I love you. I'll always love you. I didn't want to hurt you."

"Forever? Did it ever occur to you that maybe getting married wasn't such a hot idea? At least not to a woman?"

"I wanted to marry you. Did it ever occur to *you* that I'm not the first guy in the world to separate my emotions from my sex life? You are a psychologist."

"Why does everyone keep saying that? I'm a psychologist for buildings, not closeted gay men."

And now, I can't think of anything except my husband having sex in the parking garage with Michigan hoops sensation Bobby Cavale.

"Why didn't you tell me before now?" I ask, seething.

"I didn't know how to tell you," he says.

"So you just let FOX Sports do your dirty work." I smirked. "Yes—it's every girl's dream on her wedding day, to find out from Don Bell at the update desk that her husband is screwing around."

"I can't believe you're watching FOX Sports," says Michael. As though I'm the big betrayer in the family for getting my sports-related scandals from Michael's big competitor.

"Seriously?"

"I'm sorry, so sorry. I never wanted to hurt you. But if you could just do this one thing for me . . ."

"But it's a lie," I say, outraged. He has some freaking nerve.

"I know," he admits. "But if you don't, they'll fire me on an ethics violation. If you say we were separated at the time, they'll give me a warning."

"You *are* an ethics violation," I snark. "Are you in love with him?" It aches to say the words.

"No," says Michael. "It was just sex. That's all."

"I'm not going to ESPN," I say. "I'm not telling a lie to cover up all your lies."

The line is quiet. "If you don't, I'll get fired. Is that what you really want?"

"Don't put this on me," I say. "This is all you."

"I know it is, I'm sorry to even ask you. Alex, I'll lose my job," he pleads. Jesus, I'm so angry with him, but I don't know if I can bring myself to help torpedo his whole life. Or stand by doing nothing while it happens. Standing by, doing nothing, isn't exactly my forte.

"I'm not sure I want to inform your bosses at ESPN that we're getting a divorce before I tell my family," I snap.

"Divorce? Who said anything about a divorce?" he asks. He actually sounds surprised.

"You're gay!" I yell. "Of course we're getting a divorce. What did you think would happen? Tuesday: laundry day; Thursday: Costco; Saturday: gay sex orgy? You are out of your freaking mind, Michael.

Also, this seems to be a bit of an afterthought for everybody right now with the shameful media frenzy and all, but you *cheated* on me."

"I just thought maybe we could somehow work it out . . . ," he says.

"You thought wrong," I say. "As for ESPN, I'll think about it."

"Thank you, thank you," he says with a sigh. "But think fast, the flight leaves at ten-thirty."

I hang up without saying goodbye, which is juvenile and rude, and feels freaking amazing. Dialing Darcy's number, I do pros and cons in my head—should I be going to talk to Michael's bosses at ESPN? Con: Michael loses his job, and sometime in the near future I might possibly regret not being a better human being. Also, even though there is absolutely no reason to, I know I'll feel guilty anyway if Michael gets fired. I guess that's how all those political wives end up standing on the platform, next to their lying, cheating husbands—smiling tersely like first runner-up in some zombie beauty pageant. Pros: I'm an instant candidate for sainthood; if I weren't agnostic, I'd be home free. That's all I can think of, except that Connecticut is lovely in the fall—but that doesn't really seem like a good enough reason to travel out of state to perjure myself.

Darcy picks up on the second ring.

"How are you holding up?" she asks. No hello. "Are you watching the news?"

"Not anymore," I say. "Just tell me if it gets any worse, okay?"

"It will," she says.

"I told Michael I wanted a divorce, which seemed like a big surprise to him. Michael wants me to go with him to Connecticut to tell his bosses at ESPN that we were separated when he started screwing Bobby Cavale. He actually believes this will keep him from getting fired."

"It probably will," Darcy answers. "If you two were married at the time he slept with Bobby, they can and will likely fire him for violating the ethics clause in his contract. If you two were separated, they can't fire him—otherwise they'd be discriminating against him for his sexual orientation, which is illegal in Connecticut. Even if it wasn't, they'd probably want to avoid the appearance of discrimination.

Michael is talented, a rising star at ESPN. My guess is that the network is looking for a way to keep him. Which is where you'd come in."

"I really don't feel comfortable with lying."

"I know you don't," Darcy says reassuringly, "but this is more a matter of spin, of perspective. Let me be practical for you right now, do a little crisis management. It's my job, after all, and I'm good at it, and there's no way you're thinking clearly after your morning from hell. So here it is: Michael is gay, so you've always been separated, at least metaphorically. I don't think you should look at this from the viewpoint of should you lie or shouldn't you, because without context, the answer is, of course, no."

"Even with context the answer is no," I interject.

"Sure," she continues, "but I think you should look at what you want to do here, and we can sort right from wrong later."

"Spoken like someone who works in politics," I say.

"Ha. Okay, think of it this way. Big picture—first, you're going to end up paying the cheating jackass alimony because he screwed around and got himself fired. That's a payment that's going to burn like hell every damned month. And that one little white lie saves you thousands and thousands of dollars. Is that particular truth worth thirty grand a year for the next five years? Second, if you don't help Michael keep his job, which is what we're really talking about here, how will you feel about that next week after he's fired? How would you feel about it on your deathbed?"

"By next week I'd probably feel terrible. Or completely justified. I'm not sure. On my deathbed? I'd hope I'll have bigger things to worry about."

"I think that's your answer, then." says Darcy. "A year from now, or ten years from now, you will hopefully have moved forward. Maybe acquired your own twenty-year-old basketball hunk. I think if you don't help Michael now, your guilt will keep you stuck in this day forever. Let it go, let him go. Not to mention, if you do this, the stench of scandal goes away, and ESPN will do everything they can to kill the story. On the flip side, if you march in there like the wronged woman and tell them you learned that Michael was cheating on you with a college basketball player this morning, just like everybody else in the country, you'll give this story legs, and it will take longer to die down. Upside—doing this will help you both move on. That's my professional advice."

"Clearly Michael is not having any trouble whatsoever with moving on," I sulk.

"True. Right. Let's not forget that Michael screwed around. Are you medicated? Or are you out in your driveway right now, torching his stupid yellow golf pants and those ridiculous Dennis Rodman action figures and dancing around the bonfire?"

"Medicated," I say. "Tequila."

"So what are you going to do?" Darcy asks.

"I want to do the right thing," I say.

Darcy sighs. "Right is relative."

4

I grab a quick shower, throw some clothes and toiletries in a bag, and meet Michael at the Sarasota airport for the ten-thirty flight to LaGuardia. My face burns with humiliation as we wait at our gate; the news of Michael's sex scandal is blaring away on half a dozen televisions overhead. Now CNN has the story too. This isn't even real news! Why can't a seven-pound Chihuahua drag a fireman out of a burning building or something? Why hasn't one of the Kardashians gotten a back tattoo of one of the other Kardashians? Where are the politicians taking bribes and naked selfies, and celebrities short-circuiting their ankle monitors to go street racing with Lindsay Lohan when I need them most?

In any Florida airport, at least half the travelers are over eighty, so at least I could count on a big chunk of them being hard of hearing. Or asleep. As for the rest, quite a few people in the gate area are looking at the TV and then checking out Michael, trying to figure out if he's that guy on the screen. I scrunch down in my chair and pray for stealthiness, keeping my giant sunglasses over my eyes indoors, even though I'm certain I look ridiculous, like some wannabe movie star. I *feel* ridiculous, especially while trying to read my *People* magazine through the ultradark lenses. I purchased a whole stack of glossy gossip magazines at the airport gift shop, so I wouldn't have to think, make eye contact with other humans, or listen to Michael yammer on the plane.

The flight is terrible, and I wish I could nap but I can't. My mind is razor sharp with betrayal and outrage, ruminating on how many days I have before running Michael over with my car would be counted by a jury as premeditated. Michael puts his hand on my arm, which makes my flesh crawl. I have to get away from him, and the first-class restroom has a line, so I make my way down the aisle to the bathrooms in the back of the plane. Squeezing into the tiny closet, I splash some water on my face, a one-handed challenge because the water only runs when I'm holding down the lever. My wedding ring sparkles in the unflattering glare of the overhead fluorescents. My face looks green. I need a vacation. Somewhere tropical. With cabana boys. Like Mexico without all the murder.

I stare at the reflection of my wedding and engagement rings in the airplane mirror—even though they're obviously cursed, a symbol of my apparently fake marriage, they are picture-perfect, vintage platinum and aquamarine. I love those rings, I spent months picking them out myself—and I wonder if I could get away with wearing them on my other hand. Probably not.

A sad thought occurs to me. If Michael and I are going to convince his bosses that we're separated and headed for divorce, the rings are a dead giveaway that we're full of crap. Pissed, I pull at the rings to take them off, dismayed to find them stuck. My fingers are probably swollen from the flight. Or maybe from this morning's crack-of-dawn tequila shots. I squirt foul, industrial-smelling hand soap from the dispenser and lather up my hand, tugging again at the lubricated bands. Suddenly, the rings fly from my finger and ricochet off the edge of the sink like they were spring-loaded.

I gasp in horror as my elegant platinum wedding band bounces and then goes airborne, as if in slow motion, landing with a splash and a tinny clink right smack in the airplane toilet. My engagement ring, weighed down by a respectable-size round aquamarine, spins off kilter and sort of skitters across the plastic seat of the toilet before finally dropping to the floor. Oh no, oh no, oh on, oh no . . .

Peering into the depths of the toilet, I curse Michael as I spot the ring, a glittery island in a chemical blue puddle.

Argh! Now what? There's no way I'm reaching my hand down a disgusting airplane toilet. No way. Not even with opera-length rubber gloves. Not even with one of those yellow hazmat suits (not that I packed one). No way. I scoop my engagement ring off the bumpy rubber floor and check the tiny sink to make sure it's plugged. Trying to figure out how I can possibly retrieve my wedding band, I rinse and rerinse my engagement ring with the pungent hand soap, and then slip it back onto my finger for safety. Right hand.

Considering and then quickly dismissing the idea of wrapping my hand in sixty or seventy layers of toilet seat covers, I attempt to check the cabinet above the sink for some kind of stick-like implement, but it's locked. Why in the hell would anyone lock the cabinet in the airplane bathroom? Is there some international ring of airline toilet-paper thieves? Do they really think some wily criminal mastermind is going to make off with a carry-on stuffed with a couple dozen rolls of that scratchy single-ply, or a refill jug of nuclear waste–scented hand soap?

The claustrophobic airplane bathroom is beginning to close in on me like a stinkier version of the Haunted Mansion at Disney, but I'm terrified to leave before retrieving my wedding band. One flush, and it will all be over.

Pushing the little orange button to signal the flight attendant, I slide the accordion door partially open. An impatient-looking man glares at me irritably.

"So sorry," I say. "I'm going to need a few minutes. Emergency."

The flight attendant appears behind him.

"How may I help you?" she asks.

"I'm having a situation," I say cryptically. It would be disgusting and wrong to ask her to help me with such a foul task. But I know the perfect guy for the job.

5

I tell the flight attendant Michael's seat number, and poke my head out of the restroom door like a dog hanging his head out of a car window, just to get a little air. This is not a popular move. The line for the toilet has grown exponentially, and the jittery cluster of passengers are visibly and vocally perturbed that I have not yet vacated the stall, like I'm enjoying taunting them by hogging the bathroom or something. Less than a minute later, a worried-looking Michael hurries down the aisle, following the flight attendant toward the bathroom where I've barricaded myself.

"What's going on?" he asks, as he makes his way to the front of the line. "Are you okay?"

"Could I please get three little bottles of tequila? And a couple of pairs of those plastic food service gloves?" I ask the flight attendant. She looks confused, but she must think it's for medicinal purposes, or emergency in-flight DIY surgery or something, because she disappears behind the curtain.

"My wedding ring fell in the toilet," I say to Michael. The line of bathroom-goers collectively groans.

"How did that happen?" he asks.

"Do you really want me to give you the play-by-play right now?" I ask, motioning to the line of six or seven people clustered at the back of the plane.

"I guess not," he says. "What do you want me to do?"

"I want you to put on those little plastic lunch lady gloves from the flight attendant and fish my ring out of the toilet. Thankyouverymuch."

The flight attendant returns quickly with the minibottles of Jose Cuervo and the gloves, and hands them to me as I exit the restroom door. I present the gloves and two of the bottles to Michael.

"I'm going back to my seat," I say, holding open the bathroom door for Michael. "After you get the wedding band out of the toilet with those," I say, pointing to the plastic gloves, "you can sanitize the ring with the Cuervo." He looks at me like I've completely lost my mind. And maybe I have. I leave him there at the airplane toilet, armed only with little plastic gloves and minibottles of booze, and a stunned look on his face. I crack the top on the third bottle of Jose Cuervo as I saunter down the aisle to my seat, and swig it back.

It burns all the way down, but I feel like an outlaw.

6

Michael returns from the bathroom looking like he's just delivered the pope's girlfriend's demon baby with his bare hands or something. He drops the wedding band, ensconced in a wad of scratchy tissues, into my hand, and takes his seat next to me. I slip it onto my ring finger on my right hand, pull my sleep mask over my eyes, and enjoy the buzz of tequila. When I get home, I'm going to boil the ring for a half an hour and throw away the pot.

From LaGuardia, we rent a car and make the two-and-a-half-hour drive from New York to ESPN's home office in Bristol, Connecticut.

My phone starts ringing the second we got off the plane. Samantha, my other best girlfriend. She's a high-strung lunatic who owns the most popular yoga studio in town. I never go. She's too intense.

"Ohmygod. Darcy just told me. Are you okay?" she asks.

"I'm on my way to ESPN to save Michael's job," I answer. "We're in the car."

"So that's a no?" she asks.

"That's a no," I say.

"What happened?" she asks. Weirdly, my first instinct is to tell her I'll call her later, so we can talk in private, but instead I decide to let it rip. Because, really, why shouldn't I?

"Breaking news: Michael is gay, he slept with a born-again basketball player named Bobby Cavale, FOX Sports thinks I'm a man, and now we're on our way to Connecticut to lie to his bosses. Also, I dropped my wedding ring in an airplane toilet. After this, I'll need a lobotomy and advice on how to forge Michael's handwriting for the suicide note. Not in that order."

Michael does a double take on that one.

"Oh yeah, and we're getting a divorce. That's about it," I say. "What's new with you?"

"Holy hell. How are you holding up?" Sam asks me. "That lying, cheating jackass. I'll bet you want to wring his neck. I mean, I knew he was probably gay, or bi, but I never thought he'd act on it." I looked over at Michael, who was staring tersely ahead as he drove us to Connecticut.

"Jesus, you too? What tipped you off?"

"Britney, Madonna, Gaga. Not to mention his total obsession with boy bands—One Direction, R5, After Romeo, 5 Seconds of Summer. I mean, I love Michael's taste in music. But it's not exactly the playlist of a straight man. More like an eleven-year-old girl."

"Yep, that's a big red flag." I sigh, humiliated by my cluelessness. "Listen, I'm shocked, devastated, furious, heartbroken, trying not to think about it right now, or I'll curl into a ball. Which I can't do because I'm on my way to fib to Michael's bosses about how I'm totally cool with him screwing some college player."

"You're a saint. He has no idea how lucky he is that you're doing this for him."

"True!" I say into the phone, turning to glare at Michael. "He has *no idea* how freaking lucky he is that I'm doing this for him." My call waiting beeps. "Crap, Sam—my mother is on the other line."

"See? And you thought this day couldn't get any worse," she says.

"Would you please do me a huge favor? " I ask. "Would you please call everybody and let them know what's going on?"

"Sure, sweetie, call me when you get back," she says. "Love you."

"Thanks," I say. "Love you too, Sam."

I click over to the other line.

"Hello, Mother," I say. "How have you been?" Michael shoots me a look of pity.

"Michael's father called us this morning," she says tersely. "Have you spoken with an attorney?" Always her first solution to any problem. Professional habit, I guess.

"No, I haven't. I've only known about this for a few hours," I say. "And some of those were on a plane."

"Where are you going?" she asks. "Are you coming here?" Because this day isn't bad enough already.

"No, I'm going to ESPN headquarters to try to save Michael's job," I say.

"I'm writing up a contractual agreement for you. Before you talk to anybody at ESPN, you need to get Michael to sign it."

"I think you may be getting ahead of yourself, Mother. What exactly will this agreement say?" I ask. Michael shoots me a look of panic.

"It's an agreement releasing you from paying any alimony should Michael lose his job. I'm sending you a list of attorneys, and I want you to start making calls as soon as we get off the phone."

"Mother, I'm in the car with Michael. I'm having the worst shock of my life. It's not exactly the best time to start calling divorce attorneys. I'm not asking him to sign anything right now." I sigh.

"I'll sign it," Michael interjects.

"Don't be an idiot," I say to him. "You don't even know what it says."

"I'm e-mailing it to you," she says. "Stop at a print shop before you set one foot inside the ESPN building and sign three copies of that document," instructs my mother.

"I have to go," I say. "I'll think about it."

"It may seem terrible now, but this public humiliation will be forgotten and the media will move on to something else."

"It's not so much the public humiliation as the private one. I'm still getting my head around the fact that Michael is gay."

"I assumed you knew," she says.

"What do you mean, you assumed I knew? Did you know?" I ask, aghast. What the hell? Am I the only person who *didn't* know?

"Well, your father and I had our suspicions. Remember when he was in that college production of *Wicked*?"

"Yes," I say.

"Well, there you are."

I smack myself on the forehead.

"That's it, Mom? A lot of people do theater in college."

"Yes, but most men don't try out for Elphaba. Also, he was always very neat. Straight men are pigs."

"Holy stereotypes, Mother. That's not even . . . I can't even begin . . ."

I sigh deeply; it's not even worth getting into with her. "Is Dad there?"

"He's playing tennis. He sends his best. Alex, I'm just trying to protect your interests," she says coldly. "That's what mothers do." That's certainly what my mother does. Other people's mothers probably send cookies and stay on the phone with you for hours consoling you about your rotten luck and your gay husband. Mine offers up stupid stereotypes and legally binding contracts. Sometimes, I wish I had someone else's mother.

"Thanks," I say. "Bye."

"Goodbye, Alexandra." The line goes dead.

I look at Michael and he shrugs his shoulders knowingly. He's known my mother almost as long as I have: about twenty-five years too long.

My phone is constantly buzzing with texts, and at least a half dozen calls, most of which I ignore or send to voice mail.

Carter left a message while I was on the other line with my mother, and I call him back immediately. He's one of our best friends, we've known him forever. Carter is the first openly gay person we ever met. He's out, way out, whip-smart and hilarious, and kills at karaoke. If anybody saw this one coming, it had to be Carter.

"Did you know?" I ask. "Did you suspect, have an inkling?

"Sure, sweetie, everybody knew," says Carter. Oh Jesus, was I blind or something?

"Oh my gawd, did you see my husband naked?" I ask, horrified. Michael, Carter, and I met our freshman year in college. If there was ever a time for sexual exploration . . . Not that I would know.

"I may be a slut, but I have my standards," Carter says, "I don't screw around with married men. Or men who happen to be in love with my best friends."

"Aww, thanks. I believe the term you're looking for is not *slut*, it's *sexually confident*," I say.

"I'm sexually confident that I don't screw married guys," says Carter.

I sigh. "Why didn't you tell me?"

"Honestly, it never occurred to me that you didn't know. But I didn't think he'd actually screw around on you. He's always been deeply committed."

"What do you mean?"

"It's just . . . most closeted gay men I know find some other way to fulfill their needs, they just do it anonymously—with a rent boy, or at a bathhouse or a park, or a glory hole in the airport bathroom in Minneapolis, or cruising gay bars when they're in a different city. A guy may pretend he doesn't want or need sex with another man, but his body and mind will betray the lie every time."

My intestines lurch, my hands start shaking, I will myself not to vomit, or stroke out. Michael travels constantly for work, and now all I can picture is him, wearing a studded leather vest and matching chaps, cruising for dudes. Jesus, I need to get myself checked for STDs.

I shake with sobs, completely distraught. "I'm his best friend, how did I not know this about him?" Michael reaches over and grasps my hand; his eyes are fixed on the road ahead, but I can see they're welling up with tears.

"Don't beat yourself up, sweetie," Carter says. "He just jammed your gaydar. We all see what we want to see when it comes to the people we love."

By the time Carter and I hang up, I'm ready to turn my phone off and hurl it out the car window, but I need to call my grandma Leona first. There's no way my mother hadn't called her the second she hung up with me. Grandma Leona is the kindest, funniest, most loving relative I have who doesn't belong to Michael.

I hit her number and she answers on the first ring.

"Hi, Grandma," I say. "So . . . I'm assuming that Mother told you what's going on with Michael and me."

"Oh, dear," she says soothingly. "Of course, it was bound to happen sooner or later."

Et tu, Grandma?

7

The sky is as gray and stormy as my mind feels right now, and Michael and I haven't spoken for most of the car ride. My brain is so juiced up with stress hormones I can't even think straight. Apparently I'm not the only one.

"Why did you lie all those years?" I screech, like some kind of wild animal. I'm trying to be calm. I'm *trying.*

"Most of it wasn't a lie," he says.

I roll my eyes.

"Give me a freaking break. It was all a lie."

He takes a deep breath and continues, "Okay." Another deep breath. "You and I have been together for our entire lives. There's no one more important to me than you. And one of the things I've always loved most about you is how you've always known exactly what you wanted to do, even when we were kids. And it was so easy to get caught up in the excitement of your ideas and your plans."

"Our plans," I correct him.

"Yes, our plans," he says. "But sometimes they were just your plans, and you'd get so unbelievably excited and get out your little notebook and map everything out and we'd both get swept away in the enthusiasm of it all. You'd be so excited and I didn't want to say anything. And please don't get me wrong, I owe some of the best things in my life to your plans—I know I never would have had the guts to pursue my dream career on my own. I was all set to get my MBA and do my forty years at some big corporation, but you insisted that I should do the thing I loved most. You figured out the path that would get me there. You believed in me, in what I could do, even more than I dared to believe in myself. But sometimes I just went along with it all and you were so certain, or so excited about something, I just felt like I couldn't say anything."

This just pisses me off. "How is that my fault if you don't tell me when you want something different? Why is it always the fault of the person who knows what they want when the passive person doesn't say one freaking thing? Why does the person who doesn't want to be in charge, who won't take responsibility, always blame the person who does?"

"You know, sometimes I didn't speak up because I didn't have a better idea, so I thought it was better to just go along."

"And then complain about it later," I snap.

A dozen arguments, from tiffs to blowouts, over our years together zip through my mind. Me asking Michael if he wanted to go on vacation to Arizona. He'd said that sounded good, and then once we got there he said he really didn't like the desert and that we never went where he wanted to go. When we found our house, he acted like he loved it as much as I did. And then a year into the renovation he tells me he never really thought it was a good idea. A million times when I'd ask him if he wanted to go to a certain movie or restaurant and he'd say "fine" or "sure." And then afterward he'd act like at best I'd never asked him in the first place, or at worst, like I'd dragged him out of the house by his hair and forced him to eat linguini and watch a romantic comedy.

"I was afraid of losing you," he says. "I was afraid I'd lose my job or never get promoted again. I love you, I love our life together, I love to make you happy. I *wanted* it all to be true, and I thought if I tried hard enough, I could somehow make it all true. What you don't seem to understand is that I wanted the happily-ever-after with you as much as you did. More, maybe. And I was afraid, *I am afraid,* of losing you."

I'm so angry I can feel my pulse pounding in my neck. My face burns. "Don't 'oh Alex' me. You're afraid of losing me? Are you insane? You ruined my whole life because you were too chickenshit to admit you're gay before you married me!" I yell.

"I didn't think you'd be so upset," he says, shaking his head. "You have a lot of gay friends, we had that fund-raiser for gay rights at the house last year. I don't understand, you love gay people . . ."

"Please tell me you're not that dense," I say.

He shakes his head, and even as I'm saying it, I can see why he wouldn't want his job to know. Michael is a basketball announcer for ESPN, and the world of sports isn't always exactly gay-friendly. He's the biggest sports fanatic I've ever known. He loves basketball and hockey and football and tennis, and pretty much anything that involves physical skill and competition. The guy knows ice-skating competition statistics. Caber tossing. Curling. Roller derby. Seriously, ESPN has been his dream job for as long as I can remember.

But I'm not ESPN. And I sure as hell shouldn't have to sacrifice my entire life at the altar of the broadcast desk.

I'm absolutely furious. It's not like I forced him to marry me or lie to me all these years. "Why didn't you say anything?"

"You were so happy," he says. "I love making you happy. I didn't want to disappoint you. I love you. And I thought I could love you all the way." He sighs deeply, and for a second I wonder if it's manufactured. I can't believe anything anymore—even his sighs ring false.

"I was afraid," he says. "I was afraid of losing everything."

"That's bull. Carter is gay. My hairstylist is gay. Our *accountant* is a lesbian. Grandma Leona hasn't missed Drag Queen Bingo in seven years. Our families would have accepted you, I would have accepted you, the world would have accepted you, but you were so freaking worried that the boys at ESPN might not love you that you were willing to let me spend the best years of my life living a lie while you screw around on the side."

"That's not what happened," he stammers.

"That's *exactly* what happened. We were supposed to be best friends, and you didn't even care enough about me, about yourself, to be honest with me. You would rather pretend to enjoy having sex with me for the last fifteen years than admit who you are. No wonder I always had to be the one to initiate sex! It's not like you ever did! You let me feel like I was completely undesirable! I've been on a diet for fifteen years because of you! You care more about yourself and protecting your stupid, fragile ego and your career than you do about me."

Jesus, I need a cheeseburger.

"I'm sorry," he mumbles, looking out the side window to avoid eye contact. Wuss. "I'm sorry! I'm sorry! I can't apologize any more than I already have. It's done! I can't go back. You're still my best friend. I can't change who I am," he says defiantly. I hate that excuse. *It's already done so there's no point in apologizing or even having a discussion about the thing you're upset about.*

"No one was asking you to change who you were. You want me to be all cool about it—well, too late for that, buddy," I yell.

"You know what's really shitty about all this?" I ask. "All our friends are going to rally around and support you, of course, because not one of them wants to be seen as homophobic. But what's really shitty is that I have to support you too, or everyone is going to see me as some bitch. They probably will anyway. Everyone will hate me like I'm the next Kris Jenner or something, because *I* must have known, or *I* must have chained you up in the freaking closet. You come out, and somehow it's my fault. You decimate my life, and yet *you* deserve all the love and support."

I can barely breathe. "If you just decided after five years of marriage that you wanted to screw around with other women, nobody would be calling you brave or patting you on your stupid back. They'd call you what you are, a lying, selfish, cheating bastard. We wouldn't even be having this conversation. And what if I were the one who came out as a lesbian? Once again, everyone would support you!" I say bitterly. "They'd say I'd emasculated you, or ruined your life, and poor you. But once again, I'd somehow be the villain and you'd be the poor little victim. You know what? Can you even think of a single word that means the female equivalent to emasculate? I'll bet you can't. I had to look it up on my phone because I couldn't think of one. You know what it is? It's *defeminize*, a word that hasn't been used since 1907, when some misogynist wrote a newspaper article about the reasons why women shouldn't be allowed to vote," I scream. "That's just fucking wrong!"

"Alex—"

"I'm not done," I shriek, completely out of control. "You know what, I'm going to bring back that word, and use it every time some troll says a female comic isn't funny because she doesn't also look like a supermodel, or calls a woman a bitch or a dyke just because she's powerful."

"I love you," he says, his eyes spilling over with tears, his face red and blotchy.

"Don't try to screw with me by telling me how much you love me. This is about you being an asshole. Your whole stupid ego depends on your airtime. You were willing to hide who you are, ruin my life, lie to everybody we know, all just to keep your face on TV and your little ego intact. If you had told me when we were fifteen or twenty or twenty-four, I would have still loved you, we could have lived out this fantasy you seem to have about us being best friends. But now . . ."

"You are my best friend," he whimpers.

"You have to be freaking kidding me," I say. "Why would I be friends with someone who is a total liar, someone who placed his career ahead of my entire life?"

"I didn't mean to hurt you," he says. "It was never my intention . . ."

I fight back my tears, determined to say what I need to say. "You have taken everything from me. I thought I was going to have children, I thought I was going to have a life, to have a home; now I'm just the pathetic woman married to that gay guy on ESPN. Put on a dress, dance around a campfire for all I care, but don't you dare think that the reason I hate you is because you're gay. I hate you because you're a liar, a chickenshit liar who ruined my life."

"You have no idea how hard it is to be a gay man," he whines.

"Neither do you, you fucking coward."

8

He keeps trying to get me to talk to him for the rest of the drive, but I just ignore him and stare out the window while I figure out what I'm going to do once we get there. One white lie keeps Michael at the job he loves, and makes the whole torrid affair slightly less scandalous for the born-again basketball player. I hate myself for being so weak, but I actually feel a little sorry for Bobby Cavale; at the age when we're all just trying to figure out who we are, and he gets to do it in front of the entire U.S. sports media.

It's almost four o'clock by the time we arrive in Bristol. The parking lot is packed, and I'm just about to get out of the car when Michael reaches for my arm.

"Wait, please," he says. "It was wrong, selfish, of me to ask you to do this. Especially after everything you've been through today. I'm sorry. I'll handle this by myself." He hands me the keys to the rental car. "I'm not sure how long this meeting will last. There are some decent places to eat up the street. I'll call you when I'm done, and then we can head back to New York."

"Are you serious?" I ask. Great, he drags my butt all the way to ESPN and now he wants me to wait in the car or something.

"I am. I've hurt you and lied to you, and you don't deserve this. You are my best friend, and more than anything, I want to be yours again. So I'll do this on my own."

We sit in the car for several minutes while I try to figure out how to respond.

I remember what Darcy said. About getting stuck in this moment, unable to move forward.

And then I think about the thirty grand in alimony. Every year. Maybe forever.

"You don't have to go in there alone," I say benevolently. "I'll go with you." I'll probably regret it, but I sure didn't trek all the way to Bristol to sit at some T.G.I. Friday's drowning my sorrows in onion rings, mainlining Barbados rum punch while Michael gets fired. Cosmically speaking, can't I save myself by saving Michael? And if I can't save myself, at least can't I save myself the thirty grand?

We exit the car and cross the parking lot to the entrance of the ESPN campus. I trail behind Michael wondering how the hell I got here.

As we enter the building, I pull him close and whisper in his ear, "You are *so* f-ing lucky I'm doing this for you."

"I know," he says solemnly.

Michael texts his bosses as soon as we arrive, and they're waiting for us in a large conference room. There are sandwiches and baskets of cookies, bottles of water and soda, on a table just inside the door of the conference room—enough food to keep us holed up in here for a week. Who knew Armageddon would be catered?

There are four men already in the room, and one woman, and the man at the head of the table introduces himself as Tank Turner, which seems like a good name for G.I. Joe's Republican cousin. I select a bottle of sparkling water, and wonder nervously if death row inmates actually eat the T-bone steaks and fried okra and shrimp cocktails and MoonPies and banana pudding they request for their last meals, or if they're just too stressed to enjoy them. The executives look nice enough, and I try not to obsess about the fact that they will soon be asking me about my sex life, and worse, Michael's. Pleasantries are exchanged awkwardly. "Did you have a nice flight?" Uh, no. It's not a vacation, it's the worst day of my life and I'm spending it at ESPN. It's like making small talk at a funeral: you're trying to make things less awkward, and the family of the deceased just wishes they could be alone at home under the covers with a fork and an entire Bundt cake.

I've been eyeing the oatmeal raisin cookies in the bowl for the past three minutes, so I stand up to make a dash to the cookie bowl at the same, exact second Tank Turner, the tall, gray-haired man at the head of the table, sits down and says, "Let's begin." So now everyone else sits down too, while I'm standing up with my arms outstretched toward the cookie bowl. Well, that's awkward. My face colors, and I sit down quickly, pretending to adjust my seat, and clumsily knock over the bottle of water I'd just opened. A fast-moving, kamikaze puddle makes an aggressive waterfall into my lap, spreads like a hostile army all over the table, and starts dripping down the table's sides, as Michael and the executives leap from their seats to avoid water in their laps. Too late: the guy on my left ends up with a two-inch wet spot right over his crotch, which makes him look like he wasn't able to make it to the men's room on time. That will go over big at a sports network.

It would just be awkward to go get the cookie now, right? Still, they look pretty good. Grabbing a wad of napkins off the table, I fervently dab at the spill, trying to mop it up before it reaches the lap of the man sitting to my right, as the rest of the group scrambles to get papers and electronic devices out of the way of the flash flood of Pellegrino. When the spill is finally contained, Tank Turner gets back to business. I squirm around in my seat, trying to get comfortable for the inquisition, with a wet spot on my skirt the size and shape of a lobster. A gigantic, mutant lobster.

"Michael, Alex, thank you for coming to speak with us today." Michael nods like he had an option and is there to talk about his hookup out of the goodness of his heart. I don't say anything. What's the point? "I'm sorry to be so personal, er, um . . ." Tank Turner clears his throat. "But, we need to clarify some of the, er . . . details." Michael sits still as a stone, not blinking, not breathing. Oh dear God. This is going to take forever, if I don't step in and take charge.

"You'd like to know if Michael and I were separated at the time of Michael's relationship with Bobby?" I ask bluntly.

"Er, yes." Mr. Turner nods. A look of mortified panic crosses Michael's face.

"Yes. We were separated, we're filing for divorce. I knew Michael was gay at the time, and the relationship with Bobby Cavale had my blessing. Anything else?" I ask. The quickest way to cut off this inquisition surely is to just tell them what they want to hear. If I didn't take control of this mess, we were going to be here all damned day listening to Mr. Tank Turner " um" and "er" his way through Michael's sex life. I don't have the patience or the stomach for that. I hate to lie, but it seems almost worse to tell the truth.

Darcy instructed both Michael and me to call his smutty little fling a *relationship,* instead of a *booty call* or a *cheating bastard screw party,* which is my personal favorite—she said it would make it harder for ESPN to fire him. If anybody knows how to ride out a scandal. it's Darcy. She also said that me telling ESPN that Michael and I were separated at the time would be the quickest way to kill the story, which would be slightly less scandalous without the shadow of infidelity, at least on Michael's end.

"Er, no, no more questions from me," says Tank Turner as he glances around the room. "Anybody else have a question for Alex?" They all shake their heads silently. "All right, then." He smiles at me. "Thank you so much for your, er, candor today. We do need to speak with Michael privately if you wouldn't mind waiting in the lobby. Please take a plate of food with you, I wouldn't want you to get hungry while you're waiting."

"Thank you," the rest of the executives at the table echo. They all sound the same. They all look the same, even the woman. So I stand up, strategically placing my leather tote in front of the wet spot on my skirt, and grab a plate as I head toward the door. Suddenly I'm starving, and I pile the plate with two sandwiches, two oatmeal cookies (okay, three, but one of them is broken), and a bag of chips. I grab a napkin and a new bottle of water off the side table, and offer an awkward salute and something that looks a little like a parade wave as I leave the room. Well, that was awful. Balancing my teetering plate in one hand and my tote in the other, I make my way down the hallway and back to the main lobby. I wonder briefly if I should turn in my security pass, but I decide I should probably keep it in case I need to go back inside for some reason. Pulling out my laptop, I try to get some work done or at least avoid looking at the large television set blasting ESPN that is mounted on the wall. Powering up my computer, I open a charity benefit file and get to work on a set list for the orchestra. Tempo and musical selections are very important in creating an environment for charitable-giving events.

Four hours later, I'm still hanging out in the lobby. The lobster-shaped spill on my skirt has finally dried, and I've scarfed down the entire plate of food I brought from the conference room. It's probably uncouth to go back for seconds, right? My client's orchestra selection list is perfected, timed strategically with the big asks throughout the evening. I e-mail the rest of my clients to check in, or update them on details of their projects, and then reach out to some potential new clients. I hate pitching new business. But I make myself do it for twenty minutes every day.

Finally, and despite my better judgment, I spend the last thirty minutes watching clips and reading posts about Michael's affair on FOX Sports and a slew of sports blogs. The commentators ridicule Michael and Bobby, and make observations that are often outright homophobic. They would not be getting away with this over at the *Huffington Post*, but somehow, in the sports world, nobody seems to get that upset when you refer to a twenty-one-year-old as a fag. Many of the fan and viewer comments are brutal and offensive, and for the first time it hits me that Michael's trepidation about being out is genuine. Our group of friends, and the educated, progressive enclave we live in, are warmly accepting of, and include, gay people—but the rest of the world is not the same.

My instincts to protect him flare. Yes, I'm angry with him, and I have every reason to be. (Which I will be reminding him of until he dies of old age.) But no one deserves to be attacked this way, to be on the receiving end of the nastiness and cruelty that are being flung at Michael and at Bobby Cavale. Who are these awful people and why do they even care? The comments range from obnoxious gay sex jokes to quotations of scripture and assertions that Michael and Bobby will burn in hell. I can't even imagine what it must feel like to be the target of so much hatred.

What is taking so long? Could it really take four hours to fire or keep Michael?

Finally, Michael emerges in the lobby. He looks worn out and in need of a long, hot bath.

"Sorry that took so long," he says, not giving anything away. "I had to meet with the network's publicist."

"It's okay," I respond. "What's the verdict?"

"Outside," he whispers. Damn, that sounds ominous. I gather up my belongings, which are by now strewn across two chairs and the coffee table in the lobby.

"Good night, Danny," Michael says loudly to the security guard. The guard nods in return.

Michael and I push through the doors and out into the brisk evening air. Jeez, I should have brought a heavier coat. If I actually had one. Not much need for blizzard-wear in Florida.

"What happened?" I ask. "Are you fired?"

Michael looks tense on the way to the rental car, but does not utter a word until we're inside the car.

And then, he bursts into tears.

"Oh my God. They fired you?" I ask, reaching out to hug him over the armrests of the rental car, and then patting him awkwardly on his shoulder. "Tell me everything."

9

"I'm keeping my job," he says quietly through the sobs. He wipes his eyes with the back of his hand and starts rooting around in the car for something to blow his nose on. The rental car is spotless, so his choices are pretty much limited to either the floor mats or the rental agreement. Reaching into my tote, I hand him the last of a small package of tissues. Yes, I'm an *always be prepared* nerd. I never leave home without emergency supplies. Like tampons, and 3D glasses.

"What happened?" I ask. "What did they say?"

"It was just so humiliating," he says. "They asked me every detail of what happened with Cavale, and whether we met while I was working, how old he was at the time, like I was some kind of pervert, if there were more videos, if there were more players I'd slept with, and a lot of very personal questions."

"You didn't have to answer those questions. They didn't have any right to ask you that," I say indignantly, aware I had asked him the exact, same questions. I know, I know. It's weird I feel so angry I want to throw bricks at Michael's head—but I'm also fiercely protective of him and don't want anyone else to hurt him. Clearly, I'm going to need therapy, and lots of it. Maybe shock therapy, the kind that erases your memories. Do they still do that?

"I did if I wanted to keep my job," he answers. "They're suspending me from airtime for two weeks at the end of the season, and I had to sign something that says I would adhere to the ESPN ethics clause. The whole time in there I couldn't stop thinking about how hard this must be on you, and how you must have felt this morning when the story broke." He pauses for a moment to catch his breath. "I'm so sorry for how I've betrayed you. What you did in there for me was beyond friendship, and far more than I deserve."

"I agree," I say. "You owe me."

"I do," he says solemnly, and then breaks down.

"I'm sorry, so sorry," he sobs. "I never wanted to hurt you. I'm truly sorry, I was wrong."

"It's all going to be okay," I say in my most soothing voice. I just wish I believed it.

"Wait," I say. "You're off the air for two weeks after basketball season ends? And you have to adhere to the ethics clause that you're already subject to in your employment contract?"

"Yes," he says.

"That's not a punishment at all," I say. "You're not ever on the air after basketball season ends. Did they add anything new to the ethics clause?"

He shakes his head. "No."

"So aside from the admittedly mortifying inquisition, there's really no serious consequence."

"I guess so," he says. "The suspension was for what they called 'fraternization,' mostly because we gave Bobby a lot of airtime."

"But that's your producer's call, not yours. Besides, Bobby's a top draft pick."

"I know," he says.

"This is good news, right?"

"It is," he says. "But it feels like bad news. I'm lucky I still have my job."

"Well, now at least you won't have to have that pesky, 'hey, by the way, I'm gay' conversation with your bosses," I say. "Or your wife."

"Christ, I'm an ass," he says.

"Yep," I agree.

"Tell me what to do to make this right," he says. "I'll do anything. I owe you."

"Sure," I say, only half joking. "You owe me big. You owe me a soul mate."

"Done," he says, grinning. "What's your type?"

"Straight," I say, deadpan. We both start cracking up.

He shoots me a prime-time smile, fires up the rental car, and we head back to New York City, where he's booked a hotel suite near Times Square. Touristy, but fun anyway. The last flight from New York to Sarasota leaves at 8:05 P.M., so we already knew there was no way to get back from Bristol in time to make it. Weirdly, I want to protect Michael from TV and the Internet—so after we settle in to the hotel, we go out for a nice dinner at Delmonico's, where we drink too much wine and share a fantastic crème brûlée. We're tipsy when we go for a nightcap at the King Cole Bar at the St. Regis, and by the time we hit another bar at a funky little dive, we're laughing hysterically about which one of us is the bigger idiot—Michael for thinking he could be happily married to a woman, or me, for not having a clue.

By the time we take a cab back to our hotel it's almost two in the morning. In our room, Michael takes the fold-out sofa in the seating area, giving me the king-size bed in the master suite. It's beyond weird not to be sleeping in the same bed, but I guess it would be even weirder if we were. I have nothing whatsoever to sleep in, because when I packed my bag under extreme duress this morning, I apparently felt the need to bring three skirts, five shoes, a knot of costume jewelry, and a sun hat. No underwear. No shirts. No toothbrush. No nightgown. Just wanting to be out of my clothes, I make Michael give me his one clean shirt to sleep in.

That night, I lay in bed watching the chorus line of lights from Times Square beaming through the window, thinking about everything that had happened, and wondering if I'll ever find someone who will love me as much as Michael does. Someone straight. Just as I'm about to fall asleep, I hear Michael snoring softly from the sofa bed. It's the first thing that's felt normal all day.

10

The next morning I look and feel sleazy, like a walk of shame after a one-night stand. Well, I suppose that's what it feels like, I've never actually had a one-night stand. I've only ever had Michael.

I should hate him for what he did to me, but I spent all last night laughing with him and supporting him. I feel so dirty. And now I can't take it back.

Now Michael assumes we're still friends. And he will not be convinced otherwise.

11

Michael and I fly back to Sarasota on Monday morning, leaving at 6:00 A.M., which means dragging ourselves out of our hotel at four-thirty in the morning, after just two and a half hours of sleep. I'm nauseated from too many dirty martinis last night and the massive shocks of adrenaline my body keeps pumping into my gut just to keep me upright. On the ride to the airport, Michael confesses all his past encounters, admitting to several one-night stands in college, and anonymous sex when he traveled. Way more information than I want to know. I don't want these awful images in my head, so every time he drops another detail I close my eyes and picture Voldemort from the *Harry Potter* movies. It helps in a weird way.

"I thought that I was protecting you by keeping the truth from you," he says. "I didn't want to hurt you—please believe me. I've just realized that it will hurt you more if you have to learn the truth piecemeal—that every revelation will feel like a new betrayal, and I don't want to do that to you. Please know that I'm sorry for everything, I'll always love you, and I'll never dishonor our relationship again by lying to you."

It's awful, but it's a relief. I cry and cry, and Michael cries too. Hearing it all at once makes me number to the details, but at last I feel like the worst is over. He's gay. I'm not a man. What are you gonna do?

When we get to the airport that morning, I tell Michael I have a migraine, which mercifully keeps him from talking to me anymore. He dotes on me, brings me some ibuprofen and a liter of water from the airport gift shop, and carries my laptop bag onto the plane. The flight home is only an hour and a half, but I'm sleep deprived and wiped out in every sense. We haven't even taken off yet before I pass out in my seat, and I'm out cold until my own foghorn-quality snores wake me up. So ladylike.

Yesterday felt like an out-of-body experience, or one of those nightmares you wake up from sweating and howling, clutching your vibrator like a samurai sword. Once Michael and I arrive at the Sarasota airport, it hits me all at once—the shame, the devastation, the anger, the betrayal. The fact that I might never be loved, that I'd never really been loved—not all the way, at least. Or have sex again. Or have a baby. It's almost too much to bear. I'm wrung out and exhausted and I can't wait to go home and bury myself under my duvet and sleep until it doesn't hurt anymore.

"So . . . ," says Michael, as he stands beside my car in short-term parking, fidgeting awkwardly.

"You should go to a hotel," I say.

Throwing my suitcase in the backseat, I pull out of the space, leaving him just standing there in the parking garage.

12

Thirteen hours later, I wake up pissed as hell and launch myself out of bed. How dare he! The elastic from my purple satin sleep mask is tangled in my hair, and after ten minutes standing in front of the bathroom mirror trying to work it free, I'm exasperated and decide to just leave it hanging there. I can't be bothered, I'm on a mission.

High on adrenaline and fury, I stuff all of Michael's suitcases and his stupid sports team duffel bags full of dirty laundry, and grab an old box of condoms we've had in the nightstand since college, and dump them in too. Yanking his beautiful designer ties from the rack in his closet, I viciously wad them up into wrinkly little balls and cram them all in the various pockets of the suitcases and duffel bags. Ha! That will make him crazy, he's always been so freaking meticulous about his clothing. Like a beauty queen. Yes, I just heard myself. Dragging the bags out the front door, I leave the whole mess for him out on the front porch. The sleep mask still stuck in my hair flaps casually in the evening breeze. I debate adding some of Morley's cat litter to the suitcases for ambiance, but decide against it at the last minute.

But I'm not ruling it out.

I don't care where he goes, I just want him the hell out of the house.

Jackass.

"Looks like you're busy this evening," says my neighbor Zelda from the sidewalk. Her silver hair is pulled up in an elegant chignon as usual, and topped off with a sparkly barrette. Her tiny white Chihuahua, Gabbiano, is tucked under her arm.

I've always thought the name Zelda Persimmon sounded like it belonged to a witch, or an old vaudeville star. But Zelda is a formerly world famous circus performer—a beautiful flying trapeze artist who stunned and delighted audiences as the first woman in history to do a triple somersault in midair. There's even a plaque with her name on it among the other circus luminaries on St. Armands Circle.

"I'm so sorry, dollface," she says kindly as she approaches my porch. "Your grandmother called me this morning." She offers up a plate of muffins wrapped in plastic wrap.

"Did you know about Michael too?" I ask, dragging one of the duffels to the far side of the porch so it won't block my front door.

"Doll, I spent my entire career around men wearing purple satin leotards and sequined velvet capes trimmed with feathers. I'm not exactly the best judge of these things." She laughs.

Zelda always knows just what to say. I smile at her and she hands me the plate of muffins.

"Leave this for now," she says, motioning toward the door. "Let's have a treat."

"Thank you," I say.

She follows me inside, and I offer her a drink. "Milk, coffee, water, something stronger?"

She sets Gabbiano down on the floor and he skitters off to find my cat Morley. They're best friends. It's weird. Morley doesn't like anyone except Gabbiano.

"You look like you could use a glass of wine," she says.

"Probably so," I admit. Zelda makes herself comfortable on the sofa as I head to the kitchen to grab the wine, corkscrew, glasses, plates, and napkins for the muffins. Suddenly I'm starving; I haven't eaten anything since the airplane eggs this morning. Returning to the living room, I set down the plates and glasses.

I pour the wine while Zelda places muffins on the plates.

"To a fresh start," she toasts. I raise my glass and take a slug of the wine, and then bite into the chocolatey muffin. It's delicious, maybe the best muffin I've ever tasted. She reaches over, and gently untangles the sleep mask from my hair. I'd forgotten it was there.

"Thanks. Did you make these?" I ask. "They're yummy." I'm already halfway through the oversize muffin. It's like I've never tasted food before.

"You're welcome. Go easy on the muffins, doll," she says. "They're strong."

"I haven't eaten all day," I answer nonchalantly. "This is lunch. And dinner. Wait, what do you mean, strong?"

"You've had a rough couple of days. They're a special recipe," Zelda says with a mischievous grin.

"Huh?" I ask, taking another bite. These suckers are addictive.

"My sister takes a little cannabis for her glaucoma. Medical grade, of course. Good stuff," she says.

It takes a second to register.

"Are you saying these muffins have pot in them?" I ask incredulously. Suddenly, I start cracking up. Am I really eating chocolate pot muffins with my eighty-year-old neighbor? Yes, I am. And it's not even the weirdest thing to happen to me this week.

Zelda starts giggling when I start cracking up, and before long we're just roaring with laughter. We laugh ourselves silly between bites, and I've downed two muffins by the time the marijuana starts making my brain fuzzy.

I've barely processed what's happened, nothing makes any sense to me. But I'm apparently too stoned to care. I start laughing again when I tell Zelda that the only time in my whole, measured life that I've ever tried pot is with my eighty-year-old party animal neighbor. Zelda and I are rolling around on the floor with our feet propped up on the coffee table, laughing so hard I'm in danger of wetting myself.

"So you didn't have a clue about Michael?" she asks.

"Nope. Honestly, I always figured our sex life was so, um, let's say *comfortable* because neither one of us ever had any practice before we got married."

Zelda snorts, and takes another bite.

"Also, I didn't really want to open that can of worms if it turned out I was just the worst in bed ever and Michael was just being nice all these years. Of course, what would he know?"

I didn't tell her what I've really been thinking: I'm thirty-one years old, for fuck's sake. A *psychologist*. How did I not notice that my husband is gay? Am I an idiot?

"Don't you dare tell my grandma Leona that we ate pot muffins!" I say, trying to look serious, but completely unable to keep a straight face. Zelda and my grandma hit it off at a barbecue Michael and I had a couple of years ago. They've been really tight ever since.

"Who do you think gave me the recipe?" she roars.

Zelda and I hang out, wasted like college students, for another hour or so, and then she calls for Gabbiano and the two of them head out the door. She's buzzed too, so I watch her from my front door to make sure she's okay, until I see her go inside her house and turn on her porch light.

As soon as she's home, I text Michael and tell him to come get his crap, and that I don't want to see or hear him.

I'm sitting on the couch in my pajamas, as my muffin buzz starts to dissipate, watching house porn on HGTV, and wondering if my life would suck less with a renovated kitchen.

It would definitely suck less if that *Property Brothers* guy Jonathan Scott were renovating my kitchen.

A laugh gurgles up out of nowhere. Jonathan Scott renovating my kitchen sounds like a euphemism for sex. The sweaty kind. Hmmpf. Not that I would know.

Two hours later, the suitcases have disappeared from the front porch, which is devastating and a relief at the same time. I haven't left the couch, except to peek out the window.

Michael being gay has nothing whatsoever to do with me, but it burns like the worst sort of rejection.

I want to be loved. I want to be ravaged. I need validation that I'm still desirable, that I'm not frigid or stupid. I have an aching, sickening feeling that no straight man will ever want me. Or love me. I feel like I have something to prove.

Which is how I end up downloading Closr at the stroke of midnight, and texting with some stranger at one in the morning, while simultaneously raiding my refrigerator in a mad search for something topped with bacon. I know, pathetic. In my defense, I'm probably still pretty wasted. At least that's what I'll tell Darcy and Samantha if this goes terribly, terribly wrong. Closr is a dating app that connects singles with potential matches in their immediate proximity. The app notifies you if there's a compatible singleton nearby, and then their photo appears on your phone or tablet. If you think they're attractive, and they think you're attractive, the app makes a match and encourages the two matches to send an introductory text from a multiple-choice selection of casual, racy, and pithy openers—and even suggests nearby places to meet up, such as a dance club, a coffee shop, or a bookstore. When my first match appears on my phone, I'm surprised. Markmatics, as he calls himself, looks fairly normal. Cute, even. Well, cute-ish. Maybe cute-adjacent. Early forties, short brown hair, dark eyes, toothy grin. And then the Closr app suggests we meet up nearby. At the gas station. Because really, what sparks romance like fluorescent lighting and microwave burritos? And how convenient that you can nuke your dinner, pick up some fishing lures, and get beer and prophylactics all in one place.

Why are you up so late? comes the text from Markmatics.

Jet lag, I respond, feeling oddly guilty, like I'm cheating on Michael or something.

Europe? Asia? texts Markmatics.

New York, I write back.

Yeah, the New York–Florida time difference is a killer, he writes. Okay, so he's almost sort of funny.

Long day yesterday, long night, early flight. Is there a word for NYC-lag?

No but there should be, he texts. *Hey—is Closr suggesting to you that we meet up at the Exxon station too? Or is the Closr algorithm just making some unkind assumptions about my level of sophistication?*

Yes. Kind of weird.

No, it's cool. I take all my dates there.

Seriously?

No. But they do have one hell of a Slushee bar.

It's surreal to me that you can be sitting in your pajamas with a sleep mask dangling from your hair one minute, and semi-flirting with a complete stranger in the middle of the night the next. We text back and forth for an hour or so, and then I beg off and tell him I need to go to bed. He tells me he's a mathematics professor at New College, and is up late grading papers. I slept all day, but there's work I need to do, and it feels weird and rude to text a stranger so late. We agree to meet the next day for drinks, which seems like a good idea at two o'clock in the morning. Maybe it isn't. It is completely pathetic, and honestly, this guy could be a serial killer or something—but is it so wrong to want *some* kind of validation that a man, any man, *any straight man*, could possibly find me attractive? Everyone else apparently looks up all their exes and old high school boyfriends online after getting their hearts broken. But how pitiful am I? I don't even have that.

I can't just sit around letting my ovaries curdle. I'm taking charge of my love life.

13

Closr is a pain in the ass. I meet Markmatics at six for drinks at Marina Jack on the bay, and as I'm walking into the bar, my Closr app dings repeatedly with a slew of potential new matches. Slipping into the ladies' room, I swipe up (for yes) and down (for no) to clear them from my phone, otherwise the damned thing will keep making that appalling noise—*aah-OOH-guh, aah-OOH-guh*, like an old-fashioned car horn. The wails of a Richter 7 orgasm would be more subtle, but I can't figure out a way to change it without turning off my ringer completely, and that's a nonoption. There are not one but *two* different shirtless men wearing furry unicorn masks on my Closr feed, which weirds me out in a way I can't begin to describe. Is this a thing? Eighteen photos later, mostly no's, and a few *oh-hell-no*'s, I readjust my push-up bra, touch up my lip gloss, and make my way back into the restaurant to meet Markmatics. He's at the bar, and waves to me as I enter. At least I think it's him. Otherwise, some stranger is very happy to see me. Okay, he looks nice. A little pudgier than his photo, but nice.

"Hey, Alex, good to meet you in person," he says, standing as I near the bar. He leans forward like he's going to kiss me on the cheek, and then turns a bright shade of fuchsia, like he's thought better of it.

"Nice to meet you too," I say. He motions to a stool on his right and I sit down. I feel awkward—very, very awkward. And guilty as hell, which I do not understand. My husband is gay. We're getting a divorce. Why the guilt? The bartender comes by and I order a glass of rosé. Markmatics is already drinking a dark beer of some kind.

"So, Closr . . . ," he says. I nod. That's not really a question. "You're pretty," he says, and then adds unsubtly, "Why are you single?" Which feels to me like he's really asking *What's wrong with you?*

"I have webbed feet," I crack.

"Really?" he asks.

"No." I laugh, and he smiles.

So I tell him about Michael cheating on me, leaving out the part about him being gay. I'm not sure why. The cheating is humiliating enough. Besides, Markmatics is clearly already wondering which part of me is defective. I don't exactly want to drop bread crumbs. The bartender brings Markmatics another beer, and me another glass of wine, and a plate of mini–crab cakes for us to share. He's a really good listener, and before I can stop myself, I end up spilling the whole wretched story.

"Oh, that guy Michael Miller from ESPN who screwed around with Bobby Cavale? I've seen that guy," he says. "I love basketball."

Oh goody, a fan. Even as I see the inappropriateness of my over-sharing in his eyes, I can't help it, I just keep talking and talking. And then I'm crying. Right there at the bar in front of a mortified stranger, dabbing my eyes with my used napkin and trying not to get any remoulade in my eyes.

"Uh," he says

"I'm so sorry, this is the first time I've ever been out with anyone." I sniffle.

"Ever?" he asks. I nod yes and a look of panic flashes in his eyes.

"Really, I'm sorry." I sniffle again, trying to pull myself together. "I was just thinking about . . . how much I really love the curly fries here." Crap, this place is pretty nice; I don't know if they even *have* curly fries. But I have bigger problems. I smile fakely and brightly and take a big swig of my wine. "So, Mark, tell me about your five-year plan." I'm acting crazy, *I know I'm acting crazy*. And yet I can't seem to stop myself. Stop! Stop! *I can't stop*. What's wrong with me?

"My what?" he asks.

"Your five-year plan. Where do you see yourself in five years? Married? Having kids? Still teaching at the college? You know, your plan for your future?"

He looks at me like I've just told him I have a radioactive STD, and stands up from his bar stool without warning. Quick as a flash, he rummages around in his wallet for some cash and drops a fifty-dollar bill on the bar.

"I'm sorry," he says. "I just remembered I have to be somewhere else."

"Oh, really?" I ask.

"Um, yeah. My pet ferret, his name is Arnold. He's . . . um, brown. He had surgery today at the pet hospital and I just remembered that visiting hours are about to end. It's pretty serious. We're not sure if he's going to make it."

"Oh my goodness," I say. "I'm so sorry. What happened to him? Do you want me to come with you to the pet hospital for support?" Losing a pet can be very traumatic.

"Oh . . . Um, no, but thank you," he stammers.

"I really don't mind," I say.

"Well, I *would*, but, um, unfortunately. . . ." He hesitates. "Uh, the pet hospital is very strict, they won't allow any visitors who aren't family . . ."

"They won't allow anyone who isn't family . . . of the ferret . . . ," I say. Finally light begins to dawn on me. I'm a crazy lady and he's trying to get out the door.

"I'll be sure to give him your best wishes. Thanks for . . . this," he says, motioning awkwardly at the bar as he backs away toward the exit. "See you around."

Oh gawd. Well, that was an unmitigated disaster. I abandon my drink, and try to pretend like I haven't just been dumped at the bar by a complete stranger with the worst sick ferret story in history. Maybe no one *will* ever want me. Maybe Michael is just the first in a long line of men who want to get as far away from me as possible. The bartender drops off the check and scoops up the fifty-dollar bill. The tab is thirty-eight bucks.

"Keep the change," I tell him, grabbing my bag and heading back to the ladies' room to splash some water on my face before I start crying again. Inspecting myself in the bathroom mirror, I can see why Markmatics hightailed it out of the bar so quickly. My skin is all blotchy, my nose is ruddy, and my eyes are swollen and tinged with red. What a first impression. Well, that and the crying. My phone *aah-OOH-gahs* again, and I pull it out of my purse. There are eight more notifications I hadn't heard, probably because of the noise in the restaurant and the fact that I'd lowered the volume. I swipe through the photos while I hide out in the ladies' room, squatting over a toilet and waiting for my face to de-puff and my pride to heal a bit. The new Closr options are mostly no's as well, except for one possibility. A blond man called HeartDoc. That sounds promising! I hope he is actually a cardiologist and not just the owner of a super-cheesy profile name. I swipe up for yes and Closr informs me we've made a match, which basically means that he swiped yes for me too. Closr instructs me to introduce myself, and asks if I'd like to meet HeartDoc somewhere nearby. *How about Marina Jack?* it suggests. *You are 0.0 miles from Marina Jack,*" the app informs me aggressively. Yes, I know. I'm right here in the ladies' room.

A text arrives from HeartDoc almost immediately: *Do you want to have a drink at Marina Jack, or somewhere on St. Armands, or maybe downtown? Closr says we're both nearby.*

I waver for a good twenty seconds, trying to decide if it's tacky to have two drink dates in the space of an hour at the same bar. Maybe even the same bar stool. I weigh pros and cons in my head—upside: I'm already parked and I have enough time to make myself presentable before he arrives. Downside: two dates in one bar on the same night, what will the bartender think? I decide I don't care, it's worth the potential embarrassment to avoid the evening traffic, especially on St. Armands Circle, which would be jam-packed with tourists circling round and round and round in search of a parking space.

MJ sounds good, I text. *When?*

15 minutes? he responds.

See you then, I text back. Well, that's easy. One date goes bad, another one is just around the corner. I reapply my lip gloss and put a wet paper towel to the back of my neck in hopes it relieves some of the splotchiness of my complexion from my little meltdown with Ferret Guy. Do-over, I think to myself. I deserve a do-over. I mentally review my date with Ferret Guy, thinking through each scenario and how I'd handle it differently in the future. Then, I give myself a quick pep talk, pull a brush through my hair, and vow not to cry again tonight, no matter what happens. No matter what.

About five minutes later, HeartDoc texts me again. *Just pulled in. You?*

I'm inside, I text back.

Ooh, sexy, he texts. I cringe a little as I read it, wondering what the hell he means.

I don't want him to know I'm hanging out in the bathroom like a loser. I check myself over one last time in the mirror, and head out for the bar. After two or three minutes I see a guy headed in my direction. HeartDoc.

"Hi," he says, smiling. "You're here. I'm sorry, I forgot to ask your name."

"Alex," I say. "Nice to meet you. And your name?"

"I'm Dr. Ryan," he says, flashing a mouthful of the biggest, whitest teeth I have ever seen close up. Probably veneers. Is Ryan his first name? His last name? What kind of yutz introduces himself as *doctor* in a social situation? He looks at me like he's expecting me to be impressed. The wicked part of me considers reintroducing myself as Dr. Alex. Or Dr. Wiggins. Just to be obnoxious.

"Nice to meet you," I say.

"Let's grab a seat," he says, and starts walking toward the back before I have a chance to answer. He waves to the hostess, the bartender, and several patrons as we make our way through. Apparently he's a regular.

"You seem to know a lot of people here," I say. He nods and flashes the veneers again.

We sit down at a table near the window, and I decide I should probably pace myself since I've already had a glass and a half of wine earlier in the evening. When the waiter arrives, Dr. Ryan orders bourbon, neat, and I ask for a white wine spritzer, a nice light drink for a warm evening with about half the alcohol of a regular glass of wine.

"So what kind of doctor are you, Dr. Ryan?" I ask. I can hardly bring myself to call him that, but it's too funny not to.

"Ohmigod," he says. "Did I introduce myself to you as Dr. Ryan?"

I nod.

"Jesus, I sound like a tool," he says. "I spend half my day doing rounds at the hospital. All day long it's 'Hello, I'm Dr. Ryan, how are you feeling today? Hello, I'm Dr. Ryan, and how are you feeling today?' " He shakes his head and I laugh.

"Let's start again," he says. "I'm Brett Ryan, nice to meet you, Alex."

"Nice to meet you too," I say, and before I know it, the waiter is back with our drinks. We chat for a few minutes about the area of town where we live, his work at the hospital, and his favorite local restaurants. We talk about his paddleboard, and his gym, and the reclining chairs in his media room. He doesn't really ask me many questions about me, which seems a bit rude, but is not altogether unwelcome. After Ferret Guy, I'm wary of oversharing again anyway. Occasionally he asks me a question, and then uses my response to immediately springboard into more details about himself.

He asks, "Are you a working girl?"

And I say, "Yes, I'm a doctor." What kind of ass calls a woman over thirty a *girl* when asking about her job?

"Do you have the little white uniform and everything?" he asks, a little too eagerly. It's only then that I realize what he means. Ew.

"I'm an environmental psychologist," I say. "I don't wear a uniform. Or a lab coat. Is that what you meant?" I expect he'll show some embarrassment, but it seems to go right over his head.

He drains his drink. "You wanna get out of here?" he asks.

"What?" I ask in disbelief.

"I live on Lido Key, my condo is ten minutes away. Let's get out of here. We can take my car." He lays his hand on my leg and I smack my knees together in surprise. What the hell?

"I just met you," I say. "I'm not going anywhere with you." My brain sputters out half a dozen doomsday scenarios, from kidnapping and torture to Ultimate Fighting or league bowling. No thank you.

"You're hot, I'm hot, we could be hot for each other," he says, with a slick grin. Clearly not the first time he's used that greasy line. And he isn't that hot.

"Thanks for the drink," I say, "but I'm not interested in a hookup."

"Why are you on Closr, then?" he asks incredulously.

"What do you mean, why am I on Closr? To meet interesting people, get to know them, maybe fall in love someday. Why is anyone on Closr?"

"Closr is a hookup app. *Closr,* as in sex, as in 'close the deal.' What did you think it meant?"

"*Closr,* as in meeting people brings you closer together, you know, romantic relationships—*closer.*"

"It's a hookup app. Are we gonna get freaky or not?"

"Not," I say. He downs his bourbon and abruptly stands up from the bar.

"Bitch," he mutters under his breath. Misogynistic jackass. Michael would never call someone a bitch.

"Compensating," I say, loud enough for him to hear as he strides away. Not very polite, but enormously satisfying.

I am not cut out for this. Closr is for sex! This means that in less than eighteen hours, twenty or maybe even thirty men in my small beach town of Sarasota, who spend time in the places I spend time, who live or work near where I live and work—twenty or thirty potential clients or connections to potential clients—these men all think I'm looking for sex on some trashy hookup app. I am way, way out of my depths here. Which is bound to happen, considering the fact that I'm most likely the only person of my generation who has never dated online. My romantic life, which has been so carefully planned and cultivated since grade school, is now the Wild, Wild West. I can't take the chance of humiliating myself again. I'm going to have to find some other way to fall in love, get married, and have a baby, or even just have sex with a nice man sometime before I check into the old age home.

The jerk left me with the check. I hand my credit card to the bartender and wait while he runs it. As I get up to leave, I feel my phone vibrating from the depths of my purse. After rummaging around, I finally locate the phone and pull it out just in time to see HeartDoc's text: *Here's what you're missing*—along with a picture of his dick. Oh, good gawd, my first dickpic.

Or maybe it's the poor ferret, bound for the grave.

Dating sucks, and my unfortunate encounter with Dr. Creepy only confirms my worst suspicions. It's not just that no man will want me, it's worse—the only man who wants me is a disgusting chauvinist looking for a sleazy hookup. If this parade of perverts and fake ferret owners is what I have to endure in order to meet someone, I'd rather get really comfortable with spinsterhood and a vibrator.

14

I'm loathe to confess it, but I'm completely lost without Michael.

I have no idea who I am without him. How is this possible? I have a career I love and am great at; I have wonderful friends. How did I let myself be so dependent on a man that I don't recognize myself without him? My great-aunt Thelma, who marched with Gloria Steinem and burned her girdle in a demonstration in New York City, is probably rolling in her grave at the thought. Aunt Thelma surely didn't let her organs decompress for a whole day just so I could let my life revolve around some guy.

I'm a disgrace to feminists everywhere.

In the five months since Michael's bombshell and our nationwide humiliation, I've been trying to keep my business afloat despite the fact that my head is no longer in my work. I'm operating on autopilot. ESPN's publicity department did a fantastic job of killing the scandal, and after twenty-four hours only FOX Sports was interested in keeping the story alive. It died out there a few days later, as the sports media all moved on to cover the outrage over an NFL player who had been arrested for the eighth time on domestic violence charges, without ever missing a game or even a day of practice.

I've been working seventy to eighty hours a week, and then falling into bed exhausted. My brain is somewhere else, and the truth is, I feel like I need the extra work hours just to make up for the mental deficit. I find myself avoiding home—everything reminds me of Michael. At least my work keeps my thoughts occupied.

Michael shows up on my doorstep every few days to try to convince me I've forgiven him, and I waffle back and forth from blind fury, to protective sympathy, to just flat-out missing him. At first I couldn't wrap my head around forgiving him, but after months and months of being so angry and heartbroken and obsessively recounting every single detail of our relationship in the shower, talking to myself in traffic like a crazy person, ruminating over every mortifying detail when I'm supposed to be paying attention in client meetings, I'm drained of my juices and I need to shut my brain off. Michael's gay, there's nothing to be done about it, and I'm too exhausted to keep being angry anyway. I give up.

My resolve against him is melting, and I wonder if it's time to just try to let go of all the hurt and anger I feel.

What is it costing me, what am I giving up, so that I can stay infuriated with Michael? I've essentially lost my oldest and dearest friend, I'm lonely, I'm not sleeping, I'm outraged all the time, I can hardly focus on my projects at work. Is it worth all of that, is it worth everything, just to be right? Yes, Michael screwed up and he hurt me terribly and he lied, oh, how he lied. But how much am I losing every day, reliving every betrayal in my mind, coddling my heartache and indignation to keep them strong? Staying pissed at Michael is keeping me paralyzed in my own unhappiness. I'm spending hours, days at a time, too much of my time reliving the unjustness of his actions. So much of my existence is being squandered on the destruction of our marriage, leaving nothing but wasteland and embers with which to rebuild my life. I'm not helping myself. I need to let go, or I'll be mired in righteous misery for the rest of my life.

"I've always loved you and I always will," Michael tells me the first night I let him come back to the house since Connecticut. "But I was in danger of completely losing myself. Obsessively wondering if my family and bosses and you loved me for who you thought I was, rather than who I actually am. I couldn't hide who I was any longer—it was hurting more to keep my secret than to let it come out."

"Was anything with us real?" I ask, afraid of his answer but desperately needing to know.

"It was all real," he says, pulling me close to him. "I love you, you're my best friend, you're the most amazing woman I've ever known. There's nothing that's ever made me happier than making you happy."

"You just don't want to sleep with me," I say.

"I miss sleeping with you," he says. "I just don't want to have sex with you." I feel myself deflating and he speedily corrects himself, "Not just you, any woman."

"Aw, thanks." I sigh. "That makes a girl feel special."

"Put it this way," he laughs, "of all the women in the world I don't want to have sex with, you're the one I find most attractive."

"That's no good," I say. "That's like saying 'of all the blow-up dolls in the world,' or 'of all the sheep in the world . . .'"

"You're beautiful," he says, "and you have gorgeous hair and you're a force of nature; you're smart and funny and the best person in the whole world to hang out with. And I can personally guarantee that there are thousands of men in the world who would be delighted to have sex with you."

"You won't lose me," I say, snuggling into his familiar arms. As for the thousands of men willing to have sex with me, I'll have to pass on that. After Dr. Creepy and Ferret Guy, I may never date again.

Michael and I decide to try to get the divorce stuff out of the way as quickly and inexpensively as possible. I'm still in shock some days and trying to get my head around the fact that life as I've known it is over, but I also know that stalling won't change anything.

He proposes we keep our own retirement accounts, and split the investment account and our savings account fifty-fifty. This is a better deal for me because my retirement account is about twice what his is. And screw him, I deserve it. I've been socking away money in my IRA since I was sixteen and had my first job mixing malts at Custard's Last Stand. Plus, I earn more than he does—a thought that now gives me a modicum of glee.

I lay on the guilt about the fact that he has killed my chances of ever having a baby with his bullshit and lies, and demand five sperm donations from him to be frozen by a local fertility clinic for my future use. Michael is brilliant, ambitious, healthy, great-looking, and funny. Not to mention the hair. There are still days I'm so furious I can barely look him in the eye, but I'm a planner and I don't want to find myself single and staring down thirty-five with no hope in sight for motherhood. How many eggs do I have left? I wonder. Is there a person I can hire to count them? An eggologist, or something? Does being on the pill for the last ten years mean I have a few hundred extra, since it prevents you from ovulating? Or do they spoil like old yogurt?

If I'm going the frozen spermsicle route, I'd rather the donor be Michael than some anonymous Ivy League law student I pick out of a catalog. I'd rather cover my bases. And my eggs. He agrees, which is a little surprising. But maybe not. Michael always wanted kids. Maybe he's covering his bases too.

I'm keeping the house. The only thing he asks for is the rest of his clothing and the garage full of sports memorabilia that he's been collecting pretty much since birth, a few personal items, and a red leather chaise from our living room that he's always loved and I've always hated. I'm glad he wants it. Otherwise, it will be the first thing I put on Craigslist.

Darcy and Samantha take me out for a spa day and dinner while Michael goes to the house to clear out the rest of his clothes, his sports stuff, and the ugly chaise. I've finally come to terms with all of this, but I can't bear to watch him pack.

Because he just throws everything in the boxes and he doesn't label anything.

What kind of sick person does that?

Darcy, Samantha, and I sit together in a cluster of pedicure chairs, sipping pink champagne. It's kind of tart and frothy, like it maybe came out of a box. Or a soda machine.

"More champagne?" asks the attendant.

"Yes, please," I say, holding out my glass.

"Are you doing okay?" asks Samantha. "Do you want to talk about Michael moving out? Or the divorce?"

"We're having fun," says Darcy, "don't bring that crap up."

"No," I say, gulping down the rest of the champagne in my glass before the attendant brings me a refill. "I'm talked out. I've made a decision. I am not going to let this messed-up situation ruin my life. Screw that. He's gay, I'm still reasonably attractive. I'm going to get my ass back out in the world, meet somebody great, *somebody who likes women this time*, and get the happily-ever-after I'm entitled to. I'm going to rebuild my life, grow my business, finally learn how to play bass guitar. This is not going to ruin my life. I'm taking my story back."

"Cheers to that," says Darcy, raising her glass to me. "It's about freaking time."

"Damned right you're reasonably attractive. Cheers!" says Samantha, and the three of us stretch to clink glasses awkwardly over Darcy's pedicure chair. A little sloshes out of Darcy's glass and onto the vibrating faux leather chair.

"Hopefully this stuff's not flammable," she cracks.

"I wouldn't count on it." I laugh.

A week later Michael and I meet at an attorney friend's office to sign the papers, and the lawyer tells us we'll be divorced as soon as the judge sets a date for a hearing. Apparently, when you agree on everything, your marriage can be dissolved in a matter of minutes.

15

Michael shows up for our divorce wearing black leather pants. Our marriage does not end as so many do on the courthouse steps, but with one final bash at the home we owned together.

It was my brilliant idea, the divorce party. Everyone keeps saying how Zen I am, how grown-up it is that I've moved on and forgiven

Michael, and holds me up like I'm the poster girl for mental health and awesomeness. That's sort of what I was going for.

The only problem is, once the invitations went out, I found myself anxious, filled with dread, and wishing I'd never thought of it in the first place. And now I'm stuck.

Truly, I'm determined to let it all go, but sometimes it sneaks up on me and I'm so pissed at Michael for lying to me that I want to take an ice pick and jam it through his eye socket.

But anyway, here I am, all dolled up for our divorce/coming out party. My hope is that the party will bring me some sort of peace, some closure, and help me move on. But the reality of it feels like pouring salt on my wounded heart.

Our guests aren't due to arrive for another twenty minutes or so. Michael exits the bathroom, half unzipped and his belt unbuckled, tucking his shirt into his pants.

I gasp. "Oh my gawd," I say, pointing at his crotch. "What the hell is that?"

"What?" he asks. I hook my finger around a minuscule elastic strap, snapping it against his skin.

"That," I say. "Are you actually wearing a zebra-print man-kini?"

His eyes dance. "Thong!"

"Wow," I say. Because there are no other words.

"Wait," he laughs, "there's more!" He pulls what looks like a miniaturized garage door opener out of his front jeans pocket, and squeezes the little button. Suddenly, the zebra thong is alive with flashing lights in red, blue, and yellow.

"Wow. Just wow. It's like Las Vegas on your crotch," I say.

"It's a celebration! Tonight is your debutante ball!" He giggles, pouring me a glass of champagne. "You're a single girl for the first time in your life!"

"And so are you," I crack.

He smiles, hugs me close, and raises his glass. "Cheers!"

We sip our champagne and I try to stifle tears burning my eyes. I will *not* cry. I love Michael, he broke my heart, and it's over. And also I sometimes want to wring his f-ing neck. *Deep breath. Just let it all go.*

I dry my eyes on Michael's shirt, a black, skintight number I don't recognize. His blond hair is stiff with product, his eyebrows (and arms, ew) look freshly waxed, he's sporting too-cool motorcycle boots and a thumb ring.

"Oh my gawd, " I say, looking him over. "You look so gay right now."

He beams. "Thanks!"

Michael picked out my outfit for the evening, a slinky aqua dress that shows off my legs. So there's that upside to having a gay husband.

"And for the finishing touch," he says, pulling a pink box down from the closet with great flourish. Opening the box, he reveals a sparkling rhinestone tiara nestled on hot-pink velvet.

"Oh no," I say, backing out of the room. "I think only one person in the not-so-happy couple should be bejeweled," I motion toward his light-up thong, "and you've already got us covered."

"Oh yes," he says, chasing me down the hallway with the tiara. "Tonight is about fun, about new beginnings, about reintroducing the most gorgeous, charming, and brilliant woman I've ever known to society."

I shake my head. "I'm not a debutante."

"You are tonight, cookie."

"I'm not wearing that," I say.

"It's either this or the thong," he says. And I reluctantly reach for the tiara.

I hate thongs.

16

Apparently, straight people have no idea what to wear to a gay-divorce-slash-coming-out party. Friends show up wearing neon-colored feather boas and bejeweled Elton John sunglasses. At least three of our male neighbors arrive decked out in drag, which is inexplicable to say the least. It might be four. After a few glasses of champagne, seeing your neighborhood stockbrokers and bankers in blond Marilyn Monroe wigs and size-eleven stilettos, it all starts to run together.

Most of our guests are people Michael and I have known forever, and a few of my former clients who are friends. Everyone generously pretends to be oblivious to the televised sex scandal, and I'm unbelievably grateful for that. And booze. I'm grateful for booze.

Darcy and Samantha arrive, and the two of them drag me into the kitchen to refill my glass and get started on their own. Darcy's fire-red hair and outrageous wardrobe match her personality to a tee. Tonight she's wearing a strapless green sundress with coral jewelry and funky stilettos. Samantha's outfit is as perkily intense as she is. She's poured into a body-conscious, electric-blue dress, which shows off the hours and hours she spends at her yoga studio. Pert.

"I need to slow down," I say. "I've already had two glasses of champagne."

"Nice tiara, pork chop. You need to let loose, and you're not driving anywhere," announces Darcy. "We're getting you wasted." She refills my glass, and then fills Sam's and her own.

"How are you holding up?" asks Sam earnestly. "You want to pop back in the bedroom, do a few downward dogs for stress relief, loosen up a bit?" In Sam's mind, yoga cures all.

"She's fine," Darcy shoots back. "She doesn't need the downward dog or the flying monkey. Right? She just needs her friends, a full drink, and maybe a howl at the moon. Aren't you fine?" Darcy is the headmaster of the "fake it till you make it" school of thought.

I nod. "Yes. I'm fine." It's only a half lie. I am fine. I'm trying to be fine. I *will* be fine. Eventually.

"How in the world would you do yoga in that dress?" I ask Sam. "How in the world are you even *breathing* in that—" I crack up before I even finish the sentence and Darcy joins in.

"If I show you, you have to do the Pert30. Starting tomorrow." She grins, knowing Darcy and I will back down immediately. The longest either of us has ever lasted in one of Sam's boot camps is six days. Sam makes Navy SEALs cry. We'd never make it the whole thirty days.

Darcy, Sam, and I head back to the living room. Michael's dad, Fred, is sporting a new rainbow T-shirt emblazoned with GAY PRIDE for the occasion, and my grandma Leona wears her silver hair in funky spikes, her favorite gold lamé pants, kitten heels, and a fitted fuchsia jacket. Same as always. My pot-peddling eighty-year-old neighbor Zelda is flirting with one of my former clients. He's about fifty to her eighty, but in typical Zelda fashion, she seems to be charming the pants off him. She has flowered rhinestone clips in her hair, and blows me a kiss when she sees me.

I've been trying, really trying, to get myself psyched up for the party all day, but when I look around at our friends and neighbors, I'm positive everyone here thinks I'm an idiot. A sap. That I'm the single worst person in bed since the dawn of time. I know everyone must be talking about me, asking the same questions I'd ask. Asking the same questions anyone with brain matter would ask. *How could she not have noticed? She had to have known! How could she not? Did he have to watch an hour of gay porn just to get it up? Is she just completely asexual?*

I know they're wondering those things because I've been wondering too.

A dance beat flows throughout the house, and I do my best to mingle even though I'd definitely rather be in my pajamas, curled up in bed with a classic Audrey Hepburn movie and a bag of Cheez Doodles.

"How are you holding up? You look great," says Carter, embracing me warmly. "So does Michael. I've never seen him happier." I know Carter's trying to be nice and supportive, but *ugh*. Why not just punch me in the face instead?

"You look gorgeous," Michael whispers every time he passes me by.

"I'm so proud of him," says our neighbor Susan. "It's so important for everybody to support Michael. It's so brave of him to come out of the closet!"

If stage one of my Michael nightmare was all of my friends and family informing me that Michael was *so obviously Liberace-level gay* they assumed there was no way I didn't already know, then stage two is those same friends and family telling me over and over again, ad nauseam, how brave Michael is for coming out of the closet. As though he wasn't pushed. On national television.

"Way to go," says Grandma Leona, looking me up and down. "Back on the horse. I'm proud of you for supporting Michael in his time of need."

Truly, I'm grateful for the compliments, but I feel like second runner-up in the Ms. Used Tires pageant. I can't stop myself from seething every time someone tells me how much Michael needs my support, and how he's being so brave to come out. He isn't Jimmy Swaggart's grandson, raised to believe he was going to hell for being homosexual. He was raised by Unitarians, for fuck's sake.

Deep breath. I'm letting it go.

Michael rushes to my side, his face brimming with enthusiasm.

"He's here!" Michael squeals, in a way that reminds me of how the monkeys howl and jump up and down when they get excited at the zoo.

"Who's here?" I ask. Sam is off chatting with a friend, Darcy looks on with amusement.

"Remember how you said I owe you a soul mate? I'm here to deliver!" he gushes. "Come meet your dream man!" Michael drags me toward the front door, until we find a blond man with a gray fedora pushed so far back on his head I wonder how it stays on. Duct tape?

"Alex, meet J.D.," Michael gushes. Under his rat-pack hat, J.D. has precision-highlighted, *Tiger Beat*–perfect hair, shuffled artfully off to the side. His dark-rinsed jeans fit like he's been sewed into them, accessorized with one of those biker wallet chains hanging down, with a big skull on it. He's wearing a black patterned vest over a T-shirt.

Also, he seems to be wearing makeup, which is not something I normally see in a straight guy. Although, what the hell do I know?

"Nice to meet you, Alex," says J.D. slyly. His eyes meet mine with purposeful intensity. It feels like he's trying to hypnotize me or something. If I start clucking like a chicken or playing Rachmaninoff's Concerto No. 2 on a kazoo, I'll know he's succeeded.

"J.D. is a singer," says Michael.

"Singer-songwriter," J.D. corrects.

"Oh, that's interesting," I say. But it's not. There's something really off and manufactured about J.D. And Michael is fawning over him like he invented the pore minimizer or something.

"I understand you've been through a rough time," says J.D.

"Well, uh," I say, shooting Michael a dirty look. What did he tell this guy, anyway?

J.D. nods to Michael, who ignores my death stare and awkwardly taps away at the screen of his phone.

Suddenly, the music changes, and the room is filled with a vaguely familiar, bouncy pop song, heavy on the synth, low in originality. Which is when J.D. inexplicably jumps into the center of my living room, and starts breaking out the dance moves. And not just an *I'm suddenly so inspired by the music and can't stop my body from moving* type of dance. No, it's a full-on, choreographed elbow-shuffling, lasso-thrusting, running-man, boy-band bonanza.

And then, absurdly, J.D. is singing. Darcy, always the quickest person in the room, snorts with laughter, and everyone is suddenly fixed on whatever J.D. is doing in the middle of my seagrass rug.

What is he . . . ? Oh gawd, I recognize the song . . .

"Can you believe it? J.D. was in BOYS4U. Remember how much you loved them?" gushes Michael. He holds up his palm for a high-five. "Soul mate!"

"Oh my God," I say.

J.D. is pointing at me from across the room, as though he's singing specifically to me. I'm completely mortified.

"*You* loved BOYS4U," I hiss at Michael. "Not me. *You*! And we were, like, eleven."

And suddenly J.D. is *right* next to me, singing soulfully while looking intensely into my eyes. Just like they used to do it in the music videos, in front of thousands of screaming, weeping, preteen fans. I want to blink so bad it practically hurts, if only to escape his unyielding gaze for a millisecond. He is unbearably close, his broccoli-scented breath steaming my face.

Girl, he didn't treat u right
But I'll be right here
Lovin' on u all night
I won't let him hurt u no more
I'm your nirvana
Out on the dance floor
Breakitdown . . .

I feel my skin turning twenty-six shades of crimson, and gulping down my champagne does nothing to extinguish the burn. J.D. mercifully scoots back, moonwalking-style, to the center of the room, for another exhibition of cheesy dance moves to the perky, up-tempo chorus. Now he's thrusting, which was, you know, playfully risqué when synchronized with a group of four other twenty-something guys. But all alone in the middle of my living room, it's just unbelievably creepy.

"Isn't he great?" whispers Michael. "You owe me big-time, baby."

"You are out of your freaking mind," I say. J.D. begins a sort of frenzied finale, shaking his hips wildly and throwing his arms up in the air. Darcy and Sam are snickering in the corner, but the rest of the party has begun to clap in time to the music. They have no idea that an over-the-hill boy-bander isn't just part of the standard gay divorce party entertainment package, but an ill-conceived fix-up by my now ex-husband.

After what seems like forever, the music ends, and J.D. takes a bow, and then another, and another, even though the clapping has stopped. He heads toward where I'm standing with my mouth gaping open.

"Get rid of him," I say under my breath. Michael seems genuinely surprised.

"I was singing just to you," says J.D.

"That was so, um . . . special," I say. "Thank you for that." Darcy swoops in to save the day.

"Hey, Alex, you'd better come quick. I think one of the drag queens got a pashmina stuck in the garbage disposal," she interjects. Best. Friend. Ever.

"Oh, gosh . . . ," I say. "I'd better go take care of that. Please excuse me." Sam trails behind Darcy and me, and we can barely contain our giggles as we make our escape to the kitchen.

"I'm your nirvana. Out on the dance floor," Sam sings cornily. "Very catchy."

"Ha ha. So funny," I say.

And that's how it goes. A couple of hours into the party, Michael raises his glass for a toast—he grabs my hand, and I try to force a more genuine smile.

"Although most of you already know this, Alex and I wanted to formally announce that we've ended our marriage today. We still love each other, we're still best friends, but it turns out, I'm gay."

The crowd laughs supportively, and I think about how we'd announced our engagement to most of this same group of friends. I never thought we'd end this way. I never thought we'd end at all. Feeling tears form in my eyes, I force myself to smile a little wider and think about Voldemort, in the way that guys think about baseball or puppies when they're trying to distract themselves. Something about that ghastly, snake-like face, hard eyes, bald head, and the fashion show of scary robes keeps me from breaking down when I'm about to lose it. It's weird, but it works.

Michael turns to look at me, and grasps both my hands in his. "We'll always love each other, and we'll always be best friends."

I feel myself tearing up again. *Voldemort, Voldemort, Voldemort.* Michael pulls me into his embrace. We stand there hugging way past the time I start feeling awkward, while our guests cheer. *Okay. That's enough, time to get off me.* He overstays his welcome and I start to feel pissed. Well, isn't this freaking awesome? My tacit support just makes everything hunky-dory, washes away all of Michael's deception and lies. Let go, I remind myself for the millionth time tonight, just let it go.

Michael raises his glass again. "To my amazing Alex."

Our friends raise their glasses and cheer, "To Alex."

Nodding my head, I mouth the words *thank you*, gulping my champagne.

17

The doorbell rings solidly for the next hour, producing groups of guests, mostly men, I'd never met before. Beneva Fruitville, Sarasota's most notorious and popular drag queen, makes an appearance. Apparently my grandma Leona, a regular at Drag Queen Bingo, invited her. Michael is holding court in the center of the bash, seemingly having the time of his life—laughing and giddy, clearly buzzing from alcohol or outright glee, probably both. He throws his arms up, dancing with everyone from my grandma Leona to Darcy to a few of the unknown guys who have arrived at our door. Meanwhile, I play doorman, taking the coats, feeling stupid in my tiara but not wanting to seem like a bad sport by taking it off.

Grandma Leona presents us with a hilarious divorce cake she's made from scratch—a buttercream masterpiece that looks like a three-layer traditional wedding cake flipped upside down, with rainbow layers inside, and two grooms and a bride. I am so tempted to smash it in Michael's face, but I'd never waste perfectly good cake. Especially not one that practically defies gravity. I take a bite and it's delicious.

The group cheers, digs into the cake, and resumes drinking and dancing. I make the rounds a few times, freshening up the drinks and hors d'oeuvres. People kept asking how I am, and even though I know most of them want me to be okay, I feel like a few of our so-called friends are just looking for the dirty details, the plot twists of a real-life soap opera, and I'm wobbly on who to trust anymore. Maybe I'm just being paranoid. I end up telling everyone that I'm perfectly fine, even though I'm not, exactly. I'm trying to have a good time, really I am. I've never seen Michael happier or lighter. I've never felt lonelier, or more out of place.

"Alex. Stop moping. This place is crawling with hot men," says Darcy.

"They're all gay." I sulk. "I'm swearing off men. If I put half the energy into my business the last several months that I've spent wishfully planning Michael's untimely demise, and fantasizing that somehow Michael was straight and that all of this . . . never happened, I'd have doubled my bottom line for the quarter. If I can't be happy, I should at least be rich."

"True. Whatever," she snorts. "You don't have to sleep with them. I just thought you might like to have a look."

"Oh sure," I say. "A roomful of people my husband *does* want to have sex with. That will cheer me up."

"He's not your husband anymore," she says sternly. "I'm getting you a drink."

As she heads toward the bar, I sneak quietly into the pantry. It's quiet and dark, and for the first time all night I feel like I can relax. I'm digging around on the back shelf, searching for my secret stash of Trader Joe's sea salt caramels. They only sell them during the holidays, and I usually buy a dozen boxes to last me all year. But it's only February and I'm already on my last box. Stress eater. I slide the box open, and pop one of the two remaining candies in my mouth. And then the other one. Which is just where I am, face full of sea salt caramel, when the pantry door opens and a very tall man I've never seen before steps quickly inside. Okay, this is awkward. He shuts the door behind him, and in the dim light coming from the kitchen under the door, I watch him start feeling along the wall. Chewing as quietly and speedily as

I can, I'm racing to finish or at least digest some of the caramels stuffed in my cheeks before he finds the light or realizes I'm there.

I probably look like a squirrel, a shame-eating squirrel.

The light flips on, and I rapidly swallow a hunk of the candy, which gets caught in my throat. I start coughing and hacking, and my eyes begin to water.

He looks startled to have company in the pantry.

"Are you okay?" he asks. There's still a lot of caramel stuffed in my mouth, so I just nod yes. I really hope I don't have chocolate smeared all over my lips. But I can't guarantee anything.

He's tall, at least six-one, casually gorgeous with broad shoulders and ocean-blue eyes, appealing in that *I just rolled out of bed like this* way. His brown hair is cropped close, making his eyes all the more startling. Midthirties, I'd guess.

I stare at him and keep chewing my cud. When it's too humiliating to continue, I swallow the big hunk of caramel and chocolate, which moves slowly down my throat in a cohesive lump.

"Excuse me, I'm so sorry," I choke out, once the caramel clears my windpipe. "You must be a friend of Michael's?"

"Carter's, thanks. Your chafing fuel is out," he says, not quite meeting my eyes as he pretends not to notice my choking. Very gentlemanly. "Do you have any Sterno?"

I try hard not to gawk at the little cleft in his chin. God, there's nothing sexier than a nice strong jawline and a movie-star-quality chin dimple. It's my own personal kryptonite. Well, that and my gay husband.

"Thanks for noticing," I say. "I'll take care of it."

He squints at me, with those mesmerizing, deeply blue eyes, like he's trying to place me or something. With this crowd at this party, he probably thinks I'm a drag queen with a candy addiction. But then I start to panic: Do I have artichoke dip or hunks of sea salt in my teeth or something?

Darcy casually opens the door to the pantry and hands me a glass of wine without batting an eyelash at the strange scene. Music pours in from the kitchen. She steps inside, and closes the door firmly behind her. He squeezes a little closer to me, to make room for Darcy. It's getting a bit crowded in here.

"I'm the wife," I say quickly to the stranger. "So nice to meet you."

"*Former* wife," says Darcy, sizing up the man. "And she's a doctor."

"Not that kind of doctor," I add.

"It's busy in here," he says to no one in particular.

"It's the VIP room," cracks Darcy. "Don't tell anybody."

He nods politely, pauses awkwardly as though he doesn't quite know what to do next, and then exits the pantry as I start rummaging around on a low shelf, looking for another can of Sterno.

"Why do you always do that?" asks Darcy. " 'Not that kind of doctor' . . . you should stop selling yourself short."

"I'm not selling myself short. But if I don't clarify right off the bat then people start telling me about their gallbladder surgery, or their erection issues, or the most recent color of their snot. I'm an environmental psychologist. The closest I come to medical advice is to say, 'And how do you feel about that?' "

"I wouldn't mind hearing about his erection issues," says Darcy, peeking out of the pantry to catch the rear view. "Although I'd be shocked if he had any. That guy is pure testosterone." She sighs dramatically.

"Sterno Man is gay," I say. "What straight man knows about chafing dishes?"

"Sterno Man is yummy." She sighs, and nonchalantly hikes up her strapless bra. "A girl can dream."

18

"You did good tonight, kid. I know this had to be tough on you," whispers Michael's father, Fred, as he ties up the trash bags in the kitchen to take out to the curb.

"Thanks, Fred, that means a lot," I say, hugging him tightly. You have to love Fred. Here he is trying to be supportive of Michael but he's still looking out for me. Fred has been like a second dad to me from the time Michael and I first met. Would that go away too? I wonder how he's dealing with everything. We haven't talked much. It's not personal, I've barely talked to or seen anyone other than clients. I've just been trying to figure out how to get my life back together.

Fred's a retired accountant. He's a simple guy who never remarried after Michael's mom passed away, and spends his every waking hour watching sports. The fact that his only son is an announcer for ESPN is without a doubt the greatest point of pride in his entire life. At Thanksgiving he always jokes that he wants "Father of Michael Miller, ESPN Commentator" engraved on his headstone.

Michael joins us in the kitchen. "Nice shirt, Dad."

Fred smiles. "Son. Do you kids need anything else before I go?"

"We're good, Dad. And thanks again for everything," says Michael, giving his dad a long hug and walking him to the back door.

"Night, Fred!" yells Darcy, as she appears in the kitchen entry carrying a tray loaded with seven or eight drink glasses. She sets them on a tiny space of vacant countertop next to the sink, and throws herself onto a bar stool. Samantha trails behind with a couple of empty serving plates, which she sets precariously on top of a large pile of dishes in the sink.

"Are you staying in the guest room tonight?" I ask Darcy and Sam.

"Maybe," says Darcy. Sam shrugs.

Michael returns to the kitchen and Darcy howls. "Oh my gawd, you were totally flirting with that hot Cuban guy in *front of your dad*."

"I couldn't help myself." Michael laughs, downing what's left of his drink. "Don't be obnoxious," he says. "That hot Cuban guy has a name."

"My apologies," says Darcy. "What's his name?"

"I don't know!" Michael roars with laughter. "But I'm almost positive he had one."

Sam cracks up too, and the three of them sit there, laughing hysterically.

"You're not just out, you're *all the way* out." Sam laughs. "And your wife! You flirted with another guy in front of your wife!"

"Thanks for reminding me," I say, rummaging around for my wineglass. There is not enough alcohol in the world to make this less obnoxious.

"Somebody has to," Sam says , nodding toward Michael. "You need the practice. Watch and learn, baby."

"No thanks," I say.

"You might feel that way now," insists Darcy, "but you're probably going to want to have sex again before you die." She takes a gulp of a nearby drink, and then looks at Michael, and starts laughing again, practically snorting the drink right out of her nose.

"What's so funny?" I ask.

Darcy howls with laughter. "You've only ever had sex with a gay man," she says. "You're a thirty-one-year-old *virgin*!" She roars and downs the rest of her drink. Michael and Sam start cracking up too.

"What are you laughing at?" I ask him. "This is your fault. Besides, you're in the same boat."

And then it hits me. No, he isn't.

"Well, it's looking good for tonight." He grins.

"Hot Cuban guy?" asks Darcy.

"That's not our business," I say quickly. I'm standing too close to the kitchen knives to endure this conversation.

"He told me to call him after we were all done here. I just didn't want to leave Alex with all the cleanup." Michael would not stop smiling. My heart is flopping around somewhere in my lower intestines.

"You made a date at our divorce party?" I ask incredulously. Unfucking-believable.

"Chill out," says Darcy. "You're divorced. This is what happens when you get divorced. You start having sex with other people."

"It's not just sex," says Michael defensively.

"Right," says Sam. "Sometimes you have coffee."

"Or pancakes."

"This brings up a really important point," says Darcy. "There's no way for you to go out into the world and date as a normal human woman if you haven't had sex with at least one straight guy. You're a psychologist and you've managed to miss out on a pretty major part of the human experience."

"Thanks," says Michael.

"Don't take it personally," says Darcy dryly. "Between the two of you, you have no idea whether or not she even knows what she's doing in bed."

See, I knew that was what everyone was thinking. Leave it to Darcy to confirm it.

"What happens if she meets a nice guy she likes and they end up breaking up because the sex is so terrible? Or if she freaks out because she's so far out of her comfort zone—because we all know that Alex is not exactly enthusiastic with trying anything before she's positive she'll be great at it." Darcy sighs and puts down her drink. "Obviously, we have to find someone to have sex with her."

"Hello," I say. "I'm right here. In the room. Listening to this."

"She's got a lot of catching up to do," adds Sam.

"I think I can manage that on my own," I say. "When I'm ready." Like, never.

"Ready, schmeady," Darcy says. "If you wait it will just be weirder. You need to get out there right away and just do it before you start thinking about it too much."

"That's what I did," offers Michael. I glare at him and silently will him to shut up. The last person in the world I want sex advice from is Michael.

Jesus, she's probably right. I can't even imagine having sex with someone besides Michael. Except maybe Henry Cavill, but he probably isn't available. I should google him tomorrow and find out. I wonder if there's some Make-a-Wish Foundation for the former wives of gay sportscasters that arranges clandestine hookups—matching handsome, straight, and kindhearted movie stars to sleep with duped ex-wives. Someone should start that organization.

"It's official," announces Darcy. "You need sex and pronto."

"Really, I'm fine," I say. I just need to exorcise my gay ex. And get the degenerates out of my kitchen.

Darcy continues on brainstorming about my sex life with Michael and Sam as though I'm not in the room. But I am, I am in the room, and this is probably the most awkward, humiliating discussion I've ever heard. Or maybe not. I've had a busy couple of months. The glasses littering the countertops and sink full of dishes from the party are starting to weigh on me. I won't be able to sleep until I've cleaned up all this party mess. I pick up a stack of plates and head toward the sink.

"The magic number is three," says Darcy. "All men, regardless of their level of education, are hardwired to believe that three times is the exact number of times their future wives should have had sex prior to meeting them."

"I shouldn't have to go out and have sex just so some guy can feel better about himself," I say.

"True," says Darcy, "but trust me, you'll feel a lot better about *yourself*."

"Three?" says Michael incredulously. "That can't be true."

"First of all, you're gay. So your opinions on the inner workings of straight men aren't exactly on point. Second, no thirty-five-year-old man wants to deflower a virgin unless he's a pervert. Third, it doesn't matter if you've had sex with two men, or forty-seven, which is a bit closer to my number—the number they're looking for is three. Which means we need to get you laid at least twice before you start dating."

"Well, that's easy," I say. "If you can turn forty-seven into three, I can certainly boost my number up by a couple."

"I don't screw around with that crap, because I'm in politics, where everybody sleeps with everybody, and since I work seventy hours a week, everyone I sleep with is in politics. Plus, I don't give a fuck."

"So to speak." Sam laughs.

"Padding your résumé isn't going to help you here," Darcy says. "Not if your number is thirteen years of sex with one gay man. Right now you're clammy with the stench of desperation. You need to get out there. Have sex with someone who likes women for a change. Get under somebody, get over it, move on with your life."

"Ugh," I say, exasperated. "I don't want to date. I mean, sure, I want to meet someone, fall in love, get married—preferably in the next six months, so I can have a baby and get my life back on schedule. I don't want to date."

"I hate to burst your bubble here," says Sam. "But unless you want your great-uncle Ferdinand to arrange a marriage with someone from the Old Country, dating is how that whole love/marriage/babies thing is accomplished."

"So you're saying that I have to have sex with two men, and then I'll meet someone and fall in love, get married, cut to babies and happily ever after."

"Yes," says Michael.

"No," say Sam and Darcy in unison.

"That's only part of it," adds Sam. "Everybody knows there are nine men you have to date before you meet the One."

"Nine?" I ask. "I thought it was two. How did it just go to nine? I need to date eleven men? That's insane!"

Michael checks his phone for the third time in the last minute and a half.

"Just go," I say to him. "I'll take care of the cleanup."

Michael looks elated, but demurs, "No, that's not fair. I'll stay and help."

"We'll do cleanup duty," says Sam. "That hot Cuban guy may not wait all night."

"Thanks," says Michael, off his bar stool in a flash. He gives me a quick peck on the cheek. "You're a trouper, I'll give you a call tomorrow," he says, and then he's out the door.

"There are nine guys you have to date before you meet *the one* you actually fall in love with. Just sleep with two of them and you'll be all set," says Darcy. "It's mandatory, like leveling up in a video game . . . The bad boy, the quarterback . . ."

". . . the foreign guy, the tantric sex guy, the sensitive artist . . . ," adds Sam.

"Don't forget the lead guitarist, the Master of the Universe, the fireman, the guy who's so pretty but dumb as a brick, with a body that's just so unreal it makes you cry—he's generally a male model, or maybe a personal trainer," says Darcy.

"It took me ten years to get my nine," says Sam. "You're thirty-one, so it might take you a little longer."

"Thanks for the reminder," I say, tossing a cocktail napkin in her direction.

"For a second, I almost forgot that I'm old and practically undateable and that my eggs are all dried up." I turn to Darcy. "How long did it take you?"

"Hmmm, it took almost my entire sophomore year at college," Darcy says. "About seven and a half months." Sam stares at Darcy with her mouth open. "You know me," Darcy laughs, "I've always been a bit of an overachiever."

"The fish," adds Sam

"What the hell is a fish?" I ask.

"The fish is that perfect, amazing guy it can never work out with—you know, *a bird and a fish may fall in love—but where would they live?* . . . So the fish is your total dream guy, he's smart, he's handsome, he gets all your jokes, he loves to talk, he gives you a nine-hour orgasm and then makes you homemade chocolate chip pancakes and serves you breakfast in bed—but he lives all the way across the country and neither of you can move, or he's married, or next in line for the throne, or he has a terminal disease or something . . . *the fish*."

"I need to meet someone right away, if I'm going to have enough time to date the guy, plan a wedding, get married, and have a baby before I hit thirty-five. I don't have time to date nine inappropriate guys."

"Sure you do," says Darcy. "Otherwise, how else will you know exactly what you want when you find it? Besides, the Universe doesn't just drop the perfect person in your lap, it makes you work for it a little."

"The Universe dropped Michael in my lap, and he was the perfect guy." I realize what I just said the second it comes out of my mouth, and Sam, Darcy, and I start cracking up.

"Yes, he was perfect except for the fact that he's gay. But other than that . . ." Darcy roars. She picks up the bottle of wine on the counter and refills all our glasses.

"I'll make a checklist," I say authoritatively. I make a list of the nine guys.

"Hold on," I say. "The fish makes ten."

"Sometimes the fish gives up his throne, or his terminal disease goes into remission," says Sam earnestly. "That's why the fish is worth it."

"The checklist never works. Really, that is the worst possible way to find someone great," says Darcy. She turns to Sam. "Who do you know on the list that we can fix Alex up with?"

Sam pulls out her iPhone and starts scrolling through her contacts.

"Oooh," she says. "I've got the tantric sex guy. He takes classes at my studio. His name is Kai."

"What, I'm supposed to just call up some stranger and ask him to have sex with me?"

"Don't be ridiculous," says Darcy. "Sam will do that for you."

"Kai's great, you'll love him," says Sam. "But do *not* let him talk you out of using a condom, and you should stay hydrated and be sure to do some good stretching exercises before and after."

"Oh sure," I say, matter-of-factly. "Stretching, hydration, that makes perfect sense. *Are you out of your mind?*"

"No." Sam shakes her head. "Hydration is very important."

"Set it up," says Darcy.

"Wait," I say, "how do you even know about the sex and the condoms? Did you sleep with him? Because I'm telling you both right now, I'm not going out with anyone either of you have dated, or slept with."

"Kai is a client, and I never sleep with clients," says Sam.

"Except that once," Darcy and I chime in, in unison.

"Except that once," says Sam. "But Kai has quite the reputation around the studio, he's had sex with half the women there. Which is why I recommend the condom."

"Gross. Don't the women catch on? I mean, how does he keep finding new women to sleep with at the studio?" I ask.

"Word of mouth," says Sam, laughing, as she does a Groucho Marx thing with her eyebrows.

"Don't knock it until you've tried it," says Darcy. "Besides, Sam's entire freaking yoga studio can't be wrong."

Sam clutches her chest, "Not when it feels so right . . . ," she says, barely able to finish her sentence before she cracks herself up. Immediately, Darcy and I are laughing right along with her.

"My entire client list is made up of Master of the Universe types, many of whom I have slept with, so you'll have to get over that shit."

"I'm not sleeping with some man you've dated," I say.

"First, I never date my clients. Too messy. Second, you don't have to sleep with your nine, except your tantric sex guy. Some of them, you won't even want to. You just have to go out with them. Besides, don't hold yourself back on my account. If I'd thought one of these boys was the future Mr. Darcy, he'd be home decapitating rosebuds for my bubble bath, and hand-washing my unmentionables right this minute," she laughs.

"So that's two," she says. "And you may not like what I'm about to say next, but I think it's a brilliant idea anyway."

"Don't you think *all* your ideas are brilliant?" cracks Sam.

"Why, yes, yes, they are," says Darcy. "I think we need to enlist

Michael's help in this little endeavor. We're in the market for a quarterback, and he just happens to work at ESPN."

"Oh no," I say, my skin flushing with humiliation. "I can't ask him to do that."

"No worries," says Darcy. "I'll ask him."

"No, no, no," I insist. "Why do we need Michael's help?"

"Where in the world are you going to get access to a quarterback in your current life?" she asks. "Are you going to start trolling the college stadiums after practice?"

"College?" I ask. "Are you kidding? I'm too old to date a college guy."

"You're too old to get serious with a college guy. You are not too old to go on a date with one, provided he's of drinking age. Besides, there are a lot more available college quarterbacks around than pros. And they're easier to acquire. Michael has unprecedented access to every QB in the country. And, he owes you."

"Can't I just skip that one?" I say. "I'll go out with the other eight, I promise."

"No skipping allowed. You want to meet Mr. Right, get married, and have babies, you've got to get all your rides on your ticket punched."

19

Monday morning I wake up in the throes of a Voldemort sex dream. No, seriously.

I'm clutching the covers around my neck, my heart is beating wildly, and I have the oddest, still-hazy recollection of Voldemort serenading me with Michael Bublé songs and showing me his wicked side on top of the conference table of the very first firm where I interned in college.

This can only mean one of two things. Either I've completely lost it, or else I really need to have sex. With a non-imaginary non-villain.

I'm divorced. It's early, and I'm alone in my all-mine house, in my all-mine bed, with my 50 percent–mine cat Morley sleeping on the pillow next to me, where Michael used to sleep. I wonder if Morley misses Michael like I do, or if he's just taking advantage of available real estate. I reach over to pet him and try to bring him in for a snuggle, but he hisses at me, extends a claw, and then stretches back out on the pillow. Morley is not exactly cuddly. He's a shelter cat, obviously abused before we adopted him, and found on the side of the road with his brothers and sisters, all far too young to have been weaned from their mother. Karmically speaking, I always felt that if I loved and took care of Morley, despite all of his social issues, that the Universe would reward Michael and me with great children. Like Morley is a test of my patience and kindness, and if I pass the test we'll end up with a terrific family. Now my husband is gay, the clock is running out on my ovaries, and I'm stuck with a cat that crawls up on my lap like he wants some affection, but claws me like a ninja if I try to move or stroke his fur.

I snooze a little longer, not wanting to leave the quiet or comfort of my bed, but knowing I need to get moving because I'm meeting two clients today—a socialite named Olivia Vanderbilt Kensington who wants me to design the environment for a massive wildlife fund-raiser, and the other a new client, a well-funded, semifamous chef named Daniel Boudreaux opening his first solo restaurant.

Work will save me.

I hit the snooze button one last time and then drag myself into the shower, a cloud of agony hanging over my head. I have to get myself together. Michael is gay. I'm divorced. Nothing is ever going to be the way it was and I need to accept that. I spent all last night trying to figure out a new plan, what I can do to get happy, and the one bright spot in my life is my work. I love my job, I love that moving furniture, playing certain music, infusing scents, hanging particular artwork, or setting things just so can cause complete strangers to feel a connection to a space, a cause, or even behave in different ways—from alerting them to danger to putting their minds at ease. Stay a little longer in your shop, don't fall into the piranha exhibit, head to the line on the left instead of the right, peruse the pricier merchandise before heading to the cheap stuff in the back. I love my career. I love the challenge of how to affect human behavior. I love the flexibility and the power of owning my own business. Even if the rest of my life goes to shit, I feel almost certain that focusing on work will make me feel happy again. And if it doesn't, at least I'll have the ability to pay for the best therapist money can buy. Onward.

I put on my favorite yellow suit because I need an energy boost and yellow is the color that triggers optimism and confidence. Pulling my dark hair into a loose bun, I wonder if I should try some highlights at my next hair appointment. Or bangs. Just to mix things up a little. Digging through the jewelry drawer, I select a dramatic necklace with multicolor beads that looks both elegant and whimsical at the same time. My ring finger still looks bare without my wedding rings, exacerbated by the line of pale skin and slight indentation where my rings used to be. I know I'll eventually get used to it, but I still find myself surprised when I glance at my hand and my rings aren't there anymore. Is that weird for everyone? I hate that it's so obvious that I'm newly divorced.

I find myself avoiding Michael's closet. It's empty now, but I don't want to be reminded of that. With the whole big house to myself, I don't really need more storage, but it feels like it would hurt too much to just leave it empty. Oh well, a problem for another day. I pull out three pairs of shoes, my favorite splurge, and stand in front of the mirror trying to decide whether I should go with the Vince Camuto strappy pewter heels, the violet Manolos, or the funky cheetah-print heels. The cheetahs are tempting, because they're an unexpected choice and they look far better than I'd imagined they would; but given that my biggest client today is an old-school socialite, it's probably best to go with the always chic, even in purple, Manolos.

Grabbing my iPad and keyboard, I slip them into my giant aqua leather tote, along with the notebook I use to jot down notes and ideas when I'm with clients. It would be easier, of course, to just type ideas into my iPad, but clients feel you're really listening to them when you're taking notes on paper, versus feeling like you're not paying attention when you're plugging away at a laptop or tablet. And I am all about creating the best environment for success. It's the smallest details that matter.

I give Morley a gentle pat and a catnip parakeet on my way out the door, and he flattens his ears and howls at me in return. My Mini Cooper seems tiny all by itself in the garage, especially with Michael's car and all his sports stuff gone. Everywhere I look are reminders he isn't here anymore. I wonder if it was a stupid idea to keep our house. Or if trying to keep it on just what I earn will end up completely bankrupting me. I love the house. I'll get over it.

It's a perfect Florida day, and even though it's February, it's sunny and gorgeous. I put down the top on my Mini and pull one of several scarves from the glove box, tying it over my hair. I pop on my giant sunglasses, pull out of the driveway, and head down the street, feeling every inch like I'm channeling Grace Kelly.

My first meeting is at ten, with the socialite client I've spoken to numerous times on the phone but never met before. I'm really excited about this opportunity because I don't usually do fund-raisers, especially not at this level, and if I do well on this project it will open up a whole new line and bring me a ton of potential new clients. And since I've decided that building my business will be my salvation, new clients are exactly what I need.

I'm right on time, but later than I'd like because of traffic. I valet my car at the Ritz-Carlton, and hurry inside to meet Olivia Vanderbilt Kensington in the tearoom. Usually I meet clients at their place of business, but Olivia's event will be held in one of the ballrooms of the Ritz, so we're meeting here. The space is basically a blank canvas, but we'll have to marry Olivia's designs for the party with my work to create a space that will garner the highest possible donations.

The host informs me that my client has not yet arrived, and escorts me to a table near the front at my request. Since we do not know each other, I want to lower any anxiety she might feel if she had to search the entire restaurant for me—that way our meeting will get off to a smooth start.

A half hour later my client has still not arrived. And while I've been watching the door and smiling at everyone who might potentially be Olivia, I order a sparkling water with lime and pull out my iPad to make a few notes for my meeting that afternoon with the restaurateur. I check my phone periodically to make certain I haven't missed a call from Olivia, and double-check the date of the meeting on my calendar, just in case I've screwed something up. No, today is the day.

Finally after forty-five minutes, Olivia Vanderbilt Kensington strolls into the room. She's painfully thin, wearing a pale pink suit and what seems to be half her weight in pearls, multiple strands draped elegantly around her neck in varying lengths. I recognize her instantly after checking out her bio online, and stand as she approaches our table.

"Dr. Alexandra Wiggins?" she asks in a throaty voice.

"Call me Alex, please," I say. "It's so nice to finally meet you."

She looks me up and down in a way that is obviously practiced and carefully designed to evoke insecurity. She waits until the host pulls out her chair and then sits down in an elegant side motion that seems strangely choreographed.

She does not thank him, or even acknowledge him.

"Thank you," I smile, and the host smiles back. Great smile.

"Camilla Berthrand recommended you highly. I hope you're able to live up to her praise." The waiter offers her a drink or a menu and she declines both.

"Camilla was wonderful to work with, and I'm flattered," I say, ignoring the dig. "Let's talk about your project."

Her eyes light up at the mention of her event, although her facial features barely move. Botox most likely, or some very recent plastic surgery. Olivia is highly polished and well put together in such a way that it makes it impossible to tell what her actual age is. Maybe fifty. Maybe seventy-five. Not that it matters, I'm just curious. There's something about her that makes her seem like she belongs in another era altogether. Perhaps that's just how the very, very rich are. Both Michael and I come from comfortable middle-class backgrounds. So we know to put our napkins on our laps, which fork to use at most occasions, and the difference between a red-wine glass and a white-wine glass, but I always feel a little out of my league with the caviar crowd.

"I believe I mentioned on the telephone that I need your help in designing our annual Wildlife Foundation fund-raiser in June. We raised eight hundred thousand dollars at the event last year. This year our goal is to raise one million dollars. Whatever psychological magic you do, this must be an elegant event. There are important people who will be in attendance and it is critical that we maintain a very high standard."

"So my assignment here is to help you raise your donations by twenty percent," I reiterate.

"Yes," she says. "Without doing anything tacky."

I'm a bit offended but I push through anyway. Does she actually think I'm going to be adding plastic table tents or jugglers or a fast-food-inspired color scheme?

"Please be assured that your event will be as elegant as always," I say. "Most of what I do will revolve around the exhibit, bar, guest and table placement; the schedule and language of the evening; the color scheme; and the accompanying music."

"We've already scheduled the orchestra," Olivia sniffs. "The event is only four months away."

"Of course," I say. "I'll just be working with them on musical selections, pacing, and timing for various hot points throughout your event." I reach into my bag and hand her a color swatch. "This will be your biggest potential disruption," I say. "This is Pantone Emerald 17-5641. It will need to be the anchor of your color scheme, although you're free to work with any coordinating colors you choose to create the atmosphere of elegance you're seeking."

"I'm not sure I can work with green so late in the décor stage." Olivia sighs.

"You want to raise your donation levels by 20 percent, this is how it works," I say with absolute confidence. I hand her a few more green swatches as well as a business card. "These swatches are for your florist and other vendors, and this is a card for a table linen service that has our color anchor in linens and chair covers if the hotel or your vendor can't provide them."

She accepts the swatches and puts them inside a tiny Chanel pocketbook.

"Now, let's go look at our venue, shall we?" I say, signaling the waiter for the check.

Two hours later we've gone over every inch of the ballroom and I rough out some notes about potential placement of various elements, and talk with Olivia at length about the Wildlife Foundation's needs and what types of animals they are trying to raise the money for. A cute busboy pokes his head in and asks if we'll be much longer. Nice eyes. Olivia is obviously not great with strangers, but she's clearly taken with animals of all sorts, and bubbles over with excitement when talking about what her group has been able to accomplish with regard to various species. Olivia speaks as though she's lost a beloved relative when talking about the loss of the Tasmanian tiger, and I put my arm around her bony shoulders as she dabs at her eyes with a silk handkerchief.

She promises to e-mail me a list of the species they're working to save, and do her best to work with the color scheme I've provided. I don't exactly see us becoming best buddies while we're working on this project, or, ever, but at least she's relatively pleasant when I keep her focused on the animals. We wrap things up at the valet stand, and she agrees to meet again at the end of the week.

"It was so nice to meet you Olivia," I say, thrusting out my hand to shake hers. "I'm looking forward to working with you."

She offers her hand up limply, like a dead fish. "I do hope our time together will be productive," she says. A barrel of fun, that one.

By the time the valet brings my car around, it's almost one-thirty and I'm starting to panic a little that I'll be late for my next meeting with the chef. Luckily, his new restaurant is docked near downtown Sarasota, which is only a few minutes from the Ritz-Carlton, and so as long as I can find a place to park, I should make it on time.

20

I park my car at the marina, already a few minutes late, and try not to fall on my ass as I run down the dock in sky-high heels in search of my new client's floating restaurant.

Oh gawd. This is it. It looks like a garbage barge. A gigantic, hundred-year-old garbage barge. The white and blue paint is peeling, and the whole thing is filthy, and covered in mucky gray film, but there are glimmers of long-gone elegance everywhere—gorgeous leaded-glass arched windows, and badly neglected but still solid mahogany. A classic red riverboat paddlewheel. Searching around for a place to board, I finally find the gangplank entry and make my way inside.

"Hello . . . Mr. Boudreaux," I call loudly into the depths of the restaurant. It's dim, with only minimal light coming from the stunning but dingy arched windows.

"I hardly recognized you without your tiara," says a man from behind the bar, more gorgeous mahogany. I'm startled at the sound of his voice, and it takes me a second, and then it dawns on me where I've heard that melodic Southern accent before: Sterno Man. From the pantry.

"Uh, hi. Hello. You were at my party the other night," I say, flustered.

He comes forward into the dining area, brushing dust or something off his hands and onto his pant legs. He wears a black T-shirt emblazoned with a band I've never heard of. It looks soft and worn in, revealing just a hint of his well-muscled arms and strong chest. His close-cropped brown hair is a bit disheveled, which is sort of cute, and just makes him seem down-to-earth and approachable. Dear gawd, what is it with me and gay men?

"Please, it's Daniel. I'd shake your hand, but I'm all grimy from trying to get things set up in the kitchen." He grins, and his whole face lights up. "Construction and cooking do not mix."

"Nice to see you again," I say, glancing around the restaurant-to-be. At least it's in much better shape on the inside.

He absentmindedly brushes his fingers against the cleft of his chin. "Sorry for crashing. I'm new in town and my friend Carter invited me to a divorce party. I'd never been to one, so I thought it might be fun to check it out."

"Any friend of Carter's is always welcome! Or, uh, *companion*. . . ." I say awkwardly. "He's one of my favorite people. It was my first divorce party too. What did you think?"

He smiles and his cerulean eyes sparkle. "I loved the concept, and the upside-down wedding cake was a masterpiece, but I thought it didn't seem like very much fun for the bride."

"Oh no, I was just . . . tired," I explain. And humiliated. And heartbroken. And practically the only straight person in a fifty-mile radius. I take a deep breath and refocus—Daniel is a client. "At least the groom had fun," I say.

"What a complete dick," he says, shaking his head.

"What?" I ask, unsure I've heard him correctly.

"He's a dick. What kind of selfish jackass lies to everybody he knows for ten years and then expects a party afterwards? I'm sorry," he says. "That's not very politically correct of me to say, and you don't know me from Adam. You seem very supportive, and I admire that. I hope I haven't offended you. I just have a tough time celebrating outright narcissism and selfish disdain for everybody else. We're not living in the Dark Ages or some third-world country. The CEO of Apple is gay. Ellen DeGeneres is gay. Anderson Cooper is gay. And I can't even imagine what this all must feel like for you." He pauses and sighs. "I'm sorry, it's not my place. Where are my manners?"

His eyes are kind, which is unexpected after his little speech. His directness is softened somewhat by his gracious Southern accent, but I feel utterly exalted by his candor. It's the first cool burst of sanity in this whole, rotten mess. He is the one and only person through all of this to say exactly what I feel. Who didn't tell me over and over again how brave Michael is, or how hard it must be for him, while completely discounting how all of this feels for me. I've barely met this guy, and he just *gets* it.

I look at Daniel Boudreaux, stunned. Jesus, I like him a lot. He is some fantastic, truth-telling kind of man.

"Thank you, that is unbelievably kind," I say awkwardly. "More than you know. I'm so glad you were able to make it the other night. My grandma Leona made the cake, I'm sure she'll be thrilled by your compliment. Anyway, I hope you at least had fun."

"I did," he says. "And I didn't mean to be ungracious. It was a lovely party. The transvestites and the tiaras reminded me a little of home."

"Where'd you grow up, a brothel?" I quip, and instantly regret it. "Sorry."

He laughs out loud. "Close," he says. "New Orleans."

Well, that explains the dreamy accent. And why transvestites would make him feel homesick.

"Would you like to sit down?" he asks, leading me toward a small round table in the corner with five or six chairs pulled around it haphazardly.

"Absolutely," I say, pulling out my notepad and pen. "Tell me all about your restaurant."

He begins to explain his vision for the restaurant and I've never seen anyone so animated about anything in my entire life. He talks about food the way other people talk about their children. Two hours later we've opened a bottle of wine and are noshing on warm corn bread and the best jambalaya I've ever eaten in my life. Apparently construction and cooking do mix.

"So how did you become a chef?" I ask. "Oh God, this is good."

"Family business," he says, smiling, "going back four generations. My family owns several well-known restaurants in Louisiana, mostly round New Orleans. Chevalier, The Crab Pot, Royale. I've been in the kitchen most every day since I could walk. You know how some people need the TV on when they're home alone?" he asks. I nod and he continues, "I've always got to have a pot boiling on the stove to feel right."

"Why not stay in New Orleans?" I ask. "Why start from scratch in Sarasota?"

"I wanted to do something a little different than the traditional New Orleans cuisine," he says. "I love it, but I've been doing the old Boudreaux family recipes all my life. I want to do something new, something all mine, a mix of the old and the new. There's a great creative culture here in Sarasota, a lot of new talent, and of course the Gulf, so we've got some of the best seafood in the world right here in the backyard."

I'm mesmerized by the way he speaks—New Orleans is pronounced *N'awlins*. When he says backyard, it's *backyaaad*. It's the kind of voice that makes you feel instantly at home, like you're a close friend or part of the inner circle. It's marvelous.

"Why the boat?" I ask.

"You mean, why *this* boat?" He laughs.

I smile and nod. "It's going to be a lot of work."

"Things worth doing usually are." He smiles. "It was owned by an old man named Archer up near Charleston, a friend of my family's going back forever. We used to go there when I was a kid, and I always told my folks I wanted to buy this boat when I was all grown up. My family's full of amazing cooks, but old Archer made the best fried catfish I've ever eaten in my life. The old man was set to retire, he didn't have any kin of his own. He knew I loved this place, so he called me first. I bought it on the spot. The old girl needs some work, but she's gonna be the belle once we get her in shape."

His enthusiasm and vision are infectious. By the time I leave I feel more excited about this project than I've felt about anything in a long time. This is proof, I think, that throwing myself into my work is the key to being happy again, even without Michael.

I take some photos of the interior and exterior so that I can put together my plan book for the restaurant, and then Daniel and I say our good-byes. Just as I'm leaving, he disappears into the back and emerges with a loaded paper bag.

"For later," he says.

"Thanks," I say, "I could get used to this."

"I hope you do." He grins.

Ahhhh. He cooks. He has dreamy blue eyes and a chin like a movie star. He cooks . . . Why do all the great guys have to be gay?

On the drive home I think about how charming and fun Daniel Boudreaux is. And I think about the cute busboy with the nice eyes. And the restaurant host with the great smile. Jesus, what's wrong with me? It's like I'm a hormonally charged teenager or living in a bad romance novel: I suddenly can't stop myself from noticing every man around me. Which means that Darcy, Samantha, and Michael are probably right. Plus, there was that disturbing dream about Voldemort this morning. I need to lose my gay-husband virginity before I lose my mind entirely. I need to find someone to sleep with me. And the fact that I don't have the faintest idea how to make that happen is just further proof that it needs to.

21

"You were right," I tell Darcy on the car ride home. I'm driving over the Ringling Bridge, so my cell reception is a little fuzzy

"Of course I was," she replies. "I'm always right. About what?"

"I need sex, apparently."

"Say no more," she says. "I'll be at your place around nine-thirty or ten. I've got a congressman who's in trouble and I need to save his ass, and then I'll be over. Fucking Republicans, they preach all this high-and-mighty pro-marriage, anti-sin shit and they're the first ones to get caught in the men's room at Dulles with their pants down and their dicks in a hole."

I'm tempted to ask her who, but I know she'll never tell.

My doorbell rings at nine-thirty and Michael, Samantha, and Darcy are on my doorstep. It seems weird that Michael would ring the doorbell, but he doesn't live here anymore, and I guess it's what people do.

He smiles as he comes inside and my heart skips a beat. I wonder if there will ever be a time in my life when I'm not in love with him.

"What's with the Tony Stark facial hair?" I ask. Michael looks different every time I see him now. Tonight he's sporting an elaborate goatee. He grins but doesn't respond.

As usual, Darcy has brought a nice bottle of wine. Sam grabs some glasses from the kitchen and the four of us gather around the dining room table.

"Prepare yourself for the horrid world of online dating," she says.

"I don't know if I'm ready for online dating," I say. "It seems so desperate and gross."

"Desperate and gross it is," she quipped. "But online dating is basically one big man market. It's the fastest possible way to track down those nine guys you need before you meet Mr. Right."

"Definitely." says Michael.

"I'm sorry," I say to Michael, "but we've only been divorced for three days. Do you really think you're an expert on this particular subject?"

A sheepish grin washes over his face.

"I've made significant progress in the area," he says.

"Eww," I reply. "Too much information."

"You mantramp!" exclaims Darcy, raising her glass to Michael. "With the Cuban guy?" He winks as he returns the toast. He has club stamps on the back of his hand. More than one.

"A gentleman doesn't kiss and tell," he says. "But yes, let's just say that I am now approaching mantramp status."

This is a shock for me. First, because Michael always seemed pretty satisfied with once a week, although what the hell did I know about that. And second, it crushes me that he's moving on so fast without me. Doesn't he miss me at all?

"Seriously?" I ask.

He gushes, "It's like I've been parched in the desert for all this time, and now there's sparkling water all around me." My heart sinks, as I never really thought of my lady parts as comparable to the Sahara. I'm trying very hard not to feel pitiful, unwanted, and left behind. Screw him, I'm moving on.

He sees my expression and reaches out to pat me on the arm. "I'm so sorry, sweetie. I know this must be hard on you."

"Nobody's hard on her," cracks Darcy. "That's the problem."

I roll my eyes and the four of us start cracking up.

Darcy yanks my laptop out of my bag and sets it up on the dining room table.

She opens up the page to Match.com, types in some details, and then pushes the laptop over to me so I can start filling out my dating profile.

"We need a photo," says Darcy. "A good one."

"You can just pull one off my website," I say.

"Terrible idea, Dr. Wiggins," says Darcy. "We're not trying to get a man to hire you for a consulting project. We're trying to get him to want to sleep with you. Or at least take you out for martinis."

"What's wrong with the photo on my website?" I ask, slightly offended.

"Nothing," says Michael, "it's gorgeous. It just doesn't send the right message. If anyone knows how the right environment can impact behavior, it's you. And right now we need to create an environment to inspire someone to buy you dinner and rip off your clothes."

"Someone's been reading too many bromance novels," says Darcy. Sam snickers.

"Ooh!" Michael says. "We should use the one from St. Lucia last year, the one where you're wearing the white halter dress on the beach. It makes your boobs look fantastic."

"Thanks," I say, "although I'm not sure I should take a gay man's advice on what makes my boobs look great."

"Yes, you should," he says. "I still love breasts."

I'm so conflicted. Gay man. Loves boobs.

"Let's have it," says Darcy. Michael sends the photo to Darcy from his phone, and she posts it on my profile. I like the picture; the setting sun brings out the highlights in my dark brown hair, which blows in the ocean breeze so naturally you'd think I was in a photography studio with a carefully placed fan.

"That's perfect," says Sam. "Do you have one where you're riding a horse or a camel? Or sitting on a rocket ship? Those are always wildly popular with men looking for sex," says Sam.

"Aren't all men looking for sex?" asks Michael.

"Thanks, that's so helpful," I say sarcastically. "Ugh. There's so much stuff they want you to put in here: what you're looking for, all about your job and personality, likes and dislikes . . . This is going to take me hours."

"Just put in your body type, hair color, eye color, basic details, and your boob photo," Darcy says. "For our purposes, there's no reason to include your favorite book from college or the name of your first dog. Men only look at the pictures anyway. Oh, put in there that you like Italian food. "

"Why Italian food?" I ask. "I like all types of food."

"If you put in Italian food, your dates will take you to an Italian restaurant, and it's hard to find a truly bad Italian restaurant. If you leave it blank, who knows where you'll end up."

"Fine," I say. "Italian."

Sam reaches for the keyboard. "You have to check all these boxes. We don't want to eliminate anybody." From a menu of choices, she selects every possible available option.

"Camping? I hate camping. You know I can't pee outside! Fishing? And weightlifting? Give me a break," I say.

"Men love campers. Get used to it," says Sam. "Besides, you're not going to date any of these guys long enough to have to go camping."

Darcy pulls my laptop back toward her and begins editing what I've just written on my description. It's no use arguing with her.

"Michael, give me your credit card," instructs Darcy. "You should be paying for this." Michael wordlessly hands it over and Darcy types in the number. He's outnumbered and he knows it. "A month should do it. Any longer and you'll want to kill yourself." She pushes a few more buttons and says, "Done."

"Now what do I do?" I ask.

"Now you wait about two minutes for the bum rush," says Darcy. As if on cue, a little window pops up with a chat request. Darcy peers at the screen and clicks a button that says *No Thanks*. "No photo. No go."

Michael raises his wineglass "To getting Alex laid. And finding her Naughty Nine guys."

Darcy, Sam, and I raise our glasses to clink with his. "To the Naughty Nine."

"Speaking of the naughty part of Alex's Naughty Nine—Sam, where are you with the tantric yogi?" asks Darcy.

"Ooh, I'd like to meet him," quips Michael.

Darcy shakes her head at him. "Don't make me smack you. Michael; have you found Alex a hunky college quarterback yet?"

"I have some possible candidates," says Michael. "Does it have to be a Division One school?"

"No," says Darcy. "All we require is a tall, great-looking quarterback who's chock-full of testosterone. Think you can manage that?"

"And over twenty-one," adds Sam.

"I'm thinking of two right now," says Michael.

"Make it happen," says Darcy.

"Kai the tantric yogi is on board. I gave him Alex's number this morning; he'll be calling in the next day or so."

"I'm really not comfortable with meeting some strange guy just for sex," I say.

"Oh, he'll take you out for dinner too." Sam laughs. "Hope you like vegan."

Ick.

The four of us have emptied Darcy's bottle of wine, and Michael pulls another one from the fridge. The laptop dings with window after window from men requesting chats with me. We're talking and laughing, listening to Darcy's latest story about one of her clients' (who remains unnamed) unfortunate incident with his friendly neighborhood drug dealer.

"Fucking Democrats," she says. "Just because you're for legalizing pot doesn't mean it's okay to go out and score some."

"You should write a book," says Michael.

"Maybe I will." She laughs. "Of course, I'll have to change all the names to protect the not-so-innocent."

I tell Darcy, Sam, and Michael about my Closr back-to-back dates with Ferret Guy and Dr. Creepy, and the four of us laugh so hard it feels like old times.

"A few rules going forward since you're new to this. No Closr," says Darcy. "You're lucky you didn't end up covered in feathers and peanut butter in some weirdo's storage unit."

"Don't communicate online with anyone who doesn't post a photo; you don't want to end up with whoever's lurking behind door number three," says Sam.

Michael nods. "And remember, no crying on dates. It sends the message that you're a basket case."

"I am a basket case," I say.

"No asking about the five-year plan," says Darcy. "It freaks them out, makes them think you're desperate to nail them down and get married, and before you know it you've triggered some sort of pre-traumatic shock disorder."

"That's crazy," I say.

"Oh yes," agrees Sam. "Your poor date is instantly transported into a hallucinogenic nightmare where you rip off your normal date-night outfit to reveal full-on wedding gear, complete with the white gown cascading in layers of tulle, glowing devil-eyes behind a veil, complete with steel-toed wedding shoes."

"And then you shackle him," laughs Darcy, "and not in the good way, and drag him down the aisle, where he suddenly finds himself clad in a sky-blue tuxedo and ruffled shirt. The orchestra is warming up to play "Can You Feel the Love Tonight" and a clan of onlookers cackle as he is dragged to the altar, where he, who was expecting nothing more than linguine and clams, and maybe a movie, will be sacrificed to the She-God of Matrimony."

"I should write this down," I say, grabbing the iPad from my tote. *Don't be desperate.*

"Don't tell them that your husband cheated," says Sam. "It makes them think that you hate all men."

"Seriously?" I ask. "Wouldn't they just assume I hated the guy who cheated on me?" Michael's face fell. "No offense," I say.

"No, they'll think you're a bitter man-hater. Be fun. Laugh a lot," says Darcy.

We haven't quite finished the second bottle of wine when Michael announces he has to leave. "I've got a trip scheduled tomorrow."

"How long will you be gone?" I ask, trying not to sound at all like his wife.

"Three weeks," he says.

"I should get going too," says Darcy. "I'm heading back to D.C. tomorrow, and I need to finish packing."

Darcy, Sam, Michael, and I hug goodbye at the door. Over on the dining table, my laptop continues to ding every few seconds.

"Sounds like we've got some winners," says Darcy as she heads out the door. "Stick to the Naughty Nine types. Start with the bad boys. Not only will they suck you right into the present, but they're easy to spot because all they post are shirtless selfies."

"Save any hot selfies for me," Michael says, kissing me on the cheek. "Good luck, sweetie. Remember: no crying on your dates!"

"You're hilarious," I say to him. "I never should have told you about Ferret Guy." I wave goodbye to the three of them, both anxious and nauseated to see who's contacting me online.

"Don't forget," yells Darcy from my driveway, loud enough for everyone in the neighborhood to hear, "Your user name is SEXY911 and your password is BOOTYCALL!"

I'm horrified. "Seriously?"

"Nah," she laughs, "it's SEXY941."

22

There are 940 other SEXYs? I'm completely mortified and search frantically in the help section of the dating site to figure out a way to change my username before anyone sees it. Well, anyone *else*. I've already gotten five messages and another four "winks" and every few seconds a new window pops up on my screen with an instant message request. *50_Shades_Of_Hay*, *InsuranceSellr*, *AmericanGladE8R*, and *STDmuffin* all want to IM. So does *Batman*. So now I know what he does on his nights off.

Between all the ads for makeup and condoms, and the gazillion IM windows that keep popping up, covering my screen and now layered three deep, the online dating site feels like the digital version of Las Vegas. I'm completely inundated and icked out.

Seriously, there is no way I'm going out on a date with someone who'd send a wink to SEXY911. Or SEXY941, or whatever. Oh God, I don't think I can do this.

I'll be deleting them once I figure out how to change my username, but the site's help window keeps getting covered up by more IM request windows.

Fifteen minutes later, I've learned that it's practically impossible to change your username unless you open an entirely new account, and by now it's way too late for that.

I change into a camisole and soft pajama pants, disable the IM feature so that my brain doesn't explode from the onslaught, pour what is left of the bottle of wine into my glass for courage, and peruse the profiles of the men who've contacted me, looking for matches for my Naughty Nine checklist.

Apparently Darcy put no parameters whatsoever on what I'm supposedly looking for in a man in my dating profile. No age limits, height requirements, educational minimum—nothing. Basically she's cast such a wide net that no one in possession of a penis could possibly fall through. I keep reminding myself that this is all necessary so that I can move on with my life, get over my gay ex, and meet my forever person. I'm not looking for Michael or someone to spend my life with here. I'm just looking to check some boxes. Hot foreign guy. Sensitive artist. Lead guitarist. I wonder if I can just type that into the little search box. Like shoe shopping. The answer turns out to be yes, yes, you can.

I'm not certain how well the search for "bad boy" will go, unless they all choose to self-identify right there in their profiles.

SWM, 34, bad boy, rides motorcycle and will try to screw your sister.

But I type *firefighter* into the little box, and suddenly my screen is filled with men in little squares. Jeez, are they all really firemen? It seems they are. With only one goal in mind, the process of elimination is much easier. I can choose on looks alone, which feels completely crass but sort of all-powerful and fun anyway. If I'm going to get myself over the hump, so to speak, all I need to do is find someone I might like to see naked.

No blondes, that's too much like Michael. No one more than ten years older. I'm exhausted after twenty minutes, without having made any choices, other than eliminating a few guys because of blondness or middle age. There are too many options. Plus it feels too weird to reach out to some strange man. Instead, I exit out of that window and read through the profiles of the men who've contacted me while my inbox fills up with more responses. It's immensely flattering and off-putting all at the same time. Maybe there's a fireman or a lead guitarist in my inbox already. No such luck. It's mostly MBAs and entrepreneurs.

Enough online dating for the night. I take a long bath and contemplate whether or not Project Naughty Nine is just a terrible idea or the worst idea ever. Damp from the tub with my hair wrapped up in a towel, I search out Morley in hopes he's in the mood for a snuggle. I grab a spoonful of salted caramel ice cream out of the freezer just in case he isn't. Morley, previously nowhere to be found, materializes on the bed when I yell the magic words *ice cream*. The cat can be bought.

I hold him on my lap as he licks the ice cream off the spoon, and stroke his black and white fur. When he's finished, he claws me with his hind legs, hisses, and settles in on Michael's old pillow, delicately cleaning leftover ice cream off his face with his paws. Not exactly what I was hoping for, but close enough. There seems to be a lot of that in my life lately.

23

The next morning, I'm slightly hung over, exacerbated by the fact that the FedEx man is ringing my doorbell at precisely 6:30 A.M.

From Darcy. Odd. I immediately rip open the packaging to find an economy-size box of condoms in an assortment of sizes, colors, and, ahem, textures.

The FedEx guy cracks up. "Somebody's going to have a great week." My face burns with humiliation.

"It's for a client . . . ," I mumble. He gives me a formal salute and heads back to his truck, just as I realize that saying a monstrous box of condoms is for a client is about the most ill-conceived idea ever. Great, so now my FedEx man thinks I'm a sex worker or a porn star.

Trudging over to the kitchen, I toss the condom cornucopia on the counter, fire up the coffeemaker, toast myself a bagel, and slather it with cream cheese. Morley, a lover of cream cheese, finds his way to the dining room table and purrs against my leg just like a regular, mentally stable cat. I pull off a piece of the bagel and drop it in front of him, and he bats it across the tile floor like a hockey puck before pouncing on it and devouring it as though it were freshly caught prey. The adventures of an indoor cat.

I'm weirdly flattered that my dating profile has been getting some attention while Morley and I were sleeping. Online dating certainly is convenient. That profile has been working 24/7. I peruse the messages, one more depressing than the last.

Ugh, my brain hurts. I definitely should not have finished that second bottle of wine last night. I have a client meeting at nine-thirty, and feel like I really need a long, hot shower. Am I the only divorcée whose alcohol consumption quadrupled post-separation? Or is lushdom just a part of the healing process?

My inbox is brimming with firefighters. Magically, they seem to know that I was checking out their profiles last night, and six of them have contacted me first thing this morning, with messages ranging from "hey" to one long, heartfelt e-mail about how hard it is to risk your life every day when you have no one at home to love you. It's sad, really. Not that I'm interested in being that person. It's just, I feel for any guy who sits down at three o'clock in the morning to pour his heart out. Two of the six firefighters are good-looking. One, especially so.

After showering, I sit down at the table to review the messages and winks on my profile. I've decided that the winks are just too mealy and surely must be the strategy of someone who is too lazy or timid to reach out, and just wants to cast as wide a net as possible. The irony of this is not lost on me, but I delete them anyway.

I review the rest of the daters who've sent messages, basing my eliminations on looks and the Naughty Nine checklist alone. When I'm finished with the elimination round, I have two possible candidates—the hot, dark-haired firefighter who is thirty-one and recently divorced like me, and a twenty-six-year-old surfer-slash-bartender who only qualifies to date me because he's gorgeous and has the body of a sex god. I almost push the button to delete his message but then I reconsider. This is just about the checklist and sex and getting a few experiences under my belt (why do all these kinds of expressions suddenly sound dirty?), I'm not going to marry the guy. Why not sleep with a twenty-six-year-old bartender, with the sandy hair, rocking body, and chocolatey brown eyes? I check out his profile to see where he works, just in case it's a place I like to go. I'm incredibly uncomfortable with the whole Naughty Nine thing. I'll die if he turns out to be someone who works at one of my favorite restaurants. Luckily for me, upon further examination of his profile, it seems he works at one of the tourist bars on Siesta Beach, the Daiquiri Deck, a place I almost never go. His name is Billy, which strikes me as sort of juvenile for a grown man with a job, but I remember my mission and give the guy a break. I'm not going to marry him, I'm just going to go out on a date and possibly try to seduce him. Maybe.

24

"I'm definitely not going to sleep with him," I insist to Darcy. "He has the IQ of a sand gnat."

"What does that have to do with his biceps?" she asks.

"Nothing," I say.

"Exactly."

"I'm not doing this," I say.

"Oh, you're definitely going on a date. Firefighter or the pretty-but-dumb guy. Pick one," she says. "Pick one or I'll pick one for you."

"Fine," I say. "I will."

"Great," says Darcy. "You have twenty-four hours to make a decision."

"I'm not one of your politicians," I say.

She laughs. "If you were one of my politicians, I would have already made the decision for you."

The next day I wake up to a text from Darcy: *Who's the lucky guy?*

25

The lucky or not-so-lucky guy is Jeffrey, the thirty-one-year old, recently divorced super-hot fireman. At the last minute, I leave a note on my refrigerator written in red Magic Marker with a printout of Jeffrey's profile photo: *Dear Police, In case you find me in a ditch, the person you should interrogate first is Flashpoint77 on Match.com, 555-941-2221.*

We meet for dinner at Carigulos, one of my favorite Italian eateries. Michael and I used to come here on a pretty regular basis, so I figure somebody on the waitstaff will notice if I end up bound in firehose in the trunk of some guy's car. I'm the first to arrive, and I take a seat at the corner of the bar. Research shows bartenders gravitate toward the corners, so it will be easier to keep the drinks coming. My nerves are shot, so I go ahead and order a glass of white wine. It's half gone before a gentleman taps me on my back.

"Alex?" he says.

"That's me," I say. "Thank you, but I'm waiting for someone. We're not ready for our table yet." He's very short, maybe five-six on a very tall day, and from my perch on the barstool I have a lovely view of his oddly shaped bald spot. It's very dim in the restaurant, but it almost looks like there's something painted on his head.

"I'm Jeff," he says. It takes me a second to comprehend that he's my date. This is mostly because he looks nothing at all like his hunky photo in the firefighter uniform—he's a good fifteen (or thirty) pounds heavier, couldn't reach five-eleven with a step stool, and there's no way in hell he's thirty-one. Maybe fifty-one. His height really throws me, and I wonder if he was standing on a couple of phone books in the group photo he'd posted. Or maybe he just has a lot of really teeny-tiny friends.

He pulls up a bar stool next to me, and I try not to gawk as he struggles to mount the seat. There's more of the black paint stuff on the side of his forehead, and I'm just about to hand him a napkin when I realize *it's artificial hair.*

Like the kind you see on late-night infomercials—the kind you spray on from a can. Like bug spray. Or Mace.

"So," he says. "You look exactly like your profile. That's a nice change. Most of the women I go out with have been photoshopped, if you know what I mean."

"I know exactly what you mean," I say, trying very hard not to stare.

"There's nothing like showing up for a date and finding out she's fifty pounds heavier and ten years older." He smiles broadly and I can see he's missing a tooth. He's supposed to be a firefighter. Why is he missing a tooth?

"Yes," I say. "I imagine that's a shocker . . ." I'm not sure whether to order another round of drinks and laugh my ass off, or just break into tears. We've only been here a minute and a half and I'm already speechless. It takes a massive amount of concentration on my part not to stare at the tooth hole.

"So," he says, signaling the bartender. "Your profile says you were divorced?"

"Yes," I say. "My husband is gay."

"Well, then he's a moron," says Jeff. "If you were my wife, I'd never go gay." I'm only mildly intrigued about the level of attractiveness Jeff believes to be a requirement to maintain one's sexual orientation, but there's no way I'm getting into it. I'm going to finish my drink and get the hell out of here.

"You're divorced also?" I ask as I drain my wineglass. How long do I have to stay to check a guy off my Naughty Nine list? Three minutes? Five? Through the appetizer round?

"The bitch cheated on me," he says. "Can you believe it?"

"I can," I say as I drop a ten on the bar for the bartender. "Interesting meeting you, Jeff. Thanks for the date." It's hard to believe that there is anyone worse at dating than I am, but I've just hit the jackpot.

"Wait," he says, grabbing my arm. "Don't you want to get dinner?" He pauses, raising his eyebrow at me in a way that makes my skin crawl. "Maybe get to know each other a little better?"

He catches me completely off guard and lands a kamikaze-style kiss—his slobbery mouth planted half on/half off mine. I flail backward on my bar stool in response, just as my lower lip gets snagged in the hole left by his missing tooth. Ugh! My whole body shudders in disgust. *Ughhhhhhhh!*

"No thanks, Jeff," I say, extricating my offended lip with my finger, standing up, and backing away slowly like he's an escaped mental patient. "I've got an early morning."

I barely make it to my car before I completely fall apart and burst into tears. I wonder what happens if you put hand sanitizer on your lips.

26

"It can't have been the worst date ever," says Darcy. "What about that state representative being groomed for Congress that I went out with from Arkansas—you know, the guy who wanted me to have a threesome with his wife? And then left me with the three-hundred-dollar tab after I turned him down flat? *That* was the worst date ever."

"Fine," I say, "you win. That's why I'm quitting now. I don't care if I never meet anyone. I'll just spend all my time on my business, get incredibly rich, and then execute Operation Spermsicle or adopt a little Ethiopian baby like all the celebrities do. I don't need some man. I'm fine all by myself." I'm still sitting in my car on the street where I parked near the restaurant, trying to pull myself together after my meltdown. And I don't feel fine. I feel more alone than I ever have in my life.

"You can't quit," says Darcy. "You haven't accomplished your goal. I'll be back from D.C. tomorrow, we'll figure it out then."

"I don't care if I'm a gay-husband virgin," I say. "I'm not doing that again."

"You picked him," she says. "You have to be able to read through all the bullshit and lies if you're going to date online."

"That's what I'm trying to tell you," I say "I'm *not* going to date online."

"Hold on," she says, "let me get Michael on the phone." I wait on hold for a minute while she conferences Michael in.

"He's up to speed," she says. "And we have a plan."

"I'm so sorry about your awful date, sweetie," says Michael.

I couldn't stop myself from crying. "I miss you so much. I can't do this."

"I know," he says. "I'm so sorry. I wish there were something I could do."

There's a long pause on the line, the three of us silent. There is something he could do. He can suck it up and get his ass back in the closet. I shouldn't have to suffer like this.

"Enough," says Darcy. "We've figured this out. Michael and I are each going to pick someone for you to go out with from the site. We'll set up the dates and you just show up."

"I don't think that's a good idea," I say.

"Who knows you better than we do?" asks Michael.

He has a point. I agree to go on two more dates, one picked by each of them. And in return, they agree not to pressure me anymore about losing my GHV if the dates they arrange flame out. No pun intended.

On Friday morning I get up early to make the rounds on all my job sites—to meet with clients, check on progress, and develop next steps. I'm meeting with Olivia Vanderbilt Kensington to discuss the wildlife fund-raiser, although I wish I wasn't. She's called and e-mailed me multiple times a day since our first meeting early in the week, although only half of her communications pertain to her actual event, the rest being everything from complaints about her housekeeper to her frustration with homeless people. I'm not sure that she actually has the opportunity to encounter many homeless people on her five-minute drive from tony Longboat Key, where she lives, to the Ritz-Carlton, but I suppose anything is possible. From the way she speaks, you'd think there were roving bands of homeless hooligans causing mayhem, peeing on the bougainvillea, and attacking tourists. Come to think of it, maybe when she says "homeless people" she probably actually means the tourists who flood our city every winter, enjoy our beaches, and eat in our restaurants during the balmy months when every other place in the country is buried under three feet of snow. That wouldn't surprise me a bit.

After Olivia, I head over to a new psychology office where I'm staging the environment to evoke feelings of calm and trust. And finally, last stop of the day, I'm heading to the client I'm most looking forward to seeing, Daniel Boudreaux and his floating restaurant-to-be.

I arrive at the Ritz-Carlton to meet Olivia for breakfast.

Heading into the restaurant, I see Olivia has already set up camp at a table in the back. I wave when she looks up to meet my eyes, and she looks at her watch.

Am I late? I take a quick peek at my phone as I head toward the table. Nope, right on time.

"I wasn't sure if you'd make it," she says, shuffling the papers in front of her.

"Here I am," I say, sitting down at the table, "nine o'clock as scheduled." She sniffs and returns to her papers. Goodness, she's hard to like.

"I've been thinking," she says, "and I'm simply devastated, but we're going to have to change the dinner menu. The emerald tablecloths are going to make the fish look ghastly."

"I don't think that's necessary," I say, trying to use my most soothing voice, the same voice I'd use if I were trying to talk a crazy person out of a tree.

"Of course it is," she snaps. "And I'm going to need feedback from you on my wardrobe selections right away," she says. "These things take time."

Oy. This again.

"The green is lovely," I say, "as is the silver," I continue, as she scribbles notes on a tiny Crane notepad.

"I'm not dressing to match the tablecloths," she says.

"It's really not necessary," I say. "Wear whatever you'd like, save for red. Red is a color of power and we're asking your guests to help the powerless so the messaging is wrong. Anything else is fine."

"Well, I had planned to wear the green," she says, petulant. "Now that's impossible because of those tablecloths. Can't we just change those instead?"

Ah, the real issue.

"What you wear to the fund-raiser has far less effect on donations than the color anchor of the event. If you want to raise your donations by twenty percent, this is part of the plan on how we accomplish that."

She sighs deeply, so that the next table or two might hear her despair.

"Fine," she says, moving on to show me table settings and flower arrangements, and the seating chart she's been working on over the last few days.

"You put your biggest donors here?" I ask, pointing to the golden triangle on the map. The guests at those three tables alone can easily put Olivia over the top with her fund-raising goal. She nods to confirm. Much of my focus will be on the experience that the guests at those high-priority tables will be having.

"Perfect," I say. "You're doing an amazing job and this will be a fantastic event."

"It must be," she says. She gathers up the rest of her papers and snaps her portfolio closed. "I have a spa day scheduled, would you care to join me?"

Wow, that's weird. I'm not sure if this is just her being polite, or if it's an awkward attempt at friendship. I didn't think she really even liked me, and Olivia Vanderbilt Kensington hardly seems like the type to pal around with the help.

"Thank you, that's so kind of you to offer," I say. "Unfortunately I've got client meetings booked all day."

"Perhaps another time, then," she says. The expression on her face doesn't change at all, and it's hard to tell whether she could care less, or if her facial muscles are just chemically paralyzed. Botox is as common as seagulls in Sarasota, but most of the women I know who use the dermatologist's little helper still have full range of expression. Except squinting, of course.

She gathers up the rest of her things, bids me goodbye, and sort of floats out the restaurant door. Must be something they teach future debutantes at cotillion.

I quickly transcribe my handwritten notes into the color-coded client files on my iPad. I love the cloud, despite the fact that I don't actually understand how it works, because it magically syncs all of my client files and checklists. For someone like me who prides herself on organization, the cloud is the greatest invention since the label maker.

My next stop is the new psychology practice I'm designing. For once, it's nice to work with fellow psychologists who trust the science. There's far less hand-holding than with some of my other clients. We're in the final stages of construction and I can't wait to see the progress—including two innovative outdoor therapy rooms, tropical gardens especially designed to treat women with self-esteem issues, eating disorders, and anxiety. Interestingly enough, male brains don't respond to nature cues in the same way. As far as I know, the outdoor therapy gardens are the first of their kind. The innovation has the potential to bring me not only new business, but some significant recognition within my own field as well. The research backing the concept is solid, but before now, no one had ever put it into practice in this way. Sarasota has the perfect climate for this particular element, because the weather is quite pleasant year-round. For the steamier summer months, there's a retractable shade as well as cooling space vents. Besides the fact that it's just pretty amazing, and will be a real differentiator for the practice, I believe the space has a huge potential to help people feel better about themselves. The more time women spend in nature, the stronger their self-worth becomes. I love that I can help make a positive change in people's lives, even in a small way, long after my work here is done.

Pulling into the parking lot of the therapy office, which is jammed with painter, contractor, and landscaper trucks, I pull into the last available space and put the top up on my Mini. The last thing I need is a two-inch layer of construction dust covering the interior of my car. Grabbing my shoulder bag, I head inside.

The entryway is gorgeous, with high ceilings and soothing pale blue paint. Although it hasn't been moved in yet, the furniture in the lobby will feature small seating clusters with soft, tactilely pleasing fabrics and round edges, so that patients will immediately feel at ease upon arriving.

"Hey, Doc," says Joe, my contractor. "It's coming together, right?" Joe is a small guy in his late fifties, with graying hair and a clipboard permanently fused to his right hand. He's worked with me for the last few years and really gets what I'm going for. Plus, he's a total perfectionist, which I love in a contractor. It means every detail is right without me having to spend all my time at the site, which saves me dozens of hours over the course of a project.

"Hey, Joe. It looks amazing," I say. "I can't wait to see it all done."

"Ready for the tour?" I nod, and he hands me a hard hat. "We're pretty well done out here in the lobby except for the finishing, but the small offices are still being drywalled. I was just about to do the inspection." I follow him down the hallway and we step into the first therapy room. The drywalling is complete, the windows have been put in, but none of the finishing work has been started yet. The work looks good, Joe's crew has done a fantastic job as always—but my eye goes to the ceiling and it feels wrong.

"Hey, Joe, what's the ceiling height in here?" I ask. He checks his clipboard and looks up. "It's supposed to be seven feet nine inches, but these look like nine feet." In an instant he has his measuring tape pressed to the wall.

"I think you're right. Yep, nine feet," he says. "Sorry about that, Doc, I'll get this taken care of right away. New drywaller, he just finished this room an hour ago." I know Joe would have caught the error if I hadn't, but I was hoping the problem was just in this one room. We didn't have much of a cushion with our deadline.

"Thanks," I say. "Remember, it's twelve feet in the lobby, nine feet in the hallways, seven foot nine in all the therapy rooms."

"Got it," he says to me, and then pulls the radio from his belt. "Nate, can you meet me with the client at the room you just finished?"

"Sure thing, boss," says the voice on the radio. Joe marks the drywall with a pencil while we wait for Nate the drywaller.

Joe and I discuss other details on the project, and Nate appears in the doorway a few minutes later. Totally worth the wait. Nate looks like a supermodel with a tool belt. He's tall, very tall, maybe six-four, with light brown hair, striking green eyes, and full lips that make me wonder what it might be like to just hurl my laptop bag on the floor, throw my arms around his neck, and kiss him.

Whoa, Alex, I think. First, completely inappropriate—Nate is an employee. Second, Darcy and Michael were right: if I don't get this whole sex thing out of my system pronto, I'm going to end up acting like a complete lunatic the second I find myself within fifty yards of any decent guy with long-term potential.

Still, it can't hurt to look a little. While Joe reviews the specs with him, I quickly scan Nate from head to steel-toed boots. White T-shirt speckled with paint, revealing finely muscled arms and just a peek of well-toned abs when he raises his hand to mark the wall. Dark jeans that look like they were designed with his body in mind. Like *all* jeans were designed with his body in mind. *Sigh.* If TLC ever gets a peek at Nate, he'll have his own show in a reality-TV minute.

"Doc?" says Joe. Oh gawd, I must have zoned out.

"Um, yes." I say. "I was just thinking about the, er, project and the, um. . . . ceiling height issue."

"So sorry about that," says Nate. "My bad. I made the assumption since the hallway height was the standard nine feet that the offices would be as well. It's no problem at all to fix it, I'll get it taken care of today." He's looking directly at me as he apologizes, and I can feel myself getting lost in those gorgeous green eyes. Like some kind of smutty hypnosis.

"Great, great," I say, trying to tear myself away from his gaze. "Try not to bump your head." I laugh awkwardly. "On the ceiling." Awkward pause. "Because you're so tall." Jeez, that was smooth. What am I? A gawky middle schooler, or an accomplished professional woman who owns her own business?

"I'll try." He grins. "Not to question your judgment or anything," he says, "but you do know that seven-nine is a very low ceiling height, right?"

"I do know that," I say. "But lower ceiling heights are conducive to intimacy, connection, and emotional safety, which is what we're trying to evoke for the patients here. If the room helps patients to open up more, they can be helped in fewer or shorter sessions, and get to the real work of therapy much faster. The main and outdoor therapy spaces have higher ceiling heights, of course, because we don't want the people who work here to feel boxed in, and the outdoor therapy spaces have a different objective." The doctor is in.

"Cool," Nate says. He smiles at me and I smile back, unable to be the first to break our mutual gaze.

"Doc, tour?" interjects Joe, and I can feel myself blushing.

"Thanks, Nate," I say, following Joe out of the room.

"Feel free to check my work anytime," he says. I don't respond as I trail Joe down the hallway, but I can't stop myself from thinking of all the ways I could do just that.

As Joe mentioned, the rest of the therapy spaces have been framed out, but not yet been completed. Joe opens the door on the left at the end of the hallway, and we step down into what will soon be one of the outdoor therapy spaces. The landscapers are outside placing plants and digging the holes for the large royal palms. I scan the space, and seeing some inappropriate greenery, I pull a pad of sticky notes out of my tote and begin marking the plants that have to go.

Nicky, my landscaper, appears from behind the small fountain that is being installed. A stout, swarthy New York transplant, he's straight out of Central Casting if you are looking for a Mob Guy #3—but the man loves plants and flowers, and despite his gruff demeanor, he's a sweet, sensitive artist whose chosen medium is foliage.

"Hey, Doc," Nicky says. I generally prefer to be called Alex, but Joe the contractor always calls me Doc and so the rest of the crew just follow his lead. "Whadya think?"

"It looks amazing," I say. "I love what you've done with the color, it feels like an oasis out here. You're a vegetation virtuoso." He smiles widely, proud of his artistry.

"Got any notes?" he asks.

"Literally," I say, laughing as I hold up the pad. "I stuck Post-its on a couple of small varieties you have on the ground over there." He cracks up because I'm such a stickler for those kinds of details, and he takes great pleasure in endlessly teasing me about it. We've worked together for so long now that he doesn't need to even express the joke in words anymore. Anytime I hand him a spreadsheet, a color-coded map, or tagged greenery I want moved, he skips right to the punch line. I don't mind, I know my control freak tendencies can be comical at times. I also know it's a big part of why I am where I am. It's all in the planning.

I laugh along and let Nicky have his fun, and then continue: "I see where you're going with this, but we can't have any plants with sharp edges, so none of those spiky ones over there, and definitely no cactus."

"I love the flowers on those," he says. "We need a pop of color."

"I know," I say gently. "The color is gorgeous, and I'm totally up for it if you want to replace them with something softer. Think breezy, round, feathery, tropical oasis."

"Done," Nicky says, with a finality that seems better suited to confirmation of a Mafia hit than a flower selection. But I have total faith in him, the man is a greenery savant.

27

It's almost four by the time I leave the psychology office job site, which is looking better by the day. It seems like a wreck now, but I've done enough of these jobs to know that we're in the final stretch and the project will be completed to perfection in a week to ten days.

I have two more stops to make at completed project sites, just to touch base with my clients. Neither will take more than ten or fifteen minutes, which is good because I have a meeting with Daniel Boudreaux at his new restaurant at five and I don't want to be late. I hate to be late.

I've done numerous restaurants in my line of work and I've found that the meetings always tend to happen later in the day, I suppose due to the necessary nocturnal habits of those in the culinary industry. I find myself looking forward to my meeting with Daniel, not just because he's so interesting and his enthusiasm for his work is so contagious, but because I cannot stop thinking about the jambalaya he made last time we'd met. I haven't eaten all day since my breakfast meeting with Olivia Vanderbilt Kensington and I'm completely famished.

Parking quickly at the marina, I walk down the dock to Daniel's restaurant, enjoying the bay breeze on my skin and watching the sun play on the water. What a gorgeous afternoon. The paint on the outside of the boat has been stripped since my last visit, and is in the process of being refinished, although there are no construction workers to be seen. I board the boat and peek inside the indoor bar area.

"Daniel?" No answer. I walk back toward the kitchen, but there's no sign of him there either. Checking my schedule on my phone, I wonder if we've gotten our times mixed up. Heading back outside to the deck, I walk around the back side of the boat, holding carefully to the mahogany railing. The back deck is larger than the front, with room for probably eight tables, although there is only one for the moment. Daniel is leaning over the railing, shirt off, hauling something up over the side. The sun reveals a glint of auburn in his short brown hair.

"Hey, Daniel," I say, and he jerks his head back unexpectedly, causing him to lose his footing and go over the railing headfirst. I scream as he falls into the drink, and rush over to the railing where he'd been leaning just a second before.

There he is, grinning from ear to ear, treading water in the bay, with a thick rope in his right hand.

"Hi," he says. "I didn't hear you come in."

"Oh Daniel," I say, covering my mouth with my hand in horror. "I'm so, so sorry."

"We've got crabs!" he yells, holding the rope high in the air. "Right off the boat!" He looks so happy I can't help but laugh. "Come on in, the water's nice," he says, trying to tempt me with a playful splash in my direction.

"Thanks, I'll pass," I say. "The water's a little nippy for me this time of year." The tourists never seem to mind when the water reaches the low sixties, but I'm a warm-weather girl and prefer it when the temperature of the Gulf and the bay are closer to bathwater. Or at the very least in the midseventies. It will be at least two months before that happens.

Daniel's dark hair clings to his face, and he shakes the water off his head like a Labrador. Nice arms, I think, as I watch him tread water. Gay guys certainly keep themselves in fantastic shape. He swims easily to the side of the boat and pulls himself up on the ladder, water droplets clinging to his chest and abs. Still hanging on to the rope, he brings himself effortlessly over the side of the railing and onto the deck, and pulls the crab trap up out of the water behind him. His khaki shorts are completely soaked through, and they hang low and loosely on his hips. I have to force myself, consciously, not to ogle him. Seriously, I need to get ahold of myself and quit drooling over gay men.

"Look at that," he grins adorably at me and gives a low whistle. "We're having crab for dinner."

"I'm so sorry about surprising you," I say. "I didn't mean to startle you."

"Don't you worry, darlin'," he says, his intensely blue eyes full of mischief. "I like surprises."

I must be hallucinating, because it feels like he's flirting with me. Darcy was right, I do need practice with regular straight men. Otherwise, I'm doomed to repeat history.

28

Daniel grabs his shirt with one hand and drapes it over the crab trap. "I'm just going to get changed, and put these on to boil. Are you hungry?"

I nod, glad I don't have to pretend like I wasn't hoping he'd cook for me again. He really seems to like it, and it's been tough for me to eat dinners at home lately. Something about just me at the dining table. Which means I end up eating ice cream out of the container, or popcorn and a glass or two of wine. Like it's less lonely somehow if I'm standing up. It's funny because I've always eaten alone with no problems at all. Michael was on the road a lot, and there aren't too many client dinners in my business, so I ate by myself. But there's something different about it now; it's more desolate, because unlike before when Michael was just traveling, now I know for certain there is no one coming home to eat with me. Ever again. It's weird, the stuff that bothers you when you're alone, even things that never bothered you before.

There's a tiny spiral staircase in the back of Daniel's kitchen, which apparently goes up to a small studio apartment above the dining area. I'm sitting at the table on the back deck near the railing, the same one where we'd sat last time, when I see him come through the kitchen door. Towel-dried hair, fresh shorts, and a clean green T-shirt that highlights the depths of blue in his eyes.

"I'll put the pot on, *cher*." The main doors of the dining room are open to the boat deck, and a lovely breeze flows through. Daniel bangs around in the kitchen and I feel all the stress leaving my body, gently kneaded away by the rocking of the boat. Daniel emerges with plates, napkins, and silverware balanced in one hand, and a couple of brown bottles in the other. "Nothing goes with fresh crabs better than beer," he says. "That okay with you?"

"Fine by me," I say. "Can I help you with anything?"

"Sweet of you to offer, darlin', but I've got it covered." He places the beers and the dishes down on the table, sets up the silverware and napkins in a few deft moves, and then disappears back into the kitchen. The smell is divine, spicy and delectable. He's back in an instant with a tray laden with crabs, corn on the cob, and sautéed asparagus. My mouth is watering. It strikes me what an act of intimacy it is to cook for someone—to invite them into your space, feed them, make them to feel welcome. There's something about how he moves and speaks that is so intriguing and charming, so welcoming.

He joins me at the table and lifts his beer to mine, "To fresh food and a fresh start." I clink my bottle against his. I'll definitely drink to that.

29

"So you had no idea that he was gay?" Daniel says. His deep blue eyes spark with interest.

"Not a clue," I say, bringing my second bottle of beer to my lips. "You'd probably be able to spot it from across the room," I say. Gaydar, and all that. I'm probably getting too familiar with him, but there's something about him that makes me feel like I would tell him anything. He asks these incredibly direct questions, things that some of my closest friends have never even thought to ask, and I'm inexplicably compelled to share all these deeply personal thoughts. He's like human Xanax or something. "Yeah, I didn't notice anything and it was right in front of me all these years."

He laughs. "Well, when I saw your husband for the first time he was wearing a sparkly pink princess crown and black leather pants, dirty dancing with a drag queen. So that might have tipped me off."

"Just a little," I say. "I feel so stupid." Tears sting my eyes, and I am mortified. *Get it together, Alex!* Grabbing my napkin off my lap, I dab at my eyes and force myself to refocus. "I'm so sorry, I don't usually cry in front of clients."

"That's okay, *cher,* you've earned a few tears," he says in that soothing Southern drawl. He reaches over and delicately strokes my forearm. "I don't usually swim in front of mine." He grins. "I'm so embarrassed."

I can't help but laugh, his face is so open and kind, and I feel myself drawn to him once again. Oh my God, what the hell is wrong with me? I have to get out of here.

30

"Seriously," I tell Darcy. "I'm lusting over my client. My *gay* client. I have completely lost my mind. I'm going to end up screwing up this amazing project that I'm superexcited to be doing because I can't stop myself from fantasizing about him."

"Which one?" she asks.

"Sterno Man."

"Oh, he's gorgeous," she says. "How do you know he's gay? It's not like you have a great track record with these things."

"He was Carter's date to my divorce/coming-out party."

"Okay, so he's gay."

"That's what I've been saying. I know I wasn't exactly in favor of this before, but have you and Michael made any progress on finding me a . . . date? I feel like my mojo is off, like I don't know up from down anymore, black from white—"

"Gay from straight?" says Darcy. I nod in agreement. "I think on some level there's some part of you that believes you don't deserve a great guy of your own," she says.

"Why the hell would you think that?" I ask. "I deserve a great guy. A great job. A great life."

"You do," she says, "but think about it. You marry a gay man. Your first dates as a single woman were with trolls. And now you're getting yourself tangled up with another gay man, a client, no less, which means whatever neuroses you're currently afflicted with are apparently spreading to your work."

"What's wrong with me?" I ask. "I'm not doing this on purpose."

"You got knocked down. Hard. And sometimes it takes a few tries before you can get back up."

"This kind of stuff doesn't happen to me! My life isn't some continuous stream of fuckups. I think before I act. I make plans and follow them through. I always have a backup plan, a contingency backup plan, a spare tire, and a sewing kit. This kind of clusterfuck is only supposed to happen to people who don't have a plan. I have a plan!"

"Crap happens to everybody. Your spouse is gay, or he cheats with the nanny, or he rips off the IRS. You deal with life as it comes. It breaks you in half or it just feels like it does. I'm all for planning, contingency planning, emergency contingency planning—but you have to grow up. Sometimes, it just doesn't matter what your plans are. The Universe or God or just the luck of the draw doesn't cooperate, and you just have to wade through the muck until you get to the other side. Sometimes life sucks. Can you avoid disaster with careful planning? Sometimes. And sometimes the tornado just comes down and rips your house away. And you get the fuck up, and rebuild."

"I don't know what to do anymore," I say.

"Make a new plan," she says. "And stop falling for gay guys."

31

I wake up at five-thirty the next morning to the sound of my cell phone ringing, and it sends me into a panic. It's Olivia Vanderbilt Kensington. The socialite. My first instinct is always to answer a client call, but it's not even light outside yet, and the last thing I want to do is give Olivia the impression that it's okay for her to call me at all hours. She's already blowing up my phone and my e-mail dozens of times a day, much of it with details and questions of things we've already covered, or topics completely unrelated to our project. Like the fact that she wants me to go shoe shopping with her to pick out something to wear to the fund-raiser. Way outside my scope of work. I'm torn, because she's a big fish in town, and if she likes my work she can send a lot of lucrative new business my way. That said, I'm working on a flat rate, at a discount because the work is for a charity, and with the number of hours I've spent on this project, and specifically on Olivia's many, many demands, I'm already losing money. I turn the ringer off and flip the phone over so I don't have to watch it light up, then roll over and try to go back to sleep.

I can't stop thinking about what Darcy said about some part of me being convinced I didn't deserve to be happy or have a great guy in my life. When I turn it over in my mind, it doesn't feel true, but I'm also having a tough time reconciling the reality of my life as of late with my perception. Maybe there *is* a part of me that thinks I don't deserve to be happy. The good news is, it's not my brain. I know I'm a good person. I'm kind and smart and hardworking. People tell me I'm attractive, that I'm a good friend, and fun to be around. I have wonderful friends and a mostly loving family. I deserve to be in love too. And the fact that my first love didn't work out doesn't make it a mistake. It makes it an experience.

And if I truly want to move forward in that area of my life, fall in love, maybe start a family, I need to get serious about getting myself out in the world as a grown-up single woman. Michael has moved on. I should too.

32

I planned to work from home to focus on marketing and cultivating new business, but instead I've decided to feng-shui the crap out of my house. Yes, I'm a scientist and much of this is little more than hocus-pocus; but it's hocus-pocus that's been practiced for thousands of years. And as a scientist, not only do I know that modifying your surroundings can create a huge impact on your emotions and behaviors, I also know that there is power in setting your intentions—in thinking about what you want to manifest in your life. At least that's the way I'm justifying spending my entire morning taping long sheets of aluminum foil to the underside of my dining room table; rearranging my photo collages to get wood out of my metal areas and metal out of my wood areas; and trying to figure out how in the world I can incorporate purple, green, and red around my pool deck without making it look like it belongs at a Las Vegas casino.

This is the dirty little secret of most educated, professional women I know; even doctors and scientists, like me. We still check our horoscopes like the weather; we probably believe a tarot card reader could understand us, and even see a glimpse of our future—but only if she's naturally gifted, the "real deal" and recommended by a friend. And we are willing to believe in feng shui. Whatever works, we say. Some things cannot be explained. And anyway, what's the harm in repainting the guest bath blue instead of beige if there is any chance at all, even a small one, that it might help you snag that big promotion?

I pull a feng shui book called *Move Your Stuff, Change Your Life* off my bookshelf, a joke gift from Darcy a few years ago. Three hours later I've mapped out the *bagua* of my home, made a to-do list of feng shui offenders that are obviously screwing up my life, and set to correcting my biggest problems through tactical redecorating and odd fixes. The thing I like about feng shui is that it makes you think about what you want in various areas of your existence. Get happy. Find love. Make more money. Get along better with your relatives. And figuring out what you want is the first step to making it happen.

My toilets are an issue. Apparently, all my wisdom is being sucked down the drain with the scrubbing bubbles. Well, it's no wonder my life is a wreck. I "cure" the toilets with tiny red ribbons tied around the pipes in the back where no one will see them. Obviously, my biggest need for feng shui falls in the love and relationships area. The love section of my house contains not only a toilet, but Michael's old office, which has become my dumping ground for all the stuff that reminds me of him, as well as the laundry room, home of Morley's litter box.

Cosmically speaking, I think I've found my problem.

33

I clear out all the junk in Michael's former office, box it up, and stick it in the garage, which juts forward from the front of the house, making it delightfully exempt from feng shui. With every box that goes outside, I feel freer and more in control of my life. With the boxes out of sight, they're no longer acting as a constant reminder of my marriage, or clogging up my romantic life either. Clutter weighs you down. Usually I'm kind of a neat freak, but lately my house has devolved more and more into utter disarray. There's a correlation, of course, between your mental state and your surroundings. Highly stressed people are likely living in a mess. Creative people tend to be cluttered but organized; there's a pattern to the constellation of stuff even if it is not discernible to anyone else. Super-organized types like to have a place (and a label and an inventory chart) for everything and can't go to sleep if there's an unwashed dish in the sink. That would be me.

I decide to relocate Morley's cat box to the garage, and call my contractor, Joe, to ask him to swing by or send one of the crew over to install a cat door once they finish work for the day at the psych office job site. I'm hoping there will be no repercussions from Morley. He's not a fan of change, and it's not beyond his capabilities to plot and execute some dastardly form of kitty revenge. Once Michael's office, former office, is cleared out, I head out for a field trip to the home improvement store. I need red paint, stat.

An hour later my cart is loaded down with a gorgeous shade of tomato-red paint, extra brushes, sunny yellow contact paper for my kitchen drawers and cabinets, a small palm tree and ceramic pot for my fame and reputation area, and the Taj Mahal of cat doors, a $300 contraption called the Royal Door Mount. If they installed cat doors at the front entrance of the Waldorf Astoria, this would be the one they'd use. The sales guy tells me that for Florida this type of door is a must—and I'll easily recoup the cost in my air-conditioning bills in the first year alone. I'll have to take his word for it.

Back at the house, I put the palm tree in its new home, with the intention that my business will grow. I leave the contact paper on the kitchen countertop, and bring in drop cloths, paint rollers, and a tray, and set them on the floor of Michael's now-empty former office, along with the red paint and new brushes I just bought. The feng shui book says that I need red or pink in this area, and lots of it. I debated doing a fabulous hot-pink room, something uber-feminine and totally glamorous, but I ultimately opted for the red, which I knew from my own research is a little steamier. When we view the color red, our bodies have a physiological response that is similar to sexual attraction. Our hearts beat a little faster, our pupils dilate. If I'm going to feng-shui this joint, I might as well go all in.

I take off my shoes and slip into an old tank top and cargo shorts, my go-to painting outfit, and pull my long hair up into a bun so I don't end up accidentally dipping it into the paint. After laying out the drop cloth and removing all the outlet covers, I open the paint, stir it up a bit, and pour it into the tray. The color is gorgeous, and even though it's a departure from the rest of my decor, which tends to be more muted, I think I'm going to love it.

I start rolling the walls with paint, my favorite part since it provides such instant gratification. You can see what the room is going to look like when it's finished almost immediately. That's me, I guess. Always looking to the end. The office is a pale gray, but I've bought really good paint, so it covers easily with the first coat. Three walls done, and I stand back to admire my handiwork. Not bad at all. The room is still unfinished around the baseboards and crown molding, but the rolling is halfway done. Michael has a much steadier hand than I do, and it was always his job to do the detail work. Funny the things that make me miss him.

I'm just about to start on the fourth wall, which is going to be a bit trickier because it has built-in shelves all the way to the ceiling, when my doorbell rings. I put the roller at the top of the tray and pad through the house in my bare feet.

"Thanks for coming, Joe," I say as I open the door. But it isn't Joe. It's Nate, the tool-belt supermodel drywaller.

"Hi, Nate," I say, flustered. "Uh, so sorry, I was expecting Joe."

"He had to stop by another job site, some emergency." Nate smiles, all six foot four of him casually leaning up against the frame of my door. "So I volunteered."

"Thanks," I say. "Um . . . that was really nice of you." I lose my concentration, mesmerized by his eyes for a second. Or maybe seven hours. I have no way of knowing. It's like being abducted by aliens and dropped back in the exact same location you were snatched from.

"Are we doing some painting today?" he asks.

"How'd you know that?" He reaches out and gently pulls a fleck of red paint from my hair. His hand so near my face makes my heart race. I can feel myself blushing and hope he doesn't notice.

"Lucky guess."

I invite him in and he follows me toward the kitchen. As we walk, I realize I have splatters of paint on my toes and all over my arms, and who knows where else. Michael always says it's a personality paradox that I'm such a messy painter—everything else about me is organized, color-coded, and alphabetized.

"I just need a pet door installed. Here's the door to the garage," I say, then point to the large box on my kitchen counter. "There's the cat door."

"No problem," he says, "it shouldn't take too long. I'll let you get back to your painting."

"Thanks. Do you need anything?" I ask. "Screwdriver, glass of water, box cutter?"

Ahem. Bicep massage?

"Nope, I'm good," he says, "I've got everything I'll need in the Jeep."

"Okay, I'll leave you to it." He heads back toward the front door and I return to my painting. He's back inside a few minutes later, banging around in the kitchen.

I'm way up on the ladder, taping off the built-ins, when I first hear the sound. Nate is laughing, deep and loud enough to hear clearly all the way to the other end of the house. What in the world could be so funny about a cat door?

Stepping down from the ladder, I return to the kitchen. There's Nate, the Adonis in a tool belt, standing in front of the kitchen counter where I'd put the box with the cat door—doubled over with laughter, cracking up so hard his whole body is shaking. His amusement is infectious, and I begin to smile before I even know what is happening. I step around his tall frame to see what's so funny.

Oh . . . Fuck. It's the gigantic, brightly labeled, economy-size, mortifyingly extensive, multicolored selection of condoms—courtesy of Darcy. I'd forgotten all about them.

My hand flies to my mouth, my skin burning with humiliation. Jumping around Nate, I push the box off the breakfast bar to the floor, where it lands with a loud thud—as though the fact that it's no longer on the counter might erase it from his memory entirely.

"Oh my God," I stutter, trying to spit out some plausible explanation that might make the situation less mortifying. "I don't know what to . . . it's just . . . it was a joke from a girlfriend . . . I sort of got divorced last week." Jesus Alex, *stop talking.*

"Don't sweat it." Nate grins. "That's the exact same box I buy."

Ew. "Really?"

"No, I was just joking, trying to make you feel better."

"Not possible unless that joke comes with a shot of tequila."

And maybe a foot massage.

"That can be arranged." He smiles. "You could stock up a truck stop for a year with a box that size."

"I know. My friend Darcy is quite the comedienne."

He starts randomly opening kitchen cabinet doors until he hits pay dirt. I'm too mortified to be bothered by the intrusion. Two shot glasses and a half-empty bottle of tequila. My instinct is to stop him, and send him away, but then I think, *why the hell not*? I'm divorced and a hot guy handy with power tools wants to drink tequila with me.

"Why do you need to drink?" I laugh. "I'm the one dying of humiliation here."

"Trust me," he says. "I'm scarred for life. Besides, I can't let you drink alone."

34

Two shots of tequila later we decide to order a pizza. Nate installs Morley's cat door while we wait for the delivery guy from Solorzanos to arrive. It always takes forever but it's worth it. *Sooo* worth it.

There's a part of me that wants to hang out in the kitchen and just watch Nate work, but the tequila and his cheekbones have begun to go to my head and I don't want to say anything stupid. Well, anything else.

Heading back to the office, I resume taping off the built-ins so I can finish the painting before I go to sleep. It's slow progress. I'm positive that tequila will do nothing to improve my already-sloppy technique, so I'm careful with the tape.

"Nice color," says Nate, poking his head inside the doorway. "Although I can't decide if it looks better on the walls or on you."

"Fortunately, there's both." I laugh, posing dramatically with my paint-speckled arms. "Are you finished already?"

"Cutting a hole in the door and installing a few screws is not exactly the most challenging thing I've done all day," he says, helping himself to my paint supplies and coming up with a small trim brush. "You're going to be up all night if you tape off every shelf," he says. "I'll cut in, and you do a second coat with the roller." My mind wanders at the thought of Nate up on a ladder.

"You don't want the tape?" I ask. He shakes his head no, and steps up a few rungs on the ladder, easily reaching the crown molding. His technique is perfect, quick and methodical, with great attention to detail.

"You're really good at that," I say.

"I went to art school at Ringling," he says. "Construction is just how I pay the bills."

He's halfway around the room before I finish rerolling even one wall. By the time I've finished two walls, he's done the upper and lower trim for the entire room, and is working on the wall behind the built-ins.

I stand back, ostensibly to survey our work, gratuitously admiring Nate's sculpted back, his legs, his, er, ass.

Nate turns around, and the doorbell rings just in time to save me from having to awkwardly explain why I'm staring at the guy on the ladder rather than, you know, painting.

"Do you want to eat in the kitchen, or here?"

"If you don't mind, let's eat in here," he says. "That way we can finish this up tonight." Now you're talking, buddy.

Heading to the front door, I pay the Solorzanos delivery guy for the pizza, grab paper plates and napkins from the kitchen, and bring the whole shebang into the office. Nate puts the lid on my bin of paint supplies for a makeshift picnic table, and settles himself, cross-legged, on the floor.

"Can I get you a drink?" I ask as I set the pizza box on the bin. "Beer? Wine? Water? Tequila?"

He laughs. "Beer is good. Tequila too."

On the ten-second walk back to the kitchen, I try to figure out exactly what he meant. I should just ask him, but I'm feeling stupidly self-conscious. Either beer *or* tequila? Both beer *and* tequila? I hedge my bets and bring both. Grabbing a cold six-pack of amber ale from the fridge, and the bottle of tequila off the kitchen countertop, I'm already back to the office before I realize I've forgotten glasses for the tequila. Oh well.

"Please help yourself," I say. He opens the box and grabs a couple of slices. It's almost nine-thirty and we're both famished. I can't remember eating anything since breakfast. Unless you count the tequila.

I eat three slices of the large pizza, which is some kind of new world record for me; Nate polishes off the rest. I finish my first beer too fast, weirdly nervous. After Nate's second beer, he says, "What's your story? You just got divorced?"

"It's a long story," I say, "and not a very fun one." There's nothing to do with my hands and I need a diversion, so I grab another beer out of the cardboard holder. "How 'bout you, Nate? Have you ever been married?"

I gaze just a second too long at his mouth, waiting for him to speak. He grins. "I'm not really that guy."

"Neither was my husband," I crack. Don't go there, I admonish myself. This little paint and tequila dinner party feels sort of promising, and the last thing I need is to start bawling into the pizza box.

Nate laughs and reaches for the bottle of tequila.

"Should I go get some glasses or are we drinking this right out of the bottle?" I ask.

"Let's do," he says, bringing the tequila bottle up to his lips, his perfect lips, for a drink and hands it over to me. I try my best to take a ladylike swig, but such a thing isn't possible with a half-gallon bottle of tequila. F-ing Costco. I settle for not dribbling any on myself. I start to hand the bottle back to Nate, and instead of taking it, he pulls me to his body, and kisses me softly on my lips.

At first, I'm unsure whether or not I should kiss him back—my brain takes a microsecond to do a pros and cons matchup to determine whether *drinking tequila and making out with someone who is indirectly sort of an employee, but technically a subcontractor so not really*, is advisable. The tequila wins, and I kiss him back with a steamy intensity I've never experienced before. *Oh. My. God. So this is what kissing a straight guy is like.* He brings me closer to him, his mouth hot and insistent and all over mine—and I end up sort of sitting on his lap, and suddenly I'm straddling him, the two of us surrounded by paint stuff and pizza crusts. We're kissing frenetically, his hands all over my body in the most delicious way, on the small of my back, along the curve of my waist, centimeters away from my breasts. I'm pawing at his shirt, like some sex-crazed lunatic. He pulls the shirt off in one swift motion, revealing his chest, muscled and lean—it's as fantastic as I'd imagined. Hello, Adonis.

"Oh my God," I inhale. I've spent my entire adult life with a gay man, and yet I've never seen a chest like this outside of a multiplex.

He reaches toward me and tugs gently at the tank top I'm wearing, pulling it off, over my head. My ponytail holder gets caught in one of the armholes and I'm suddenly straitjacketed with one arm up in the air with my face wedged close to my armpit, blinded by my own top, the other arm down, while Nate laughs and attempts to unstick me. I feel my skin turning crimson, burning with humiliation, when suddenly I'm free, my dark hair falling down over my shoulders and my tank top in Nate's hands.

"You're beautiful," he says, studying my face, then letting his eyes linger on my black lace bra. He tosses my shirt to the floor, and kisses my shoulders and décolletage, softly at first and then more insistently—one hand holds me close around my waist, the other slides over my breast against the lace of my bra.

His breath is heavy on my skin, my panties are soaked, and my entire body is electric with anticipation. My hands are all over his chest, stroking the muscles in his back, and I nuzzle his ear as he works his way down my neck. Deftly, he unclasps my bra, and lifts my breasts to his lips, and runs his tongue teasingly over each nipple, one, then the other, as I arch my back in ecstasy. I can't stop myself from watching him take my breasts with his mouth, grazing his lips back and forth across my hardened nipples, until I'm wet and ripe. It's the sexiest thing I've ever experienced in my life.

As my breath quickens, he's back at my mouth, kissing me fiercely, his tongue exploring my lips, then my neck, the lobe of my ear.

We look at each other, both hot and panting, and he grins at me. "If only we knew where to find a condom. Or eight hundred."

Looks like this feng shui thing is working already.

35

I may be terrible at dating, but I am awesome at sex.

"You didn't!" shrieks Darcy.

"I did." I can't stop grinning. I feel like a whole new woman. A woman with a vagina. I can't believe I was so resistant to the idea in the first place. "It was *A-M-A-Z-I-N-G*. It was like three hours of foreplay, which beat Michael's old record by about two hours and forty-five minutes. I swear he kissed every single inch of my body. And, when we were all done, he finished the painting. With his shirt off."

"Really? Because usually they just roll over and start snoring. He must really be hoping for a round two."

"Maybe," I say. "That wouldn't be the worst thing in the world."

"Did he sleep over?" she asks.

"No, I told him I had an early meeting and kicked him out at two in the morning. I was freaked out that things might get weird in the daylight. And the absence of tequila." Darcy howls with laughter.

"That was probably a good move. I don't know if you're ready for a sleepover. Keep it casual for now."

"We ate pizza off a paint bin, drank tequila from the bottle, and had sex on the floor. You can't get much more casual than that."

"Just be careful, doll," she says. "I'm glad you had fun, I'm glad you're moving forward, I just want you to tread carefully. You don't want to be like one of those people who've lived in a cult all their lives and they get out into the real world and OD on Cheez Whiz and bologna sandwiches until their hearts explode."

"I'll try to lay off the Cheez Whiz," I say.

"That's all I ask," she says. "I'm just looking out for you."

"By the way," I say. "Thanks for the condoms."

Darcy snorts.

36

I'm feeling a little squirrelly about going to the psych office job site. Obviously I need to check on my projects, just as I always do. But normally I wouldn't go back so soon. The truth of it is, I want to see Nate. And I think it will be awkward as hell to see Nate. It's been almost twenty-four hours since he arrived at my house, and he hasn't called. I don't know if this is normal, or something I should worry about. Darcy says it's no big deal. Maybe he doesn't have my number. I wonder if he feels weird about calling me since I'm sort of, but not really, his boss. Actually Joe is his boss. It didn't occur to me until after the fact that I'd be completely mortified if Joe ever finds out that I slept with one of the guys on his crew. Hopefully Nate isn't the type to kiss and tell. Or have wild, crazy, tequila-fueled sex and tell.

37

Even the promise of soy burgers and a life-changing, three-hour orgasm is barely enough to overcome my aversion to the overwhelming fetor of patchouli and incense.

Kai the tantric yogi and I meet at the Green Zebra Café. I'm early, he's ten minutes late. But I'm fresh off my night of tequila, sex, and paint rollers and brimming with newfound confidence.

Kai is exactly as Sam described him, with sandy, shoulder-length wavy hair and soft brown eyes. He's lean, about five-ten, maybe five-eleven, and wearing a flowy white shirt and linen-colored pants that are probably made of eco-friendly hemp or bamboo fibers or something. He orders us a round of Balancing Arts Elixir shots from a waitress who knows him by name. I'm hoping the "secret ingredient" listed on the menu is rum, but it's probably just lemongrass or ginger root or something. Kai spouts Zen platitudes like he's a human meme generator.

And I'm getting the feeling that while wheatgrass and tantric sex might be Kai's go-to first date, starting a cult is probably his second.

"Sam's told me a lot about you, Alex," says Kai, gazing at my eyes. He barely blinks, and I begin to feel weirdly exposed under the intensity of his gaze. What exactly did she tell him? "You have a beautiful aura around you," he says.

Jeez, I'm not sure I'll be able to make it through the entire date, or the bonus round, with a straight face. I mean, is this guy for real?

"Thank you, Kai," I say, because what else do you say? He reaches across the table and clasps my hands in his, staring deeply into my eyes. My nerves are starting to get to me. In theory, I agree with Darcy and Sam. I'm an adult woman, and sex is part of the human experience. And after my night with Nate, it's pretty obvious I've missed out on a whole lot by spending my entire grown-up life sleeping with a gay man. But in practice, I'm just not sure I can go through with it.

"You've been through a great deal of pain this year, but you are a powerful woman, and you will rise above these troubles. Your goddess spirit will find peace and happiness, because that is what you deserve," he says earnestly.

And your lucky Lotto numbers are 47, 13, 63, 12, and 2, I think to myself.

Dinner is weed-like and wholly unsatisfying, and I'm fantasizing about eating a big juicy steak throughout the entire meal. We agree to go back to Kai's place, because I don't want this weirdo in my house, and while I'm not sure I want to go through with this, I *am* sure that if the Naughty Nine are all that stand between me and a real relationship, I want to get them over with as quickly as possible and get on with my life.

I follow behind him in my car; the drive is only five or six minutes. I was really hoping it would be longer.

Kai's condo is exactly what you'd expect if the Dalai Lama decided to set up a sex den in Florida.

The whole place smells like incense and lemons, New Agey music is playing from speakers positioned near an odd cream-colored floor couch. He invites me to change into a robe to better relax, and directs me to a powder room decked out with a hook with several hangers, a basket filled with miniature toiletries, and two neat rows of bottled water. I crack myself up momentarily remembering what Sam said about staying hydrated.

A cotton waffle-weave robe is folded neatly along with a pair of spa slippers on top of a small, round table. It's reminiscent of the day spa I go to sometimes—all Kai is missing are the little lockers and the key on the curly plastic thing that you put in the pocket of your robe when you go in for your seaweed facial.

I should probably be offended that he's so presumptuous, but what's the use? We both know why I'm here. When I emerge from the powder room, he's also wearing a waffle-weave robe and spa slippers, and I can't help but giggle at the sight of him. Because, come on, he looks ridiculous. There are bronze and ceramic statues of Buddha everywhere; dream catchers and crystals hang in front of windows darkened with bamboo shades. He's lit half a dozen candles and dimmed the lights, and he motions for me to come and join him on the squishy floor couch.

"Relax, Alex," says Kai, "free your mind from all the tethers of earth." I squint my eyes closed, trying not to crack up about the whole "tethers of earth" thing. It sounds like he's readying me for a trip to the mothership. "Take a deep, cleansing breath," he says, "and open your eyes to the sensual beauty all around you."

He's going to have to quit talking if he wants me to keep a straight face.

We sit cross-legged facing each other, and he's massaging my palms with some sort of weird smelly oil as he stares into my eyes for what seems like hours. It's oddly intense, and hypnotic, but my brain is having none of this. It's not for me, at least not with a complete stranger. Maybe I just need to see where this thing with Nate the toolbelt supermodel goes. Or maybe I need to wait until I'm in love.

"I'm sorry," I say, "I just think I need something deeper." Kai nods at me, with understanding in his eyes, and just as I think he's about to stop with the tantric hand massage, he swiftly maneuvers me backward, placing my feet on his chest, pulls my hips towards his groin as he squats like a savage.

"Whoa," I say. Not exactly what I meant, but I'm morbidly fascinated. What the hell is he doing?

"This is one of the deepest positions in the Kama Sutra," he says. He shifts himself to enter me, and my brain is still squeamishly hesitant to even go through with this. And just as I'm about to tell him I don't want to, *nothankyouverymuch* but I'd really like him to stop, he grasps the soles of my feet and starts vigorously massaging them.

Which is his first mistake. Well, that and the Gandhi pants.

I'm insanely ticklish, and before either of us knows what's happened, my left foot shoots out reflexively, and I kick him smack in the nose.

I watch in horror as his nose begins gushing blood. I mean, it's everywhere.

"Ohmygod, Kai, are you okay?" I'm completely mortified. He seems stunned. Scrambling to my feet, I rush to the kitchen to grab a towel. I run the cloth under cold water for a few seconds and quickly run it back to Kai.

"What the hell?" he says in a nasally voice. "What the hell?" The towel is soaked with blood in less than a minute. This is bad, really bad. I start rummaging around in the kitchen in a panic to find something to stop the bleeding, and rush back with a roll of unbleached paper towels and a bag of frozen organic peas.

"I'm so sorry," I say effusively, "I didn't mean—"

"You broke my nose," he yells.

"I'm so sorry, it was an accident," I say. "I'm really ticklish. I didn't mean to . . . Do you want me to drive you to the emergency room?"

"Yes," he hisses. I awkwardly shred strips of paper towels for him while he stuffs the little pieces up his nostrils to stop the bleeding—and then I retreat to the powder room to quickly wash the smelly oil off my palms and yank on my clothes.

I emerge seconds later and lead Kai out to my car. He's still wearing the waffle-weave bathrobe and spa slippers, and he groans as he presses the bag of frozen peas to the bridge of his nose.

We drive to the emergency room in utter silence.

Dating is exhausting. And weird as hell. How do people ever meet and fall in love, anyway?

After the whole tantric-yogi emergency-room fiasco, I'm ready to take a break, or just give up altogether. But Darcy has arranged a date for me with one of her many clients, Robert Warren, a conservative wunderkind from the other side of the state. He's *so* not my type. But he checks that "Master of the Universe" box, so Darcy is insisting that I go—and frankly it will take me less time to just go on the date than it would to try to talk her out of it.

I google him and he looks like a Ken doll in a Brooks Brothers suit. Judging from the hundreds of photos online, he seems stiff, and humorless, and boring as hell. Oh well, I can survive anything for a few hours. I mean, how bad could it possibly be? At least it can't be worse than Kai the tantric yogi and our ill-fated ER date.

The congressman's assistant calls me to set up the details. She's efficient and polite, and informs me that Robert Warren will be driving to Sarasota from West Palm Beach on Saturday. He'll pick me up at my home around noon, and we'll be going to some sort of outdoor festival, weather permitting. She asks me to please wear a dress, which I find incredibly arrogant and obnoxious—but who knows, maybe the congressman is worried we'll be photographed together or something and wants to make sure I look appropriate.

On Saturday, my doorbell rings at noon on the dot, and I appreciate that his timing is so precise after a three-hour drive. It takes a special sort of skill to be that prompt.

As I open my front door, my mouth drops open from shock—because standing on my porch is a cross between a Norse god, the Grinch, and one of the odder characters from *Lord of the Rings*.

38

"Gunner Starlord at your service, Lady Alexandra," he says, bowing deeply.

WTF? His face is completely covered in some sort of greenish-black makeup, and he's sporting a Viking helmet with those little horns on the sides, and black boots caked in mud. He's draped in multiple brown cloaks and lace-up leather armor, a single fingerless black leather glove, and a red cape draped over his arm. He carries a puffy, oddly shaped sword-like object, and a puffy, oddly shaped shield adorned with a crest comprised of two crisscrossed hammers and a bear eating a lion. Because, sure.

"Robert?" I ask tentatively. *Please say no, please say no, please say you have the wrong house . . .*

I'm going to kill Darcy.

He stands up a little straighter, puffs out his chest, and smiles, "Yes, Robert Warren, so nice to meet you, Alex. Darcy has told me so much about you."

"Ah, that's so nice," I say. I wish I could say it was nice to me *him*.

"You must be wondering about my appearance," he says.

"It did cross my mind," I say.

"I'm Gunner Starlord, Human Warrior of the Isle of Black Elder."

"I'm confused." Gunner Starlord?

"I'm a LARPer, and there's an imperial battle for the realms today," he informs me. "We mustn't be late. There is much at stake."

"I thought you were a congressman," I say, still trying to wrap my head around the costume. And the foam sword. And the whole "*Call me Gunner Starlord*" thing. Darcy's probably laughing her ass off about now.

"LARP means 'live action role-playing,'" he says.

"You mean like a Renaissance fair? Or one of those historic battle reenactments?"

He sniffs condescendingly. "It's a little *more involved* than that, Alex."

"Ah, I see," I say. But I don't see. I don't have any idea what he's talking about. He looks like an escaped mental patient.

"Are you going to invite me in?" he asks. Now, that's a question for the ages.

"Yoohoo! Hello, Alex!" my neighbor Zelda calls from the sidewalk as she walks her little dog, Gabbiano, past my house. Gabbiano tugs at his leash, wanting to come in to play with Morley. I wave back as she grins and raises her eyebrows at my costumed, shield-carrying date, all decked out in his medieval garb.

"Uh, sure," I say to Robert/Gunner Starlord. "Please come in."

He steps inside, and casually sets his sword and shield against my hall table.

I'm trying to keep an open mind, really I am. *Really*.

Robert/Gunner Starlord explains that we'll be attending a LARP for our date, that the red cape is for me to wear, and that he's already taken the liberty of creating a character for me. He'll explain on the way.

This, I've gotta hear.

On the entire forty-five-minute drive to wherever in the hell he's taking me, Robert regales me with his character Gunner Starlord's highly detailed backstory, including his family history, epic foam-sword battles, rivalries with other imaginary people, and romantic encounters with witches, fairies, and magical healers.

He's speaking in vocabulary I can barely follow, a breakneck dissertation on concentrated fire and destroy shields and one-hundred damage or two-hundred damage; levels and points; elves and barbarians and witch hunters.

I'm trying to be a good sport and absorb as much as I can; this feels oddly like one of my weird Voldemort dreams. Robert/Gunner Starlord reaches over to the glove box and pulls out a thick book, handbound in an uneven piece of leather, dropping it in my lap. I flip through it, curiously; it's probably two hundred pages—a highly detailed rule book for the imaginary world we're about to enter. Oh dear Lord, what has Darcy gotten me into?

We park and once we exit the car, Robert/Gunner Starlord hands me a character card and the red cape, and a small dagger made out of foam and duct tape.

"For your protection," he says solemnly. "It's a boffer."

"Excuse me?" I say.

"A boffer, that's what these types of weapons are called."

According to the card he's given me, I'm a healer, which means I get to attend to the imaginary wounded after their battles. I'm not sure what that entails, but I'm here, so I might as well play along. I pull on the red cape. Even though I feel like an idiot.

It's surreal as we walk into the elaborate campsite, set up like a small village and populated by all sorts of medieval and fantasy characters, many of whom apparently spent the night. In the woods. I don't even like regular camping—and it occurs to me that it's probably really hard to sleep on the ground while wearing fairy wings. Or horns. Gunner Starlord leads me through the crowd, and a woman wearing a black bustier, a feather cape, and a pointy hat hurls oatmeal mixed with green glitter at me, as she recites an incantation.

"*Jalla kaboobba whencas odium . . .*"

"Hmmf, don't mind her," Starlord whispers in my ear. "That's just Morgana. She's only a level-three wizard. Her spells can't harm you." I start cracking up and immediately my hand flies to cover my mouth when I realize that Gunner Starlord is deadly serious.

39

My date with Congressman Robert Warren, aka Gunner Starlord, was, by far, the most bizarre six hours of my life.

I mean, how often do you get to see your date battle it out with foam hammers and swords with another grown man dressed up as a Minotaur, like it's some magical medieval fight club?

The second he drops me off at my house and pulls out of the driveway, I'm on the phone to Darcy and Sam.

"How'd it go?" asks Sam.

"You seriously would not believe it if you saw it for yourself," I say. I tell them about the LARPers, the elaborate costumes and makeup, my observation that the unparalleled fashion of choice for witches, fairies, and elven women is a dead heat between the breast-hoisting bustier and the wench gown. "I don't know that it's even necessary to put them on display," I joke. "I think a lot of those guys may not have even encountered a real live woman before. It might just be too much for them to handle."

I replay every detail of the battle royal between the congressman and the Minotaur, the spell-caster who seemed to have it in for me, and as much as I could remember about the excruciatingly detailed backstory of Gunner Starlord.

"Gunner Starlord?" roars Darcy, "*Gunner fucking Starlord?*"

"Yep," I answer, laughing so hard I can barely catch my breath.

"I heard he was a weird one, but I had *no idea.*" Darcy laughs. "Please, please tell me you took a picture."

"I'm texting it to you now," I say. "Show no one. This does not leave the three of us."

"Nice cape," cracks Darcy.

My misadventure with Gummer Starlord was like a bad omen of what was to come.

To say that my dates with the sensitive artist and the lead guitarist did not go well would be the understatement of the year. The sensitive artist (okay, mentally unstable graphic designer, but close enough) wept inconsolably for forty-five minutes over a two-year-old breakup, and didn't stop until the busboy cleared the table. Now I know how Ferret Guy felt.

Twenty minutes into the date at the finest table Hooters had to offer, the wannabe rocker, who asked to be called Kryptic, enthusiastically suggested I recruit our waitress for a BDSM threesome back at his place.

"Are you wearing panties?" he asked me while lecherously swirling a chipotle garlic chicken drummette in bleu cheese dressing.

"Are you wearing an ankle monitor?" I shot back.

"I've got the largest collection of nipple clamps on the East Coast," he whispered.

"I'm sure your mother is very proud," I said, wishing I'd taken Darcy up on her offer to buy me a stun gun for my birthday. You know, just in case. Although this creep would have probably liked it. Ten minutes later I was back in my car, speeding toward home.

Michael keeps promising to find me not only a replacement soul mate, but also a quarterback, and he hasn't delivered on either. I'm not holding my breath.

But at least my Naughty Nine list is now down to a more manageable Terrifying Threesome: The bad boy. The quarterback. The sexy foreign guy.

Well, foursome if you count the fish.

It's too bad that I can't count Ferret Guy and Dr. Dicpic against my Naughty Nine, but apparently nobody truly *needs* to date a math teacher or an Internet pervert before they find true love.

I keep thinking that if I stay busy, I won't be sitting around obsessing over my embarrassment about the fact that Nate hasn't called. Yet. It's not working.

Two days later Michael finally (finally!) comes through on his promise to introduce me to a quarterback. No sign or word of the soul mate he promised. Dane Cooper is the injured, first-string quarterback for the University of South Florida. He apparently broke his foot while he was being sacked by the East Carolina Pirates, which is why I've agreed to meet him at his house instead of a restaurant or bar—the cast makes driving difficult. Anyway, it's some sort of dinner party with his "crew," which is, I guess, another way of saying his teammates.

The drive to Tampa is about an hour, which gives me plenty of time to think about the insanity of going on a blind date, arranged by my gay ex-husband, with a twenty-one-year-old college student—and psych myself up for the evening. I need to check off the quarterback on my Naughty Nine list, so I put the fact that he's unbelievably young—not to mention Michael's idea of a good date for me—out of my head. As I pull in to the parking lot of his apartment complex, something dawns on me for the first time . . . *I wonder what's in it for him.* A thing for older women? The hope that Michael will give him some airtime? I'm in no position to judge someone else's motives, being that I'm only here to satisfy some silly requirement on the Naughty Nine list.

After climbing two flights of stairs, I've arrived at the door of 3K, Dane's apartment. Thumping hip-hop seeps down from upstairs, there are pizza boxes and beer bottles on the stair landings, and the place has the sort of beigey, run-down, burritos, old cigarettes, and vomit aura of every college apartment complex you've ever seen or lived in. And can't wait to escape the second you get your diploma.

What in the hell am I doing here?

I knock on the door and it takes Dane a good thirty seconds to answer. I'm remembering I saw a Waffle House on the side of I-75 on the way up here and fantasizing about drowning my dating sorrows in a double order of hash browns, just as Dane finally opens the door. Another ten seconds and I would have lost my nerve and headed back home.

"Hey," he says, "thanks for driving so far." Okay, good start. He's polite. Well, polite-ish. He's pretty tall, probably six-four, with the strong, chiseled chest and arms of a guy who's been doing two-a-days since he was about five. He's wearing a USF T-shirt and baggy athletic shorts. So, it's not a *formal* dinner party. I'm feeling a bit overdressed in my wrap dress and heels.

Dane's hair is dirty blond, and he's got the patchy starter beard of a teenager. He motions for me to come inside, grinning adorably. Nice smile. Great teeth. He's wearing some kind of headset, with the microphone pushed up. Like the kind coaches wear on the sidelines.

He steps back from the door, and I notice the clunky blue cast on his left foot.

"No problem," I say. "How's your foot?"

"Uh, it sucks. But the painkillers are cool," he says, dragging his foot back to the couch. I follow him inside and close the door behind me. "You look pretty hot," he says.

"Thanks," I say, feeling weirdly self-conscious as I look around the room. Oh gawd, *he's so young.*

The apartment is heavy with the gaminess of testosterone laced with pot, decorated with liquor bottles and dirty laundry, and dark. Bent white blinds drawn closed cover the windows. He sits down on a brown-and-orange-flowered velveteen sofa that predates him by a couple of decades, and props his cast up on a dinged-up coffee table with brass detail on the corners. I sit down at the far end of the sofa, and check out the apartment. The furniture is mismatched, banged up, and solely functional. But he has a huge TV mounted to the wall, another gigantic TV perched on a stand on top of a black entertainment unit right below it, a massive sound system, and three different gaming systems—it's a virtual shrine to manly electronics.

"Are you a meat lover?" he asks casually. He checks his phone and then sets it down on the coffee table next to another headset like the one he's wearing.

"What?" I ask. Gross. What is this, some kind of pervy frat boy come-on?

"Pizza," he says. "Are you okay with the Meat Lover, or do you want something else, like cheese or veggie? Lotsa girls like the veggie."

"Oh," I say, embarrassed. "Anything's fine, thanks."

He picks up his phone and calls in the pizza order. Two pizzas, both covered in meat.

"You want a beer?" he asks.

"Sure," I say. This date will go easier with alcohol. He stands up and hobbles over to the refrigerator, his cast clunking on the tile floor. He pulls out two bottles of beer, and now I feel guilty, I should have offered to get up. The poor guy has a broken foot, after all. He twists the caps off the bottles and hands one to me.

He sinks back down into the sofa, grabbing a remote off the table. The TV is on, and a buff, animated soldier loaded down with machine guns and grenades shifts back and forth on screen. The soldier looks antsy, like he really needs to find a restroom or something.

"We're going to play *Call of Duty: Advanced Warfare* with my clan," says Dane.

"Clan?" I ask, horrified. "Like *the* Klan?"

"Naw," he says, "that's fucked up. We're playing with my clan, my crew, my boys." I must still look confused. "My friends," he clarifies.

I feel about seventy right now.

Dane hands me a headset, like the one he's wearing, "Here ya go. Put it on."

"Oh, I'm not really much of a video game player," I say, fiddling with the headset.

"That's okay," he says. "We really just need a fill-in. We've got a ranked match tonight streaming on Twitch and Matty got carpal tunnel."

The only three words I understood in that sentence were *okay*, *really*, and *match*. Oh, and *carpal tunnel*. What the hell is Dane talking about?

"Huh?" I say eloquently.

"Just put it on," he says. "It's cool, I'll help you out. We'll do all the work. We just needed another warm body so we didn't get disqualified on this round."

"That sounds important," I say, "and I don't want to mess it up for you." Actually, it sounds pretty ridiculous, but I'm keeping my mouth closed on that one.

"It's cool," he says. "The clan we're playing tonight kinda sucks, so there's nothing to worry about. We've got this."

I tentatively put on the headset as he powers up the other TV.

"You look cute," he says.

"Thanks," I say, feeling like I'm back in high school.

"First thing you need is a gamer tag," he says.

"What's that?" I ask.

"Your screen name," he answers, looking at me expectantly. "Mine is QB_SNiiP3R," he says proudly as he selects it on screen. "No pressure, though, yours doesn't have to be as cool."

"Lucky me." I laugh. He's staring at me, waiting for me to answer; my mind blanks out and I can't think of anything funny or witty. Actually, I can't seem to think of anything at all. "Uh . . ."

"It doesn't have to be perfect," he says. "You can always change it after tonight if you don't like it." That's rich, like I'm ever going to need a gamer tag after tonight.

"Uh. . . ." Jeez. I can't think of anything. Anything at all. Dane shifts in his seat; he's clearly getting impatient.

"SparklePony?" I say tentatively. An inside joke with Michael, but it's the only thing I can think of. I'm terrible at remembering usernames, so Michael made everything from Netflix to our cell phone account *SparklePony* so I wouldn't forget.

Dane rolls his eyes, but looks amused. "Okay, SparklePony it is."

He enters my username, picks a generic avatar, and then hands me the controller, explaining rapid-fire how the thing is supposed to work. "This stick is how you move your camera—if you click it, it will do your melee attack or zoom; right stick click is melee so you can beat someone with your gun instead of shooting them in the face. Left stick is move. If you click it you can sprint. If you're in sniper mode, it holds your breath. *A* is double jump to give yourself a little rocket boost, *B* is crouch, *X* is the critically important reload button, *Y* lets you switch your weapon. Left bumper is your exo-ability, right bumper is your lethal equipment. Left trigger is 'aim down the sight,' right trigger is the most important button of all, 'fire weapon.' Those are the basics."

The basics? He's practically speaking in tongues. Right button to fire is pretty much all I got out of that. And something about holding my breath.

He points to the top TV screen. "That's us, D34TH2C@MPERS." A video feed of Dane's face is on one side of the screen, the game is in the center.

He points to the other TV below "That's you."

"*Death to campers*?" I laugh. "I mean, I hate camping as much as the next person—especially the sleeping outside part—but I don't wish a zombie apocalypse on them or anything."

Dane responds without taking his eyes off the top screen, "Not that kind of camping. 'Campers' hide in one spot trying to kill you when you respawn. Or they're in a shitty spot where you can't get to them, and they kill you a bunch of times. Not cool."

The game hasn't started yet, but comments start scrolling on the right side of the screen, mostly in jibberish. Except one.

Γũpernaturaı̣̄Pâragoņ: *SparklePony? What kind of lameass brony name is that?* OMFG QB_SNiiP3R *you brought a* CHICK
~*ȀtomįcChimera*~: *sparklepony???? lmao is she gonna make us sandwiches at intermission?* WTF?

I'm hearing stereo, Dane next to me, and Dane through the headset, "Be cool, you guys. You can't be talking about my special lady like that, you douchebags. Matty's out with carpal, we need a warm body. You wanna cancel the stream tonight?"

Dane is defending my honor against these sexist little monkeys, which is kind of sweet. Except he did it by calling somebody a douchebag, which is pretty awful. I've only been here ten minutes and it already feels like the longest date of my life.

~*ÅtomįcChimera*~: *Move the camera, lets see how warm she is.*

Ba@Frenzy: *Shut up and play*

"Just ignore them. They're a bunch of immature assholes. Ready?" asks Dane.

"Ready or not," I say.

"Just stick with me."

The action starts. And it does not go well.

It looks like we're in a jungle or something, but full of sand and overturned trucks and bombed-out buildings. All I can see is the end of the gun my character is carrying. In the headset, all the guys are talking to each other, talking smack, telling each other what to do, swearing up a storm, which makes it even harder to remember which buttons to push to make myself move or shoot. At first I can't figure out how to move my character at all, and then once I do I just keep running around, trying to follow Dane's character, which isn't as easy as it sounds.

"Fire, fire," yells Dane, looking directly at me. I indiscriminately mash a bunch of buttons, unsure of which one is supposed to fire my weapon. Suddenly a grenade goes off, taking out our entire team. I can't even see who fired it.

"What the fuck, Dane?" yells somebody in the headset. Dane starts swearing and the first round is over.

"You're not supposed to take out your own guys," he says to me tersely.

"Wait, what . . . that was me?" I ask.

"Yeah, that was you. Just be more careful," he says.

"Sorry, guys," I say into the microphone. "Sorry, my bad." For the first time in the game, everyone is silent.

The next round isn't much better. I'm stuck in a corner and I can't seem to make my way out. We're inside and I keep going around and around what looks like an endless room with no doors or windows. I'm starting to feel dizzy.

"Get outta there!" yells Dane.

"There's no door," I say. "I'm trapped! I think I'm trapped in a circular room! There's no way out." And then *boom!* I'm dead. This time it only took me about fifteen seconds to get myself killed. The comment section goes wild.

Dane stands up, dragging his cast and pointing to the upper TV screen, which shows his character's point of view. There's my character crumpled in a heap, apparently trapped in a corner. No circular room. Just a corner. Lots of windows, at least two different doorways, and a bombed-out wall. Not trapped.

"Look straight ahead," Dane admonishes me. "If you look straight up at the ceiling you can't see where the hell you're going."

My untimely death is probably the best thing to happen to D34TH2C@MPERS, because without my help they manage to blow up a bunch of stuff, kill a lot of bad guys, and make some serious progress in completing their mission. I sit on the couch beside Dane while he plays, pretending like I'm interested. I'm trying to watch to see what he does so that I won't get myself killed in, like, three seconds next time, but his fingers move with lightning speed on the controller.

There's a knock at the door.

"Will ya get that, babe?" Dane asks, never taking his eyes off the screen or his hands off the controller.

I stand up and answer the door. Pizza delivery. Dane is engrossed in the game, so I take forty dollars out of my purse and pay the guy. He looks thrilled at a ten-dollar tip, he's clearly used to delivering to college students.

I bring the pizzas over to the coffee table and set down the boxes.

I search the kitchen for plates and napkins, but come up short. I probably have wet wipes in my purse, but feel weird about the idea of whipping them out.

"Thanks," says Dane, still glued to the screen. I sit there watching him, smelling the pizza, for another twenty minutes until Dane's character gets killed. He pushes open the box and grabs a slice.

"Do you have napkins or paper towels?" I ask.

"Nah," he responds, licking some sauce off his finger. He's watching the action on screen, and swears as the rest of his team gets killed off a second time.

The final round goes a bit better. Dane shows me once again how to make my character run and jump and change direction, and suggests that I avoid shooting or bombing anyone, for the safety of the team. This is the best idea I've heard all night.

"Just stick behind me, don't worry about doing anything else," he says.

"Okay," I agree, trying not to let myself read the mean stuff people are saying about me in the comments section. Who knew people could be so cruel with just punctuation marks and emoticons?

"Eyes straight ahead," he says, making a weird signal with his hands like he's special ops or something, and not just some gamer guy sitting on some dead relative's horrid old couch.

"Eyes straight ahead," I repeat, following closely behind Dane. The herky-jerky movement of the game is starting to make me feel seasick, but I keep trotting behind him like we really are saving the world from evildoers.

Dane, and the other guys on our team, GuerillaBl̉ád̉é, and ~*IronȞolySin*~, are clustered together behind a wall of rubble when we're suddenly surprise-attacked by snipers.

"Run!" yells Dane, and I take off backward. The three of them are shooting and swearing, and I keep scrambling along the side of a long building, trying not to look up.

Two things happen almost simultaneously: at the end of the long building, I suddenly find myself face-to-face with one of the bad guys—Dane, GuerillaBl̉ád̉é, and ~*IronȞolySin*~ are screaming something about a bomb carrier . . . and then all three of them are wiped out in rapid succession by the sniper.

"Fuck!"

"Jesus, you've got him at point-blank range!" screeches one of the voices in the headset. "We've got him!"

"Shoot him!" Dane yells at me. "The guy right in front of you, kill him! Kill him and we win!"

I look down at the controller, trying to remember what to do.

"*Shoot him!!!!!*" yells Dane, as I aim my weapon and mash the FIRE button. A spray of bullets peppers the sky. Two seconds later the bomb goes off and I'm dead.

A string of expletives burns through my headset, and over on the other end of the couch, Dane's head is in his hands.

"I'm really sorry," I say.

He looks crestfallen. We sit there in silence for a few seconds, and then he reaches over and pulls the controller from my hands.

"I don't think this is going to work out," he says.

39

My best date so far was a fix-up jointly orchestrated by my neighbor Zelda and my grandma Leona, who arranged a night out with Leonardo, the thirty-two-year-old Brazilian grandson of a lady in their scuba diving class. Or maybe it was their country-and-western line dancing class. Or their sensual cookery class.

Anyway, we met for dinner and drinks at a club downtown, followed by samba dancing, and a moonlight stroll down around St. Armands Circle, all the way to Lido Key. We connected immediately, talked about everything under the sun, and laughed like we'd known each other for years. He was smart and funny and romantic, not to mention his broad shoulders and gorgeous brown eyes that reminded me of melted chocolate.

Leonardo's English was solid, his accent was dreamy, and unlike me, he was a skilled dancer, imbibed with both confidence and natural rhythm. He was also on his way back to Rio in less than twenty-four hours. Naturally, the best date I'd had since this whole mess began was leaving the country with no plans to return to the U.S. anytime in the foreseeable future. We shared stories and laughed all night, watched the sun come up from the beach, and spent every waking minute together we could before it was time for him to go to the airport. He looked deep into my eyes as he swept me into his arms at the DEPARTURES curb, gently brushing my lips with the most slobbery, frothy, drooling kiss I've ever experienced. Even counting toddlers. And Saint Bernards.

And then he was gone.

It's funny how going out with someone who is so close to what you're searching for, but *not quite right*, makes you yearn for something meaningful.

40

Nate hasn't called. I haven't called. It got weird.

I've avoided the psych job site and Nate the tool-belt supermodel drywaller for eight days. The job is practically finished, and if I don't show up soon, Joe and the rest of my crew are going to think I've joined a cult or something.

I didn't want to go to the job site until Nate called me. And he never did.

Eventually, I just had to suck up my pride and do my job.

The key, I've decided, is to be totally professional. Get in, get out, just focus on the work. And at all costs, avoid looking Nate in the eyes. His animal magnetism is Medusa-like—if I gaze upon him even once, I'll be a goner.

I pull in to the job site and I'm thrilled to see that Nicky has already completed the landscaping outside. It's gorgeous, just what I hoped for—peaceful and tropical, like the grounds of an elegant hotel. Checking my face in the mirror one last time before I go inside, I smooth my hair and add a dot of lip stain. Stalling a bit longer, I smile wide at myself in the rearview mirror: nothing stuck in my teeth. All predictable embarrassments avoided, I grab my bag, step out of the car, and go inside.

"Hey, Doc, it's looking good, right?" Joe says to me as I enter the lobby.

"It's looking great," I say. The entryway is finished and the furniture has been delivered, covered in plastic wrap and stacked in a precarious-looking tower, out of the way on the far side of the room. I can't wait to put the room together today—it's always one of my favorite parts of any job. It's also the last part. Joe escorts me through the rest of the offices. The ceiling height has been corrected, and the therapy offices are cozy and inviting. We head back to the therapy gardens and I begin to wonder why I haven't seen Nate yet. Not that I'm going to ask. There's a big part of me that hopes I won't see him at all, avoiding the potential for utter humiliation in front of my favorite contractor and his entire crew.

But there's another part of me, albeit a tiny one, that's hoping to accidentally run into Nate. The fact that he hasn't called me after we had sex is too humiliating for words. Maybe he'll see me and suddenly realize he wants to be with me. Not that I have a burning desire to be with him or anything—it would just be nice if he called, you know? It's probably best to avoid him.

Nicky is in the outdoor therapy rooms, finishing up the last of the plantings. Like the landscaping out front, it's stunning and serene, the perfect place to spill the contents of your heart. Nicky has installed an extensive drip system for the plants, moderated for the particular needs of each plant so that the areas would require less intrusion for maintenance of the foliage. It was Joe's idea, and I think it's brilliant.

Joe leads me through the rest of the therapy rooms and work areas. I'm almost all the way through the building when I see him, standing on a stepladder, prepping the last bit of plaster for paint.

"Looking good, Nate," says Joe. Nate turns at the sound of Joe's voice, and grins when he sees me.

"How's it going?" Nate says to me, raising an eyebrow flirtatiously. I feel my skin flush, and stare straight ahead, hoping Joe hasn't caught the scent of my humiliation. Oh God, this is the worst. Nate might as well have just boisterously announced to the entire crew that we screwed around. Really, it couldn't have been more obvious unless he'd beaten on his chest from high atop the ladder, and then squirted spermicide in my hair.

"Just doing a walk-through," says Joe. "Looks good."

"Really good," I mumble. My skin burns scarlet in disgrace. *Just a few more hours, and I'll never have to see Nate again.*

Joe confirms with me that all the painting at the rear of the building will be completed in an hour or so, and dry enough to move in the furniture in a couple of hours. The rest of the rooms are now done. I head back up to the lobby to oversee the staging of the office. Handing out extra copies of my floor plans to the crew, I direct them to set up furniture in the individual offices.

As I'm arranging the seating groupings in the lobby, I mentally lecture myself to never have a one-night stand again. Sure, there are women who are totally cool with it, own their own sexuality and all that—and more power to them. It just isn't me. Obviously, I need some kind of emotional connection to go along with the physical one. I'm still far too vulnerable for no-strings sex. I've just gotten out of a no-strings marriage.

I no longer care about being a thirty-one-year-old woman previously afflicted with gay-husband virginity, or the fact that the one straight guy I had sex with isn't even interested enough for a second date (or, if I'm being completely honest with myself, a first date,) or even a courtesy call. And I no longer care that Darcy and Michael think my number of sexual partners is too low—I'm done with Operation Naughty Nine. I'm not going to modify my past, my life story, or pad my sexual résumé just so some guy-to-be-named-later won't run screaming from my shortcomings. If I'm going to date, have sex, or even fall in love again with a man, any man, he's just going to have to accept me for all my weirdnesses.

40

Over the next few months, I throw myself into my work. Olivia Vanderbilt Kensington, my socialite client running the Wildlife Foundation benefit, is an endless pit of neediness. She calls me at all hours of the day, every day. We meet twice a week, sometimes three times, and she requires far more hand-holding than all of my other clients combined. She changes details, like the specific accent flowers she wants in the centerpieces, and then changes them back, and then changes them back again, updating me constantly on the endless minutiae of her day and her thought processes. She's not a happy person; eventually I start wondering if maybe she's just lonely, and complaining is her way of connecting with the world.

I feel sorry for her in some ways, but it doesn't make her endless demands any less taxing.

My favorite client, Daniel Boudreaux, and his fanciful floating restaurant, is something else entirely. I stop by at least two or three times a week, and Daniel always treats me with some sample of whatever new menu item he's trying out for the restaurant. I'm endlessly inspired by the space and the chef himself, and find myself sketching variations for his restaurant in nearly every free moment. It's exciting to work with someone so creative and passionate, a counter to the emotional drain of clients like Olivia Vanderbilt Kensington. I try to focus on the outcome with her, rather than the experience. If the Wildlife Foundation benefit is a big success and meets its goal of a 20 percent fund-raising bump, it will open the floodgates for more high-end fund-raising business for me, which in turn will bring me more corporate business. The job is murder, but the potential payoff is worth it.

41

After stopping by a small ad agency downtown that has me on retainer to rearrange furnishings of their common creative areas every couple of months to boost creativity, I decide to make an impromptu visit to Daniel Boudreaux's restaurant—down at the marina, less than half a mile away. It's nearing eleven, still too early for lunch, but a girl can dream.

I park, put up the top on my Mini, and pull the scarf from my hair. As I get out of the car, my hair whips in the wind coming off the water. Trying to smooth it out with a hairbrush would surely be a losing battle, so I decide to just let it fly. The day is gorgeous, already mid-seventies, and I watch a pelican swoop down and skim the surface of the sparkling water. This is the first time I've ever stopped by Daniel's job site before noon, and I wonder if he's up and moving around yet. Restaurant owners and chefs are almost always night owls, by nature or by circumstance.

No need to worry. As soon as I near the floating restaurant I can see the boat is teeming with construction workers, busy on the deck.

I make my way up the makeshift gangplank and onto the boat, and the workers wave and nod as I tiptoe through the mess to the rear deck. I'll check the kitchen next, but it feels like less of an intrusion to look outside first.

Daniel's there, in a white T-shirt and loose olive-green shorts, his toned back turned to me. He's fussing with a long banquet table loaded high with sandwiches and salads, veggies and a too-elegant bucket filled with ice and bottles of water. Clearly he's expecting company.

"Daniel," I say just above a whisper—I hardly want to send him nose-diving over the railing again. Hardly.

"Hey, Alex," he says, smiling as he turns around. He rambles over to where I'm standing and gives me an easy hug, like we've known each other forever.

"Uh, hi," I say, pulling myself more slowly than I should from his embrace. He smells good. Too good. I have to get a hold of myself.

"You're just in time for lunch," he says, grinning.

"Oh, no." I stammer, feeling my face flush from embarrassment. I don't want him to think I'm some pathetic orphan, conveniently showing up around mealtimes. "I was just at a project site a half mile away and I thought I might stop by to set a meeting with you to go over the, er, concept and the plans for the restaurant. I'm so sorry to intrude . . . it looks like you're having guests."

"This?" he shrugs. "I was just putting out a spread for the workers. I find most people work better when they're well fed."

"That's so nice of you," I say, eyeing the table. Mufalleta and po'boy sandwiches are piled high, there's a huge iced bowl of boiled shrimp, greens and salads galore, and loads of fresh fruit and veggies.

"Stay, won't you?" He smiles and my face flushes again.

"I really wouldn't want to intrude," I say. "Besides, I don't want you to get the idea I'm always expecting you to feed me anytime I drop by."

"I'd sort of like that idea," he says. "You're one of my favorite people to feed." I can't stop a smile from bubbling up.

"Stay, *cher*," he says, grasping my hands gently in his. "Besides, you don't want to miss out on my spicy shrimp."

"Well," I grin back at him, "if you insist." He selects one from the bowl and playfully pops it into my mouth. Divine. "Oh. That's good," I say. "Really good."

"Let me just call the workers for lunch, and then we can sit down and talk for a bit about our plans for the ol' girl."

"No woman likes to hear a man disparage her age," I crack.

His response is a wide-open smile. He gently pats the railing, "She knows I think she's a beauty."

I laugh.

He excuses himself and disappears around the side of the boat, returning less than a moment later followed by a swarm of workers who look like they might trample one another to get to the mouthwatering spread Daniel has so generously laid out.

"Please help yourselves, boys," he says, a split second before they rush the table. "There are plates and silverware at the left end, and sweet tea and water at the other end." He grins at me and I grin back. Daniel is the consummate host, he never seems happier than when he has guests. He takes so much joy from feeding people, and I wonder if the rest of his family is the same. That joy, plus his family's legendary skills in the kitchen, is undoubtedly the reason for the Boudreaux family's incredibly successful restaurants.

After the workers have helped themselves to the food, and sit strewn around the boat deck smiling and talking, Daniel and I prepare our own plates. Anytime I pass something by, he swoops in and scoops a little of it onto my plate and says, "Oh no, *cher*, you don't want to miss this one."

He's right, of course, everything is delicious. The workers linger over their meals, and return to the table for seconds and thirds. There's still enough food left to host at least another twenty people.

Usually I use Joe and Nicky, my regular construction crew, for projects, but they're already busy on another site and working on a boat requires special skills that my guys aren't necessarily experienced in. Plus, the last thing I need is Nate, the tool-belt supermodel drywaller, hanging around here all day, making me feel like a loser.

Since my work on Daniel's restaurant focuses on soft finishings like lighting, table placement, and color scheme, Daniel's own team is refurbishing the boat. The work is going well. The wood has been sanded and is in the process of being refinished. Battered wood is being replaced as necessary, but Daniel is insistent on restoring as much of the original boat as possible, especially the gorgeous leaded-glass windows, which add so much charm and character.

Daniel and I sit at our usual spot, the one table on the back deck, laughing and joking, and watching the sun play off the water as the boat rocks gently with the waves.

"Mmmm," I say, scooping the last bite of creamy potato salad into my mouth.

"That's what I like to hear." He laughs.

"Have you decided on the name for the restaurant yet?" I ask. "We can't delay much longer."

"I'm thinking of calling it Boudreaux," he says.

"That works." I smile. "So could we please drill down a bit on the kind of atmosphere we're trying to create here? Obviously we've talked a lot about the broad strokes, but need to get into more elaborate detail."

He looks dreamily toward the water. "I want it to be the place where people have the best night of their lives."

"That's terrific," I laugh, "but not very specific. Is it elegant? Casual? Family? Somewhere in-between?"

"Yes," he says, breaking his gaze from the water to look at me.

"Yes to which?" I ask.

"Yes to all. I want it to be the kind of place that feels like an old Southern family. The relatives are a little quirky and imbued with their place in history; the furniture is decadent but it's a little worn, a gem from another age, a gazebo in the backyard that's been the site of first kisses, naps on sunny days, and heart-to-heart talks, a giant magnolia tree in the yard. I want this place to be somewhere you could hold an elegant wedding or show up in bare feet after a day of fishing or hanging out at the beach. I want my guests to feel like they're friends, come as you are in a tux or flip-flops, have some great food, and some great music. I want a sense of romance and whimsy, the kind of place where you could propose or bring your entire family, where musicians come to jam with each other for fun after they're done with their gigs downtown."

I'm speechless, which is unusual for me. Generally my clients' goals are more benchmark-specific—increase productivity or revenues, boost donations, drive shoppers to the pricier goods. His vision is so clear that I can feel what he means in my heart and in my bones, without yet being able to quite put together in my head how it could be executed on this floating restaurant.

"And the typical restaurant benchmarks," I ask, "like, wanting to turn the tables in sixty-eight minutes?"

"If my guests leave after only an hour, they're not having enough fun," he says.

It's so novel, even for me. Daniel's project isn't about money or turnover, it's about the experience for his guests. More than anything, I want to bring his vision to fruition. My mind sparks with the thrill of the challenge—this project is the exact reason I love environmental psychology—using surroundings to evoke such specific types of emotions.

"Can we make that happen, *cher*?" he asks, his ocean-blue eyes dancing with excitement.

"Yes," I say, feeling slightly less sure than I sound, but determined to see it through. I need to create an environment that evokes all the best parts of Daniel himself, as well as this boat he loves.

"Do you have anything left, furnishings or anything really from the original restaurant?" I ask. "I'm thinking it'll be really helpful to see anything that's still here; maybe you could tell me what you loved so much about the place growing up."

"Of course, *cher*. There's a storeroom behind the kitchen with all the stuff ol' Archer left in the restaurant. I didn't have the heart to throw it out but I wasn't sure what to do with it all."

"Can I take a peek?" I ask. "Maybe there's something that will work for us."

Daniel leads me back to the storeroom, a large closet behind the kitchen. He opens the door and pulls a string from the ceiling to turn on the light. The small room is a treasure trove, jammed with antique furniture, tarnished silver candlesticks, boxes of knickknacks and treasures, a stack of menus dating back fifty years, and a beautiful portrait of a woman standing on the deck of the boat, her hair blowing in the wind as she holds fast to the railing.

"Who's this?" I ask, gently running my finger against the bronzed frame of the painting.

"I think that was Archer's wife," he says. "She died young, they never had any children and he never remarried. I didn't know her; she died long before I was ever born."

"These things are amazing," I say, making my way around the stacks of boxes to see what's hiding near the back wall of the storage room. I suddenly teeter in the cramped space, terrified of nose-diving into a pile of boxes, yet unable to reach the wall to maintain my equilibrium—and quick as lightning, Daniel reaches out and grabs my hand to steady me. His skin is warm and soft, and holding his hand sends an electric sensation up my right arm. He holds my hand firmly until I regain my balance, which takes me a heartbeat longer than it should have.

"Thanks for keeping me from falling," I say.

He smiles warmly. "Sometimes we just can't stop ourselves from falling, *cher*."

42

I pick through the rest of the boxes to get a general idea of what's in them, making mental notes about how I might incorporate some of the pieces into Boudreaux. Pulling a greenish mermaid statue out of a box, I hold it up for Daniel to see. It's weighty and gorgeous, a stunning piece of vintage art.

"What do you think of this?" I ask. It's likely copper, judging from the verdigris patina. And the fact that it weighs as much as I do.

He laughs, his blue eyes twinkling mischievously. "It's so funny you would pick that up. I've always loved that statue, it was my favorite when I was a kid. I was actually planning to bring it upstairs to the studio once I got all moved in."

"You'll have to fight me for it, it would be perfect for the restaurant." I laugh, handing the heavy statue over to Daniel so I can make my way back through the boxes and to the doorway.

"You don't strike me as the arm-wrestling type. What type of battle did you have in mind?"

"Sing-off?"

"No deal, *cher.* I can't sing a lick. Cook-off?"

"Oh, that's fair." I laugh. Daniel puts the statue down just outside the doorway and extends his hand to me. My heart flutters and misses a beat or two as I reach out to hold his hand. What the hell?

"Yahtzee?" he asks.

"Oh, you're on," I say confidently. "That's my game."

"That's *my* game," he says. We stand there for a second, not blinking. He's still holding my hand.

I take a deep breath and try to reclaim my focus. "I have another request, but it's personal, so feel free to say no."

"Well, now I'm intrigued," he says. "Do tell."

"Behave yourself," I say, dropping his hand. "Would you mind showing me your living space?" I ask tentatively. "I feel like it would help me get a better sense of your style, who you are when you're alone. Does that make sense? If it's too much to ask, it's no problem at all. I just thought it might . . . help."

He winks at me, and takes my hand again. "Anything you need, *cher.*" He gently takes the lead, and I trail behind him up the narrow spiral stairway at the back of the kitchen. His hand is warm, and holding it feels like the easiest thing in the world. Too easy. I'm going to get myself in trouble.

"Are you sure I'm not intruding?" I ask. Maybe this isn't a good idea after all.

"Not a chance," he says.

The studio upstairs feels larger than it seems from the outside. There are more of the gorgeous leaded windows all the way around the room, offering a 360-degree view of the bay, the dock, and downtown. It's stunning. The floors are a dark hardwood and the little wall that remains between the massive floor-to-ceiling windows is painted a creamy white. A few of the windows are propped open on either side, and a balmy breeze drifts through the room, gently fluttering the sheer cream-colored curtains that hang almost from the ceiling. The ceiling is made of wood, in a more intricate pattern than the floor, but painted the same creamy white as the walls—rather than matching the dark stain of the floors. There are three good-size skylights in the ceiling, stretching across the length of the room. Unlike the rest of the window glass in the room, the skylights look like fairly recent additions. Daniel grabs a small remote to show me the skylight view, and demonstrates how they can either open for fresh air or be covered by mechanized shades.

"I like to look at the stars when I lie in bed," Daniel explains, and my heart flutters. The bed is centered against the wall, with a woven headboard, and a simple duvet in creamy white like the curtains, and at least half a dozen pillows in the same white cases. There's something so inviting about the bed, I suddenly feel tempted to just crawl under the duvet and take a nap. Maybe it's the salty air, or just the feeling of ease I always feel around Daniel. Or maybe my string of terrifying dates has left me sleep-deprived.

A small side table, made from reclaimed wood, sits to the left of the bed. It's stacked high with books, which reach the top of an oil-rubbed bronze swing-arm reading lamp.

"I like your table," I say. He smiles.

"An artist from Vieux Carré made it from old signs and wood he'd salvaged after Hurricane Katrina. Everywhere you looked there were just heaps of rubble, of what used to be memories and homes and businesses—and this guy looked at all those piles of heartache and saw something beautiful." He gently touches the front of the drawer and says, "This piece of wood right here came from our restaurant on St. Peter in the Quarter. It reminds me of my home, and I love that from so much destruction came something beautiful. Plus, there's not a chance Mama and Chef would have let me just pry off one of the floorboards at the Chevalier for sentiment, so I guess I'm lucky there was some way I got to have a bit of it with me."

"You call your father Chef?" I ask.

"I grew up in kitchens." he laughs. "It's a term of endearment. And honor. My father called my granddaddy Chef too." His voice is tender when he speaks of his family.

I reach out and gently stroke the wood of the table, I'm not sure why—maybe just an effort to soak up some of its history. It has the patina of time and humidity and is smooth to the touch.

On the other side of the bed, there's an overstuffed chair and ottoman in the corner covered in something that looks like green sailcloth. There's a large armoire, a piece of furniture that looks like it would be out of place in the studio apartment of a floating restaurant, but seems right at home with the rest of Daniel's things. It's an antique, probably a family heirloom from the grand old Southern home he talks about sometimes. His clothes have to go somewhere, the four walls are covered in windows, so it isn't exactly ideal for a closet. A blue surfboard leans casually against the armoire, as though it's waiting to go out.

"Eventually I'd like to put some French doors and a little balcony out here," he says. "But that's for another day, I guess. I'd have to find some way to reclaim the leaded-glass windows for the doors. I couldn't stand to part with even one, never mind two."

On the opposite side of the room is an inviting sofa and wide coffee table, a pair of cane-backed plantation chairs, and a large bookshelf that separates the sleeping space from the living space. There are photographs everywhere, artfully grouped and hung in silver frames on every available inch of wall space. Some are landmarks in the French Quarter, some are old black-and-white photos of what are presumably Daniel's relatives going back generations, in and around his family's various restaurants. I can't stop myself from searching out a romantic interest for Daniel among all the photographs. They give nothing away, other than the obvious—Daniel loves his home, his family, the beach, and the legacy of his family's eateries.

The apartment is small, but open and airy, bathed in bright sunlight and fanned by the Gulf breeze coming through the windows—evoking that large screened porch on the beach cottage where you spent the best summer of your life. Aside from the large collection of photos, and the overstuffed bookshelf, the furniture has simple lines and works beautifully in the space. It's masculine and nautical, inviting, simple, and comfortable, an eclectic mix of old and new. It's like Daniel.

We make our way back down the tight spiral staircase to the kitchen.

"Let's talk about the menu. What have you finalized?" I ask.

"All my favorites, fresh seafood, crab cakes, N'awlins classics like crawfish etouffee and jambalaya, fried catfish, pecan pie and doberge. Some more experimental stuff, tropical-Cajun lobster infusions and the like." My mouth is watering.

His eyes dance as he talks more about the food, and how cooking for people makes him feel. "Speaking of my favorites," he says, "do you feel like coming round on Saturday night for a little get-together here about eight? Invite anyone you'd like, I've always found the best way to make new friends is to throw a party. Casual, of course. Are you free?"

"Um, let me check my calendar." I take a peek at my phone and pull up my calendar. Yep. Empty. For every Saturday night for all eternity. "Yes, I'm free that night. Can I bring anything?"

"Just your gorgeous self, *cher.* Leave the rest to me." He smiles, his palpable charisma pulling me in like low tide. Or a riptide.

43

"Tell me again exactly what happened," insists Darcy. The two of us are sitting on my lanai, deconstructing every conversation and clue we have about Daniel, starting with the first time I ever met him, at the divorce party. Darcy has a way of stripping someone's psyche bare, analyzing their behaviors and demystifying their personality with such depth, precision, and authority that there seems no room for the possibility that her analysis might not be true. She's almost always right. I think that's why she's so effective in politics. And friendship.

I go over, detail by detail, every meeting I've had with Daniel. The smiles, the little hugs, the electricity I feel when he touches me, the way he looks at me sometimes that makes me feel like he might be flirting with me.

"And you're positive he's gay?" she asks.

"Yes." I say with conviction. "No. Maybe."

"Okay, obvious solution, uh, why don't you just ask him?"

"I can't," I say, exasperated. "First, he's a client and if I ask him if he's gay or he has any idea at all that I have some mad crush on him it could completely screw up our working relationship. I like him, I like this project. I don't want to mess it up."

"But what if he's not gay, and he's interested in you too, and you're sending him such weird signals he doesn't know whether to pursue it or not?" she asks, refilling her wineglass.

"I don't know," I say. I stand up from my lounge chair and head over to dip my toes in the pool.

Darcy joins me at the pool's edge. She runs her fingers through her shock of red hair. "Why do you think he's gay?"

"He was Carter's date to the party."

"Are you sure?" she asks. "Maybe Carter just invited Daniel because he was new in town and didn't know anyone."

"Maybe," I say. "But almost all the men at the party were gay."

"Correlation does not equal causation," she says. "The sexual orientation of the partygoers has no impact on whether or not Daniel is gay."

"I know." I sigh. "What do I do?"

"Here's an obvious thirty-second solution: why not just ask Carter?" asks Darcy.

"Ugh, too humiliating. Either Daniel is gay, and I'm a total idiot, *again*. Or he isn't gay, and I'm just too clueless to be able to tell the difference. No thanks."

"Go to Daniel's party," she says. "Wear something fabulous. Let your hair down a bit. Be open to whatever happens."

"You know that going with the flow isn't exactly my strong suit."

"I do," she says, softly patting my arm. "But you'll never get a new ending if you keep starting with the same tired beginning."

44

It feels like a date, but I know it isn't. At least, my brain knows.

I arrive at Daniel's gathering at precisely eight with a nice bottle of Mollydooker Shiraz called Carnival of Love. It was seventy-five bucks, but the bottle reminds me of New Orleans and the sommelier at the wine shop told me it was a fantastic wine and the perfect gift for a foodie. I took his word for it, I don't have much of a palate. I just wanted to get something Daniel would really like.

I've stressed for two days about whether or not I should bring someone to Daniel's gathering. Not that I have anyone to bring, mind you. Darcy left town this morning. Eventually it was too late to ask anyone else, and I decided to just go alone. I'm wearing a pale blue halter dress, one of those go-to outfits that forgives my flaws and plays up my best features, and always makes me feel confident and beautiful. The dress flatters my skin and makes my legs look long and lean. My hair falls down to my shoulders in waves, and I complete the look with a pair of strappy wedges, a silver necklace, and a chunky turquoise bracelet. I'd like to say I'm not dressed up for anyone in particular, but that would be a lie. What am I doing to myself?

It's just begun to grow dark, and I step cautiously up the gangplank. Daniel has strung white retro-looking globe lights across the deck, which gives the boat a lovely, romantic glow. The night air is warm, still a bit humid, and the scent of some sweet tropical flower mixes with the seawater lapping against the boat. The unmistakable music of Louis Armstrong floats in the air, but there are no other sounds of people, of other guests. Oh my gawd. I'm such a dork. Have I shown up on the wrong night? I flush at the thought, and I'm just about to turn around and sneak quietly off the boat when Daniel appears from the back deck.

My breath catches in my chest. I've never seen him dressed up before, he's always wearing shorts or jeans when I come to the boat for our meetings. He cleans up nicely, looking every inch the famous restaurateur—wearing a tailored shirt and pants in a deep midnight blue, with a light gray tie. He's freshly shaven, not sporting his usual stubble, which I find endearing. God, I'm hopeless.

"Oh, hi," I say awkwardly. "I thought I'd just stop by to say hello . . ."

"Alex!" he says, embracing me warmly. I reach up to return the hug, finding my hand resting on the back of his arm, noticeably firm beneath my touch. "I'm so glad you made it, *cher*," he says.

As usual, I linger too long in his embrace; the night is so warm, the rocking of the boat so lulling, I have to stop myself from swaying to the music. Daniel smells really good—a masculine cocktail of saltwater, citrus, and probably just full-on testosterone. Finally, after too long and yet not long enough, he steps back and I hold out the bottle of wine. He smiles and whistles. "This is one of my favorites, thank you."

"Thank you so much for inviting me," I say.

"It wouldn't be the same without you, *cher*." He smiles and the light from the globes catches his deep blue eyes. I could just drown in them. "You look luminous tonight."

I blush and mumble, "Thanks." There's something so easy about his manner. I get the feeling he could say pretty much anything, no matter how wicked or corny, and it would still come out as charming and genteel.

He offers his hand to me, which feels so old-school and manly. "Shall we?" I gingerly allow him to take my hand, trailing behind him as he leads me to the rear deck of the boat. "Watch your step, *cher*," he says as we make our way back. There are five tables, all covered in the vintage ivory linen tablecloths I selected from the stash of treasures in the storage room. They're stunning. A small bar is set up on a side table, and a lavish banquet table is layered in different shades of blue chiffon tablecloths and a lovely presentation of hors d'oeuvres. It all looks delicious. Seeing the boat in the evening, with the stars twinkling above and the elegant arch of the Ringling Bridge in the distance, I'm finally visualizing Boudreaux coming together. The restaurant is going to be everything Daniel wants it to be.

"Would you like a glass of wine?" he asks. He drops my hand as I nod, and pours me a glass from an open bottle. "Try this one," he suggests, "I think you'll like it." I take a sip and nod in agreement. It's really good.

"Thank you. Am I the only one here?" I ask, taking another slow sip. "I'm so sorry, am I early?"

He looks down for a split second, and then up again, until his eyes meet mine. "I might have told you eight o'clock when I told everyone else eight-thirty."

"I'm sorry," I say, without knowing why. Nervously, I set my glass down on the bar. "Do you need help setting up?"

"Dance, *cher*?" he asks, his blue eyes playful. I nod and he pulls me gently into his arms. He's warm. We sway to the music and the gentle rocking of the boat. His hand rests on the small of my back, in that sweet spot that makes you feel feminine and protected and adored all at once. He's respectful in his distance, but with every sway back and forth, we move closer to each other, a millimeter at a time. I feel myself melting into his arms, and the tension between us is delicious and innate and disorienting all at once. I examine the line of his jaw, a tiny dimple on the left side of his cheek when he smiles, the sexy cleft in his chin, the firmness of his back, wanting to drink in every detail to relive for later in case this never happens again. Daniel is confident in his movements, but delicate in his touch, as though he's hesitant to go too far. His breath warms my ear, and I smile as I feel him inhaling the scent of my hair.

He pulls me closer still. "Is this okay, *cher?*" he asks, his lilting voice just barely above a whisper.

I don't know what to say. I nod, but I don't actually know what *this* is. What is it? Just a dance? A prelude? Is he just warm and gracious, and am I so desperate, naïve, or misguided that I'm confusing platonic friendship for something more? The fact that I find myself drooling over my client and fantasizing that Daniel is flirting with me doesn't make it so. I can't trust my instincts, they're surely steering me off a cliff. Should I really rely on my thumping heart, lust-addled mind, and frenetic hormones? Or do the smart thing and just shut this down right now, eat dinner, beg off dessert, get the hell out of Dodge, and avoid risking the humiliation and heartbreak of falling for yet another gay man?

I close my eyes, pretending to be contemplating a decision, in the same way you promise yourself you'll get up and out of bed in one minute and that you're just resting your eyes, when you know full well you're going to fall back asleep within seconds and it will take a wailing snooze alarm, the promise of bacon, or the threat of unemployment to coerce you out from under the covers. Just another minute of dancing, and then I'll stop. One more song. After this next song. I rock in his arms under the stars and the blanket of night air, unwilling or unable to tear myself away.

"Hello? Danny, where are you?" A familiar voice pierces our private little bubble and I step back quickly. Daniel keeps hold of my hand a second longer and twirls me slowly before releasing me. I love to be twirled; doesn't every woman? I can feel myself flushing and hope it isn't evident on my skin. Daniel looks at me and smiles, his expression playful.

"We're back here," Daniel says loudly in the direction of the voice. He leans in close, his lips brushing over my ear and sending shivers down my neck as he whispers to me in his soft Southern cadence, "That was a sweet and unexpected lagniappe, *cher*."

I'm going to have to look up that word when I get home. I'm pretty sure it means appetizer. Either that, or rack of lamb.

Daniel strides toward the front of the boat to greet his guests. Just as he reaches the edge of the interior dining area, a group of three round the corner.

"Alex!" exclaims Carter. "I'm so glad you're here! Out on the town!" He's flanked by a dark-haired man who looks vaguely familiar, and a woman I'd never met before. Carter makes his way to me quickly and gives me a tight squeeze.

"Good to see you, Carter," I say, as he kisses me on each cheek with great flourish. He did always have a flair for the dramatic.

"Good to see you too, Alex. How are you holding up, sweetheart? You look amazing. Don't you just love this little floating palace?" he prattles on without waiting for a response. That's Carter, I'm used to it. "I can't wait to see what you and Daniel do with it. It's going to be fabulous." He turns quickly to the two guests behind him. "Lolly and Santiago, this is my very dear friend Alex, and our host, Daniel. This is Lolly, she's a graphic designer who works with me." Lolly smiles and Carter continues, "And this handsome fellow is Santiago."

"Nice to meet you both," I say, shaking Lolly's hand, then Santiago's. "Have we met before?" I ask. There's something about him that is so familiar.

"He was at your party," interjects Carter. Suddenly, my pulse roars in my ears, and I feel the light-headed, tingly sensation that comes before passing out. I search around desperately for my wine and grab the glass from the bar, swigging it down as my brain races in horror.

Oh God. Santiago is the Cuban guy. The Cuban guy Michael made a date to have sex with at our divorce party. The one he flirted with like mad in front of me, in front of all of our friends and family. The man whose name Michael could not remember.

One should not chug an entire glass of wine at an elegant dinner party. I start hacking and coughing, having practically waterboarded myself out of sheer humiliation. Am I ever going to live this down? Am I ever going to be free of Michael? Carter, Lolly, and Santiago look on at my oncoming breakdown with mild concern.

Daniel is at my side instantly. "Are you okay?"

"Seasick," I choke out.

Confusion colors his expression.

"Why don't you just come with me?" he asks, leading me around the front of the boat, through the dining room, and back through the kitchen, setting me on a stool. "Are you okay? Are you really seasick?"

I'm sure this is baffling to him, as I'm on the boat three or four times a week and have never, ever complained of seasickness. I should have come up with something more plausible. Scurvy, maybe. Rapid-onset scurvy.

I nod my head no, still coughing in fits and starts. The kitchen is buzzing with activity from the line, and several servers make their way around us, as though we're part of the furniture. Daniel hurriedly brings me a glass of water, and I take a sip, and then another. I hang my head in embarrassment, and he kneels down in front of me.

"I'm so sorry," I say. What the hell is wrong with me?

"What's going on?" he asks.

"It's nothing. Carter brought a friend, Santiago, tonight. Santiago and Michael apparently . . . made a date . . . at our divorce party. It's stupid. I was just taken off guard."

"I understand," Daniel says, holding the glass of water for me. His eyes are kind, and it makes me feel even more ridiculous. But how could he possibly understand?

"I'm sorry. This was a bad idea," I say. "I should go." I need to regroup. This is no way to behave in front of a client.

"Please stay, *cher*," he says. "Eat something and you'll feel better. You want me to toss him over the side of the boat? Maybe poison his appetizer?" He grins at me, and offers up the glass of water again. I giggle, in spite of myself.

"We can probably let him live," I respond.

"Well, isn't that generous of you." He laughs and offers his hand to me. "Come on, you've already gotten the most awkward situation possible out of the way in the first five minutes of the party, now you can relax and just have a good time. I'll make sure you don't end up sitting at the same table with Santiago."

"That's kind of you," I say, "but it's really not necessary. I'm fine, I don't want to trouble you."

"It's no trouble, *cher*," he says, smiling. "I was looking for a good excuse to sit next to you anyway."

45

Daniel and I exit the kitchen, as Carter and his little entourage cheer me on.

"She lives!" he says, extending his arms to hug me. Santiago and Lolly applaud enthusiastically, joined by several other guests who arrived while we were in the kitchen and have no idea why they're clapping.

Carter hugs me and kisses me on the forehead, whispering, "Forgive me, Alex, I never would have brought Santiago if I'd known you were going to be here."

I nod without saying anything. It's the only way to ensure I don't burst into tears.

"Also, I had no idea Michael told you they'd hooked up," he says.

"So that's a little awkward." I nod again, and search around for my empty wineglass. I probably need a refill.

Daniel makes introductions all around, as a few more people arrive. His construction manager, Scully, is there along with some of the crew, the metals artist who's creating the Boudreaux sign, and several chefs I recognize from popular restaurants around town: the Cariguilos are here, as well as Michael Klauber and Phil Mancini of Michael's on East, and Alyson Zildjian, a talented Sarasota caterer. Sarasota is a small beach community, and many of the guests already know one another well. Cliff Roles, man about town and the city's most outrageous and colorful photographer, alternates between mingling with guests and snapping pictures, some of which include him. There are about thirty guests in all, and I know or have heard of about ten of them. It's a colorful, creative, and boisterous crowd, comprised of probably every person Daniel has met since he moved to town a few months before. The wine flows and the food is heavenly.

I'm chatting with Lolly when I spot him out of the corner of my eye: Dr. Creepy. Daniel is on his way toward me with a glass of wine, when Dr. Creepy sees him and makes a beeline in his direction. Creepy doesn't notice me until it's too late.

"Brett," says Daniel warmly, "glad you made it."

"Thanks for the invite," says Dr. Creepy.

Daniel touches my shoulder gently, "Alex, this is Brett." He gasps audibly. Well, this is going to be interesting. "Brett, meet Dr. Alex Wiggins, she's an environmental psychologist and her firm is helping to design the milieu for Boudreaux." I turn to face Dr. Creepy head-on. There's no getting out of it now.

"We've met," I say, trying not to let on how much I despised him. Or the fact that it took me the better part of an hour to figure out how to get the picture of his junk permanently off my phone. Somehow the image had gone to the cloud, and by the time I got home, the slimy little weasel (and his slimy little weasel) was added to my laptop and my iPad, not to mention most likely permanently archived somewhere on my backup drive. It would not go away.

"So how do you two know each other?" I ask.

"He's part of the boat restoration crew," says Daniel. "The guys call him 'Barnacle Brett.' He's scraping the barnacles off the boat, getting her all cleaned up." He laughs and pats Brett on the shoulder. "I think this might be the only time we've ever had a conversation when you weren't wearing a wetsuit."

Dr. Creepy, aka Barnacle Brett, looks mortified, and I cannot contain my smile. It's awful, and petty, I know. But it's also deeply satisfying. And, it explains why so many people knew him at Marina Jack—he probably cleaned the barnacles off half the yachts in the marina.

Barnacle Brett excuses himself quickly, mumbling something about needing to find the men's room. I wish Darcy were here to see what just happened. She'd be laughing her ass off.

Sitting down at a table next to Carter and Lolly, I'm certain that Santiago will be close by, but I'm determined not to care. I watch Daniel make his way around the deck, chatting easily with new friends and acquaintances. He's a natural host, charming and funny, effortlessly gracious and welcoming. You'd never know by looking at him that he's only been in town for a few months. He schmoozes like a local.

The evening is perfect, not too warm, and it's clear enough to see the stars over the Sarasota Bay on one side of the boat, and Sarasota's famous kissing statue over the other. The party guests cluster in small groups of old friends and new, laughing and talking, enjoying the food, the wine, and all the evening has to offer.

Carter and I are cracking up about some old story we've forgotten all but the punch line to, and the group of us squeeze in together when Cliff Roles comes by to snap a few photos. I try surreptitiously to size up Santiago without him noticing—weirdly curious about what attracted Michael to him. He's on the short side, but muscular. He has a thick Cuban accent, and a loud and easy laugh. Also his pants are very, very tight.

Michael is a gay man fresh out of the closet. Maybe the pants are all it took.

Cliff stays to dish for a while; the man is the deepest well of gossip in the city. He knows everyone, and has seen everything, and loves to recount every wicked, Technicolor detail. Occasionally I look up in the middle of one of Cliff's stories to see Daniel glancing over at me. He smiles and goes back to his conversation, but there's a palpable energy that seems to tether us together, even though we're on opposite ends of the boat deck. Maybe I'm the only one who feels it. I have to get a handle on myself. He's a client. A gorgeous, dimpled, probably gay client. Eventually Daniel makes his way to our table, and takes the seat next to mine. There's already a wineglass at the place, but Daniel swiftly relocates it to the next seat over. I'm not the only person who notices. Both Carter and Cliff Roles are rapt with interest.

"Lovely party, Daniel," says Carter. "How are you enjoying working with Alex? She's incredibly talented, isn't she?"

"Incredibly talented," Daniel agrees. I feel myself blush at the compliment, and attempt to change the subject.

"How did you and Carter meet, Daniel?" I ask. Carter laughs out loud at the memory, and it takes him a few seconds to respond.

"I think the first time was at Pridefest in Jackson Square," says Carter. "I remember you wore that pretty purple T-shirt that showed off all your muscles and made the boys cry. And I recall there was a certain chef trying to scale a statue and ride double on the back end of President Jackson's horse."

Pridefest. Purple muscle shirt. Daniel is definitely gay.

Daniel smiles, flashing a dimple. "I'm pleading the fifth on the Andrew Jackson statue. But I will say that we're still very close friends." He laughs. He looks at me. "Carter was dating my brother Gabriel right after college. He visited us in New Orleans several times, and we stayed in touch after they broke up. I gave Carter a call when I decided to move to Sarasota. He always raved about the city, and between that and the beach, it was one of the big reasons I considered opening a restaurant here."

"Oh Gabriel," says Carter dramatically, "that boy broke my heart."

"*Cher*, as I recall, you were the heartbreaker in that relationship. Weren't you over the moon about some guy you knew from college?"

Daniel clutches his heart and sighs dramatically. "The one who got away?"

"Who was that, Carter?" I ask. "I don't remember you falling for anyone in college."

"Oh, there've been so many, I don't remember," says Carter, shaking his head. He looks very much like he wants to change the subject.

"Love at first sight as I remember it." Daniel laughs. "He broke poor Carter's heart. The guy says he was straight, and that was that. Carter tried to move on, and he started dating Gabriel, but never quite got over his first love."

"Daniel, you cad," exclaims Carter. "You know for a fact that my first love has always been, and will always be, La Mer skin-care products."

"A true love story. Just look at his pores!" interjects Santiago, and the whole table is laughing. But suddenly Carter won't meet my eye, and I begin to wonder if the straight guy that Carter's been in love with since college is Michael. My Michael. Did Carter flat-out lie to me that day when I asked him if he'd ever screwed around with Michael? Has he been lying to me the whole time I've known him? Maybe Michael broke Carter's heart too.

I try to control my breathing as my mind reviews every interaction between Michael and Carter since the day we met him. Nothing stands out—even now, knowing what I know, I can't think of anything that proves or even hints that Carter and Michael might have had a spark between them. Not only that, but Carter isn't on the list. When Michael finally came clean about everything on the way to the airport in New York, he didn't mention anything about Carter. And judging from the hour of far too much excruciating detail as Michael purged himself of guilt, I'm certain he didn't leave anything out. Not even the stuff he should have left out.

But this is just too much of a coincidence. Carter had a crush on a straight guy in college. Michael is gay but pretended to be straight. The three of us have been inseparable since we met freshman year. What are the odds that Carter *isn't* talking about Michael? Not good, I know that for sure. My brain starts spitting out potential red flags, and I try the best I can to keep it together. Between Santiago and Carter—am I really sitting at a party, at the very same table, with two other people who've potentially slept with my husband? Did Michael actually screw three of us? It's too mortifying to think about, and yet I can't seem to stop myself. If it turns out my husband and one of my best friends hooked up in college, I'm never going to be able to trust anyone, ever again.

"Who was it?" I ask Carter. He looks up, but avoids looking at me directly.

Daniel looks at me with surprise, and then realization crosses his face. His mouth drops open. "Oh no," he says, low under his breath.

"It was a long time ago," says Carter. This is not the answer I want to hear. "I barely remember the guy's name."

Was it Michael? I want to ask. But I don't, because I don't want Daniel's elegant little dinner gathering to devolve into a Jerry Springer situation. Cliff Roles and Santiago lean forward with anticipation, as though they're expecting a bombshell. I need to know, but I don't want to find out in front of all these people. I need to be somewhere I can have a nervous breakdown in private, if need be. Optimally, somewhere with emergency rum and pie à la mode delivery.

Carter looks at me. I look at him. He shakes his head no and I don't push it any further. That will have to happen later.

46

"Who's up for dessert?" asks Daniel quickly, signaling one of the servers. He turns to me. "This is my favorite song, *cher,* would you take a turn around the floor with me?"

I nod yes, grateful for the chance to escape the table before I say or do something to embarrass myself. Or Daniel. Carter raises an eyebrow and his glass as we depart.

I feel like an exposed nerve. It's a lovely party, and I don't want to ruin it. I should go. Maybe Daniel will send me home with a dessert-filled doggy bag. Or several.

Daniel takes my hand and leads me to a spot near the bar where a few people have begun to dance. The music is a bouncy funk song that sounds sort of like the Neville Brothers, but I don't know for sure. Daniel pulls me gently into a closed position, which I apparently remember vaguely from my pre-wedding ballroom dancing lessons. He has one hand on my back and his other holding my right hand. He starts grinning as we glide around the dance floor, just moving to the music with no particular pattern—occasionally breaking for twirls, and once for a small dip.

"I'm sorry about the Carter thing," he whispers. "It didn't even occur to me . . ."

"It's fine," I say, hoping both desperately and proactively that Carter had a crush on some other straight guy he knew from college. "I'm grateful for your kindness, but you have other guests and I think it's probably time for me to go. I don't want you to feel like you have to keep whisking me away from the parade of awkward that has become my personal life," I say. "Besides, that way you don't need to dance with me, you could dance with Carter instead."

"His legs aren't as nice as yours," he says, laughing. "Oh, I've stepped in it now. That was completely inappropriate and unprofessional wasn't it?"

"Thanks for the compliment," I say, blushing. "I'll let it slide."

"I *want* to dance with you," he says earnestly. "Wait . . . you think I'm interested in Carter?"

"Aren't you?" I ask. "He was your date to my divorce party, wasn't he?" At least now I'll get an answer to the *Is he or isn't he?* question that has been plaguing me since the first day I came to Daniel's floating restaurant. *Please don't be gay, please don't be gay, please don't be gay* . . .

He stops dancing abruptly, while we're in the center of the cluster of people, but keeps one hand at my back and holds my hand with his other. The guests keep dancing around us.

"I'm straight," he says. "Very, very straight. Just because I cook and let my brother buy me jeans does not make me gay." He laughs. "I'm gay-friendly, gay-supportive, often gay-adjacent—but I'm as straight as they come."

And all of a sudden, my brain is practically belting out the "Hallelujah Chorus." Not gay! Not gay! Not gay!

And he's not gay even with abs like a sex god.

Hallelujah! Hallelujah! Hallelujah! Hallelujah!

And we shall make out forever and ever.

Hallelujah! Hallelujah! Hallelujah! Hallelujah!

"Wait, you let your brother pick out your jeans?" I laugh.

He looks a bit embarrassed. "Jeans, suits, shirts. We're the same size, and Gabriel has really good taste. If he weren't a chef, he'd be a stylist, or a set designer. Also, he's been known to clean out my closet and replace anything he deems unsuitable." He cracks, "I have to hide my flip-flops when he visits."

"I can't decide if that's sweet that you let him dress you, or just really, really odd," I say teasingly.

"Oh, it's sweet," he says, laughing. "I'm a sweetheart, I tell you. Gabriel's been supervising my wardrobe since he was in seventh grade. My whole family's, actually. At the time, it just felt like a way we could be supportive of his creativity. Now that I'm an adult, I appreciate the fact that I hardly ever have to shop for suits. They just magically show up on my doorstep—sorry, my gangplank—courtesy of UPS, and conveniently charged to my credit card."

"So all those cool-guy band T-shirts you have, those are all strategically picked out by your tasteful brother?" I tease.

"No, *cher*, that's my department. He picks the suits, and the ties, and the dress shirts. And shoes. He's always sending me shoes. And Diesel jeans, which it never would have occurred to me to buy if not for Gabriel. But the T-shirts, and the board shorts, and the flip-flops are all me."

I've seen Daniel in jeans. I should send his brother a thank-you note. Or a really big fruit basket.

"What?" I say with feigned awe. "You pick out your own flip-flops?" He grins in response.

We're standing still in the middle of the dance floor when the song changes to a slow ballad. Daniel pulls me closer and the two of us begin to sway to the music. Dancing with him is so easy, so effortless, so elemental. My breath catches in my chest as he holds me close. Suddenly I'm no longer aware of the people around us, just the feel and the warmth and the scent of Daniel, and the way he's holding me near to him. I don't care that he's a client, or that I've only learned in the last three minutes that he isn't gay. I don't care about any of it, and I let myself just sway and sway, lavished in his embrace. I want him to kiss me and I'm profoundly surprised by how rapidly the desire overtakes me. My list-making, pros-and-cons, rational brain is overruled. I don't want to think about anything other than how I feel in that exact moment—exquisite and romantic and full of possibilities.

The ballad ends too soon, followed by another up-tempo jazz number. I reluctantly take a step back from Daniel, and his fingertips linger at the small of my back for another heartbeat. My breath holds in my chest as our eyes lock on each other's—as though we're both waiting for the other to be the first to glance away.

Cliff Roles snaps a photo of us, startling me. He pats Daniel on the shoulder. "Lovely party, Daniel. I've stayed too long and drunk too much, and I'd love to do it again soon. Thank you for your hospitality." Daniel gently lets go of my hand and turns to give Cliff a hug. I'll be trolling Cliff's social media pages the second I get home in search of the image he just snapped of us dancing, hoping against hope that the picture is in focus, flattering, and discreetly downloadable.

"So glad you could be here, Cliff," says Daniel. "How are you getting home?"

"I rode with Alyson," he says. "She's at the dessert table right now, trying to deconstruct your pralines."

"I'm happy to give her the recipe," Daniel says.

"She's a purist," he laughs, "I think she likes to guess." Cliff gives Daniel a pat on the back and a warm handshake, and then turns to hug me.

"You're looking fabulous, darling," he says. "I was so surprised to hear about Michael."

"You and me both," I say. Cliff laughs at my response and then wanders off toward Alyson.

"Nice guy," Daniel says to me. I nod. We return to our table and Carter announces that he's exhausted and has to be leaving too, as Lolly and Santiago stand up and gather their things. I suspect that Carter's sudden departure has something to do with the uncomfortable discussion about the man he was in love with in college who may or may not have been my (now former) husband. I don't want to think about it anymore tonight; I'll deal with that potential disaster later.

"I'll call you tomorrow," says Carter as he kisses me on each cheek. I nod.

"Nice to meet you both," I say to Santiago and Lolly. They both hug me and say goodbye. It's weird, hugging a guy who slept with Michael. But not as weird as you'd think. Daniel excuses himself to make the rounds with his guests once again. It's almost midnight and the partygoers are complimenting the chef and saying their goodbyes.

I finish my wine, my third glass, I think, while chatting with a local author named Darby Vaughn, who's funny and bright, and the kind of person you meet and ten minutes later it feels like you've known them all your life. I sneak a peek as Daniel talks with the group of local chefs he invited. He looks up and smiles at me as though I'd called his name.

"That's some serious chemistry," says Darby to me. "Are you and Daniel together?"

"No, no." I shake my head. "He's a client." As though that somehow explains everything.

"Client, hmmm. He keeps looking over at you." She smiles. "Definitely some serious sparks."

My cheeks flush. I feel it.

Darby's friends begin to congregate at my table and then after a few moments, Daniel joins the group. As they thank him for the party, I grab my clutch and my wrap, and wait my turn to say goodbye to him.

Before I can speak, he leans forward and whispers in my ear, "Please don't go, *cher*."

47

The remaining guests ready themselves to leave, hug their host, and disembark into the warm night. My heart thumps achingly at the possibility of what might lie ahead. I visit the ladies' room to smooth my hair and freshen up. Also, because it's easier to hide out in the restroom than nonchalantly hang around the boat deck *not leaving* while everyone else is saying goodbye. Apparently dating involves spending a lot of time in the bathroom, which is something I had not anticipated.

I readjust my cleavage, brush my teeth using one of the tiny disposable toothbrushes I always keep in my bag for emergencies, and touch up my lip stain. Emerging a few minutes later, I'm surprised to find that the boat deck has cleared out almost completely. Servers are cleaning up what's left of the dessert table, clearing wineglasses and empty plates. A wide smile appears on Daniel's face as soon as he sees me, and he crosses the deck to join me.

Suddenly I feel awkward and self-conscious, even though I've been alone with Daniel at the restaurant dozens of times before.

"Thanks for inviting me tonight," I say. "I had fun, and it's so easy to see how amazing Boudreaux is going to be once it opens."

"Thank you for being here," he says. "I'm glad you stayed. I thought you might take off after the surprise Santiago visit, and then the thing with Carter. I'm so sorry I even brought that up. After that mess, I'm lucky if you ever come back."

"I don't scare that easily," I say, with more boldness than I feel.

"I'm very glad to know that," he says. He glances around at the servers cleaning up. "They'll be done in fifteen minutes or so."

He seems anxious for them to leave.

48

I smile at Daniel, unsure of what to say.

"Would you like a drink or anything?" he asks. "Maybe some dessert? I noticed you didn't have any." I shake my head no. But I could get used to this, a guy who worries about whether or not I've had enough dessert.

I feel awkward, incredibly awkward.

"Why am I here?" I ask, a little too bluntly.

"I'm sorry," he says quickly, apologetically. "Do you not want to be here?"

"I'm just confused," I say. "Is this about work?"

"Is that why you stayed?" he asks.

"I stayed because you asked me to," I say. A perfectly ambiguous answer. I'm suddenly afraid of giving myself away.

I hold tight to the railing of the boat, looking out into the dark bay. The night sky is sprinkled with stars and I wonder what it might be like to lie on my back on the boat deck and just look up.

Daniel stands next to me, wordlessly, looking out over the water. On the other side, the artful arch of the Ringling Bridge spans into the darkness. He reaches out and takes my hand, entwining my fingers in his, and the two of us stand there awhile longer, still in the moment.

His hand is warm, gentle, and I smile at how giddy I feel at this small romantic gesture.

"There's something about you that feels like we've known each other a very, very long time," he says softly.

"Years long, or reincarnation long?" I ask, only half joking.

He smiles. "Lifelong."

"Why do you think that is?"

"I think, *cher*," he says, "that there's something about you that feels like home to me."

"You mean I remind you of New Orleans?" I ask, both confused and wanting him to say more.

"No, I mean, when you're around I feel comfortable and excited and part of something, if that makes any sense to you."

I nod.

The crew finishes cleaning up and leaves for the night, and Daniel and I move to our usual table by the railing, sipping our wine and not saying much.

I'm still not sure exactly why he wanted me to stay, although I'm hoping that it has more to do with the dance than the restaurant project. I've decided to play it casual, stay loose, and see where Daniel is going with this. Which will only require me overcoming basically every single aspect of my personality.

"I'm glad you came tonight," he says.

"Me too."

"Is this weird," he asks, "with us working together?"

"Not yet," I quip. "But you know me."

He laughs. "I do." He sips his wine and fiddles with his cocktail napkin. "So, did you really think I was gay?" His mouth is set in a smile, but his eyes are serious.

"I wasn't sure," I say. "I mean, I would have been fine with it either way."

He looks crestfallen. "Really?"

"Sure, I've worked with lots of gay chefs before." I smile to myself. It's been thirty whole seconds and I haven't professed my massive crush on him, or tackled him to the ground to kiss him or anything! Clearly, I'm on a roll.

Daniel takes a deep breath and reaches across the table to touch the back of my hand. "There are a hundred reasons why I should bring this up later," he says. "We're working together, you've just gone through a really rough divorce . . . but every time we're together I just want to spend all day talking to you. And when you leave, I can't stop thinking about the next time I'll see you. I kept feeling there might be something between us, but now that I know you've been thinking I'm gay this whole time, I'm wondering if I was just imagining it all."

I smile. "I did think you were gay. So imagine how confused I was. I kept thinking, am I actually flirting with a gay man? And then I'd think, *well, it wouldn't be the first time*."

"Not gay." He smiles.

"Not gay." I nod.

There's another awkward silence between us, and after a seemingly interminable pause, Daniel speaks again.

"So, I don't want to make our working relationship awkward. I like you a lot. I'd like to spend more time with you if you're up for it. And if you're not interested, or you feel that it would compromise you professionally or make working together uncomfortable, or if you might be interested but it's just way too soon, just say the word and I'll keep it to myself. Forever, if you'd like. Or until tomorrow. Either way."

"You're a client," I say.

He grins. "Only for one more week."

All is quiet but for the waves lapping against the side of the boat. Daniel's chair is angled toward mine, close enough for our knees to touch while we're talking. I try not to look at him gratuitously, but he's funny and handsome and has these crazy sexy blue eyes and the anticipation of what he might say or do next is driving me to mad contemplation. There's something so delicious in the waiting and wondering.

For a long time we sit there not saying anything, enjoying the quiet of the bay and the occasional steamy knee bump.

Daniel puts his hand near the armrest of my chair and gently strokes my forearm with his index finger.

"Are you chilly, *cher*? Do you want my jacket?"

"Thank you, I'm fine," I say. Despite the fact that I'm not the least bit chilly, I'm tempted to borrow Daniel's suit jacket just to feel his warmth, even by way of an article of clothing, to inhale his scent more subtly than, say, taking a big snort next to his neck the next time he leans forward. I wonder if men think the same way, if Daniel would notice the heat of my body inside his jacket, or if he'll smell my perfume lingering long after I've gone home.

"Do you mind if I ask why you thought I was gay?" he asks.

"I think initially I assumed so because you came with Carter to the divorce party. When we first met, I didn't feel even a flicker of interest on your part. There was the Sterno . . ."

"My manners were atrocious that night," he says. "I apologize. I was struck mute by how distraught you looked, I couldn't think of anything to say. It was odd, actually, I'm rarely at a loss for words. Lifetime spent in the hospitality industry, I suppose."

"And then, there's the calling everyone *cher*, from me to the construction workers to Carter . . ."

"That's an old and fairly unbreakable family habit. I was teased unmercifully about it in college. I tried to stop when I was in school at Boston University, and eventually I just gave in. If it offends you, let me know and I'll do my best to call you Alex instead. Or Dr. Wiggins, if you prefer."

"I don't mind it," I say. "I actually find it sort of charming." Very charming in the sense that it makes me go wobbly in the knees every time he says it. A tidbit I'll be keeping to myself for now. "But you have to admit," I say, "not a whole lot of straight guys call their head carpenter *cher*."

"Well, Scully is a very sweet guy." He laughs.

"I'm sure he's delightful," I say.

"Is that it?" he asks. "Colloquialisms and man dates and Sterno? Nothing else?"

"You have to know that with everything that's happened in the last few months, I'm seeing gay everywhere I look."

"Gayvision. Gaydar. Gay-colored glasses, so to speak?"

"Exactly," I say.

"So it wasn't my dancing?"

"You're a really good dancer." I laugh. "Really good."

He stands up, and extends his hand, "This is my favorite song, *cher.* Would you like to dance with me?"

I listen carefully for the song we danced to before, but this time instead of a bouncy Cajun beat it's a slow, big band, crooner kind of song. Maybe Harry Connick Jr. Sort of timeless and romantic. I stand up to dance with him and he pulls me close.

"I think you're full of it. I thought the other song we danced to was your favorite song." I laugh. He holds me delicately, but his arms are strong and firm.

"You're on to me, *cher.* I confess, any song that's playing when I'm dancing with you is my favorite song." I smile over his shoulder and he pulls me in a bit closer.

"So here it is," he whispers in my ear. "Alex, I think I could be falling for you."

49

He pulls me closer still as my heart flutters wildly. "You're smart and charming and a bit goofy, and tenderhearted, and incredibly compelling. Am I rambling? You're beautiful, so beautiful. I can't stop thinking about you."

I don't know what to say. "Thank you" doesn't seem appropriate. I feel the same way, obviously, but I'm so terrified of being hurt or betrayed that there's a part of me that just wants to shut this down, keep it on a professional level. On the other hand, my heart is practically jumping out of my chest.

He stops rocking and looks into my eyes. We're inches apart and I'm mesmerized by the tiny flecks of indigo in his blue eyes. A girl could drown in those eyes. And it wouldn't be the worst way to go.

"It's too fast, isn't it?" he says. "You're just barely divorced and you were really hurt by it, and you probably don't even want to think about maybe falling in love again someday."

Falling in love? I'm not even positive I want to date. But I nod, still unsure of what to do.

"The trouble is, I can't . . . stop thinking . . . about it. Falling."

"You should be. You're worried I'm going to push you over the side of the boat again, aren't you," I tease. He's being so earnest and sweet, and I have no idea why I feel the need to crowbar in a little levity. I'm just scared out of mind.

"A little." He smiles, and then his face grows serious. "You're not saying much. Am I going too far with this?"

He's looking at me intently, and I return his gaze, memorizing the cleft in his chin, the color of his eyelashes, the fullness of his lips.

I pause, almost afraid to answer. "No, it's not too far." He smiles at me, and begins to sway gently to the music again. My body follows his.

His hand presses tenderly at the small of my back, bringing me closer until our bodies are touching.

His lips brush my ear, sending a current of electricity from the nape of my neck to my fingertips. "Is this too far, *cher*?"

"No," I answer, "it's not too far."

He moves slowly, deliberately, his breath leaving a trail from my ear to just millimeters away from my mouth. I close my eyes, tasting his warm breath on my lips.

"Is this too far?" he asks.

"Maybe," I say, slowly opening my eyes.

"Okay," he says, taking a slow step back. Gentlemanly. Good to know.

"Kidding," I say, raising my eyebrows playfully. It takes him a second for my answer to register.

"Are you just trying to torment me?" he cracks.

"A little bit," I reply. "Is it working?"

"A little bit." He grins at me, and I smile back. He moves his lips toward mine again, at an achingly slow pace. This time, I watch his eyes intently as he draws near. His lips touch mine, gently at first, then he kisses me hungrily, evidence that we've both been waiting for something a very long time. It's soft and urgent and tender—exactly what a kiss should be. The kind of kiss I never, ever got from Michael.

Daniel still holds me near with one of his hands behind my back, and the other clasps my hand in his and holds it close to his heart. He brings my hand to his lips and kisses it softly.

"Your hands are so soft," he says.

"All the better to . . . ," I tease.

He laughs and it strikes me how delightful it is that he finds so much merriment from everyday life. After my last six months, which seem so heavy, and drenched with sadness as thick as pea soup, Daniel's inherent joie de vivre is a welcome vacation from my real life. I feel more like myself with him than I have in a really long time.

He kisses me gently on the top of my nose, my cheek, and then hesitates at my lips, in that achingly delicious limbo you feel when you know he's about to kiss you and the anticipation is practically driving you mad, even though the limbo itself is almost as intoxicating as what's surely to follow.

"I've wanted to kiss you for a very long time," he says breathlessly.

"Me too," I confess. So much for playing it cool.

"Really?" he asks playfully. "Since when?"

"Hmmm," I say, "I'm not sure it would be professional of me to admit it."

"I won't tell if you don't," he says.

"Okay," I say. "I've wanted you to kiss me since the day I startled you and you fell into the bay."

He grins, and another adorable dimple appears.

"Especially after I saw you with your shirt off," I say, shocked at my own boldness. "You?"

"You'll think I'm a cad if I admit it," he says.

"So unfair," I tease. "I told you, now it's your turn."

He grasps my other hand and gently pulls me towards him. "I wanted to kiss you the first time I ever saw you."

"You mean here?" I ask.

"No." He laughs. "At your divorce party. I thought you were stunning in a way that just knocked the wind out of me. And then I was just so awkward. You looked so sad. Of course, the timing was completely inappropriate, you'd just gotten divorced that day. I was a plus-one, and wobbly on the etiquette of asking out the hostess. And then when you walked into my restaurant, I thought maybe destiny lent a hand. I felt so at ease with you."

"You feel at ease with everyone," I say.

"That is the result of growing up fourth generation in a restaurant family and learning to be a host as soon as I could walk. I'm comfortable around most people, and I can get along with just about everyone—but I don't usually feel so connected to someone I've just met. Do you know what I mean?"

"I do," I say.

We stay there dancing and talking for a while—maybe minutes, maybe hours. In his arms, I feel as though I've lost all sense of time.

We talk endlessly, about the projects I'm proudest of, what thrills me about environmental psychology, his favorite things about New Orleans, my favorite spots in Sarasota. He tells me about how his father lent him out to other famous New Orleans kitchens like Tujague's, Brennan's, and Commander's Palace over the summers when he was a teenager, so that by the time he started college he had already worked with some of the best chefs in the country, including Emeril Lagasse and Paul Prudhomme.

"How was that experience? Was it intimidating?"

"Not really," he says. "You have to remember that I grew up with these chefs. Their kids worked in my family's restaurants, I worked in theirs. To me, they were like uncles. And having grown up in kitchens, there's really no place I feel more comfortable."

He pauses, then asks, "Do you want to take some dessert upstairs to the studio? Kick off your shoes, hang out on the couch?"

Taking my shoes off would feel great, but there's no way I'd trust myself to be alone with Daniel twenty feet away from his bed. First, the Nate debacle has taught me to be more careful. Second, Daniel isn't the subcontractor of a client, he *is* my client. At this point, my career is everything I have, the only thing in my life I have any control over, the only thing I can truly depend on. I need to tread very carefully, to take things slowly with Daniel rather than just rush right in.

"I promise to behave myself," says Daniel.

"I can't promise the same," I say. "So I'd probably better go."

"Are you sure?" he asks.

I smile, kissing him playfully. "Yes, I'm *sure* I can't promise to behave myself." He grins in response and pulls me closer.

"We should definitely go upstairs, *cher*," he says.

"I should definitely go home," I say.

"If you must," he says. "I understand. Mmmm . . . good night then." His lips linger at my neck.

"Good night," I say, kissing him lightly on the cheek.

He turns his head and kisses me on the lips, now more urgent than ever. Suddenly my fingers are stroking his hair; his arms are around my body, pushing me fervently against the deck railing as we kiss. The firm surface at my back and Daniel's passionately insistent body pressing against me, and I can barely catch my breath. I don't want to catch my breath.

My hands move down from his hair to his chest, and I snake one around his waist. I can feel the strong muscles in his back through his shirt, and I can barely stop myself from yanking up his shirt to touch his bare skin, something I've thought about near-constantly since I first saw him with his shirt off in this same spot we are now kissing. His breath is fast and heavy, matching my own. His warm fingers touch my skin where my back is exposed from my halter dress. His touch is addictively exquisite. I want to climb on top of him, straddle him, devour him.

"I should go," I say breathlessly.

"Stay, *cher*," he says. "Do you really need to leave?"

"I do," I say. If I don't leave now, I know I'll be here all night. As much as I've fantasized about Daniel in every way possible, I know I'm not even remotely ready for that yet. It's too soon, and I still don't trust my own judgement.

"Okay," he says. "I understand." He brings my hand to his lips again and kisses it gently. "Until tomorrow, then." His eyes never leave mine.

I nod and let my hands drop to my side. Gathering up my wrap and my clutch, I turn to look at him one last time before I go. He's dashing and charming and clearly wants me. I have to be some sort of lunatic to leave him pining for me on the boat deck. What if tomorrow he just acts like nothing ever happened tonight, like everything is the same?

"Thank you for a lovely evening," I say, shaking the worrying thoughts from my mind.

"Thank you for being here tonight," he says, his sensuous mouth smiling. "And for the dance."

He walks me to my car, which I think is sweet. I'm glad for the company. Although the marina is well lit and in a safe area of town, I have no idea how late it is, and it's never a good idea to be wandering around a parking lot alone in the middle of the night. As we reach my car, he leans down to kiss me on the cheek.

I should go home now, it's already so late, but I lean upward to kiss him on those full, perfect lips once more. He kisses me back, gently, sweetly, at first and then hungrily, his firm body coaxing mine up against the door of my car. I kiss him back with ache and urgency, every nerve in my body on fire.

What is it about being kissed against a car or a wall that is so thrilling, so carnal? Is it the firmness of the wall against your back, while he urgently presses into your every curve? Is it the delicious feeling of touch on nearly every part of your body? Or is it that a wall is a vertical substitute for a bed, a steamy prelude for what's to come?

At last, I tear myself away, my skin flushed and my heart thudding wildly.

Daniel looks at me with longing, but takes a step back, opening the door of my car for me. I toss my clutch inside, and get into the car.

He leans down so that we're eye to eye, puts his hand to his heart, and taps his fingers on his chest like a heartbeat.

"Sweet dreams, *cher*," he says, and then closes my door firmly. I smile, knowing exactly what I'll be dreaming about tonight.

50

Jeez, it's 3:24 in the morning. Time with Daniel went by so fast, but I can hardly believe I stayed so late. Thank goodness it's still dark; another couple of hours and I'd be making the walk of shame in last night's clothes in front of my neighbors.

Before I make my way home, I check my phone and find three voice mails from Carter, and a bunch of texts.

CALL ME, NEED TO TALK

CALL ME AS SOON AS YOU GET THIS

CALL ME, NO MATTER HOW LATE

The last message was thirty minutes ago. I almost ignore it, wanting to relive every moment of tonight with Daniel instead. But I know if I don't call Carter back, I won't be able to think about anything else. Damn my type-A tendencies.

It's way too late, but I dial his number anyway. I know why he's calling and I just want to get it over with. Worry unmercifully clenches my intestines as Carter's phone rings, and I struggle to take a full breath. Every time I start to believe I can not be more humiliated, or more hurt, some new affront comes to light. I brace for bad news.

"You're up late," says Carter as he answers the phone.

"What's up?" I ask. I'm not in the mood for small talk.

"Jesus, Alex, I'm so sorry about tonight," Carter says. "I realized almost immediately that you must have thought that Michael was the guy I had feelings for in college. You must have been completely freaking out. I wanted to talk to you about it, but I didn't want things to get even more awkward than they already were."

"Was it Michael?" I ask. "Did you guys get together in college? You said you knew the whole time he was gay. Is that how you knew?"

"It wasn't Michael I was in love with," he blurts out. "It was Daniel. I was dating Gabriel, his brother. Daniel is great; you know how great he is. Anyway, after a few visits to New Orleans I realized that I had some pretty serious feelings for Daniel, and that he was unequivocally straight. I didn't want to hurt Gabriel, or freak out Daniel, so I made up that story, a half-truth, really, about falling for a straight guy in college—the one that got away, you know. Gabriel and I broke up, Daniel and I stayed friends. At first I was dreaming that we'd have some magical Hollywood moment in a rainstorm where he realized he was gay after all and that he was madly in love with me the whole time. His shirt would be sticking to his chest from the rain, and he'd be wearing really tight jeans, and his hair would be sort of pushed over to the side. Maybe a little beard stubble." He grew quiet.

"It sounds like you've given this a lot of thought," I say, letting the image of Carter's fantasy of rain-soaked Daniel play in my mind. *What, I'm supposed to let that image go to waste?*

"A lot of thought," he says. "A *lot*. But it became pretty apparent very quickly that it wasn't going to happen. He's a really decent person, and we've been friends ever since. But he doesn't have any idea about my feelings for him, no one does. No one but you. And I think it would make things awkward between us if he knew. He's a really good friend, and I don't have feelings for him anymore. Except lust—but who doesn't?" He's rambling, even more than usual. "Please don't say anything to him, I don't want it to get awkward."

"And nothing happened between you and Daniel?" I ask. Not that it's any of my business, but I'm continually unnerved by the pernicious effects of my romantic past.

"Nothing happened. Nothing even came close to happening. Sadly for me, he's not at all ambiguous about his sexuality." I smile. Not so sadly for me.

"I won't say anything," I say, exhaling stress as thick as cigar smoke. I'm just so relieved that Carter and Michael didn't hook up. Or Carter and Daniel. Disaster averted. Finally, after all this time and drama, it seems like things are going my way.

51

Once my call with Carter is over with, I practically float the rest of the way home, replaying every perfect, enchanted moment of the night, like a romantic movie playing in my head.

When I get home, I wash my face, brush my teeth, and change into a pretty camisole nightie I haven't worn in over a year. For the first time in forever, I feel beautiful and desirable and flirtatious, and my usual post-breakup bedtime wardrobe of ratty oversize T-shirts just isn't going to cut it tonight. Ahem, *this morning.*

Putting my decorative pillows on the dresser, I climb under the covers and arrange my pillows just so. Morley jumps up on the bed next to me, and settles himself at my side. I was out very late, maybe the little guy missed me. Reaching out to touch him, I stroke his fur gently. He hisses and claws at me with his hind legs.

"I love you too, Morley," I say, pulling the sheet to my neck. I close my eyes and drift off to sleep.

I sleep until noon.

I can hardly believe my eyes when I look at the clock the next morning. Noon! Morley is meowing loudly near his bowl, and I can hear the familiar sound of one of my nearby neighbors running a leaf blower down the street. It's Florida, somebody's always running a leaf blower.

I pad barefoot to the kitchen to feed Morley, laughing at the fact that I can't seem to stop myself from grinning like a fool, thinking about Daniel and every moment last night (and this morning!), from our first dance together to the final sizzling kisses against the door of my car.

I pour a glass of orange juice for myself and take it out to the lanai to enjoy the sun and the spectacular view of the inlet and the bay. The bougainvillea is still in full bloom, massive bushes of vibrant fuchsia blossoms. Every year about this time I struggle between my compulsive need to have neatly groomed landscaping, and not wanting to touch a single stalk of the vibrant, explosively untamed leaves. The bougainvillea wins, of course, it's too spectacular to trim back. It'll return to green again soon enough. Sitting on a lounge chair, I watch the palms sway in the breeze over the water as I sip my juice, and let my mind wander back to Daniel once again, and that first dance.

The doorbell rings, which is unusual for a Sunday. Maybe it's Zelda with more pot muffins.

"Coming!" I yell as I run toward the bedroom, grabbing a robe from the hook in my bathroom and tugging it on as I scramble to answer the door.

Out of breath, I yank the front door open. It's a delivery guy, with a stunning arrangement of pink peonies. I beam. The last time I got flowers was almost eight months ago, from Michael, on the morning of our anniversary. Yep, three weeks to the day before he told me he was gay.

"Alex Wiggins?" asks the delivery guy.

"That's me!" I say, a little too enthusiastically. He hands me a clipboard to sign, and when I finish, he hands me the flowers.

"Thanks!" I say, feeling in the pockets of my robe for a tip. "Hang on," I say. I set the flowers on the kitchen counter and rummage around in my wallet for a five-dollar bill. All I have are two ones and a ten and a couple of twenties.

I grab the ten-dollar bill and hand it to the delivery guy. Why not? I'm in a spectacular mood.

"Thanks, miss," he says, pocketing the tip. "Thanks very much."

"Thank you," I say, quickly closing the door. I can't wait to read the card to see who sent me the flowers. Every cell in my body hopes the card reads *Daniel*.

The peonies are beautiful, and the scent is sweetly unexpected, almost rose-like. The florist mixed in a few pale green blooms in the arrangement, and I search around among the flowers looking for the card. At last I find it.

I slip the small card out of the envelope, and my breath catches in my chest as I read the message:

ALEX,

I'M STILL THINKING ABOUT OUR DANCE LAST NIGHT.

DANIEL

I make my way out to the lanai and lay back on the lounge chair, closing my eyes and letting the sun warm my face.

My phone rings and I pick it up to check the caller ID: Daniel Boudreaux.

"Oh Daniel, your flowers just arrived. Thank you. They're just beautiful. I love peonies."

"You're welcome, *cher*," he says in his perfectly melodic lilt. Daniel seems to hesitate and then speaks again. Like this brash, confident guy is suddenly shy. "So I was calling, because . . . would you have dinner with me tonight?"

I sit straight up on the lounge chair. Is this really happening?

"No pressure, of course," he says suddenly. "I don't want to assume anything, it's just after last night I thought you might . . . consider . . ."

"Sure, I'd love to have dinner with you," I say, far more casually than I'm feeling. But I guess jumping up and down and yelling "Woo-hoo" is probably not standard dating protocol, even if it's your first second date ever. Maybe it is, what do I know? I stand up and dance around on the pool deck in my pajamas, holding the phone away from my mouth so he can't hear that I'm breathing like a cavewoman from all my jumping around and nineties-pop-star-quality dance moves.

A group of boaters on the inlet are cracking up; they wave at me with their phones like they're at a rock concert. I feel my face turning scarlet, but I take a dramatic bow and wave back to them. I'm so happy I hardly care.

"I'll pick you up around seven-thirty?" Daniel asks.

"Sounds good," I say. "I'll text you my address."

"Until tonight, *cher,*" he says softly, his voice a quixotic melody in my ears.

52

I haven't been able to stop thinking about Daniel all day, even if I wanted to stop. Which I kind of don't.

I realize I never felt this kind of sweet infatuation about Michael. I adored him, for sure. But there was never a day in my whole life when my mind went back to Michael over and over again, thinking about his eyes, his hair, the firmness of the muscles in his shoulders. His voice, his scent, the softness of his lips, what it felt like when he was pressed up against me.

I'm giddy, my brain drenched in an intoxicating potion of endorphins I studied in school, but apparently never fully experienced until now.

I lie out in the sunshine for a while longer, trying and failing to focus on a book I wanted to finish. I can't concentrate; every other sentence is punctuated with thoughts of Daniel and my intermittent analysis of the fact that I have surely lost my mind. Eventually, I give up on the book and decide to just spend the next hour lost in my own thoughts, staring out at the view in my backyard.

When I get too warm, I retreat to the air-conditioning inside. It's fairly obvious I'm not going to get anything useful done today, so I survey the contents of my closet to figure out what I'm going to wear tonight.

I pull out half a dozen dresses, all in bright happy colors that match my optimism, and try them on in front of the mirror. I plug my iPod into speakers and dance around the bedroom to my favorite playlist—*Embarrassing Songs I Love*—a compilation of frothy, feel-good pop songs from Hansen, ABBA, Taylor Swift, Britney Spears, and Beyoncé. Basically, the cotton candy of music.

Morley stretches out on the bed and watches me as though he's considering having me committed for psychiatric evaluation. It occurs to me that I've compared myself to a crazy person multiple times in the last hour, and the doctor part of my brain wonders if I somehow equate the feeling of buoyancy and freedom I'm feeling right now to mental illness. What does that say about me? Is the feeling of emotional free-falling really so scary to me? Yes, and for once, I don't care. Call me crazy.

I pull on a hot coral-pink dress with spaghetti straps. The color is alive with hope, and I decide it's perfect for my first official I-actually-like-this-guy date in forever. I have some strappy gold wedge sandals that are perfect with the dress, and decide I need a pedicure before my date. My toes are pale blue, which is gorgeous, but it doesn't really go with my dress and I'm in the mood to pamper myself. I decide I'll forgo my usual strip mall pedicure for a more luxurious experience if I can get an appointment at the Met, a local day spa. Giving them a call, I'm delighted to learn that not only are they open on Sundays, but they have an appointment available at four, which is perfect. Clearly the Universe wants me to have fabulous toes for my date with Daniel tonight. The Universe is cool like that.

Hanging up my dress, I place it back in my closet, ready for later. I rinse my face, change into a cotton shirt, shorts, and flip-flops, and throw my hair up into a loose bun. I'm suddenly hungry, and start rummaging through the refrigerator for some lunch. Morley is instantly at my feet, as though he's been paged, sputtering and purring, looking for a treat.

Selecting a bowl of chicken salad, I set it down on the island and then go back to grab the pitcher of iced tea and a bowl of grapes. Morley is howling for attention. I pull down a plate for me, and a small bowl for him from the cabinet, grab some silverware, and drop a few scoops of chicken salad in the bowl for Morley, placing it on the floor.

Morley sort of grunts and digs in to the chicken salad. I place a large dollop on my plate along with some grapes, and pour myself a glass of tea. After putting everything back in the refrigerator, I sit down at the breakfast bar and eat my lunch.

Once I've finished, I put my dishes and Morley's in the dishwasher, wipe down the countertops, and head out to the spa on St. Armands Circle for my pedicure.

53

It's almost six when I return home from my pedicure feeling relaxed and pampered, although I can't know for sure whether it's the complimentary spa mimosa or the leg massage that has me feeling so on top of the world. I take a long, steamy shower and add a few extra steps to my usual routine, including deep conditioning my hair, a pore-shrinking masque, and a full-body exfoliation. I accidentally get a little of the pore-shrinking masque in my left eye and it burns like hell. What do they put in that pore-shrinking stuff anyway, hydrochloric acid?

Howling and jumping up and down, I first try rinsing out my eye in the stream of the shower but it's just making it worse, and then I scramble out of the shower, naked, shivering, and dripping all over the floor, to try to rinse my eye with cool water from the sink. *Ohmygod, my eye's on fire!*

I rush to the sink and cup my hand under the water, splashing it on my face over and over again—aiming for my inflamed, squinty eye, but mostly drenching my left shoulder and the bathroom floor instead. After ten minutes of this, the burning begins to subside a bit, but my eye is still red and swollen, and my vision is all blurry. This is terrible. Daniel will be here in an hour, and I look like I've just gone two rounds with Laila Ali. Or a rattlesnake that went straight for my eyeball.

Grabbing a towel to wrap around myself, I dig through the medicine cabinet and locate a bottle of saline eyewash, and then try to clean out the rest of the irritant.

Desperate, I lie on the cold tile floor in the kitchen, still wrapped in my towel, with a teabag and a package of frozen tater tots over my left eye, wondering where, at this late hour, am I ever going to find a pirate-style eye patch that matches my coral-pink dress? Morley makes his way over, rests himself on the towel wrapping my hair, and licks the icy bag of potatoes resting on top of my face until I can no longer stand (about thirty seconds) the scratchy sound of his tongue against the plastic and shoo him away.

Twenty minutes later, my eye feels better, my vision has returned, and the swelling has subsided. Disaster averted. I blow my hair dry and apply a little makeup for polish.

Ten minutes before Daniel is due to arrive, I slip on my shoes, which look fabulous with my pale pink pedicure, and select an enameled floral necklace and some drop earrings to complete the look. I dump my wallet, lip stain, keys, and phone into a woven straw clutch and set it, along with a cream-colored pashmina, on top of the breakfast bar. My heart is beating like it's prom night, and I'm hyper-aware of the fact that this is essentially my first meaningful date ever. I was never this nervous or excited to go out with Michael—I guess because we'd known each other all our lives. There is something really delicious about the unknown, the endless possibilities of where things might go, of what could happen.

Ready five minutes early, I pace around the house looking for something to do. I fluff the throw pillows on the couch, even though they don't need it. Start a load of towels. Refill Morley's bowl with cold water and an ice cube, just the way he likes it. Re-puddle the living room window treatments. I go into the guest bathroom to fluff the towels on the rack, and then do the same in the master bathroom. When the doorbell rings at seven-thirty on the dot, I'm in the middle of collecting Morley's cat toys from the far reaches of the house.

I open the front door and my heart is thumping like a rabbit's. There stands Daniel, looking dapper in a pale pink button-down shirt and a pair of linen pants.

"We match," he says. "Actually, as Gabriel would say, we coordinate."

"Did he pick out your wardrobe for tonight?" I tease.

"No," he grins, "that was all me." He leans forward and gives me a gentle kiss on the cheek. I can hardly contain my glee. "You're not going to let me live that one down, are you?"

"Not a chance. Please come in," I say, and he obliges.

"You look beautiful tonight," he says. "Great place. Very you."

"Thank you," I say, taking my clutch and wrap off the breakfast bar. He looks beautiful too, but I don't exactly know how to phrase that. He is gorgeous, and he looks completely at home in his perfectly tropical, dressy casual attire. Like he just stepped off a yacht, or out of a Tommy Bahama catalog.

Morley appears from nowhere and starts rubbing against Daniel's legs. Before I can warn him to beware of flying claws, he leans over and picks up Morley, cradling the cat in his arms while he scratches him behind the ear. Morley starts purring, his odd, broken motorboat purr, and I stand there with my mouth open. Daniel sets him back on the floor, and Morley purrs even louder, figure-eighting Daniel's legs. I'm dumbfounded.

"Sweet little guy," he says. "Shall we?" He extends his hand and I allow him to take mine.

"Wow, that's amazing," I say. "Morley never likes anyone. Not even me."

He laughs. "I'm sure he likes you as much as he likes me. What can I say? Morley clearly has good taste."

"Maybe it's your modest personality," I say.

"Or maybe it's that I handle shrimp a couple of times a day." He laughs.

Locking my front door, I follow Daniel down the front walkway to his car, a shiny black BMW. He opens the door for me and then once I'm inside, he shuts my door and heads to the driver's side. I smile to myself; the car seems freshly washed.

"Is there any place special you'd like to go?" he asks as he slides behind the steering wheel. "If not, I was thinking maybe we'd try Sangria on Main Street."

"Oh, I love that place," I say. "Tapas is one of my favorites because I like to try a little bit of everything."

"Me too," he says. "Sangria it is."

We drive downtown, which is busy even on a Sunday evening with locals and tourists. Parking karma is with us, and we find a spot a half block away from the restaurant. As we walk down the sidewalk, he gently places his hand at my back.

We're seated more quickly than I'm accustomed to, even though there's a bit of a crowd. The hostess is smiling and flirting with Daniel, who seems generously oblivious.

Once we're seated, our waiter is with us in a flash. Neither of us has even had a chance to take a peek at the menu.

"Do you want to start with some wine or sangria?" Daniel asks, and I nod yes in response.

"You pick," I say. "Not my forte." I'm starving, but feeling weirdly self-conscious about ordering food or wine in front of my famous chef date.

"Red, white, rosado?" he asks.

"What's rosado?" I ask.

"It means it contains enough of the grape skins for a lovely pink color, but not enough to call it a red. You'd call it rosé if it's French, rosado if it's Spanish or Portuguese."

"That sounds good," I say. He selects a bottle from the wine list and the waiter confirms his choice. Our waiter returns quickly and pours the wine. It's light and fresh, not too heavy. The perfect choice for a warm evening. Daniel and I each peruse our menus, and we rattle off a few different dishes to start with: the beef tenderloin with carmelized onions, a goat cheese spread, sea scallops sautéed in butter and wine, chilled artichokes. Our waiter leaves and we stare across the table at each other for a few seconds, suddenly at a loss for words.

"I'm so glad you agreed to have dinner with me tonight," says Daniel. "I was worried that in light of everything you've been through, that last night things might have been moving too fast for you."

I smile, unsure of what to say. Last night, the dancing, the kissing, all the emotion—it *was* fast.

"Thank you for the invitation," I say.

He laughs. "You certainly like to play your cards close to the chest."

"What do you mean?" I ask. I know exactly what he means.

"It means I'm going to have to work a little harder to get to know you."

"Knock yourself out," I say. His eyes dance at the challenge. It's tough not to stare at his face. Apparently I'm not the only one having this issue; the hostess has peeked around the corner at least four times to gape at him, and a nearby table of women clearly enjoying a girls' night out seem to be fascinated with Daniel as well. I can't blame them; with mesmerizing blue eyes and broad shoulders, he does cut quite the dashing figure.

The chef arrives at our table before the first dish is brought out, and introduces himself to Daniel. His chef's jacket is starched white, a dramatic contrast to his black hair and caramel skin.

"I'm Jose, the executive chef," he says in a thick Spanish accent. "We're so honored you've come to dine with us, Mr. Boudreaux."

"This is Alex Wiggins," Daniel says, gesturing to me. "Please call me Daniel. Chef, I'm so pleased to meet you, I've heard great things about your menu. I hope that you'll join us for dinner once Boudreaux opens up next week."

"Alex, very nice to meet you," Chef Jose says to me, grasping my hands in his. "I hope you are delighted with your meal." He turns to Daniel. "I'm an admirer of your family's restaurants, and of course your legacy. I will be honored to dine at Boudreaux."

"That's so kind of you," says Daniel with a wink. As Daniel and Chef Jose talk food, I see that the table of ladies to Daniel's left have taken notice of the special attention he's receiving from the chef. Sarasota is a small city, low on big shots.

"I'm preparing something special for you," says Chef Jose, "I hope you will enjoy it."

"Thank you," says Daniel. "We're looking forward to it."

I smile. "Thank you so much. It was so nice to meet you." Chef Jose nods his head and excuses himself to go back to the kitchen.

"I've never had a chef come to my table before," I say. "Does that happen to you all the time?"

"Professional courtesy," says Daniel.

"Is that a yes?" I ask.

"That's a yes." He smiles at me. "Tell me your story, Alex."

"I think you know it already," I say. "What do you want to know?"

He looks deep in thought for a moment, and then he breaks into a smile. "About you, *cher,* I want to know everything. Where did you grow up?"

"I grew up here. Some people can't wait to get out of a small town, I couldn't wait to come back after college. I love it here. Not just the beaches, which are the most beautiful in the country. I love how creative and artistic this town is. I love its weird little circus history. I love the fact that it never gets cold."

"That's what I love about it too. Do you still have family here?" he asks.

"My grandma Leona is here," I say. "She's a riot. She's the most positive person I've ever known. My mom and dad are back in San

Diego. They moved away once I went to college. I'm an only child. Well, sort of, I guess. I had a brother who died when he was two, leukemia. I was six when it happened. It was so rough on my parents, I felt like I had to be this perfect kid who never gave them any trouble because they'd already been through such a brutal, heartbreaking few years." I pause. "Weird, I don't think I've ever said that out loud before."

"That's a lot of pressure for a six-year old," Daniel says kindly.

"I met Michael that year, two weeks after my brother died. He was a life raft for me. He was funny and sweet and protective. And his family wasn't sad all the time. They were happy, and fun. And they played Scrabble and ate pepperoni pizza every Friday night. I practically lived there in elementary school. And then, a few years later, Michael's mom died. And Michael felt like the only person in the whole world who could understand what that felt like was me. It bonded us together on such a deep and profound level. We were inseparable."

"You were lucky to have each other to lean on," says Daniel. "I'm so sorry about your brother."

"It's okay," I say. "It was a really long time ago. Does that sound callous? I always feel that I should be sadder than I am. But the truth is, I was very young when he died. We never played together, because at first he was just a baby, and then he was too sick. I barely remember him, and most of those memories were in the hospital. They seem more like a dream now, or a movie you saw a really long time ago, but can't quite remember what it was about. The thing I remember most is not the loss of my brother so much—it was the loss of my parents after he died. It changed them, they were never quite the same. They were brokenhearted, hollow, disconnected. They stopped mourning after four or five years, but I have this whole lifetime of memories of sad Christmases, sad Thanksgivings, sad Fourth of Julys. Like ever enjoying anything again was strictly verboten for my parents and me, because my brother, William, wasn't there to enjoy it too. Do you know what I mean?"

"That must have been rough," says Daniel, reaching across the table to gently pat my shoulder.

"I shouldn't complain," I say. "I've had a great life. My family loves me. I've had amazing opportunities. I'm educated, I have friends who care about me, a business I'm inspired by." I smile at Daniel. "I'm well fed."

Daniel raises his glass, "To being well fed."

I raise my glass to his. "To being well fed."

As if on cue, our waiter appears with several of our selections: the goat cheese spread and the beef tenderloin. He also brings a small plate of *jalea* prepared for us by Chef Jose—a breaded seafood with marinated vegetables. Daniel and I sample the various dishes, which are absolutely delicious.

"Try this," says Daniel, raising a forkful of *jalea*. I take a bite, and even though I usually hate when anyone tries to feed me, it feels natural and comfortable, sharing with him.

"It's good!" I say. "Spicy."

"You're spicy," he says, his eyes flirtatious. I can't help but be charmed.

"How do you get away with saying stuff like that?" I ask. "Do you think it's the dreamy Southern accent?"

In a comically on-the-nose Scarlett O'Hara falsetto he says, "I declare, Miss Wiggins, I have no idea what you're talking about." We start laughing and suddenly we can't stop ourselves at cracking up over every little thing; we're laughing so hard our eyes start watering.

Our waiter swings by to drop off a few more plates, and pick up the ones we're finished with.

"I think we need to sample more food," says Daniel.

"We should try the empanadas," I suggest.

"Sounds good. Do you like scallops?" he asks, and I nod yes. "And maybe the butternut squash?"

I start laughing over nothing, Daniel starts laughing, and seconds later the two of us are roaring away at the table with no earthly idea what set us off again. I think it was the word *squash*, which is hilarious if you have a glass or two of rosado and say it over and over again like a punch line. *Squash*.

"What's your story?" I ask.

"What do you want to know about?" he asks. "I've already told you too much about my family, I think."

"Yes, let me see if I can get this straight," I tease. "Gabriel shops for your clothes. Who does your hair?"

We laugh and talk for hours and suddenly I notice that the staff are starting to prep the restaurant for close.

"Please tell me if this is too personal," Daniel says. He's still smiling but his face is serious.

"Okay," I say. "But you already know most of my low points, and you did attend my divorce party, so . . ."

"Do you think you'd ever want to be in a relationship again?" he asks.

"From what my friend Darcy says, you may be the only man on the planet looking for a relationship."

"Is that a no?" he asks. "Or a yes? Or a maybe?"

"Theoretically," I say, "the answer is yes. I loved having someone to share my day with, to joke around with, someone who got all my little flaws and weirdnesses and loved me anyway. Things were just so easy with Michael, and I trusted how I felt with him, I trusted our relationship, and now I find out I shouldn't have. So there's something in me that doesn't trust in love, doesn't trust in my own judgment, doesn't know if I can ever trust another man."

"But you'll never know if you don't put yourself out there again."

I nod, as though I'm considering what he just says, but really I'm thinking that putting myself out there has not exactly been a winning strategy for me so far.

"So, you're not dating anyone?" he asks. I reminisce about the oddball collection of weirdos and jerks I've encountered over the last few weeks.

"No," I say. "Not dating anyone." I pause. "Well, except for tonight." He smiles in response and it feels good. But it also feels scary.

"Tonight is perfect," he says.

"What about you?" I ask. I'm high on adrenaline and oddly thrilled that he's asking about my dating life. I may have no real practice with relationships with the opposite sex, but I know he's testing the waters. And that feels flattering and powerful in a way that has my skin flushed and my extremities tingling.

"It's been a long time," he says. "I've been focused on the idea of opening my new restaurant for a while. I meet a lot of really nice people, but I haven't met the right person, if you know what I mean. And sometimes I get lost in my work and everything else falls by the wayside."

"Me too," I say.

"Lately, though, I haven't been able to focus at all."

I laugh. "What's the trouble?" I ask. "Not enough sleep? Too much stress?"

"The trouble," he laughs, "is that a lovely and fascinating woman seems to occupy far more of my mind than anything else."

"Have you tried hypnosis?" I ask, still playing along.

"I'm already hypnotized. And mesmerized," he says, blue eyes burning into mine. I'm starting to feel a little mesmerized myself.

54

He reaches across the table and touches my hand, sending tremors through my body. What is it about this man?

"Alex," he says, "will you see me tomorrow night?"

"I'd love to," I say, "but Boudreaux is opening in less than a week. Are you sure you can spare the time?"

He smiles in response. "We can work all day and spend time together at night. Once Boudreaux opens, it will probably be a while before I get another night free. I'd like to spend all the ones I have left with you, if you can stand me."

"You're pretty tough to take." I laugh. "But I'll consider it." He grins.

"Thank you very much, *cher*," he says. "I'm honored."

"So am I," I say laughing.

"Is there anything special you'd like to do this week?" he asks.

"I'm open," I say.

"Well then, leave it all to me."

When the waiter brings the check a few minutes later, I reach for it automatically.

Daniel beats me to it.

"You're the client," I protest.

"I'm your date," he says earnestly. "It's our first actual date, if you don't count last night. If we're working, you can treat. If we're flirting, canoodling, romancing, I will. Deal?"

"You always cook for me when we're working," I say.

"Lucky you." He smiles. He's sweet, chivalrous, and I find it impossible to say no to those eyes.

Once Daniel has settled the bill, he puts his hand at the small of my back and and we walk outside.

"Thank you for the lovely meal," I say.

"Thank you for the lovely company," he replies.

The night is warm, but the humidity has relented and downtown buzzes with activity. There are open-air restaurants, shops, galleries, and bars lining Main Street, and we stroll along taking in the atmosphere. Daniel reaches for my hand as we walk, and my heart beats faster at the sweetness of his gesture. We've been walking west from the restaurant, down toward the bay front, and when we're five or six blocks away, the sky opens up and produces a torrential downpour. We're instantly soaked, and we duck into a small co-op art gallery to escape the storm.

The place is busier than usual; aside from the usual tourists there are lots of others who were caught in the storm as well. Wordlessly, Daniel and I look at the works by local artists, from pottery to paintings.

"It's funny, she sort of looks like you," says Daniel. The painting is a nude, and I have to admit the subject's face and body type look an awful lot like mine. It's eerie, almost.

And then I spot the mole on the subject's left hip.

Same as mine.

Oh Jesus. My face burns scarlet and dread starts to build in my gut. I glance around quickly to ascertain the artist's name. Could this just be an incredibly awkward coincidence? Maybe lots of women who look exactly like me have moles on their hips too. Like we're all made in the same factory or something. Finally, I spot it, on a plaque near the bottom of the display, along with a photo of the artist. Nathaniel Roche.

Oh, holy hell. Nate, the tool-belt supermodel drywaller is an artist? Jesus! I didn't think he was *really* an artist. Not an *artist* artist. I thought he just meant that in the same way every waiter in LA says they're an actor. This can not be happening.

I feel the blood draining from my extremities, and it's pretty clear I'm about to have a full-blown panic attack. This nude painting is of *me*. My hair, my mouth, my breasts (which, I must admit, don't look half bad), my tiny mole on my left hip. I know Nate saw the mole because he spent a good deal of time that night tracing it with his finger. Oh Jesus. Did he sketch me while I was in the shower or something? Was it all from memory? I feel so violated. And mortified that Daniel, a guy I really, really like, is essentially seeing me naked on our first real date. Not cool.

"Are you interested in this piece?" asks a female voice from behind me. She's an older woman, maybe seventy, with curly gray hair, a rainbow-colored infinity scarf, and paint-speckled fingernails.

"It's lovely," says Daniel to the woman. He leans over and whispers to me, "It is incredibly beautiful, but maybe not your taste, not something you'd hang in the living room?"

"Would you like to meet the artist?" asks the woman. "He's here tonight."

Oh sweet Jesus. Nate is here? We need to leave. Right now.

"Not tonight, thank you," I say, dragging Daniel toward the door. "We have to be going. So sorry!"

Daniel looks confused but smiles politely at the saleswoman, and then follows me out into the rain anyway. The torrential downpour stopped as quickly as it started, and now it is merely sprinkling.

"Do you mind walking in the rain a bit?" I say to Daniel, dragging him down the street.

"Not at all," he says. "I love walking in the rain. Do you want to tell me what happened back there?"

"It was just . . . odd . . . ," I stutter. "It did look a lot like me, and I just felt really . . . awkward."

"I understand," says Daniel.

He probably can't, really, unless a one-night stand happened to paint him in the nude also, but I appreciate his kindness. If he has any suspicions that the woman in the painting is me, he isn't saying a word about it. And for that, I am grateful.

But I am going to kill Nate.

55

Daniel and I walk back to his car holding hands, and I hardly want to let go once we reach the passenger door—as though it might never happen again. Daniel closes my door and gets into the driver's side.

As he starts up the car he says, "It went by too fast."

I know just what he means. The traffic is light and we arrive at my house around fifteen minutes later. Daniel parks his car in my driveway and walks me to my front door. I pull my keys out of my purse and stick the house key in the lock. I debate with myself as I turn the key—should I invite Daniel in or not? Asking him in for a cup of coffee or a nightcap would be the polite thing to do, but I'm worried that if I let him past my front door that things will move too fast between us. And unlike Nate, I really care for Daniel. I don't want to let my outright lust get the best of me before I have a chance to get to know him better.

"Thank you for a lovely evening," I say.

"Thank you for having dinner with me tonight," he says, as he leans forward ever so slowly. His lips are an inch or so from mine, and every cell in my body wants him to kiss me. I lean forward just a bit, bringing my lips closer to his. We stand like that until the agony of anticipation is too powerful to overcome. He slides his arm around my waist and leans in to kiss me, his body pressing deliciously against mine. I let myself melt into his embrace, my arms around his neck.

We stand out there for a long, long time, kissing against the door. I drink in every detail of the moment, the scent of his skin, his soft yet insistent mouth, the length of his eyelashes when he closes his eyes to kiss me, the firmness of his back and arms. I want to invite him in, but I'm certain of what will happen if I do. My body is as ready as it's ever been, but my brain is warning me to go slowly, take my time, get to know him better before I leave his clothes in shreds at the bottom of my bed.

"Invite me in," he whispers softly in my ear. His kisses trail from my ear down my neck, leaving a wake of shivers and goose bumps in their path. My flesh is on fire, and it would be so easy to say yes. I want to say yes.

"It's too . . . soon," I say breathlessly, "I need to slow things down."

He smiles and his blue eyes dance in the porch light. He leans forward and kisses me gently on my lips, slowly moving to my cheek and kissing me again, and then nuzzling my neck. "We'll go as slow as you want, *cher*."

He steps back, kissing me once more, softly, on the cheek. "Until tomorrow, then."

"Tomorrow," I say wistfully, wondering if I'm out of my mind for letting this delicious, gorgeous man go off into the night. I sigh, step inside my front door, and watch him leave through the open door.

He steps back from the front porch and walks to his car.

"Sweet dreams," he says, just before he opens his car door.

"Sweet dreams," I reply.

He grins. "I'm certain of that."

Wistfully, I watch Daniel leave.

And the spilt second he pulls out of my driveway, I'm on the phone with Darcy.

"Nate is a painter."

"Hunky tool-belt Nate?" she asks. "Wait . . . I thought he was a drywaller."

"No, I mean he paints portraits."

There's a long, long pause on the other end of the line.

"What kind of portraits?" she asks.

"Nudes," I say.

"Oh shit."

56

I feel this incredible new buzz of sexual tension every time I'm around Daniel that I never experienced before with Michael. I didn't know any better. I didn't know it could be different, that it *should* be different. Maybe, like me, Michael didn't know either, until he did.

Everything is fun with Daniel, not just our nights out together, which have been incredible—but the mundane stuff too, like the two hours we spent rearranging tables for the setup in the bar. The space is unusual, so it took a few tries. (Okay, like eighteen.) But Daniel was so patient, and he kept me laughing while he moved them all around, back and forth, until the arrangement was perfect.

Designing the environment for Boudreaux is a challenge, because what Daniel wants it to be is intangible in many ways. How I dress a restaurant signals its customers what to wear, how long to stay, how much their check will be, and what kind of experience to expect. But what Daniel wants Boudreaux to communicate is an extension of himself. Elegant but comfortable, polite, Southern, hospitable, creative, romantic, fun. The Boudreaux legacy. Those values are challenging to convey in the selection of table linens, the size and grouping of tables, the angles of the chair backs and depth of the seat cushions, the flow of foot and staff traffic from dock to deck. They are, however, embodied in Daniel, in who he is as a person and a chef. I've decided the best way to give Boudreaux the feel of Daniel Boudreaux himself is to create a neutral backdrop for his warmth and creativity, using soft, flowing whites and colors of the sea. Mixing the traditional with the new, and pulling every bit of history and charm out of that boat that he loves so much, from the polished mahogany bar to the stunning arched leaded-glass windows to the collection of photographs of Daniel's beloved family of cooks and grand Louisiana eateries.

It feels like we've spent every minute together this week, working on Boudreaux all day, and then hanging out together, laughing and relaxing into the night. It's scary to me, how fast I'm falling for him. But there's something about him that makes me feel safe, something that feels like we've known each other forever.

I'm just afraid to trust it.

I mean, I felt that way about Michael and look what happened.

Daniel seems so fearless to me. It's like he's not even worried about the possibility of things ending in a big ball of flames. I'm not sure I could ever do that.

On Thursday night, two days before Daniel's opening, we get all dressed up for a big night on the town, and end up in an epic Yahtzee battle for the mermaid statue from the storage room. We never quite manage to make it off the boat.

Because if you've ever had a Yahtzee smackdown with a guy with deep and dreamy blue eyes, you know what a turn-on that can be.

57

It's almost noon on Friday and Daniel and I are still wrapped up in the sheets and each other's arms. We stayed up late, all night and into the morning, making love and talking about everything under the sun, like we wanted to know every single thing about each other before a giant meteor hit the planet and the world ended. I know it's *technically* been less than a week since our first date, even though we've known each other for a couple of months, and I wanted to take things slowly—but we've been spending practically every minute together and he feels like someone I've known forever. Maybe it's weird to feel this way so soon, even when I swore to myself I'd be cautious, but he feels safe, trustworthy, like we belong in each others' lives.

Also, he's sexy as hell and my willpower reserve is completely, down-to-the-dregs depleted. Not even emergency measures like granny panties or hairy armpits could have kept me out of his bed by this point.

Sunlight streams through the skylights and the breeze off the bay gently billows the sheer curtains to the rhythm of the sea. I lean against Daniel, nestled in the crook of his arm, and he tenderly strokes my hair and plants tiny kisses on the side of my face, as though he's memorizing every detail. I've never slept on a boat before, and even though the ship is large and steady, there's still a barely perceptible movement with the water—I slumbered more deeply and had more vivid dreams than I could ever remember having had before.

"Are you hungry, *cher*?" asks Daniel, and I nod in response. I'm starved. Daniel sits up to get out of bed, and I marvel at his firmly muscled back and strong shoulders. The kind of muscles that come from working hard, a lean strength earned from enjoying every opportunity of living life by the ocean: paddling a surfboard, windsurfing, kayaking, and swimming out to the sandbar.

"*How could you, Daniel?*" a furious, clearly distraught woman screams from the top of the spiral stairs. She storms in, her face red with rage and heartbreak. She's tall, maybe six feet, with long black hair cut bluntly, angry dark eyes, and the pale skin of a vampire. I have no idea who she is to Daniel, but I feel like the worst sort of woman. Panicked, I gather the bedsheet around me, and scramble to find my clothes, which are strewn about the floor.

"Sasha, please calm down," says Daniel, holding a pillow in front of his manhood. Like that's going to save him. This woman is pissed, and from the looks of it, she has every right to be.

"I will not calm down," she screams at him. "How could you do this to me? Who is this . . . woman?" She says it like it's a dirty word, and I feel the shame coloring my complexion.

"I'm sorry, so sorry," I mumble, yanking on my dress and scooping up my shoes, my bag, and horrifically, my bra, which is lying just a few feet in front of this tall, screaming woman. She glares at me as I speedily retrieve it. I have no idea where my underwear has gone, but I'm sure as hell not going to stick around to find out.

"Alex, wait," says Daniel, but I'm already halfway down the spiral staircase. Barefooted and brokenhearted, I sprint past the workers on the boat and run down the dock in my bare feet. The ground is searing hot, and I hop onto a little patch of grass to slip on my shoes. I promise myself I won't cry until I'm safely alone in my car, but the tears start coming and I can't stop them. I lecture myself that it's only been a week with Daniel, there's hardly anything between us, that I clearly don't know him as well as I thought I did if he would do this to another woman, and involve me, just as I'm getting back on my feet again. By the time I reach my car, my body is wracked with sobs. Desperately searching for a Kleenex or even an old drive-through napkin to stop the snot now streaming out of my nose, I tell myself that it isn't just Daniel I'm upset about, that the experience with the screaming woman just brought up my feelings about Michael. But on a cellular level, I know that isn't the truth. I'm crushed that Daniel is not the person I thought he was. I liked him, I really liked him. And even though we've only been romantic for less than a week, what we have together felt bigger than the amount of time we'd acted on our feelings. What we have together felt real.

I allowed myself to let go with him. And I hate the fact that my instincts have steered me off a cliff once again.

58

"He's an asshole," says Darcy. "You can do better. I'm coming over tonight and we'll drink mojitos and talk smack about him."

I'm sitting in my car at the stoplight near the kissing statue.

"As much as I appreciate the offer," I say, "I can't drown my sorrows in mojitos tonight. I have the wildlife fund-raiser and I should have been at the job site an hour ago. I'll bet Olivia is completely freaking out."

My phone buzzes, speak of the devil. It's Olivia herself.

"I'll call you later," I say to Darcy. "My client is on the other line."

"Which one?" asks Darcy.

"The socialite," I say.

"Well, that manicured ball of insanity should keep your mind off anything to do with Daniel," Darcy says. "Call me later."

We hang up, and I switch over to speak with Olivia Vanderbilt Kensington.

"Olivia, hi, how is everything going?" I ask, driving home as quickly as traffic will allow. I need to get home, shower and change, and make it back to the Ritz-Carlton for Olivia's event as quickly as possible. I should never have spent the night at Daniel's. For lots of reasons.

Olivia is in full-blown panic mode.

"Where *are* you?" she hisses. "My event is in six hours!"

"I'm on my way," I lie. "I'll be there within the hour and I'm yours for the rest of the day."

"Unacceptable," says Olivia curtly.

"I'll be there as quickly as I can," I say. "See you soon." The phone line goes dead suddenly. Did she hang up on me? What grown-up person goes around just hanging up on someone, just because they're angry? My irritation at the manners breach is short-lived; mostly I'm relieved to get off the phone with her. I love my clients, at least most of them. But I know I'll feel relieved once Olivia's event is over and I don't have to deal with her ten calls a day and her random and irrelevant dog grooming skirmishes and hatred of tourists and ball gown issues, ninety-nine percent of which have absolutely nothing to do with me or the Wildlife Foundation. I'll smooth things over with her once I arrive at the Ritz-Carlton. I've done a dozen events there over the last few years, and I'm always pleased by how elegantly and efficiently they pull together my event plans. Olivia's wildlife fundraiser is going to be amazing, and I have full confidence she'll get that 20 percent bump in donations she hired me for. One more day, and I'll be done with her.

As much as I prefer to be at an event site all day on the day of, I've already been at the Ritz every day this week preparing the staff. They completed most of the setup before I left yesterday evening. And we were fortunate that the main ballroom wasn't booked on Thursday, so we were afforded an extra day to prepare. Christie, the hotel's fantastic events manager, has my highly detailed notebook for every element of tonight's benefit, and the staff at the Ritz are top-notch at execution.

Besides, most of my work has already been completed; all that is left is to ensure that every detail is perfect before we open the doors to guests for cocktails at six-thirty.

There was really no need for me to be at the Ritz at the crack of dawn. But I feel guilty about it anyway. And life would be a little sweeter right now if I were at the job site, rather than in Daniel's bed, thirty minutes ago.

My phone buzzes again, and I look down to see if it's Olivia calling again. Daniel's devastating face appears on my phone. I hit IGNORE and toss the phone in my purse. I can't bear to speak with him right now. I need time to pull myself together. Thankfully, the wildlife event offers me a valid reason to ignore his calls. I already told Daniel I'd be busy all day today. I'm crushed.

Five minutes later I pull into my driveway, and my phone buzzes again. Daniel again. I ignore that call as well. The grand opening of Boudreaux is tomorrow night, and while I'll have to spend a good chunk of the day at the floating restaurant tomorrow prepping for the big event, I won't have to see Daniel again after tomorrow night. My heart sinks. Oh Jesus. Will that woman who barged in this morning be at Daniel's opening? Will she be hanging around the boat all day, glaring at me while I try to do my work? What a nightmare. Of course, she probably has every reason to glare at me. I'm apparently the other woman.

An odd thought strikes me and I wonder if this was how Bobby Cavale, the basketball player that Michael had the affair with, felt when he learned that Michael was married. Did Michael at least tell Bobby so that he could go into whatever they had with his eyes open? Or did Michael spring it on him like he had me? A horrible thought crosses my mind. What if Daniel is married? I never even asked, I just assumed he wasn't. I feel sick at the thought. Not that it isn't bad either way. I'm not sure if a ring and a piece of paper deepen the heartbreak over infidelity, I think it probably sucks either way.

I hurry into the house, drop my bra, my bag, and my wrap by the front door, and head for the shower. Morley, who clearly misses me, follows me into my master bathroom, and rubs up against my bare legs.

"Hey Morley," I say as I lean down to pick him up, "did you miss me?" He purrs for a split second, and then hisses at me, extending his back claws to deliver a nasty scratch on my belly. "Good to see you too," I mutter as I set him back down on the bathroom floor. "No," I say, my voice rising. "It's not good to see you when you scratch me and hiss at me." Now I'm yelling. At the cat. "I love you, and I take care of you, and I deserve some respect!" Morley looks at me like I've lost my mind.

I feel better, weirdly better, as I shower quickly, taking special care to rinse Morley's most recent scratch, which is bleeding just a little. Take that, rotten cat.

I decided to forgo shaving my legs because I figure no one will get close enough to notice and I'm pressed for time, but I shave my armpits because I can't stand not to. Drying off quickly with a fluffy white towel, I grab a vibrant red skirt and jacket, and throw them on the bed as I track down a strand of silvery beads, a funky statement ring, and a pair of pewter-colored heels that I can stand in all day while still looking fabulous. I dry my hair quickly, and pull my event go-bag out of my closet. Usually when I do fund-raisers like this, I need to work all day getting the event set up, and then quickly dress for the benefit itself. My go-bag has everything I need for a quick change and up-do: perfume, deodorant, wardrobe tape and emergency supplies, a pair of ballet flats, a strapless bra, a small metallic Jimmy Choo clutch that goes with everything, and a palate of smoky evening makeup, all labeled and neatly organized inside. It saves me time not having to pull the items together every time I have an evening event.

Once my hair is dry and my makeup applied, I dress in the suit and add the jewelry and shoes I've chosen.

Red is the color of power, and I need it to reign in Olivia Kensington Vanderbilt quickly once I arrive on site. Her panic and neediness will only slow things down. Red is the leader, red is the boss, red is in charge.

I pull my favorite pair of sparkly, strappy heels from my closet and my go-to little black dress for the evening. I'm set.

Thirty-five minutes later I'm out the door, lugging my usual working tote and my evening go-bag, along with a garment bag containing my dress for the benefit slung over my shoulder. I hang the dress and the go-bag in the backseat, and stick my tote in the passenger seat. My phone is ringing again and I decide to ignore it. I run back into the house to refill Morley's bowls with fresh water and food, and then at last, I'm ready to go to the Ritz-Carlton to meet Olivia. It's not even one o'clock yet, and I'm already wishing for the day to be over.

I speed off toward downtown and the Ritz-Carlton, happy that the midday traffic isn't too bad. It's only fifteen minutes later when I pull into the valet stand at the Ritz. I gather my belongings from the back of the car, and head into the ballroom. My phone is buzzing yet again, but I'm too loaded down to answer it. It's probably Olivia anyway.

"You're here!" says Olivia as I enter the ballroom. "I thought you'd never arrive."

"I'm here," I say. "It's going to be a wonderful event."

"I certainly hope so," she sniffs.

The ballroom has been transformed. The emerald tablecloths, or more specifically, the Pantone Emerald 17-5641 tablecloths, look rich and warm. Large double-sided photos of giant-panda faces hang from the ceiling. This is part of what is called priming; studies show that charitable giving increases when there are "eyes" in the room. Hence the panda photos. They're beautiful images, by world-renowned wildlife photographer Andy Rouse, and they're not only compelling but inescapable. The specific color of green I've chosen psychologically primes guests to be more generous, in a similar way. I'm managing the pedestrian traffic flow in the room with a combined understanding of group dynamics and physical barriers. Elements as simple as a tall floral arrangement and the volume of music in a certain area will encourage the flow of guests to pass through the sea of emerald, directly past the succession of panda photos, then to the bar, and then to the "capture" area, where the guests, who will now be both primed and lubricated, can be personally cultivated by Olivia and other Wildlife Foundation board members for their generous donations. The pandas are the showstoppers, but other large images of beautiful and endangered animals line the walls as well. Olivia gave me a full list of the species her organization is working to save, like the desman, which reminds me of a cross between an anteater and a sewer rat, with all the photogenic appeal of both. The desman, while benefitting from the funds raised tonight, will not be lending its beady little eyes to our cause.

The golden triangle, as we call it, is the cluster of tables at the front and center of the room. They are for the organization's most generous and frequent donors, and much of our 20 percent bump will come by way of their wallets. We want them to feel like rock stars. Personalization is key to success with this group, so I made flash cards with their photos, names, and personal information and provided them to all the board members and Olivia's staff—basically, anyone from the Wildlife Federation who would be interacting with the guests. I've quizzed Olivia and her crew repeatedly, and they now knew every key donor by face, name, occupation, marital status, and dinner selection. Just the day before, I spent an hour with them playing a sort of "donor bingo" to help them memorize, doling out chocolate kisses to winning staff members who correctly identified five key donors in a row. Olivia, scrawny as she is, is surprisingly competitive when it comes to chocolate treats.

Not only do the staffers need to know the guests by face, they need to work to ensure the guests know one another as well, not only their names, but all the areas they have in common. Peer group expectation can be instrumental in increasing donations, and our event is doing everything we can to leverage that.

I review Olivia's speech for the evening once more, reminding her yet again to ask the audience to think about how babies make them feel, which has been found to double donations in many settings. It seems like an odd question at a benefit for endangered wildlife, but it's my job to work it into Olivia's speech as naturally as possible. That question is magic. The same is true for words that evoke religious imagery—which makes people behave more generously, too—and I've sprinkled some of those words throughout Olivia's speech as well.

By four o'clock, everything is ready. The room is perfect, the staff is prepped. Olivia retires to her suite upstairs to ready herself for the party. Now that everything is done, it probably would have been easier for me to just return home to get ready for the benefit, but after my late arrival this afternoon, I don't want to cause Olivia any more stress. She's already so nervous she might start molting.

Bringing my cocktail dress and my go-bag to the ladies' powder room, I change into my evening clothes, touch up my makeup with a smokier evening eye, and pin my hair up into a simple chignon. I add jewelry and my ballet flats, and I'm ready to go by four-twenty. Two hours to kill before the event. I'll change into my heels just before the guests arrive. I quickly repack my bag and check my phone. It's been buzzing all afternoon, and I've ignored it until now. There are a half-dozen voice mails from Daniel. Part of me is desperate to know what he has to say, but I'm not sure I can hear his voice and keep myself together for the long night ahead, so I ignore them for now. Self-preservation. There are four texts from Daniel as well, and I allow myself to look just at the first one.

It reads, *Alex, I'm so sorry about today, please let me explain.*

Not a chance, buddy.

There's also a text from Darcy:

Have a great event tonight. Big things are coming your way.

There are two messages from Fred, Michael's dad, but when I listen to them there's just a bunch of hissing and wind sounds, like he was butt-dialing me while driving with his booty hanging out of a convertible going seventy down the interstate. I'll call him later.

When I emerge from the powder room, Olivia is still up in her suite. I settle myself in a seating area just outside the ballroom, pull out my iPad, and make some notes for Daniel's opening night tomorrow. I also make a few follow-up calls to be certain everything will be ready, so that I can spend as little time on that boat as possible. Usually, I stay for my clients' events, but I'm planning to leave as soon as the guests arrive and the opening night celebration for Boudreaux is under way. I can't bear the thought of staying any longer than absolutely necessary—I'm embarrassed and hurt, and the last thing I need is to spend an evening mooning over lying, cheating Daniel. I knew, I just knew, he was too good to be true. They always are.

I laugh bitterly to myself. I'm awfully cynical for a woman who's only seriously dated two men in her entire life. Still, at this rate, two is enough. Count me out.

Taking a deep breath, I force myself to concentrate. Focus on the work. The work will save me. I review the plans for Boudreaux, finding very little to tweak. My week with Daniel had left me so exultant that the work is inspired. I finally feel that I've been able to capture the essence of who Daniel is for Boudreaux. Well, who I thought he was, at least. I can hardly wait to see it executed Saturday night. Boudreaux is going to be spectacular. Too bad I'm never going to set foot on that glorious boat again after tomorrow night.

Cliff Roles, society photographer, arrives about six, a half hour before guests are scheduled to arrive.

"Hello, darling," he says in his charming English accent. "Gorgeous event tonight," he says, kissing me on both cheeks.

"Hello, Cliff," I say. "I'm so glad you're here."

"Wouldn't miss it, darling," he says.

As always, I ask him to snap some shots of the empty ballroom to include in my portfolio. The Wildlife Foundation benefit is a big event that will likely attract a lot of other society clients. It's an important opportunity for me.

While he takes pictures, I swap my ballet flats for strappy heels, and stash my go-to bag and tote under a skirted table in the staff area.

Olivia arrives in the ballroom at six-ten, just as Cliff is finishing up his photos for me. They do the double-kiss cha-cha, and chat for a few moments. Cliff is completely in his element at the society shindigs. Everyone loves Cliff. And they pay homage if they have any hope at all of inclusion in the society pages. Cliff asks Olivia and me to pose together for a photo, which is surely a greater favor to me than to her. But I'm glad for it. Even if my eyes are half closed or my posture makes me look like a hunchback, that picture will be going up on my Web site. Now all I need is for all my hard work to create a 20 percent increase in donations. This part is always scary. Because even though I believe in the science, there's always a risk when you tie your success to the behavior of other people. Humans are, by and large, manageable. But they can also be unruly, illogical, and often unpredictable. And quickly influenced by outside forces. Which is part of what makes my work so challenging. The very elements that help me to succeed can also easily and quickly precipitate my failure. It's basically like herding squirrels. Or coaxing them to wear little top hats or purple sneakers. And then convincing them to hand over their hard-earned nuts.

Olivia's staff, the orchestra, and the bartenders are in place at six-fifteen, and I make the rounds giving last-minute instructions. I tell the bartenders to pour generously, and remind the conductor to make sure he hits the selections on my playlist, chosen for their ability to evoke specific emotions, at the precise cues I've outlined.

The guests begin to filter in at six-thirty, and I watch them react as I'd hoped to the emotionally charged imagery of the great pandas. The early guests follow my traffic plan precisely, which thrills me. It's the earliest guests who determine the traffic pattern for the rest of the evening—the guests who arrive after those first crucial few just follow along in their footsteps. Olivia's team is on hand, and judging from the conversations taking place, the donor flash card drills are having their desired effect. Cliff is working the ballroom, snapping pictures of donors enjoying the open bar and the company of their well-heeled peers.

Everything is coming together perfectly. Even Olivia, for once, looks pleased. Her face, pulled tight from years of costly maintenance, has almost stretched into the makings of a smile.

And then, everything falls apart.

59

It's Daniel.

He enters the ballroom, unfairly handsome in his tailored black suit. He moves with confidence and a little swagger, and it's devastating to just stand there and watch him. He spots me a few seconds after

I first see him and he makes a beeline for me, cutting through the tables.

This is not happening. Moving quickly toward the staff area in the back, I hope against hope that he won't follow me. I've spent all day trying to block what happened at his place out of my head. I'm not ready to talk to him, and there is no way I'm discussing today's humiliation in the middle of one of the biggest events of my career.

He makes better time than I do, unjustly so, because I'm tiptoeing along in high heels, and he's unfairly blessed with longer legs and more practical shoes.

"Alex, I need to talk to you," he says. His blue eyes are so earnest, and I have to focus very hard not to let myself get sucked under his spell.

"I'm working," I hiss, still making my way back toward the staff area.

"Alex, please stop," he pleads. "I just need to talk to you." I spin around and motion for him to follow me behind the wall.

"What are you doing here?" I demand.

"I bought a table," he says. "I knew this was your event and you weren't taking my calls. I just needed to explain—"

"I'm *working*," I say more loudly. "This is my job. You can't be here right now. I need to focus and you being here makes that impossible."

"I'm so sorry," he says, reaching out to touch my arm, "if you'll just let me explain."

I yank back my arm. "Don't touch me," I snarl. "You can say whatever you want to say to me tomorrow. Right now, I need you to leave. If you have any respect for me at all, if you care even a little bit about my feelings, you'll go. I can't deal with . . . this . . . tonight."

His eyes fall downward. "I'm so sorry, *cher*," he says quietly. "I'll go. I didn't want to upset you. I just wanted to . . . talk."

"Thank you," I say, letting out a sigh of relief as he turns to walk away.

"You look so beautiful tonight," he says. And finally, after lingering too long, he walks away.

And while I'm mostly outraged that he would just show up here tonight, a small part of me is heartsick to see him leave. I hide out unseen behind the wall leading to the staff area and watch him go. To my surprise, he stops to speak with Olivia Kensington Vanderbilt for a minute or so before he exits. She embraces him warmly as though they've known each other for years. The man certainly does get around. My curiosity piqued, I wait until Daniel exits the main doors and then casually with a purpose make my way over to Olivia.

"Was that Daniel Boudreaux I saw?" I ask, attempting to appear nonchalant.

"Yes, it was," says Olivia. "What a lovely young man."

I push my luck with her a little further.

"What did he want?" I ask. Olivia glares down her nose at me.

"I don't see how it's any of your business," she says, "but he gave me a lovely donation for the foundation. Five thousand dollars."

I'm completely taken aback. "He did?"

Olivia rolls her eyes at me. "Are we ready to start the program or not?"

60

I'm fortunate that my work for the benefit is completed, because I can't get Daniel out of my head. Standing at the edge of the ballroom, I sip a glass of ice water and make sure that everything goes off as scheduled.

The program moves from drinks and dinner into the presentation and auction. By the time the auction is at full steam, the guests are deeply connected to the plight of the animals, and primed for generosity. Once the auction is finished, the orchestra plays on so that donors can continue to socialize and dance. The bar too stays open. Olivia and her team work the tables; the golden triangle now wrung out, they make their way around the perimeter of the ballroom to squeeze every last donation they can muster.

I sit down at my table, relieved that the evening has seemingly gone off without a hitch. Which is probably my first mistake.

61

No one is certain what set off the fire sprinklers, but all of a sudden it's raining in the ballroom. The guests start scattering, squealing and running for the exits, and the hotel staff circles around the room in a panic, checking to see if someone has accidentally pulled down one of the fire alarms. There's no fire anywhere to be found. The catering manager radios the assistant hotel manager to stop the water, but it takes several minutes and half a dozen phone calls to contact the alarm company responsible for monitoring the system. The system can't be overridden off-site, for some reason, probably due to the same malfunction that set it off in the first place. So by the time the alarm company representative is on-site, the water is two inches deep in the serving bowls, and the entire room looks like the main dining room of the *Titanic* after it struck the iceberg and sunk to the bottom of the ocean.

Olivia is howling in the corner, her hairpiece drenched and hanging off the side of her head. Her soaked silver gown sticks to her scrawny body, and her eye makeup runs down her face in gray-blue streaks.

She lets out a bloodcurdling scream and screeches across the room as soon as she sees me: "This is *all your fault*. You're *fired*!!!!!!"

62

I've never been fired before. From anything. It's awful. I feel terrible and worthless and helpless.

Intellectually I know that the random malfunction of a fire sprinkler system doesn't have anything to do with me, but the humiliation I felt when Olivia Kensington Vanderbilt screamed my name across the Ritz-Carlton was going to poison my confidence with self-doubt for the rest of my years.

How could this happen? Everything was going perfectly. The irony is, I was just planning to leave when the sprinklers went off. My job was done. Donations were wrangled, the program was over, all that was left was dancing and gabbing, neither of which were under my purview. Plus, it had been a really, really long day. I needed a hot bath and a glass of wine and a really good night's sleep since my weekend from hell was only halfway finished.

"I'm sorry that this happened, Olivia," I say, not wanting to sound defensive, but also not willing to shoulder the blame for something I had absolutely no control over. "I'm going home," I say. "I'll speak to you on Sunday after we've both had time to think this through."

"You'll speak to me now," she yells.

"No," I say weakly. "I'm going home now."

I grab my go-bag and my tote, which, thankfully, are dry under the cover of the table where I left them. That's a relief. My whole life is on my iPad, as well as all the details for Boudreaux's opening night. I thank the Universe for the lucky break and stick to the perimeter of the room, where it's slightly less boggy, using my garment bag as a waterproof shield for my belongings as I make my way outside. The line for the valet seems miles long, understandable since three hundred benefit guests all decided to leave at once. I give the valet twenty bucks in exchange for my keys and walk to the parking lot in search of my car.

I spot him first, leaning casually against my car in the dim light of a streetlamp, holding a bouquet of pale pink roses and looking better than any man has a right to. Jesus, this isn't fair. His sea-colored eyes are searching mine, the color so intense I can still discern it ten paces away. I stop dead in my tracks just a few feet from him. His tailored suit hangs perfectly on his lean body, and I will myself not to be swayed by his obvious physical charms. Deep breath. I remind myself of this morning's humiliation, and in particular, the look on the face of the woman who surprised the two of us in bed. There's no way I'll let myself be responsible for causing that expression of hurt again. I know that feeling of betrayal. I know it as well as anyone.

"Why are you here?" I ask, sounding tougher than I feel.

"I'm sorry," he says. "I had to speak with you. If you'll just let me explain . . ."

"Daniel, I asked you to go. I've had a very long day, and a very long night, and a long day planned for tomorrow. I will listen to what you have to say tomorrow. Not tonight. Tomorrow. I'll be at Boudreaux at ten in the morning."

"And we can talk then?" he asks, his voice tinged with melancholy.

"It's your dime," I say cruelly. "Can I go now?"

He steps away from my car door, and I hit the button on the key fob to unlock it. Once it clicks, Daniel opens my door. I stop myself from glaring at him in response. He's a client, and I just have to make it through one more day.

I fling the go-bag and the garment bag in the backseat, and slide my tote and my tired body into the driver's seat. It's hard to believe that I was in bed with this man less than twelve hours ago. Now it seems like a lifetime.

"I'll see you tomorrow, then," says Daniel.

"Tomorrow," I reply coldly. He hands me the bouquet of pink roses, which are beautiful and delicate and surprisingly fragrant. I toss it in the passenger seat, and he gently closes my car door. I pull out of the parking space and drive away, never looking back.

63

It's never good when the phone rings at two o'clock in the morning. Someone has almost always died.

"Alex, can you come right away to the hospital? There's been an accident." It's Fred, Michael's father. "Sarasota Memorial."

"I'll be right there," I say. Fred won't tell me what's happened over the phone, which leads me to fear the worst. As quickly as I can, I get dressed, putting on jeans and a T-shirt, and pulling my hair up into a ponytail. My hair is still slightly damp from the long shower I took before bed. I finally got the tension knots out of my neck after almost an hour, and now I feel them coming back. I drive to the hospital in silence and darkness, my brain generating dozens of gruesome scenarios, the worst of which is that my best friend in life has died without me by his side. I am too numb to cry, too numb to call anyone. I feel like the only soul on the road.

I hardly slept at all before Fred's call, my mind shadowed with imaginary arguments between Daniel and myself where I scream at him over and over again, *How could you do this to me?* My brain produces no answers, of course, just the same heartbreaking questions over and over again on a cruel loop.

Pulling into the ER parking lot at Sarasota Memorial, I search in vain for Fred's car. I find an open spot and pull in, and rush inside the emergency room as fast as I can on wobbly, slow-moving legs. My heart is pounding so hard I think it might explode. Can you have a heart attack at thirty-one?

"Michael Miller," I say to the nurse at the front desk. She checks something on her computer and then waves me over to the waiting room.

"Are you family?" she asks.

"I'm his wife," I lie.

"Someone will be out to speak with you shortly." She gives nothing away, which I guess is probably a job requirement.

"Is he alive?" I blurt out.

The nurse's face tenses but her voice remains exactly the same, "Please be seated, someone will be out to speak with you shortly."

64

I close my eyes and pray silently, something I never do. I cannot bear the thought of living my life without Michael. We were supposed to grow old together. Even though we aren't still married, I think we both assumed that was how it would work out.

I call Fred, Michael's dad, and his phone goes straight to voice mail. Leaving a message, I tell him I'm in the waiting room. Next, I try texting, having no idea if Fred even knows how texting works. Again, I let him know where I am, just in case the message gets through to him.

My worry-addled brain spits out disastrous possibility after possibility of all the terrible things that could have happened to Michael. Car accident, poisoning, hotel bathtub electrocution. I remember a time not so long before when I halfheartedly wished for Michael's demise, and now I'm filled with guilt over the possibility that I somehow had a hand in whatever tragedy has befallen him.

I check my phone every few seconds searching for a response from Fred. An infomercial about prostate health blares from the television bolted to the wall overhead. The waiting room is like a collection of walking dead that time of night. Strange, quiet people with dark circles under their eyes and looks of despair, filling out endless paperwork. A small dark-haired child, who looks to be about three, snuggles with her mother while trying to get comfortable against the hard plastic chairs.

In twenty minutes, no one has come to get anyone. I walk to the nurses' station again.

"I'm here for Michael Miller," I say. "Can someone please tell me what's happened to him? Where is he?"

As the nurse checks her computer screen, Fred appears through the large double doors that lead inside the hospital. His large body appears older than his years; his eyes are bloodshot and his skin is ruddy from crying. I've never seen him look so distraught, not even when Michael's mother died.

I rush into his arms, "Oh my God, Fred. What happened? They haven't told me anything." He hugs me tightly, not letting go for a long time, sobbing into my shoulder. It must be bad, very bad.

"Michael was in a car accident coming home from the airport tonight. A drunk driver broadsided his car as he went through an intersection," says Fred. His emotions overtake him again and he sobs without being able to speak for a few moments. "The police found syringes in the back of the woman's car." I feel myself going woozy and struggle to say focused while Fred attempts to regain composure.

"He's in surgery now," Fred continues, and I let out a breath of relief. Michael is alive; no matter what else might have happened, he's still alive. Relief floods my body and I begin to cry. "He's got a shattered pelvis, four broken ribs, his arm is broken, his hip was dislocated, one of his lungs is bruised, his spleen ruptured, his sternum is fractured . . . concussion . . . he was impaled by a piece of metal in his abdomen . . . there's more but I can't recall exactly," he trails off.

"Is he going to be okay?" I ask. Jesus, with all that, Michael is lucky to still be alive. I can barely bring myself to ask the next question. "Is he going to live?"

"The doctors won't say," he cries. "They'll know more once he's out of surgery."

"Do they know how long it's going to take?" I ask tearfully. "When we'll be able to see him?" I'm paralyzed with disbelief. How could this happen? What was that driver thinking? Why did it have to be Michael? Fred takes my hand and leads me through the double doors to the surgery waiting room. It's significantly smaller than the ER waiting room, with soothing art that looks like it came off an assembly line, and small brown sofas instead of hard plastic chairs. It's empty except for one person, a man with dark hair, crying into his hands. He looks up as soon as Fred and I enter the room, and instantaneously I feel like I might throw up.

It's Santiago, the man Michael made a sex date with on the night of our divorce party.

"What's he doing here?" I say under my breath. Fred squeezes my hand.

"Santiago and Michael are together now," he says.

"We're in love," Santiago says defiantly. This is too much for me to process, with Michael in surgery, fighting for his life. I collapse onto the sofa opposite the one where Santiago is sitting. Fred gingerly sits down beside me.

"Were you with him when it happened?" I ask Santiago. It doesn't seem likely; he doesn't have a scratch on him.

"We were talking on the phone when he was hit," says Santiago. "He just landed at the airport and was calling to tell me he was on his way over." My stomach lurches. It still stings to think about Michael with anyone else. I hate myself for it, but I feel defensive and angry that Santiago is here. Who is he to Michael? A hookup? What right does he even have to be here? Fred and I are Michael's family, not him. He's just some . . . interloper.

"I heard it happen," Santiago weeps, "I heard the crash, and I heard Michael screaming, but he couldn't hear me." He sobs and his whole body shakes with grief. Without thinking, I move to the sofa where Santiago is sitting and put my arms around him. And before I know it, I'm sobbing with him.

A petite, red-haired woman enters the room carrying a clipboard.

"I'm so sorry to bother you," she says in a quiet voice. "I just need to complete some paperwork." She comes to sit down next to Fred and asks him, "Do you have Michael's insurance information?" Fred shakes his head no. He's devastated, barely functioning.

"I have it," I say. "I think I might still have his card in my purse, let me check." Santiago looks surprised as I dig around in my wallet and fish it out.

She asks the usual medical history questions, nearly all of which I know because I've been there all his life. Broken arm when he was eleven. Concussion at seventeen. Exercises every day. Moderate drinker. Doesn't smoke. Allergic to penicillin. Fred stares numbly at the wall and lets me handle the paperwork and the questions. It feels good to help in some small way, and for me, doing something, anything, is better than just sitting here helplessly waiting for bad news. Santiago watches me quietly as I speak with the hospital worker, and for the first time I wonder what this nightmare must be like from his perspective.

"Do you know how long it will be before we hear something?" I ask her, once the paperwork is completed.

"I'll try to find out something for you," she says kindly. She leaves the room, and Santiago, Fred, and I sit in silence. It's unbearably tense. The waiting room is too warm, and it smells weird, like feet and antiseptic.

"Can I get anyone some coffee or water from the cafeteria?" I ask.

Fred nods. "Thanks, Alex. Coffee would be nice."

"Santiago?" He shakes his head no and buries his face in his hands again. I pick up my purse and go off in search of the cafeteria. The hospital halls are dim and eerily quiet. After some wandering around, I locate a sign that directs me down a large hallway to the cafeteria. There are a few people clustered at tables, and one quiet worker sits at the cash register, reading a magazine. Coffee is self-serve, and I get some for Fred, with cream and two sugars, just the way he likes it. I pick up a couple of bottles of water for Santiago and myself, and select three turkey sandwiches from the refrigerated case. I'm not hungry, but Fred or Santiago might be. I pay for the food, and the cafeteria worker is kind enough to set me up with a carrying tray for the drinks, and a bag for the sandwiches. She dumps in a handful of condiments and napkins. I thank her and quickly make my way back to the waiting area, where Fred and Santiago are sitting silently.

"Any word yet?" I ask. Fred shakes his head no. Handing the coffee to Fred and a water bottle to Santiago, I ask if anyone is hungry. Santiago nods yes and I pass out the sandwiches.

"Eat something, Fred," I say. "You need to keep up your strength." He nods obligingly, unwraps the sandwich and bites into it. Santiago follows suit.

Eventually the hospital worker returns. Unfortunately, she doesn't have much of an update to share.

"He's still in surgery," she says. "His surgeons are doing everything they can to repair the damage. His doctor will come to update you as soon as they know more. He'll likely be in surgery for several more hours. The best thing you can do is try to get some rest." She pats me on my shoulder and leaves the room.

"Rest is a good idea," I say. "Fred, why don't you stretch out on that sofa, and Santiago, you can take the other one. I'll take the chair over here. There's nothing we can do for Michael right now." Fred finishes his sandwich and I go to the nurses' station in search of a few spare pillows. Fortunately, the cranky nurse who was at the desk when I arrived has been replaced by a young male nurse. When I explain why we're there, and ask him for a few extra pillows, he disappears into the back and emerges with three small, flat pillows. I thank him and take them back to the surgery waiting room, giving them to Fred and Santiago. Fred decides to take my advice, reclining his large body on the small sofa with his legs draped over the side. Santiago, a much smaller man, lies down as well, on his side with his feet poking forward. He fluffs the small pillow and stuffs it under his head.

Swigging half my bottle of water, I scan the doorway of the waiting room in search of a light switch. There's no way any of us are going to be able to rest with the fluorescent lights glaring overhead. Once I spot the switch, I flip it off. There are still a few small emergency lights illuminated, but the absence of fluorescents makes the room much dimmer and the slim possibility for sleep a bit more likely. I take my spot on the chair in the corner, propping the pillow under my head against the wall like you'd do on a crowded airplane. Closing my eyes,

I know I won't be able to sleep. My mind runs a loop of memories of Michael and me. First day of kindergarten. Laughing so hard we lost our breath, perched in the tree house in Michael's backyard. Michael's mom's funeral. Our first kiss. The day we got married. The day Michael broke my heart. Snuggling on the couch under a blanket watching old black-and-white movies. Cooking steaks on the grill on our very first night in our new house. All of it, going round and round my mind like a carousel.

I love Michael. I always have and I always will. And I promise the Universe that I'll be a better human being if Michael survives.

I thought I was still awake, but I must have finally dozed off at some point because I'm startled when someone flips on the light switch. It's a doctor, midfifties, in blue scrubs. His gray hair pokes out from under his surgical cap. Fred springs up off the couch to his feet. Santiago rises more slowly.

"Michael's still in surgery, but it looks like he's going to pull through. He had some internal bleeding, which we were concerned about, and we'll have to keep him here for the time being, but he's made it through the worst part and we think he's going to be okay."

Fred hugs the doctor tightly, and I thank him over and over again. Santiago still looks like he's in shock. The doctor runs through the list of Michael's various injuries and the resulting treatment, but I'm so relieved I barely register a word of what he's saying.

Michael is going to be okay. He's bruised and broken, but he's alive, and that is all that matters.

The doctor excuses himself and Fred, Santiago, and I stand together in the center of the room, holding on to one another and weeping with relief. We laugh, we cry, we hug, and we cry some more.

Fred and Santiago decide to get some breakfast while we're waiting for Michael to get out of surgery. I stay behind to send Daniel a text to let him know I won't be at Boudreaux at ten this morning as planned. The hard setup for Daniel's restaurant was completed earlier in the week, table clusters and items that impacted traffic flow. All that's left are the "soft" items, tablecloths and floral placement, which Daniel's waitstaff will be implementing anyway. I would just be there to supervise. Daniel's head waitress, Tina, and I have already gone over the plan, down to the smallest details, and the entire staff has copies of my event notebook, complete with photos of finished looks, tabbed and indexed in their own three-ring binders. And while the control freak in me hates to miss the setup for Boudreaux's opening night, I know everything will be exactly as I've planned it. And there is just no way I'm leaving the hospital before I have a chance to see Michael, hold his hand, and know he's going to be okay.

It's not even 5:00 A.M. yet, way too early to call. Next, I text Darcy, Sam, Carter, and Grandma Leona to let them know that Michael has been in an accident and is in surgery, but that he's going to be okay. I try to think of whom else I should contact. Michael's boss? My parents?

I have so many feelings. Loneliness, sitting there in the stillness of the empty waiting room. Relief, I guess, knowing Michael is going to pull through. Sick to my stomach, probably because of the cocktail of adrenaline, fear, and stress hormones circulating in my system. I have the oddest urge to call Daniel, just to hear his comforting voice with its gentle lilt. And then the memory of yesterday and the screaming woman comes roaring back into my consciousness, reminding me why that isn't possible. The Boudreaux opening-night party will be the last time I'll see him. At least on purpose. In a town this size, it's impossible to avoid someone forever. After the restaurant opens that night, my work with him will be finished. I feel a surge of melancholy mixed with relief that it's only one more night.

Grabbing my purse off the chair where I left it, I wander down the hallway toward the cafeteria, where Fred and Santiago have gone. I'm not really hungry, but in search of comfort instead. I hope they have pastries.

Fred and Santiago sit together at a table in the center of the room, eating what looks like breakfast sandwiches and talking like old friends. A twinge of jealousy hits me like an electric shock. When did they get to be so close?

Waving to them as I enter the room, I head to the cafeteria line to see if I can find something that looks appealing. Nothing much. I pour myself a glass of orange juice to give my blood sugar a jolt, and select an almond Danish from the case. Almonds have protein. Protein is healthy, even if said almonds are glazed in icing.

Joining Fred and Santiago, I set down my Danish and wipe the table where I planned to sit with a paper napkin, brushing away some crumbs of unknown origin.

"Alex, I'm sorry I forgot to ask. Have you met Santiago?" asks Fred as I sit down at the table and begin to pick at my Danish.

"We have met," I say. "Remember, he was at our divorce celebration? And then Carter reintroduced us at a dinner party for one of my clients, Daniel Boudreaux." Santiago nods.

"Good, good," says Fred, as though he can think of nothing else to say. The silence is killing me. Some part of me always feels the need to keep the conversation moving.

"Santiago, how long have you and Michael been together?" I ask.

"We met at your party, as you say," he says in his thick Cuban accent, "and we have been together since then. So, four months." I nod. "We are in love," he adds. It sounds almost defensive to my ears, but what do I know? And maybe he does feel like he needs to defend his relationship with Michael. Fred and I, we've known Michael for his entire life. As much as it feels to me like Santiago doesn't belong here at the hospital, it isn't my call to make. It's Michael's. And it's time for all of us to move on.

I ask Santiago about his work, and how he ended up in Sarasota. I talk to Fred about sports, mostly priming him with questions about his favorite baseball team and listening intently as he explains how the team is faring, injury status, and draft prospects. It's soothing, listening to him rattle on without much more input from me. Almost like sitting at the breakfast table with Michael. Santiago joins in sometimes, clearly passionate about baseball himself.

Around six-thirty, the three of us amble back to the surgery waiting area. The room is still empty, but the pillows we left from our stay overnight have been cleared away. With Fred and Santiago settled back on the sofas, I go down the hallway in search of a restroom. My teeth feel like they're wearing little wool socks, and I want to rinse off my face and brush my hair.

Hospital mirrors are unkind, and aside from my now-cockeyed ponytail and the bags under my eyes, my skin has a sort of greenish pallor to match the taste in my mouth. I dig a silvery package containing a mini–disposable toothbrush out of my purse, laughing to myself while recalling how Michael always teases me mercilessly about my need to overprepare for any possible contingency. Feeling significantly better after brushing my teeth and rinsing my face with cool water, I brush my hair and pull it back once again into a neat ponytail. I neglected to put on deodorant last night after I showered since I was heading right to bed. Sleeping in a hospital chair in a too-warm waiting room, plus the stress of the last few hours, has me feeling grimy and my armpits sweaty. There are no paper towels, only hand dryers, so I put a quarter in the machine and buy myself a sanitary napkin, wetting it with cool water and using it to give myself a birdbath in the sink. And that's just where I am when a nurse comes in to tell me that Michael is finally out of surgery—standing at the sink with my T-shirt hiked all the way up over my bra, giving myself a once-over with a wet maxi-pad.

65

Gathering my things quickly, I follow the nurse down the hallway to the surgical waiting room. The same surgeon from before is standing with Fred and Santiago, updating them on Michael's condition.

"He's in recovery now," says the doctor. "We'll keep him there for a while longer and then we'll be moving him into a room upstairs. Nurse

Lori will take you now. He's made it through the surgery, and should make a solid recovery."

Fred and Santiago nod.

"What does that mean, solid recovery?" I ask. "How long will it take for him to heal? How long will he need to be in the hospital? Will he have any permanent damage? Were his mental faculties impaired?"

"Healing time is dependent on the patient, and we won't necessarily know all the answers to your questions until he's woken up and we can see where he is. He was barely conscious when the ambulance brought him in, and he's still under anesthesia now. I'm sorry I don't have more specific information for you. He'll be in the hospital for at least another few days at the minimum, probably about a week. You might want to bring some of his things from home to make him more comfortable."

"Thank you, Doctor," I say. Fred and Santiago thank the doctor also, and he nods in response and excuses himself quickly.

"Okay," says Nurse Lori, "we'll have Michael moved up to the fifth floor in about an hour. His room number is five fifteen, and if you'd like to come with me, I can bring you upstairs."

Fred, Santiago, and I follow the nurse to the elevator, and down the hall to what will be Michael's hospital room. It's after 7:00 A.M., and the halls on the fifth floor are bustling with nurses, doctors making their rounds, and aides distributing breakfast trays. The room is nice, for a hospital room, and there's only one bed, which is a relief. Michael is a light sleeper and wouldn't do well with a roommate, some stranger's family and friends visiting all day long, *Wheel of Fortune* blaring from the TV.

My phone buzzes with a text message from Daniel:

Is Michael okay? Let me know if you can. Don't stress about the opening today. I'll handle it if you can't be here. Family is more important than anything else.

And another:

I'll be thinking about you. Please let me know if there's anything at all I can do for you. ANYTHING.

I respond, all business:

Thanks, I appreciate it. Michael's out of surgery. Tina has my event book and staff has been prepped. You should be all set to go. I'll try to stop by later to check on everything before the opening.

After a while, someone comes to take away the bed in Michael's room. I pace the hallways to work off some excess energy. I'm so conflicted about Daniel, and I want nothing more than to put him out of my mind. My mind, unfortunately, is not cooperating.

By seven-thirty, my phone starts buzzing with calls. First Carter, who has a complete and utter freak-out, and then Darcy, who says she'll cancel her day and head over about eleven. I'm not sure what Michael has scheduled for the day, so I leave a voice mail for his boss, whom I met in Connecticut when he was grilling me about Michael's sex life. I let him know that Michael was in an accident, hit by a drunk driver, and that he's in the hospital, and that either Michael or I will call him as soon as we know more. It feels like a wifely thing to do, calling his boss from the hospital, but it also feels like the job for his oldest and best friend.

By eight, Fred, Santiago, and I are starting to get nervous. It's been an hour and a half since Michael got out of surgery, and we haven't had an update since then. Another hour passes, and then another. By ten, I'm starting to freak out. I've already been to the nurses' station for updates a half-dozen times, but they don't seem to know any more than we do. And if they do, they aren't telling. Fred and Santiago sit waiting in Michael's room, while I continue to pace up and down the hallway. Sitting still, not doing anything, is not my forte.

Finally, Michael and his hospital bed come rolling down the hallway, pushed by an aide who looks like he probably plays lead guitar in a thrash metal band on the weekends. He has spiky black hair, and a touch of leftover eyeliner. A tattoo on his forearm is just visible at the edge of the white long-sleeved shirt he has under his scrubs. His name-tag reads RICK, but I'd bet anything he goes by something far cooler.

"Michael, oh my God, I was so worried about you," I say, rushing the gurney. His eyes are closed, but he moves a little when he hears me call his name.

"Hey, buddy," says the hospital aide with a kind smile. "Looks like you've got a visitor."

Michael's facial muscles are slack, and his eyes are woozy and unfocused as they flutter open. I want to dive onto the hospital bed right there in the hallway and hold him close, but I don't know where his injuries or sutures are, and I don't want to hurt him. He's covered in bandages, and his left arm is in a sling of some kind. He looks terrible.

"Alex," he murmurs. "I'm *so* glad you forgot to put the scissors in the blender. It's too cold for that. It's *too* cold. Don't forget the marshmallows. I love you."

I have no idea what he means by all that, but I translate it to mean he's happy to see me, and thrilled to be alive. And I'll delight in torturing him about the marshmallows for the next sixty years or so. It's the least I can do.

"I love you too," I say. "I'm so glad you're okay."

"Aww," he slurs. "I'm okay. Are you okay?"

"I'm okay now," I say, tears welling up in my eyes. "I'm okay because you're okay." His eyes close again and I reach out to touch his hand, holding it gently in mine the entire way back to Michael's room.

"So, the anesthesia takes a little while to wear off," laughs Rick, the aide.

I take a deep breath and smile. It's all going to be okay.

66

"Look who I found!" I say, as Rick pushes Michael's hospital bed into the room. Rick locks down the bed and rehangs Michael's IV. Fred stands at Michael's bedside with tears in his eyes, not saying anything at all. But the relief is all over his face.

Santiago rushes to the side of Michael's bed, speaking softly to him in Spanish, "*Oh, querido, querido . . .* ," which I think is both incredibly touching and yet a tiny bit hilarious, as Michael does not speak a word of Spanish. Santiago kisses Michael all over his forehead, and watching it feels a little bit like having an out-of-body experience. Here I am on one hand, witnessing this sweetly intimate moment, and on the other, a practical stranger is kissing my former husband. Fred is handling it pretty well. Maybe he's already seen plenty of Michael kissing someone other than me. Maybe, no matter how much time has passed, I'll never really get used to it. Or maybe I will.

The three of us huddle by Michael's bedside as he dozes in and out. Mostly out. Nurses enter and leave, checking Michael's IV, his bandages, and his blood pressure. They write their names on the little whiteboard hanging on the wall of Michael's hospital room, but there are so many of them it hardly seems helpful.

"He needs his rest," says one of the nurses. "You folks should take it downstairs for a while."

"Do you have his house key?" I ask Santiago, who nods yes. "When he wakes up, he'll want his pillow. He never leaves home without it." As soon as the words leave my mouth I realize that Michael was returning from a trip when his car was struck by the drunk driver. He probably had his pillow with him.

"Where's his car?" I ask.

Fred shakes his head. "No idea."

"I don't know," Santiago says.

"When the police called you about the accident, did the person leave their name?" I ask Fred.

"Yes," he says. "The officer left a message." He retrieves his phone and hands it to me. "It's the last one," he says.

Listening to the voice mail message from 1:51 that morning, I take down the number of Detective Lynn Brown.

"I'll run it down," I say.

Detective Brown answers on the first ring. I ask her about the accident and she gives me the name and number of the tow company that is storing Michael's car. I call them next. Their lot is only a few miles away. I wonder if I still have Michael's car key on my key ring.

"Fred, why don't you stay here in case Michael wakes up," I say. "Santiago, you can go to Michael's place and pick up some clean pajama bottoms and T-shirts, some socks and underwear, maybe his extra phone charger, anything you can think of to make him more comfortable.

"And I'll go to the tow company lot downtown and see if I can pick up his pillow and his shaving kit with his toothbrush, razor, deodorant—you know how picky Michael is about shaving. And I'll see if I can track down his smart phone," I say.

Fred kisses me on top of my nose. "Alex, I don't know what I'd do without you."

"You never have to find out," I say, and give him a quick squeeze. Santiago nods and gives Michael a kiss on the forehead.

"Be right back," he says.

I squeeze Michael's hand. "See you soon." He never opens his eyes.

Santiago and I walk down the hallway together to the elevator, but I decide to stop off at the cafeteria before heading out to my car.

"I'll be back soon," I say to Santiago. He hugs me awkwardly and waves goodbye. The cafeteria is crowded now, with a midmorning rush. I pour a large cup of coffee for Fred with cream and two sugars, grab a banana just in case he gets hungry, and run them upstairs to Michael's room before leaving to go to the tow yard.

Fred gets teary when I walk into the room with the coffee.

I kiss Fred on the cheek. "Don't worry," I say. "It's all going to be okay."

As I walk down the hallway toward the elevators, I hope it's true.

67

The tow yard is in a sketchy part of town I'm not entirely familiar with, on a side road in an industrial section sandwiched between downtown and the airport. Michael's small silver Honda is visible as soon as I make the corner, and the devastation of the mangled car takes my breath away. The driver's side is entirely caved in, and the door has been pried off. Looking at the wreckage, it's impossible to see where Michael's body had been, the twisted metal left little room for a person. A garment bag still hangs from the hook behind the driver's seat, and it sways gently in the breeze.

I park my car diagonally next to his in the lot, and get out to survey the rest of the damage. The hood of Michael's car is mashed in and crumpled, although only from the driver's side. As I circle the car, I marvel that from the passenger's side, the car seems perfectly intact.

"Can I help you?" yells a grimy man walking in my direction.

"This car belongs to my husband, Michael Miller," I say matter-of-factly. "He was in a car accident last night, he was taken to Sarasota Memorial. This is his car. I'm just here to pick up some of his things to take to the hospital."

"I'm gonna need to see some ID," he says. I whip out my wallet and produce my driver's license. "You says his name was Miller," he says. "Your name is Wiggins. If yer married, why don't you have the same last name?"

"Because," I say authoritatively, "it's not 1955." He blinks, seemingly unsure of what to do next. "His shaving kit is in the backseat," I say, "and I see his suit hanging there," I pointed. "I have to get his things and make it back to the hospital before Michael wakes up. Do you need me to sign something?"

"Uh, yeah. I'll go get it," says the man as he lumbers off toward the office. The key to these types of situations is to just assume that the person you're dealing with is going to cooperate. If you fully commit to that idea, they usually do.

Being the boss translates to areas outside of your work. And if you're somebody like me, you can't just turn it off.

As there is no longer a front door on the car, there's no need for a key. I pull Michael's suit through the hole left by the wreckage. The bottom of the bag is shredded, exposing bits of Michael's favorite navy suit. He'll be upset about that. I set the garment bag down in the front seat of my car, and go back to see what else I can retrieve from Michael's Honda. Reaching over to unlock the passenger-side door, I struggle not to cry. There's blood on the dashboard, on the emergency brake, on the steering wheel. Michael is lucky to be alive. I'm lucky that Michael is still alive.

I walk around the car and enter on the passenger side. Michael's shaving kit and iPad are just sitting on the backseat as though nothing at all has happened. I grab them both and look for his phone. His pillow has fallen to the floor in the backseat, but it's no worse for the wear. The pillowcase has some small black smudges on it, although I can't immediately determine what caused them. Michael's phone is sitting on the passenger-side floor, still plugged into the charger. I load everything into the front seat of my car and leave Michael's car where it is. I pull a small tarp from my trunk and do my best to secure it to Michael's car with a roll of leopard-print duct tape, also from my trunk. At least that way the interior won't be completely trashed if it starts to rain. It's not much, but it's something.

The tow yard employee is back a few minutes later with a clipboard. I scrawl my signature on the page.

"Any idea when you'll be picking this up?" asks the guy. He hands me a card.

"I'm sure the insurance company will be here in the next few days. We'll let you know," I say vaguely.

My hands are shaking as I drive away.

68

Before heading back to the hospital, I swing by my house to pick up a few clean pillowcases for Michael. I choose the softest ones, so they'll feel like home to him.

Fred is napping in the chair when I get back to the hospital. Michael is still asleep. I look him over tenderly, weeping at his many injuries. He looks broken in so many ways. I sit silently in the other chair, the one near the foot of Michael's bed, and watch him as he sleeps. The nurses told us earlier he has morphine in his IV bag, because his injuries are so severe.

"You're here," Michael whispers, slowly opening his eyes. He seems disoriented, and his voice cracks.

"I'm here," I whisper. "Do you want some water?" He nods yes, and I fill the cup on his bedside table from the pitcher of ice water the nurses brought earlier. He seems confused that his left arm is in a sling, and his right hand won't bend because it contains an IV needle. "Let me help you," I say, holding the cup of water up to his lips. He takes a long sip, and then another one. He looks around the room, and sees Fred sleeping in the corner.

"Let me wake up your dad," I say. "I know he wants to see you."

"Wait," Michael says. "Wait just a few minutes. Let me get my bearings."

"Do you remember what happened?" I ask softly.

"Somebody T-boned me," he says slowly. "They were going really fast . . . Ambulance."

"Drunk driver," I say. "They brought you here last night. Your dad and Santiago have been here all night. Santiago just went to your house to get you a few things. He'll be back soon."

"Did you tell everybody what to do, harangue the doctors, redecorate the place?" he asks.

"I see your sense of humor fared better than your spleen," I say. "I brought you your pillow. Maybe I should take it back," I tease.

"Thank you," he says, his eyes misty. "I wouldn't be me without you."

"Ditto," I say. I might not be Michael's wife anymore, but we'll always be family.

"How's my hair?" he cracks.

I give him the once-over. "You're such a TV nerd. Never let it be said that you weren't born to be in front of a camera. You know, you don't have a scratch on your face. Not one. How is that even possible? And who gets into a life-threating accident without even messing up his hair?"

He smiles. "I can't move my arms, but at least my hair looks good."

"At least." I laugh. "And on the plus side, I think you're a shoo-in for that big anchor job. Those guys don't need to move their arms, right?"

Fred stirs from the corner.

"You're finally awake, pal. How are you feeling?" He rises and stands on the other side of Michael's bed.

"Sore," Michael says. "But glad you're here."

"You scared me there for a while," says Fred, smiling, his eyes welling up with tears. "Try not to do that again."

"I'll do my level best," says Michael. He begins coughing and I hold the cup of water to his lips again. He takes another sip. "Thank you."

There's a soft knock at the door, and then Darcy, Sam, Carter, and Santiago enter the room. Darcy is carrying a small green vase filled with white roses.

"Do you think Michael remembered me in his will?" cracks Darcy. She fills up every room she enters with her personality and presence.

"No, he's leaving it all to me," Carter laughs. "Except for that terrible red chaise. You can have that."

"Nobody wants that ugly thing." Sam laughs too.

"Oh good, you're alive," Darcy says to Michael. She sets down the flowers on the bedside table, leans over the bed, and kisses Michael on the cheek. "There's still time to change your will." Carter pats the top of Michael's head gently, and Santiago sets down the overnight bag he's carrying on the floor near the window, and then plants a kiss on Michael's forehead.

"The gang's all here," says Michael, smiling weakly as we crowd around the bed.

"You're the most attractive near-death patient I've ever seen," remarks Darcy. "What did you do, call for hair and makeup the moment you got out of surgery?"

I laugh out loud. Michael and Carter do too.

"You look like a soap opera star or something," she says.

"Do you need anything?" asks Fred.

"I've got everything I need right here," Michael says.

There's another knock on the hospital door, and a volunteer enters, awkwardly carrying a very large basket. She's about seventy, no more than five feet tall, with curly white hair and hot-pink jogging shoes. The basket is almost bigger than she is.

"We're going to need a bigger room," cracks Darcy. Carter takes the oversize basket from her arms and sets it down on the table.

"Thank you, ma'am," Carter says.

The basket is overflowing with food: long sandwiches wrapped in paper and tied with raffia, tall containers of salads, napkins, silverware, and small plates, all beautifully displayed.

"Who's it from?" asks Darcy, digging through the basket. "This looks amazing."

Carter reads the card:

MICHAEL—HOPE YOU'RE FEELING BETTER.
BEST WISHES, DANIEL BOUDREAUX

"Awww," teases Michael, "Your boyfriend sent me a bouquet of sandwiches." Everyone laughs and my skin flushes scarlet.

"He's not my boyfriend," I say.

"That's not what I hear," says Michael playfully. Darcy remains uncharacteristically silent. "Santiago told me all about it," says Michael.

"He says you two were steamy on the dance floor last weekend." Santiago grins sheepishly at me.

"Aren't you supposed to be resting quietly about now?" I ask Michael.

"I heard it too, from the man himself," gushes Carter. "Daniel Boudreaux is smitten."

"Well, he's something, all right," says Darcy. I shoot her a stern glance across the room. She gets the message and doesn't say another word on the matter.

"He's a client," I say. "Nothing more."

"Well," says Carter, "I've known the man for ten years and I've never seen him fall this hard for anyone."

"Look at this, there's shrimp and crab salad, po'boys, this one looks like ham and Brie," says Darcy digging through the basket, mercifully changing the subject. "Who's hungry?"

"I am," says Fred, heading toward the food. Sam starts pulling plates, napkins, and silverware out of the basket, laying them out on the table. Fred selects a fried oyster po'boy.

"Mmm, delicious," Fred says as he bites into the sandwich.

"Michael, do you want anything?" I ask.

"No, I'm not hungry at all. Maybe leftover from the anesthesia or something. You all dig in, though," says Michael. He groans a bit as he shifts his weight in the bed.

"Are you okay?" I ask. "Do you want me to call a nurse?"

"I'm just really sore all over," he says, "the pain seems to be getting worse." He smiles. "I feel like I've been in a car accident or something."

"You're hilarious," I say, pushing the nurse call button on the TV remote.

"I love this bread," says Darcy, biting into a shrimp salad sandwich. "Crunchy on the outside, light and melty on the inside."

"Daniel makes it himself, traditional New Orleans style," I say.

"I'll say one thing," says Darcy with her mouth full, "that boy can cook."

Carter and Santiago each help themselves to sandwiches. Carter chooses the ham and Brie, and Santiago picks something that looks like roast beef.

The seven of us perch in various places around the room, me at the end of Michael's hospital bed. Darcy hands me a crab salad sandwich, one of my favorites. The room goes silent as we enjoy the food.

"Okay, okay, give me a bite of that," Michael says to me. I move nearer to the head of the bed and hold the sandwich out for him to take a bite.

"Ooh, that's good," says Michael. "That's maybe the best sandwich I've ever had." He takes another bite. "Don't break up with him just yet, Alex. I think Santiago and I might need him to cater a housewarming."

I almost choke on my salad when he says that, but before I have a chance to ask Michael what in the hell he's talking about, a stout nurse with gray hair pulled into a severe bun enters the room. She makes her way through Darcy, Sam, Santiago, and Carter and disconnects Michael's IV line, without so much as a greeting. She hangs a new IV bag on Michael's stand, pushes a few buttons on the monitor, and then begins taking his blood pressure.

"Would you like a sandwich?" I ask. "We've got plenty."

"No thank you," she answers curtly. "Mr. Miller has been through a severe trauma and an extensive surgery. He needs to rest. No more than one visitor at a time for the next day or two." She's like a drill sergeant. "Say your goodbyes."

"I'm fine, really," says Michael, who seems to get woozier before our eyes.

"Your IV bag was empty," says the nurse. "For some reason it wasn't connected to the monitor when they brought you back from post-op." Michael's eyes are closed before she finishes her sentence.

"Is he okay?" asks Fred.

"His pain medication will make him drowsy," says the nurse. "He was alert before because it was wearing off. His body needs to heal. He needs to sleep."

Darcy, Sam, and Carter stand up to leave. Darcy gives Michael a quick peck on his forehead.

"Feel better," she says.

"We'll be back later," says Carter. They hug Fred and me, and Carter hugs Santiago. Michael is out when they leave the room.

I hate to even think about leaving when Michael is hurt and in the hospital. Where else would I be but at his side? But I don't want to slow his healing either. And if the nurse thinks Michael should only have one visitor at a time for the next few days, we should probably listen to her.

"Fred," I say. "Do you want me to stay, or do you want to stay and I'll come back and sit with him later?" I ask. Pausing for a second, I consider Santiago's feelings. "What about you, Santiago? How should we do this?"

"I'm going to stay either way," says Fred. "I want to be here if he wakes up again."

"Would you like me to bring you a change of clothes, or some toiletries?" I ask Fred.

"I'd appreciate it," he says.

"I'll go now," says Santiago, "I can come tonight and stay here if Fred wants to go home to sleep later."

"That sounds like a good idea," I say. "I have to go to Daniel's opening tonight to make sure everything is in place, but I'll stop by the hospital before I go. And I can come back afterwards if Michael is up to it."

Fred nods.

"I need to swing by the restaurant to make sure the setup is on track, and I'll pick up your things at your house and drop them back here in an hour or so if that works," I say.

"Thank you," says Fred. I kiss the top of Michael's head as he sleeps. He doesn't move at all. The nurse finishes checking Michael's vital signs and leaves the room, apparently satisfied that we're clearing out. Santiago kisses Michael again and we both hug Fred before leaving the room. We don't say a word as we walk together down the hallway toward the elevator.

69

I need a shower, but I want to check on the Boudreaux project first, so I head up Bayfront Parkway toward the marina. The midday sun is shining brightly and the water sparkles in the distance, embellished by the collection of large sculptures that dot the waterfront, on loan from all over the world.

As I pull in to the marina parking lot, my mind is abuzz with nervous energy. Maybe it's the lack of sleep. Or an adrenaline hangover from the fear and stress of Michael's accident. But most likely it's because just twenty-four hours earlier, I ran off that boat in a state of semi-undress, humiliated and ashamed, as a strange woman screamed at Daniel. It will be a giant relief when the project is finally completed and I can be done with it. Just one more night. I only have to make it through one more night.

I step across the gangway and the deck is bustling with workers finishing preparations for opening night. I'm happy to see the red event binders I provided to all the staff members are in use across the restaurant.

Nicky, my greenery artist, has already been to the site and worked his magic—lining the dock and walkway with fragrant potted white magnolias, and creating a more intimate environment inside with feathery palms. It's perfect, just as I envisioned. The magnolias are not just beautiful and fragrant, a lush cue of the experience to come; they're an homage to Daniel, and the old Southern home with the magnolia tree he spoke of so often. The environment is not only primed for patrons of the restaurant, but for Daniel as well. On board, workmen are busy securing the silver frames for the black-and-white photographs of Daniel's family and culinary legacy inside. Timewise, it's too tight for my comfort, but the framers were unable to come until today. So today it is.

"Alex!" says Tina, Daniel's headwaitress. I spin around to find her behind me—in her arms, a box containing an eclectic mix of silver candlesticks.

"Can I help you with that?" I ask. She shakes her head.

"I've got it," she says. "I'm blown away by the transformation here. This place is going to be gorgeous."

"Thanks," I say. "It's coming together. Is the staff having any questions with the event book? It looks like your crew is a bit ahead of schedule, which is always nice. It seems we're right on track."

"We're all pretty clear on what you want," Tina says. "The photos and diagrams in the red binders really helped a lot."

"Great work," I say. "I'm going to do a quick walk-through, and then I'll be back later tonight."

"Chef's in the kitchen," she says. "Do you want me to let him know you're here?"

"Uh, no, thanks," I stall. "I'll check in with Daniel after I've had a look around." I'm hoping to get out of here as quickly as possible. If I can avoid Daniel, all the better. It's not exactly professional, but it is self-preservation.

The starboard side of the boat, which is what you'd see when you first come on board, is finished to perfection. The tables are set with vintage white linens, mixed in with pale blues and aquas at scattered tables. Smaller tables are adorned with mismatched silver candlesticks with pale blue tapers; larger tables have sea-blue vases and white hydrangea blooms.

Black-and-white photos are grouped artfully along the freshly painted walls where foot traffic will flow, a revealing combination of historical photos from the Boudreaux family's grand restaurants, to more whimsical snapshots, such as the one where Daniel, his brother Gabriel, and a slew of young cousins were photographed at about four years old, sitting all in a row at a prep station in one of his family's kitchens, all decked out with chef hats and little neckerchiefs.

Next, I walk through the inside area, near the bar. The framers are nearly finished, and will move to the rear deck to install the last of the black-and-white photos when they're finished inside. The photographs are stunning, and the framers have done an excellent job. I numbered and color-coded all of the pictures with accompanying diagrams to show them exactly where each photo was supposed to be hung, and they've followed my instructions exactly.

Maddeningly, the tables inside the bar area are nearly all covered with tablecloths and centerpieces, but the configuration is all wrong. Someone has pushed many of the smaller tables together, creating fewer, larger tables in one big island in the middle of the room. I go outside to the rear deck in search of Tina, and ask her to send a couple of staff members inside to help me relocate the tables.

"What happened here?" I ask.

"It's a standard bar setup," says a waiter whose name I can't recall. Exhaustion, I guess. Usually, I'm very efficient at remembering names.

"Let's stick to the event bible, please," I say. "We're going for a very specific environment here, that's not exactly business as usual." I open the red binder to the bar setup diagram, and point to the layout. "We need this setup exactly."

"Sure thing," says the waiter. "Sorry about that." They pull the linens and centerpieces off the massive center tables and reconfigure them as I've requested.

"Thanks, guys," I say. "I need to check out the back deck and then I'll be back to make sure everything in here is as it should be. Let me know if you need anything." I'm a bit frustrated. I spent the entire last week arranging and rearranging those tables for the ideal configuration. And I'm in no mood for rogue furniture movers. Less than twenty-four hours earlier I was fired, publicly, from a high-profile job. If I'm going to redeem myself, everything, and I mean everything, for the Boudreaux opening has to be perfect. And I'm already off my A-game.

After tweaking the placement of a few palms, I leave the waiters rearranging chairs and resetting the tables, as I move to the rear deck. The port side of the restaurant is completed, with the exception of the addition of the framed photos. It's breathtaking, and I couldn't be prouder.

It's then I hear a familiar voice behind me.

"Alex?" says Daniel. "Why didn't you tell me you were here?"

70

I spin around to face him and my heart skips a beat. He's wearing black pants, his chef's coat, and a toque blanche. He pulls off his toque as I turn to face him.

"Nice hat," I say. "You look like a real chef."

"My family is down for the opening tonight. Chef, my father, is old school. I usually just wear a black skullcap. But he gave me this toque to wear tonight. It's the one he wore when he opened his first restaurant."

"That's really sweet. Very sentimental." I say. "Look, I was just heading out. I wanted to stop by and check to make sure everything was going to be ready for tonight." He nods, wordlessly, and I continue, "I only got a few hours of sleep last night, so I'm going to go home, take a quick nap and a shower, and I'll be back before the opening starts."

"How's Michael?"

"He's in pretty rough shape, but he'll be okay," I say. "Thank you for sending the basket of sandwiches. It was really thoughtful." It was. Here he has his first restaurant opening in just a few hours and he takes the time to make a basket of food for someone he barely knows.

"I cook for the people I care about," he says. "I wish I could have done more." His deep-blue eyes are serious. Tentatively, he moves another step closer to me. My breath catches in my chest and it's agony. I wish yesterday hadn't happened at all.

"I'm glad you're here," he says. "But you didn't have to be. I understand."

"You're my client. Your opening is important to me."

"Your client," he repeats slowly, shaking his head. "Could I please just explain about yesterday . . ." Unwelcome tears begin filling my eyes, and I wipe them away quickly, embarrassed for Daniel or anyone on the staff to see them.

"Can we not have this conversation now, please?" I whisper. "I'm exhausted, I'm wrung out, I just want to get through tonight. After that, we don't need to see each other again."

Daniel's expression is crestfallen, and he slowly takes a step back. I turn quickly and walk away, leaving him standing all alone on the deck of Boudreaux.

71

I cry in my car on the entire drive to Fred's house. My chest aches and my nose is running, but I can't stop. Everything hurts so much. I tell myself it's just the stress of Michael's accident, not enough sleep, and having two major client events in twenty-four hours. But the flurry of thoughts that occupy my mind aren't about slumber or work.

I pick up a change of clothes for Fred, and pack his toothbrush, razor, and cell phone charger, and then head back to the hospital to drop them off.

Fred naps in the corner, snoring softly, but Michael is awake. The drill sergeant nurse is nowhere to be seen. I put the bag with Fred's things on the table, and sit at the foot of Michael's bed.

"How are you feeling?" I ask.

"My whole body hurts like hell," he says. "I think the pain meds are starting to wear off again."

"I'll call someone," I say.

"I already did," he says. "I'm sure they'll be here soon." I refill his water glass and help him take a few sips.

"Can I get you anything?" I ask. "Are you hungry, do you need an extra pillow?"

"I'm fine," he says. "I'm sorry if I embarrassed you about Daniel earlier. I didn't mean to."

"I was embarrassed," I say, "but not for the reasons you think." I tell Michael, in excruciating detail, what happened the day before, every awful moment. It's a relief to talk to him, I've missed it more than I realize. He listens and pats the top of my hand with his, until his IV monitor starts beeping.

"Be careful," I say. "You don't want to pull out your IV."

"I'm so sorry, sweetie," he replies. "What did he say?"

"What do you mean?" I ask.

"After it happened. Who was she? What was the story? Did he explain himself?" Michael asks.

"He tried to, I guess. I ran off so quickly. I was humiliated. The poor woman was obviously in distress and I didn't want to make it worse. *I* was in distress. And then he showed up at my event at the Ritz last night and wanted to explain, but I didn't want to hear it. Then he tried again today when I went to do the walk-through before the opening tonight."

"He crashed the Wildlife Foundation benefit?"

"Not exactly; he bought a whole table, came by himself, and then gave Olivia a five-thousand-dollar donation. And then he waited outside for me with flowers, but still . . ."

"But . . . ," says Michael.

"But I told him I just wanted to get through tonight's event," I say. "What does it matter? What possible explanation could he have that would make me okay with this?"

"Maybe he had a relationship with the woman and it's over. Maybe it wasn't what you thought it was. Maybe she's a crazy chef groupie. Or maybe he *was* with her and then he met you and couldn't imagine his life with anyone else," he says. "I certainly know how that feels."

"Yeah, that turned out great," I say. "And I don't think chefs have groupies."

"Oh, they do," he quips. "Some of those Food Network ladies are out of control." I smile at Michael, I can't help myself. He always has a way of joking me out of a bad day.

"Look, I don't know Daniel," says Michael. "I only met him once that night at our party, and to be honest I wasn't checking out his personality."

"Great," I say.

"But Carter's been friends with him for ten years, and he says Daniel's one of the good guys."

I weep and Michael leans forward to hold me, except he can't move his arms so it's really just more of an off-center shoulder bump. "I can't go through this again," I say. "I won't survive another betrayal. It's better to just end it now, before I get in any deeper. If I fall in love with someone, I need them to love me back. Just me. I have to be enough."

"I'm so sorry," he says, "I wish I'd never hurt you. I wish I'd never lied to you. I feel responsible." He sighs. "Look, you have to at least listen to Daniel's explanation. Give him the benefit of the doubt. If you listen and it's not good enough, fine. If you don't believe him, fine. But you at least have to listen. If you don't, you're giving up on something real, something that could make you happy, without giving it a chance. There's nothing I want more than for you to be happy. You deserve to be loved, all the way."

"It's too late," I say. "Even if I bought whatever explanation Daniel served up, which frankly, I can't imagine—I already told him I didn't want to see him again after the party tonight."

I'm wiping the tears from my eyes when Santiago and the drill sergeant nurse enter Michael's room together. Santiago steps to Michael's bed and gives him a tender kiss on top of his head.

"Glad to see you up, *querido*," Santiago says. Michael beams at him like a high schooler in love.

"How's your pain?" asks the nurse, "on a scale of ten, ten being the worst?"

"About a nine," answers Michael. Santiago hovers around Michael, fluffing his pillows and refilling his water pitcher. Seeing Michael and Santiago together, how sweet they are, how obviously taken they are with each other, makes me long to fall in love again too someday. Unfortunately, my fate doesn't seem to agree.

72

I kiss Michael on the cheek, and hug Santiago goodbye. Fred is still snoozing in the chair in the corner of the hospital room and I don't want to disturb him.

By the time I arrive home, I'm so cross-eyed and foggy from lack of sleep that my bedroom seems too far away from the front door. I make the trek across the house anyway, knowing I'll sleep more soundly in my own bed than I would on the couch, even though it's comfy, and inviting, and only ten feet away.

When I awake four hours later at five-thirty, I'm spooning Morley, and still wearing my jeans and T-shirt from last night. For once, Morley doesn't seem to mind. My alarm has not yet gone off, and it isn't until I hear the doorbell ring that I realize what woke me up.

Still a bit disoriented, I wander to the front door and open it.

"Hello, Cinderella," says Carter with flourish, "It's time to get ready for the ball." He's sporting a blue suit with a bright pink tie and classic Wayfarer sunglasses. Darcy stands next to him on the porch, with a garment bag flung over her shoulder and a bottle of dark rum under her arm. I motion them inside, and they sweep into the house and take over the kitchen as I trail behind.

"Get in the shower, you look like a hobo," instructs Carter. "We're leaving in an hour. Sam is meeting us there."

"I'm making my famous mai tais," says Darcy. "Carter and I will be having a little cocktail while you get ready. If you hurry, you can have one too."

"Thanks." I laugh, heading back toward the bathroom. I brush my teeth for a solid three minutes and then slip into the shower. The warm water feels good. I'm remarkably refreshed after my four-hour nap, and although I'm hesitant to see Daniel, I figure he'll be very busy all night, and I can't wait to see Boudreaux in all her glory. I'm really proud of my work there.

When I emerge from the shower, I wrap my wet hair in a towel, slip on a short cotton robe, and head to my closet for inspiration. Laid out on my bed is the slinky aqua dress I haven't worn since my divorce party. The one that hugs every curve and makes my legs look a mile long.

"Carter, have you been going through my closet again?" I yell toward the kitchen. He and Darcy appear in the doorway of my bedroom, mischievous looks on their faces.

"Michael insisted," says Carter. "He says if he croaks tonight that you wearing that dress is his dying wish."

"He's not dying," I say.

"He is eventually," says Carter solemnly. "We all are." He keeps a straight face for all of ten seconds and then he and Darcy start cracking up.

"Fine," I say, "I'll wear the dress. Did Michael want to pick out my shoes too, or were you guys going to let me handle that?"

"It's Michael's other dying wish that you wear the strappy silver stilettos. But get a move on, we're on a tight schedule."

Darcy hands me a mai tai. "For courage," she says.

"Thanks," I say, accepting the glass. I head back into the bathroom, brush and dry my hair, and apply some makeup.

"Twenty minutes!" yells Carter from somewhere near the kitchen. "We're leaving in twenty minutes." Carter is the only person I know who is more obsessive about punctuality than I am.

I pull on a strapless bra, panties, and a silk slip before putting on the gorgeous aqua dress. I know why Michael picked it for me. It's his favorite because he says I always look so confident when I wear it, like I could take on the world.

I accessorize with my favorite aquamarine drop earrings, a bejeweled silver cuff with stones the color of the ocean, and a delicate Tiffany starfish necklace on a barely-there silver chain. To finish, I select a teal-blue ombre clutch with a silver chain, and the strappy silver sandals

Michael had suggested. Really, what's the point of having a gay ex-husband if you can't rely on him for fashion advice?

I slip on the stilettos, and put the essentials in my clutch—lip gloss, wallet, mini-toothbrush, phone, keys. My pedicure from last week still looks great, no need to touch it up.

Heading into the kitchen, where Darcy and Carter are hanging out, I'm five minutes ahead of schedule. Carter will be so pleased. Darcy's changed into a stunning, off-the-shoulder white dress and tall salmon-colored wedges in a funky geometric pattern. She looks amazing, as always.

We toast to Michael's health, and then head out the door to Carter's big black Lincoln Navigator.

Traffic is light, and it only takes about ten minutes to get from my house to the marina. Carter, always the gentleman, drops Darcy and me off by the dock entrance so we won't have to tromp through the marina parking lot in our high heels. We wait in the shade while Carter parks the car, and the three of us walk down the dock to Boudreaux together.

We arrive at six-thirty, although the party and first seating aren't until seven-thirty. I need to make sure everything is in place, and Carter promised Daniel he'd arrive early for moral support.

"The magnolias are a great touch," says Carter.

Tina, the headwaitress, is standing at the hostess stand when we arrive at the gangplank.

"This is Alex," she says to Brenna, the hostess. "Please take her to her table."

"*Fancy*," says Carter. "You have your own table." We cross the gangplank, and the view is stunning. The vintage linen and sea-colored tablecloths flutter gently in the breeze, the centerpieces are perfection, the ivory cane-backed chairs look elegantly formal and comfortable all at once.

"Oh, Alex, it's gorgeous," says Darcy.

"You've really outdone yourself," says Carter. I smile, pleased as

I can be. I love that moment when the vision in my head for a space or an event becomes a reality.

Brenna takes us along the wall with the framed black-and-white photographs, and across to the rear deck with the view of the bay. She leads us to the table where Daniel and I so often sat together, in the corner, near the railing.

"Here you are," she says.

"Oh no," I say. "We're happy to sit at one of the interior tables. This is the best table in the house; we should save it for a VIP at tonight's event."

"Chef Daniel was very specific." She smiles. "*Very* specific."

"Thank you," I say. Carter and Darcy make themselves comfortable. I sit down and hang my clutch. Everything is so beautiful, I can't stop gazing around.

"Look at this," says Darcy, pointing to a silver-framed photograph on the wall behind us.

"Oh my God," says Carter.

I turn to look to see what the two of them are so enamored of, and I'm stunned to see a black-and-white print of the photograph that Cliff Roles snapped of Daniel and me while we were dancing—that very first night we kissed. The vintage globe lights strung along the deck shimmer in the background. Daniel and I are both smiling in the picture, completely entranced by one another.

Daniel had it framed in silver like the others, the photographs of his beloved family and their culinary legacy, and hung it right next to our usual table. I'm touched.

"I told you," Carter says. "Smitten."

"I'll say," says Darcy.

"I'm going to the bar," Carter announces. "Does anybody want anything?"

"I'd just like some Perrier with a twist of lime for now, please," I say. "I need to do a quick walk-through to make sure everything is in place before the event starts."

"Do your thing," says Darcy. "You know where to find us."

"Yes," teases Carter. "At *Alex's* table." Smiling, I roll my eyes at him and excuse myself to do the walk-through.

I'm so thrilled by how everything has turned out. Both decks are flawless, and the inside bar area has been reconfigured according to my plan. One of my signature red binders sits open on the bar. I close it and stow it on the shelving underneath. The mermaid statue with the verdigris patina we found in storage is elegant in her permanent place near the inside entrance. My Yahtzee victory the other night assured her a home in the restaurant, rather than upstairs in Daniel's studio.

Cliff Roles arrives on board around six forty-five and I ask him to please take as many shots of the decks and bar area as he can before guests arrive. Cliff and I have a standing deal when he photographs my events. In addition to the work he does for the society pages, I pay him extra to shoot the rooms themselves. It works out well for both of us. Cliff makes some extra cash for taking photos at an event he was shooting anyway, and I get some amazing photographs for my portfolio. Boudreaux is the most stunning restaurant I've ever done, and I want to capture every exquisite detail for posterity.

"I'm so glad you're here tonight, *cher*," comes Daniel's unmistakable voice. "It wouldn't feel right without you."

I turn toward his sweetly melodic tenor, a masculine siren song in the key of Louisiana drawl. He's debonair as you'd expect culinary royalty to be; his dark hair urbane, his cleft on stun, and his charisma at full wattage. He looks polished and dapper in a slim cut navy suit. It's all I can do not to just rip it right off him.

"You're breathtaking," says Daniel.

"Thank you," I say. "You're pretty breathtaking yourself." Jesus, I can hardly contain myself. I give myself a quick reminder of what transpired the morning prior.

"You're wearing the same dress you wore the first night we met," he says. His deep-blue eyes are so intensely captivating, I can hardly focus. The fact that he remembers what I wore the first time he ever saw me makes me blush.

"Before everyone arrives, I hoped you'd allow me to explain about yesterday," he starts. I think about what Michael said about giving Daniel a chance. Actually, I've been thinking about it all afternoon.

"Okay." I nod.

"It was not what you thought—" he starts to say, as he's interrupted by a cohort of Southerners crowding around him, blessed with the same movie-star chins, dimples, and bourbony New Orleans accents.

"*Cher,* is this her?" asks a striking older woman with dark hair pulled back in a sophisticated chignon.

"Daniel, Daniel, are we finally meeting your Alex? We've waited all day, son. Where is she?" says a man in chef's whites.

Daniel's skin flushes a little, which I find completely endearing.

"Yes, this is Alex. Alex, this is my family," he says. "I'd like to introduce my mother, Genevieve Boudreaux; my father, Etienne Boudreaux, who everyone calls 'Chef'; my brother and, as you know, wardrobe consultant, Gabriel." I smile a little when he mentions the wardrobe consultant bit. "And this is my grand-mere, the incomparable Miss Georgina Boudreaux."

"So nice to meet you all," I say, shaking hands all around. It's so lovely that they've all made the trip from New Orleans to support Daniel on his opening night.

They're a gorgeous bunch, dressed mostly in kitchen clothing, with the exception of Gabriel, Daniel's brother, who's nattily turned out in a linen suit, bow tie, and a straw fedora—every inch the Southern gentleman.

Daniel's father wears chef's whites, the traditional black-and-white houndstooth pants, and a toque blanche. He looks like Daniel, thirty years older. He's still lean and strong, not quite as tall as his sons, his own dark hair peppered with gray. Daniel's mother is slender and elegant. She wears classic red lipstick, and has on a chic black dress and heels, covered with a full-length white apron. His grandmother, a stout woman in her seventies, wears a long black cotton skirt and a white chef's coat.

Daniel's grandmother grasps my arms with both her hands, and kisses my cheeks. "*Cher,* you and my Daniel have created a beautiful restaurant. I wish you much success."

"Thank you." I smile. I'm not sure that she knows that my part ends after tonight, but I don't want to spoil the mood.

"The detail is magnificent," says Chef. "You and Daniel had quite the vision. I never believed old Archer's boat could be turned into such a showplace."

"I think Daniel always knew," I say. He beams with pride.

Genevieve pulls me to the side as Daniel converses with his father and brother. I feel instantly at ease with her. Like Daniel, she has the talent of making you feel you were a lifelong confidante.

"This place is so much Daniel, such a tribute to our family history. You've truly captured Daniel's raison d'être."

"Thank you," I say. "That means a lot to me."

"I love the magnolias outside, *cher,*" she says. "So beautiful. They reminded me of the sixty-five-year-old magnolia tree we have in our yard at home."

"Daniel spoke of it often," I say. "It felt important to him." A wide smile lights up her entire face.

"Did you see the picture of the two of you?" Genevieve whispers in my ear. I nod, surprised she noticed it. She smiles a dreamy, faraway smile. "He's very sentimental, my son. Steadfast. He has the gentle soul of an artist."

It's clear she adores him. And who could blame her?

"There will be no restaurant if there's no cook in the kitchen," announces Daniel's grandmother, Miss Georgina. "Come now, *chers,* we've met Daniel's young lady, we have work to do." She hugs me tightly and disappears behind the kitchen door. Chef smiles at Daniel, and kisses him proudly on each cheek.

"You must try the tropical-Cajun lobster," he says to me. "It's a revelation. My son is a great talent."

"All right, Chef's had too much cooking wine again." Gabriel laughs loudly; Daniel and his father join in.

"Be still my heart, is that the sublime Miss Genevieve Boudreaux?" says Carter dramatically as he enters the bar area.

"Carter, so glad to see you, *cher*!" says Genevieve, embracing him warmly. Chef and Gabriel encircle Carter, patting him on the back and greeting him like a beloved relative.

"Meet Darcy, she's my plus-one tonight," announces Carter. "But don't worry, y'all, I haven't switched teams on you." The Boudreauxs greet Darcy, and Carter makes introductions all around.

"What do you think of Alex's work? She and Daniel make a great team, no?" says Carter.

"Boudreaux is a jewel," says Chef. "In fact, Genevieve and I want to discuss a new restaurant project with Alex. We saw those red binders all over today, and the level of detail, right down to the flow of guests and server traffic, is truly impressive."

"What can we say?" jokes Gabriel. "Chef loves his seating charts." He's hilarious. I can see why he and Carter hit it off, and why Gabriel and Daniel are so close.

"It's seven, Chef, we'll be opening in thirty minutes," says Daniel.

"Are you ready, son?" asks Chef. Daniel nods, and Chef hugs him tightly.

"We're so proud of you, *cher*," says his mother. She holds him close and kisses him on each cheek. Chef and Genevieve hug me too, and then disappear behind the kitchen door. I marvel at how warm and supportive they are.

"You're taking the door," says Daniel to Gabriel. "Brenna will shadow you tonight."

Gabriel nods. "Mother is supervising dessert prep and then she'll join me up front."

Daniel hugs his brother wordlessly.

"Don't worry, *cher*," says Gabriel. "If it's a fiasco, we have enough liquor to keep us all tanked for a week."

"Comforting." Daniel smiles.

73

Darcy and Carter return to our table, and after some last-minute instruction, Gabriel leaves to manage hosting duties. It's fascinating to watch the Boudreaux family work together. Even on opening night, they all take charge of different areas, working together like an exquisite medley of flavors.

We're alone once more, Daniel and I.

"Your family is amazing," I say, and he grins. Their affection for each other is obvious.

"There's not much time left before the guests arrive," he says. "But I really wanted to talk about what happened yesterday."

"Are you sure you want to discuss this right now?" I ask. "We can talk after the party if you want. I promise I'll stay to listen. You sort of have a lot going on right now."

"I can't bear to leave this unresolved," he says. "I know what you must be thinking—"

"Daniel, you're needed up front," says Gabriel, poking his head inside the doorway. "Press is here."

"Go," I say. "It's your big night. We can talk about it later."

He smiles. "It's *our* big night." He reaches out and squeezes my hand, and then follows his brother outside.

74

I head out to our table, where Carter and Darcy are enjoying their drinks and the thrill of good gossip.

"I told Carter about the Daniel situation," says Darcy. "We need his advice." This was what I both love and hate about having such a close-knit group of friends. There are no secrets. Even when you want secrets.

"Has Daniel told you his side of the story?" asks Carter.

"No," I say. "Why, do you know what it is?"

"No," he answers, downing the rest of his drink. I squeeze the lime into my Perrier and take a sip. I need ice.

"He tried to tell me just now," I say, "but then he got pulled away to do an interview."

"We think you should listen to him," says Darcy matter-of-factly.

"I'm sorry, aren't you the one who told me to run screaming in the other direction?" I ask.

"I've reevaluated," she says. "Half my clients are guys who cheat on their wives and girlfriends, and I'll be the first one to tell you that's a losing proposition. But this doesn't feel like that. If the screaming lady was important, she'd be here. And if she was anywhere to be found, you'd be hiding out in the powder room or in the back of a taxi headed for home. But she's not here, is she?"

"Not that I've seen," I say. "But if I disappear tonight, you should probably drag the bottom of the bay."

"Will do," says Carter cheerfully.

"He's introduced you to his family, he put a clearly intimate picture of the two of you in a very public spot," Darcy says. "I think there's more to this story, and you need to find out what it is."

"I'll listen to what he has to say, but I can't think about this right now. If the Boudreaux opening tonight isn't a complete and spectacular success, I'm cooked," I say. "After last night, I might as well close up shop."

"Are you out of your mind?" asked Darcy.

"Yes," I say. "Why do you ask?"

"One of my clients called me today because she wants to hire you for all her major fund-raisers next cycle. It's a bit funny because she had no idea we even knew each other. It could be big for you. Fantastic money, great exposure."

"Who?"

"She's a Democratic congresswoman from Miami," says Darcy. "Young, smart, very savvy. She's well funded and running for Senate next cycle. Anyway, she sits on the board for the Wildlife Foundation and she was at your little underwater shindig last night."

"Oh gawd," I moan. "So much for that job. What a disaster."

"Well, my client told me that disaster raised almost one-point-two million dollars last night. That's a forty percent bump over last year's numbers. Do you know how huge that is in this economy? Plus, the flood at the Ritz made the front page of the newspaper, so you'll probably get a few sympathy donations from that as well."

"Did it really?' I ask. "That's humiliating. Wait . . . forty percent? That's astounding. We were aiming for twenty."

"Well, you overshot it. The flood story ran on the front page, below the fold, with a photo of you and the skinny socialite. Fabulous dress, by the way."

"Thanks. You mean Olivia Kensington Vanderbilt, the Wildlife Foundation chair?" I ask. Darcy nods.

"She fired me last night. Publicly. She screamed, 'You're fired,' across the grand ballroom at the Ritz-Carlton."

"Well," snorts Darcy, "apparently she counted all that money and this morning she was singing your praises."

75

There's little Sarasota loves as much as a new restaurant opening. The steady stream of tourists, spectacular weather, and availability of fresh seafood from the Gulf draws a much higher caliber of restaurants than one would generally find in a town this size. Boudreaux has the added appeal of a waterfront location and a celebrity chef with movie-star looks.

The first seating at seven-thirty is packed rail to rail. I make my rounds to watch the crowds, look for flaws in the traffic flow, and observe the diners' experiences to make certain that Boudreaux is providing the unique culinary experience Daniel aspired to.

Genevieve and Gabriel are the consummate hosts, welcoming every guest like an old friend. With Chef and Miss Georgina supervising the kitchen staff for the night, Daniel is free to ingratiate himself to his guests, ensuring their experience is perfect. He's tirelessly charming, and I watch him move about the restaurant for hours, making personal connections with every guest. It's brilliant. These diners feel like friends, and they'll return for years to come.

I've tasted everything on Daniel's menu, due to his charming habit of feeding me whenever I'd stop by the boat to work, and the fact that he and his new staff ran through the entire menu multiple times during our final week of preparation. As I watch the food come out to each table, I'm impressed with Chef and Miss Georgina's execution of Daniel's original recipes. They're exactly as he envisioned. Prepared as though Daniel had plated each meal himself.

As I make my rounds, Daniel and I keep finding each other's gaze in the crowd, even from across the room. The connection between us is captivating, galvanic—as though we're bound together by some powerful force perceptible only to us.

Later, I'm standing near the wall, waiting for the crowd to pass so

I can return to my table. Just a few steps away, Daniel charms some guests with a tall New Orleans tale. He reaches backward, unobserved, and lightly touches my hand, a simple gesture that sends shivers over my body as powerful as on the first night we danced.

It will be hours before the last guest will leave. Daniel's opening night is a resounding success. The patrons and the media are raving about the food, the view, the wine list, and especially, the chef.

As the crowd finally begins to thin out around 1:00 A.M., and no new guests are arriving, Daniel appears at our table.

"Do you have a minute?" he asks.

"Do you?" I laugh. He takes my hand and I follow him through the kitchen, to his studio upstairs.

76

"Are you exhausted?" I ask.

"I'm energized. This is the biggest night of my life so far, and all I could think of was spending it with you," he says, still holding my hand in his. We stand in the dark, near the doorway of his studio, the only place on the boat where we can talk privately.

I feel like a live wire, being alone with him.

"I'm so sorry. I can only imagine what you must have thought, yesterday," he says.

"I thought that I trusted you, maybe too soon, and that trust had been betrayed," I say. "Is that what happened?"

"You haven't known me long, but I'm loyal as the moon is to the sun," he says.

That's sweet, sort of old-fashioned and poetic. But I'm not sure I'm buying it.

"So who was she?" I ask.

"Her name is Sasha," says Daniel. My heart sinks. This isn't off to a good start. I was praying for something along the lines of *mistaken identity* or *Food Network groupie*. He brings my hand to his cheek, and I take a deep breath. Just listen, I think to myself. *Just listen*.

"She's a restaurant critic at the *Time-Picayune*. We were involved for about two years; it was stormy, toxic, painful," he says.

"The thing is, I should have known better. My mother and Gabriel both warned me about dating her. I didn't listen. She's very intense, torrid, passionate, emotional, which truth be told, was what initially attracted me to her. She was beautiful, she could be incredibly charming. But she became enraged easily, she was highly jealous, and created huge scenes at Chevalier and Royale more than once. My family wasn't having it; obviously, a screaming fit in the middle of the dining room during the dinner rush was unacceptable," he says. I nod and listen, unsure of what to believe.

"I'd break it off, she'd follow me—show up where I was working, call me over and over again all night long, scream at me for hours, appear at my apartment in the middle of the night whenever I tried to break it off. We'd get back together and sometimes it would be good for a while, and sometimes we'd just get sucked right back into this vortex of a constant, poisonous cycle of fighting and making up, fighting and making up."

"Why did you stay?" I ask.

Daniel continues, "I don't know. There were times when I stayed with her because I didn't have the energy to leave her. Eventually, my father told me he was going to have to call the food editor at the *Times-Picayune* to let him know what happened at the restaurant the last time she exploded. He was obviously conflicted about it. I was angry at first, but I understood, of course. There was no way she wasn't going to get fired. I can't blame Chef—aside from the big scenes, and who knows what she would have written about our restaurants, or a new opening, if she was angry—she was really out of control by then."

"I'm sorry," I say.

He speaks slowly now, "She cried and told me it was only because she loved me so much and she knew she was losing me. I didn't want her to lose her job. There was part of me that felt responsible. I asked my father not to call her boss, to give her another chance, and told him I'd leave town and open a restaurant outside New Orleans."

"But you love New Orleans," I say.

"I love my family more," he says. "And I'd never risk our family legacy."

"So you left?" I ask.

"It was okay. We'd been wanting to expand, and it got my family out of an awkward position, and allowed me to end the relationship. I felt suffocated, I had to get away from her."

"What happened when you told her you were leaving?" I ask.

"Nothing, at first," he says. "I just left. I changed my number. I traveled for a bit, was a guest chef for a time at a couple of different places—the Boudreaux family name does open a lot of doors. I thought that if I came right out and told her I was ending the relationship that she'd retaliate against my family's restaurants. But if I just left, I figured she'd eventually move on. That all that anger would dissipate, that maybe she wouldn't hate me as much."

"So not exactly as planned," I say.

"And then when Archer called me about the boat, I knew it was time to open my own restaurant. And I knew Sarasota was the place I wanted to do it."

"Can you blame her for thinking the two of you were still together?" I ask, "I mean, since you never actually ended it."

"It's been a year and a half since I left. I haven't spoken with her. Before I came here, I hadn't stayed any one place for more than six months. But maybe I should have said something. I still don't know if it would have made things worse, or preclude what happened the other day. But if I could go back and change something to prevent yesterday morning from happening like that, I would."

"So what happened after I left?" I ask. I'm torn. I feel incredible sympathy for Daniel if what he's saying is true. But I have no real way of knowing if it is. And that scares the hell out of me.

"I told her that you and I were seeing each other, that I didn't love her anymore, that I was serious about you, and that I'd do anything to convince you of that." My heart skips a beat at that revelation.

"What did she do?" I ask. I'm so confused. What would Sasha's side of the story be? Did she really think after all that time, after everything that happened, that Daniel somehow belonged to her? If Sasha were a man, she'd probably be arrested for stalking. It was an uncommon act of kindness and generosity on Daniel's part, to save her job and move away from the city he loved to protect his family's restaurant legacy. But I'm unnerved by what seems like Sasha's utter audacity, bursting right in, and I'm afraid there's more to the story than he's telling me. If I'm going to trust him at all, I have to trust him at his word, and that is terrifying and disconcertingly familiar. I'm not sure if I can do it.

Or if I should.

"She was upset," he says. "But we talked for some time yesterday, and I think she understood. And even if she doesn't, I've already moved forward."

We stand there in the darkness, and he silently holds my hand. My mind is awhirl with my doubts and fears. Is he telling the truth? Is it foolish to leave myself vulnerable to any man? Is my heart overruling my brain because it knows better, or because it doesn't?

"I'm so drawn to you, Daniel," I say. "But I don't know that I can trust you. And I just can't survive another betrayal. I just can't."

He shakes his head, "Has it ever occurred to you that you're so afraid of being hurt by love that you're willing to sacrifice everything amazing that comes along with it?"

I know he's right. I just don't know if I'm willing to risk it.

"I know where your soft spots are, *cher*. I promise you can put your faith in me," he says.

Steadfast. That was the word Daniel's mother had used to describe him. It's an unusual word, one of another time. And yet my instincts are telling me that it suits Daniel perfectly.

I think about how close Daniel is with his family, how clearly they adore and respect each other, how the black-and-white photo he mounted next to our table feels like a declaration, how with the exception of yesterday morning, I've never gotten a single inkling that Daniel is anything but the good man I believe him to be.

"Alex, I'm in love with you," he says softly. And suddenly, there's nothing I believe to be truer.

Maybe it's the accent.

77

Things may not have worked out exactly how I planned, or even close to how I planned, but they still worked out pretty well, even without me being in charge of everything.

I'm happy, actually happy. My business has taken off, after all the effort I poured into it over the last year. I've built something lasting that sustained me though my stormiest days. It feels good. If nothing else, I've learned that I can depend on myself even when I can't depend on anyone else. Even disasters can become triumphs.

I have my best friend back, and he's finally happy being himself. And that's all we really want for the people we love, isn't it? Michael's accident was scary as hell, but it brought all of us closer together. It made me realize how important Michael still is to me. And that even though things didn't work out as I planned, they still worked out. It's ironic that Michael was the one who ended up convincing me to take a chance on Daniel.

After what happened with Michael, I'd felt like I was always the one putting myself out there, taking all the risks, and being crushed as a result. I'm already naturally cautious, and betrayal made me more so. But what I didn't realize until now was that Daniel was taking big risks too. I wasn't alone, out there all by myself. He put his family's legacy on the line to try something completely different, he put his faith in me and my unusual little company to give form to his dream, and he let himself fall in love, an act of bravery considering the person he fell in love with was broken and unsure and distrustful.

He had faith that all of it would work out.

And it did.

It's okay to let go sometimes. Sure, it's not my strong suit. I'm more comfortable with my schedules and backup plans and my color-coded binders and my old-school label maker. But letting go, doing things that scare me, taking risks even if I might get hurt—if I can just have a little faith that things might not turn out as badly as I fear—well, the payoff can be very, very good. Crazy good.

78

I take a deep breath and finally allow myself to just let go of all the fears I've been grasping onto so tightly over the last year. My fears are not protecting me. They're keeping me prisoner.

Because if real love isn't worth risking everything for, what is?

"Say that again," I tell him, wishing I could make out his expression in the darkness.

"I love you," he says, in that melodic voice I could listen to forever.

"I'm in love with you too," I say.

Daniel pulls me into his arms and kisses me tenderly.

And for the first time in a long time, it feels like everything might just be okay.

Maybe Daniel is my *fish* after all. And yes, maybe a bird and a fish *can* fall in love.

Where would they live? On a boat, of course.

ACKNOWLEDGMENTS

I've never been so grateful for the people who love me and support me and cheer me on as I have during the writing of this book.

Like Alex, my life was going along great until it wasn't—and the following people helped put me back together, kept me sane, made me laugh, made me cookies, and gave me a reason to get up in the morning:

Quinn and Elle, there's no one in the Universe I could love more than you. I'm so thankful for both of you—for your wisdom, your humor, your strength, your goofiness, your very cool take on the world, and the joy and happiness that you bring into my life every single day. You're the best kids anyone could ever wish for. I'm so, so lucky you're mine.

To my mom, my biggest supporter, in every way big and small. I owe you everything. I'm grateful every single day that we are family, that we have each other. You're the best, which is why all my friends always want to adopt you. Thank you, and I love you from the depths of my being. You're wise and kind and hilarious, and every day I aspire to be the extraordinary human being that you are. Not just another pretty face. (Although there is that.)

Lizzy, I love you to pieces. I always have and I always will. I'm so proud of you, and I'm so thankful for you. You make everything brighter just by being here.

Cassie, I love you so much.

To Brendan Deneen, my former agent and favorite editor—thank you for your patience (especially for your patience), your creativity, your superhuman energy, and the fact that you are an incredible champion for writers. Nobody gets us like you do. Maybe because you're one of us.

To Stephany Evans, super agent and amazing friend, thank you for your tough talk, kindness, love, and unwavering support. You're the best.

Lisa Earle McLeod, one of the most kick-ass women I've ever known, and one of my favorite inspirations for awesome, straight-talking female characters. To Heidi Godman, ditto for you. I consider myself lucky to know you both.

Abby Fabiaschi, who I adore, and my standing Friday lunch date. I'm so proud of you and so grateful for your friendship and wisdom and love. You're an incredibly talented author and I just know you're going to have a huge career.

Emily Sheets and Eric Sizzler, you know what you did. A million thanks. This book wouldn't be a book without you.

My *Daytime* show family, Cyndi, Jerry, Deanna, Alyse, Rob, Chip, Ben, and the crew. You guys are the best!

And to Mike Bracken, one of the kindest, funniest, most original people I've ever known, and one of those writers who's just so extraordinarily talented he makes it look easy while the rest of us are sweating it out. You encouraged me, teased me, egged me on, held my hand, made me laugh so hard I snorted, and read my pages more than once. Mostly, you made everything bright and alive and hilarious again, and I love you madly for it.